M. JOHN HARRISON

Copyright © M. John Harrison 2005
All rights reserved

The right of M. John Harrison to be identified as the author of this work has been asserted by him in accordance with the Copyright, Designs and Patents Act 1988.

The Course of the Heart © M. John Harrison 1992
Signs of Life © M. John Harrison 1997
This collection first published in Great Britain in 2005 by
Gollancz
An imprint of the Orion Publishing Group
Orion House, 5 Upper St Martin's Lane, London WC2H 9EA

A CIP catalogue record for this book is available
from the British Library

ISBN 0 575 07594 5

Typeset at The Spartan Press Ltd,
Lymington, Hants

Printed in Great Britain by
Clays Ltd, St Ives plc.

www.orionbooks.co.uk

ANIMA

Also by M. John Harrison

The Committed Men
The Centauri Device
The Ice Monkey
Viriconium
Climbers
The Luck in the Head
(with Ian Miller)
Travel Arrangements
Light
Things That Never Happen

CONTENTS

The Course of the Heart   1

Signs of Life   227

THE COURSE OF
THE HEART

Contents

PROLOGUE: Pleroma   5

PART ONE: In the Wake of the Goddess   13
   1 Misprision of Dreams   15
   2 N'Aimez que Moi   29
   3 'Michael Ashman'   44
   4 Dark Rapture   59

PART TWO: The Poor Heart   71
   5 China's in the Heart   73
   6 The Facsimile   82
   7 Number 17, Hill Park   96
   8 On the White Downs   107
   9 The Place of the Cure of the Soul   121

PART THREE: The Course   131
   10 It Always Happens to Someone Else   133
   11 The Slave of God   149
   12 Trasfigurante   164
   13 Fatalité Intérieure   180
   14 Burnt Rose   190
   15 Every Web Remained Unbroken   201

EPILOGUE: Kenoma   219

PROLOGUE
Pleroma

When I was a tiny boy I often sat motionless in the garden, bathed in sunshine, hands flat on the rough brick of the garden path, waiting with a prolonged, almost painful expectation for whatever would happen, whatever event was contained by that moment, whatever revelation lay dormant in it. I was drenched in the rough, dusty, aromatic smells of dock-leaves and marigolds. In the corner of the warm wall, rhubarb blanched under an upturned zinc tub eaten away with rust. I could smell it there.

Some of the first words I heard my mother say were, 'A grown woman like that! How could a grown woman act like that?' She was gossiping about someone in the family. I can't remember who, perhaps one of her younger sisters. It was the first time I had heard the phrase. 'A grown woman.' I imagined a woman cultured like a tomato or a potato, for some purpose I would never understand. Had my mother been 'grown' like that? It was an image which ramified and expanded long after I had understood the proper meaning of the phrase.

My mother loved films. She loved the actresses Vanessa Redgrave and Glenda Jackson as much as the characters they played. She was a tallish, thin woman herself, but otherwise nothing like them. Against their grave and bony calm, always breaking out into rage or delight, she could set only the tense provincial prettiness shared by nurses and infant teachers. Her name was Barbara, but she had her friends call her 'Bobbie'. When I was older I found the effect of this as sad as her neatly tailored trouser-suits and deep suntan. She was frightened the sun would make her haggard but she sat out in it anyway, in the garden or on the beach, turning up her face in a static flight reflex of vanity and despair.

The women she liked Redgrave and Jackson to play were queens, dancers, courtesans, romantic intellectuals determined to better themselves to death like huge rawboned moths inside the Japanese lamps of their own neuroses. Sexuality seemed to be the strongest of their qualities, until, at the crux, they diverted all the sexual momentum of the film into some metaphor of self-expression – an image of dancing or running – and gave the slip to both the filmic lover and the audience. Much more important was to remain at the focus of attention, and for this they were in competition even with themselves. Having captured the centre stage they were ready to abandon it immediately, dance away, and still ravenous, demand:

'No. Not her. Me.'

The year I was twelve, my mother was thirty. I remember her walking up and down on the lawn at the front of the house shouting, 'You bloody piece of paper, you bloody piece of paper,' over and over again at a letter she was holding in her right hand. It was from my father, I suppose. But clearly something else was at stake. 'You *bloody* piece of paper!' Eventually she varied the emphasis on this accusation until it had illuminated briefly every word. It was as if she was trying for some final, indisputable delivery.

Her sense of drama, the transparency of her emotion, unnerved me. I ran round the garden pulling up flowers, desperate to offer her something in exchange for whatever loss she was suffering. 'Have my birthday,' I remember shouting. 'I don't want it.' She looked puzzledly at the broken-stemmed handful of marguerites. 'We must put them in a vase,' she said.

My role was the role of Vanessa's male lead, Vanessa's audience. I was to follow my mother's retreat through the diminishing concentric shells of her self. The layers of the onion, peeled away, would reveal only more layers.

'A birthday's the last thing I want, darling.'

The letter was left out on the lawn all afternoon, where the rain could pulp it. When my father stayed away for good, she took to saving her skin, carefully applying a layer of honey-coloured make-up every morning, only to remove it even more carefully at night. Liberated perhaps too late by best-selling feminist novels, she wore wide American spectacles with tinted lenses to protect her eyes and emphasise the fine, slightly gaunt structure of jaw and cheeks.

'I am a sadder but a wiser woman,' she wrote to me from a holiday villa in Santa Ponsa, perhaps over-estimating the maturity of a boy seventeen years old. 'We never get to know people until it's too late, do we?'

I was flattered by these sentiments which, unfinished and adult, implied but somehow always evaded their real subject. Long after I had given up trying to puzzle out what she meant, I was still able to feel that she had confided in me.

'But there you are, my dear. As you grow up I expect you're finding that out.'

By then I was already playing truant two or three afternoons each week from the grammar school. I couldn't have explained why. All I ever did was walk about; or sit hypnotised by the Avon where it ran through the local fields, watching the hot sunlight spilling and foaming off the weir until a kind of excited fatigue came over me and I could no longer separate the look of the water from its sound and weight, its strange, powerful, almost yeasty smell. This I associated somehow with the 'grown woman'. She had developed with me. That yeasty smell, that mass, was hers. She didn't so much haunt as stalk my adolescent summers, which were all rain and sunshine and every minute the most surprising changes of light.

My mother, unaware of this, told people I was young for my age; and indeed during my first term at Cambridge I spent most weekends at home, travelling by rail on Friday evening and early Monday morning. The train often stopped for a few minutes near Derby. I don't remember the name of the station. Two old wooden platforms surrounded by larch, pine and variegated holly gave it an air at once bijou and mysterious: it was the branch-line halt of middle-class children's fiction forty years ago. Sitting in the train, you had no idea what sort of landscape lay behind the trees. The wind rushed through them, so that you could think of yourself as being on some sandy eminence away from which spread an intimately folded arrangement of orchards and lanes, of broad heathland stretching off to other hills. Afternoon light enamelled the leaves of the holly. Everything was possible in the country – or garden – beyond. Foxes and owls and stolen ponies. Gorse and gypsy caravans in a rough field. Some mystery about a pile of railway sleepers near the tracks, shiny with rain in the green light at the edge of the woods!

I wanted it desperately.

Then the light passed, the wind dropped and the train began to move again. The trees were dusty and birdlimed. All they had hidden was a housing estate, allotments, a light engineering plant. A woman with a hyperactive child came into the carriage and sat down opposite me.

'Just sit down,' she warned the child.

Instead it stared defiantly into her eyes for a moment then wandered off to make noises with the automatic door.

Early in my second term I bought a stereo. I quickly learned to put on the headset, turn up the volume and listen again and again to the same piece of music, each repetition of a significant phrase causing soft white explosions all over the inside of my skull.

Whether the music was the first movement of Bruckner's Fifth or only the Bewlay Brothers, the result was the same. The actual cortex, the convoluted outer surface of my brain, was somehow scoured and eroded by these little painless epiphanies. I half-hoped that if I listened long enough or got the volume high enough, it would be worn as smooth as a stone by them, so that I would never be able to think again. My ideal at that time was to remain conscious – perceptive, receptive – while no longer conscious of myself. I never achieved that. The music always lost its effect. The explosions ceased to scour. My brain began to grow itself again. I woke up to myself, staring out of the window at the green light rippling through the trees.

Girls eighteen or nineteen years old swam down towards me through it, their arms and legs moving in lazy, thoughtless strokes. When I thought about them they were red-haired, smiling, sleepy-eyed as a Gustav Klimt. A year later I lay on the floor with one of them.

It was early June, bright but humid. The air had been like a hammer for days, the streets stunned and dazzled into silence. She lived with some other people, but the house was empty all through the week. Her room, which was at the front and shaded by the great canopy of a horse-chestnut tree, stayed dim and cool for much of the day. For an hour in the morning the shadow of the slatted blinds moved across the sofa with its Indian cushions, on to the fringed maroon and orange rug and then on again, to dwell over her parted legs and scattered underwear. A little after two o'clock a thin, incandescent line of sunshine sliced into the upper part of the room, caught the dusty paper birds of a cheap mobile and flared them briefly into enamel and gold. That was it.

'This room reeks of sex.'

'It reeks of us,' I said.

I had known her for a week and two days. Half awake alone in my own bed I would catch the smell of her, and in a moment of shocked delight, remember her whispering, 'Fuck me! Fuck me!' in the middle of the night. Wherever I was I could close my eyes and visualise precisely the curves at the base of her spine where it seemed to hold its breath before it arched out into the smooth, heavy muscles of her behind. I loved her contact lenses. I loved the way she had to stop in the middle of the street to slip one out into the palm of her hand then lick it up into her mouth like a cat to clean it.

'Perhaps we should have a bath.'

At three o'clock, someone manhandled a bicycle up the steps outside and came into the house. We heard footsteps on the cool tiled floor of the hall. By then we were restless, a little tired, sticky to touch. Whoever had come in knocked first hesitantly then determinedly at the door of the room. A voice I knew asked for me.

'Don't answer,' she mouthed.

'Yaxley's ready to try,' said the voice at the door. There was a pause. 'Are you there? Hello? Yaxley says he's ready. This weekend.'

'Don't answer!' she said, quite loudly.

I sat up and looked at her. I had known her for a week and two days, and I loved everything about her.

'Shh!' I said.

She pulled me down again. 'Go away!' she shouted.

'Are you in there?' said the voice at the door. 'It's Lucas!'

'Hang on, Lucas—' I answered.

Would anything have changed if I hadn't, if I'd stayed there quietly with my hand between her legs, trying not to laugh?

'—I'm coming.'

PART ONE
In the Wake of the Goddess

1
Misprision of Dreams

Pam Stuyvesant took drugs to manage her epilepsy. They often made her depressed and difficult to deal with; and Lucas, who was nervous himself, never knew what to do. After their divorce he relied increasingly on me as a go-between.

'I don't like the sound of her voice,' he would tell me. 'You try her.'

The drugs gave her a screaming, false-sounding laugh that went on and on. Though he had remained sympathetic over the years, Lucas was always embarrassed and upset by it. I think it frightened him.

'See if you can get any sense out of her.'

It was guilt, I think, that encouraged him to see me as a steadying influence: not his own guilt so much as the guilt he felt all three of us shared.

'See what she says.'

On this occasion what she said was:

'Look, if you bring on one of my turns, bloody Lucas Medlar will regret it. What business is it of his how I feel, anyway?'

'It was just that you wouldn't talk to him. He was worried that something was happening. Is there something wrong, Pam?'

She didn't answer, but I had hardly expected her to.

'If you don't want to see me,' I suggested carefully, 'couldn't you tell me now?'

I thought she was going to hang up, but in the end there was only a kind of paroxysm of silence. I was phoning her from a call box in the middle of Huddersfield. The shopping precinct outside was full of pale bright sunshine, but windy and cold. Sleet was forecast for later in the day. Two or three teenagers went past, talking and laughing. (One of them said, 'What acid rain's got to do with my career I don't know. That's what they asked me. "What do you know about acid rain?"') When they had gone I could hear Pam breathing raggedly.

'Hello?' I said.

She shouted, 'Are you mad? I'm not talking on the phone. Before you know it, the whole thing's public property!'

Sometimes she was more dependent on medication than usual; you knew when because she tended to use that phrase over and over again: 'Before you know it—'

One of the first things I ever heard her say was, 'It looks so easy, doesn't it? But before you know it, the bloody thing's just slipped straight out of your hands,' as she bent down nervously to pick up the bits of a broken glass. How old were we then? Twenty? Lucas believed she was reflecting in language some experience of either the drugs or the disease itself, but I'm not sure he was right. Another thing she often said was, 'I mean, you have to be careful, don't you?' drawing out both *care* and *don't* in such a way that you saw immediately it was a mannerism learned in adolescence.

'You must be mad if you think I'll say anything on the phone.'

'I'll come over this evening then.'

'No!'

'Pam, I—'

She gave in abruptly.

'Come now and get it over with. I don't feel well.'

Epilepsy since the age of twelve or thirteen, as regular as clockwork; and then, later, a classic migraine to fill the gaps: a complication which, rightly or wrongly, she had always associated with what Yaxley helped the three of us do when we were students. She must never get angry or excited. 'I reserve my adrenaline,' she would explain. It was a physical, not a psychological thing: it was glandular. 'I can't let it go at the time.' Afterwards though the reservoir would burst, and it would all be released at once by some minor stimulus – a lost shoe, a missed bus, rain – to cause her hallucinations, vomiting, loss of bowel control. 'Oh, and then euphoria. It's wonderfully relaxing. Just like sex,' she would say bitterly.

'OK, Pam. I'll be there soon. Don't worry.'

'Piss off,' she said. She was dependent on reassurance, but it made her angry. 'Things are coming to bits here. I can already see the little floating lights.'

As soon as she put the receiver down I telephoned Lucas.

'I'm not doing this again,' I said.

Silence.

'Lucas? She isn't well. I thought she was going to have an attack there and then.'

'She'll see you, though? The thing is, she just kept putting the phone down on me. You've no idea how tiring that can be. She'll see you today?'

'You knew she would.'

'Good.'

I hung up.

'Lucas, you're a bastard,' I told the shopping precinct.

February. Valentine's Day. Snow and sleet all over the country. For thirty minutes or so, the bus from Huddersfield wound its way through exhausted mill villages given over to hairdressing, dog breeding and an under-capitalised tourist trade. I got off it at three o'clock in the afternoon, but it seemed much later. The face of the church clock was already lit, and a mysterious yellow light was slanting across the window of the nave, as if someone was doing something in there with only a forty-watt bulb for illumination. Cars went past endlessly as I waited to cross the road, their exhausts steaming in the dark air. For a village it was quite noisy: tyres hissing on the wet road, the bang and clink of soft-drink bottles being unloaded from a lorry outside the post office, some children I couldn't see, chanting one word over and over again. Quite suddenly, above all this, I heard the pure musical note of a thrush and stepped out into the road.

'You're sure no one got off the bus behind you?'

Pam kept me on the doorstep while she looked anxiously up and down the street, but once I was inside she seemed glad to have someone to talk to.

'You'd better take your coat off. Sit down. I'll make you some coffee. No, here, just push the cat off the chair. He knows he's not supposed to be there.'

It was an old cat, black and white, with dull, dry fur, and when I picked it up it was just a lot of bones and heat that weighed nothing. I set it down carefully on the carpet, but it jumped back on to my knee again immediately and began to dribble on my pullover. Another, younger animal was crouching on the windowsill, shifting its feet uncomfortably among the little intricate baskets of paper flowers as it stared out into the falling sleet, the empty garden.

'Get down off there!' Pam called as she hung my coat up in the tiny hall.

Both cats ignored her. She shrugged.

'They act as if they own the place.' It smelled as if they did. 'They were strays. I don't know why I encouraged them.' Then, as though she were still talking about the cats:

'How's Lucas?'

'He's surprisingly well,' I said. 'You ought to keep in touch with him, you know.'

'I know.'

She smiled briefly.

'And how are you? I never see you.'

'Not bad. Feeling my age.'

'You don't know the half of it yet,' she said. She stood in the kitchen doorway holding a tea towel in one hand and a cup in the other. 'None of us do.' It was a familiar complaint. When she saw I was too preoccupied to listen, she went and banged things about in the sink. I heard water rushing into the kettle. While it filled up, she said something she knew I wouldn't catch: then, turning off the tap:

'Something's going on in the Pleroma. Something new. I can feel it.'

'Pam,' I said, 'all that was over and done with twenty years ago.'

The fact is that even at the time I wasn't at all sure what we had done. This will seem odd to you, I suppose, but all I remember now is a June evening drenched with the half-confectionery, half-corrupt smell of hawthorn blossoms. It was so thick we seemed to swim through it, through that and the hot evening light that poured between the hedgerows like transparent gold. I remember Yaxley because you don't forget him easily. But what the three of us did under his guidance escapes me, as does its significance. There was, undoubtedly, some sort of loss: whether you described what was lost as 'innocence' was very much up to you. Anyway, that was how it appeared to me: to call it 'innocence' would be to beg too many questions.

Lucas and Pam made a lot more of it from the very start. They took it to heart.

And afterwards – perhaps two or three months afterwards, when it was plain that something had gone wrong, when things first started to pull out of shape – it was Pam and Lucas who convinced me to go and talk to Yaxley, whom we had promised never to contact again. They wanted to see if what we had done might somehow be reversed or annulled, what we'd lost bought back again.

'I don't think it works that way,' I warned them, but I could see they weren't listening.

'He'll have to help us,' Lucas said.

'Why did we ever do it?' Pam asked me.

I went down the next day. The train was crowded. Across the table from me in the other window seat, a tall black man looked round smilingly and cracked his knuckles. He had on an expensive brown silk suit. The seats outside us were occupied by two middle-aged women who were going to London for a week's holiday. They chattered constantly about a previous visit: they had walked across Tower Bridge in the teeth of a gale, and afterwards eaten baked potatoes on the north bank, admiring a statue of a dolphin and a girl; they had visited Greenwich. On their last day it had been the zoo in Regent's Park where, gazing diffidently into the little heated compartments of the reptile house, they were surprised by a Thailand water lizard with a skin, one of them said, 'like a canvas bag'.

She relished this description.

'Just like an old green canvas bag,' she repeated. 'Didn't it make you feel funny?' she insisted. But her friend seemed bored.

'What?'

'That skin!'

At this the black man leaned forward and said, 'It only makes me feel sad.'

His voice was low and pleasant. The women ignored him, so he appealed to me, 'I couldn't say why. Except that a lizard's skin seems so shabby and ill-fitting.'

'I don't think I've ever seen one,' I said.

'What if evolution were ideological after all?' he asked us. 'With aesthetic goals?'

The women received this so woodenly that he was forced to look out of the window; and although he smiled at me once or twice in a preparatory way, as if he would have liked to reopen the conversation, he never did.

Later I went down the carriage to the lavatory, and then on to the buffet. While I was there the train stopped at Stevenage; when I returned to my seat I found that the women had moved to an empty table, and the negro had been replaced by a fat, red-faced man who looked like the older H. G. Wells and who slept painedly most of the way to London with his hands clasped across his stomach. He had littered the table with sandwich wrappers, plastic cups, an empty miniature of whisky, the pages of a newspaper. Just before the train pulled in, he woke up, glared at me suspiciously at this mess, and pushed something across to me.

'Last bloke in the seat left this for you,' he said. He had a thick northern accent.

It was a square of folded notepaper, on which had been written in a clear, delightfully even hand, 'I couldn't help noticing how you admired the birch trees. Birchwoods more than any others are meant to be seen by autumn light! It surprises them in a dance, a celebration of something which is, in a tree, akin to the animal. They dance even on cold still days when the air leaves them motionless: limbs like illuminated bone caught moving – or just ceasing to move – in a mauve smoke of twigs.'

This was unsigned. I turned it over but nothing more was written there.

I laughed.

'Was he black?' I asked.

'Aye, kid,' said the fat man: 'He were.' He hauled himself to his feet and began, panting, to wrestle his luggage off the rack. 'Black as fuck.'

As the train crawled the last mile into London, I had seen three sheets of newspaper fluttering round the upper floors of an office block like butterflies courting a flower. The Pleroma demands of us a passion for the world which, however distortedly, reflects it. I still remember the intelligent eagerness of the negro's smile – how he always had to talk about the world – the way his sharp-edged elegant cheekbones seemed, like tribal scars or a silk suit, to be more designed than organic.

Though he hated the British Museum, Yaxley had always lived one way or another in its shadow.

I met him at the Tivoli Espresso Bar, where I knew he would be every afternoon. The weather that day was damp. He wore a thick, old-fashioned black overcoat; but from the way his wrists stuck out of the sleeves, long and fragile-looking and dirty, covered with sore grazes as though he had been fighting with some small animal, I suspected he had no jacket or shirt on underneath it. He looked older than he was, the top half of his body stooped bronchially, his lower jaw stubbled with grey. I sometimes wonder if this was as much a pretence – although of a different order – as the *Church Times* he always carried, folded carefully to display part of a headline, which none of us ever saw him open.

At the Tivoli in those days they always had the radio on. Their coffee was watery and, like most espresso, too hot to taste of anything. Yaxley and I sat on stools by the window, resting our elbows on a counter littered with dirty cups and half-eaten sandwiches, and watched the pedestrians in Museum Street. After ten minutes a woman's voice said clearly from behind us:

'The fact is that the children just won't try.'

Yaxley jumped and looked round haggardly, as if he expected to have to answer this.

'It's the radio,' I reassured him.

He stared at me the way you would stare at someone who was mad, and it was some time before he went on with what he had been saying:

'You knew what you were doing. You got what you wanted, and you weren't tricked in any way.'

'No,' I admitted.

My eyes had begun to ache: Yaxley soon tired you out.

'I can understand that,' I said. 'That isn't at issue. But I'd like to be able to reassure them somehow—'

Yaxley wasn't listening.

It had come on to rain quite hard, driving the tourists – mainly Germans and Americans in Bloomsbury for the Museum – off the street. They all seemed to be wearing brand-new clothes. The Tivoli filled up quickly, and the air was soon heavy with the smell of wet coats. People trying to find seats constantly brushed our backs.

'Excuse me, please,' they murmured. 'Excuse me.'

Yaxley became irritated almost immediately.

'Dog muck,' he said loudly in a matter-of-fact voice. I think their politeness affected him much more than the disturbance itself. 'Three generations of rabbits,' he jeered, as a whole family were forced to push past him one by one to get the table in the corner. None of them seemed to take offence, though they must have heard him. A drenched-looking woman in a purple coat came in, looked anxiously for an empty seat, and, when she couldn't see one, hurried out again.

'Mad bitch!' Yaxley called after her. 'Get yourself reamed out.' He stared challengingly at the other customers.

'I think it would be better if we talked in private,' I said. 'What about your flat?'

For twenty years he had lived in the same single room above the Atlantis Bookshop. He was reluctant to take me there, I could see, though it was only next door and I had been there before. At first he tried to pretend it would be difficult to get in.

'The shop's closed,' he said. 'We'd have to use the other door.'

Then he admitted:

'I can't go back there for an hour or two. I did something last night that means it may not be safe.'

He grinned.

'You know the sort of thing I mean,' he said.

I couldn't get him to explain further. The cuts on his wrists made me remember how panicky Pam and Lucas had been when I last spoke to them. All at once I was determined to see inside the room.

'We could always talk in the Museum,' I suggested.

Researching in the manuscript collection one afternoon a year before, he had turned a page of Jean de Wavrin's *Chroniques d'Angleterre* – that oblique history no complete version of which is known – and come upon a miniature depicting in strange, unreal greens and blues the coronation procession of Richard Coeur de Lion.

Part of it had moved; which part, he would never say.

'Why, if it's a coronation,' he had written almost plaintively to me at the time, 'are these four men carrying a coffin? And who is walking there under the awning – with the bishops yet not a bishop?'

After that he had avoided the building as much as possible, though he could always see its tall iron railings at the end of the street. He had begun, he told me, to doubt the authenticity of some of the items in the medieval collection. In fact he was frightened of them.

'It would be quieter there,' I insisted.

He sat hunched over the *Church Times*, staring into the street with his hands clamped violently together in front of him. I could see him thinking.

'That fucking pile of shit!' he said eventually.

He got to his feet.

'Come on then. It's probably cleared out by now anyway.'

Rain dripped from the blue-and-gold front of the Atlantis. There was a faded notice, CLOSED FOR COMPLETE REFURBISHMENT. The window display had been taken down, but for the look of things they had left a few books on a shelf. I could make out, through the plate glass, W. B. Yeats's *The Trembling of the Veil* – with its lyrical plea for intuited ritual 'Hodos Chameliontos' – leaning up against Rilke's *The Notebooks of Malte Laurids Brigge*. When I drew Yaxley's attention to this accidental nexus, he only stared at me contemptuously.

Inside, the shop smelled of cut timber, new plaster, paint, but this gave way on the stairs to an odour of cooking. Yaxley fumbled with his key. His bedsitter, which was quite large and on the top floor, had uncurtained sash windows on opposing walls. Nevertheless it didn't seem well lit. From one window you could see the sodden façades of Museum Street, bright green deposits on the ledges, stucco scrolls and garlands grey with pigeon dung; out of the other, part of the blackened clock tower of St George's Bloomsbury, a reproduction of the tomb of Mausoleus lowering up against the racing clouds.

'I once heard that clock strike twenty-one,' said Yaxley.

'I can believe that,' I said, though I didn't. 'Do you think I could have some tea?'

He was silent for a minute. Then he laughed.

'I'm not going to help them,' he said. 'You know that. I wouldn't be allowed to. What you do in the Pleroma is irretrievable.'

'All that was over and done with twenty years ago, Pam.'

'I know. I know that. But—'

She stopped suddenly, and then went on in a muffled voice, 'Will you just come here a minute? Just for a minute?'

The house, like many in the Pennines, had been built right into the side of the valley. A near-vertical bank of earth, cut to accommodate it, was held back by a dry-stone revetment twenty or thirty feet high, black with damp even in the middle of July, dusted with lichen and tufted with ferns like a cliff. Throughout the winter months, water streamed down the revetment day after day and, collecting in a stone trough underneath, made a sound like a tap left running in the night. Along the back of the house ran a passage hardly two feet wide, full of broken roof slates and other rubbish.

'You're all right,' I told Pam, who was staring, puzzled, into the gathering dark, her head on one side and the tea towel held up to her mouth as if she thought she was going to be sick.

'It knows who we are,' she whispered. 'Despite the precautions, it always remembers us.'

She shuddered, pulled herself away from the window, and began pouring water into the coffee filter so clumsily that I put my arm round her shoulders and said, 'Look, you'd better go and sit down before you scald yourself. I'll finish this, and then you can tell me what's the matter.'

She hesitated.

'Come on,' I encouraged her. 'All right?'

'All right.'

She went into the living room and sat down. One of the cats ran into the kitchen and looked up at me expectantly. 'Don't let them have milk,' she called. 'They got some this morning, and anyway it only gives them diarrhoea.'

'How are you feeling?' I asked. 'In yourself, I mean?'

'About how you'd expect.'

She had taken some propranolol for the migraine, she said, but it never seemed to help much. 'It shortens the headaches, I suppose.' As a side-effect, though, it made her so tired. 'It slows my heartbeat down. I can feel it slow right down.' She watched the steam rising from her coffee cup, first slowly and then with a rapid plaiting motion as it was caught by some tiny draught. Eddies form and break on the surface of a deep, smooth river. A slow coil, a sudden whirl. What was tranquil is revealed as a mass of complications that can be resolved only as motion.

I remembered when I had first met her:

She was twenty then, a small, excitable, attractive girl who wore moss-coloured jersey dresses to show off her waist and hips. Later, fear coarsened her. With the divorce a few grey streaks appeared in her astonishing red hair, and she chopped it raggedly off and dyed it black. She drew in on herself. Her body broadened into a kind of dogged, muscular heaviness. Even her hands and feet seemed to become bigger.

'You're old before you know it,' she would say. 'Before you know it.'

Separated from Lucas she was easily chafed by her surroundings; moved every six months or so, although never very far, and always to the same sort of dilapidated, drearily furnished cottage, so you suspected she was looking for precisely the things that made her nervous and ill; and tried to keep down to fifty cigarettes a day.

'Why did Yaxley never help us?' she asked me. 'You must know.'

Yaxley fished two cups out of a plastic washing-up bowl and put tea bags in them.

'Don't tell me you're frightened too!' he said. 'I expected more from you.'

I shook my head. I wasn't sure whether I was afraid or not. I'm not sure today. The tea, when it came, had a distinctly greasy aftertaste, as if somehow he had fried it. I made myself drink it while Yaxley watched me cynically.

'You ought to sit down,' he said. 'You're worn out.'

When I refused, he shrugged and went on as if we were still at the Tivoli:

'Nobody tricked them, or tried to pretend it would be easy. If you get anything out of an experiment like that, it's by keeping your head and taking your chance. If you try to move cautiously, you may never be allowed to move at all.'

He looked thoughtful.

'I've seen what happens to people who lose their nerve.'

'I'm sure,' I said.

'They were hardly recognisable, some of them.'

I put the teacup down.

'I don't want to know,' I said.

'I bet you don't.'

He smiled to himself.

'Oh, they were still alive,' he said softly, 'if that's what you're worried about.'

'You talked us into this,' I reminded him.

'You talked yourselves into it.'

Most of the light from Museum Street was absorbed as soon as it entered the room, by the dull green wallpaper and sticky-looking yellow veneer of the furniture. The rest leaked eventually into the litter on the floor, pages of crumpled and partly burned typescript, hair clippings, broken chalks which had been used the night before to draw something on the flaking lino: among this stuff, it died. Though I knew Yaxley was playing some sort of game with me, I couldn't see what it was. I couldn't make the effort, so in the end he had to make it for me. He waited until I got ready to leave.

'You'll get sick of all this mess one day,' I said from the door of the bedsit.

He grinned and nodded and advised me:

'Have you ever seen Joan of Arc get down to pray in the ticket office at St Pancras? And then a small boy comes in leading something that looks like a goat, and it gets on her there and then and fucks her in a ray of sunlight?

'Come back when you know what you want. Get rid of Lucas Medlar, he's an amateur. Bring the girl if you must.'

'Fuck off, Yaxley.'

He let me find my own way back down to the street.

That night I had to tell Lucas, 'We aren't going to be hearing from Yaxley again.'

'Christ,' he said, and for a second I thought he was going to cry. 'Pam feels so ill,' he whispered. 'What did he say?'

'Forget him. He could never have helped us.'

'Pam and I are getting married,' Lucas said in a rush.

2
N'Aimez Que Moi

What could I have said? I knew as well as they did that they were only doing it out of a need for comfort. Nothing would be gained by making them admit it. Besides, I was so tired by then I could hardly stand. Yaxley had exhausted me. Some kind of visual fault, a neon zigzag like a bright little flight of stairs, kept showing up in my left eye. So I congratulated Lucas and, as soon as I could, began thinking about something else.

'Yaxley's terrified by the British Museum,' I said. 'In a way I sympathise with him.'

As a child, I had hated it too.

Every conversation, every echo of a voice or a footstep or a rustle of clothes, was gathered up into its high ceilings in a kind of undifferentiated rumble and sigh – the blurred and melted remains of meaning – which made you feel as if your parents had abandoned you in a derelict swimming bath. Later, when I was a teenager, it was the vast shapeless heads in Room 25 that frightened me, the vagueness of the inscriptions. I saw clearly what was there – 'Red sandstone head of a king . . .' 'Red granite head from a colossal figure of a king . . .' – but what was I looking at? A description is not an explanation. The faceless wooden figure of Rameses emerged perpetually from an alcove near the lavatory door, a Rameses who had to support himself with a stick: split, syphilitic, worm-eaten by his passage through the world, but still condemned to struggle helplessly on.

'We want to go and live up north,' Lucas said. 'Away from all this.'

*

As the afternoon wore on, Pam became steadily more disturbed.

'Listen,' she would ask me, 'is that someone in the passage? You can always tell me the truth.'

After she had promised several times in a vague way, 'I can't send you out without anything to eat. I'll cook us something in a minute, if you'll make some more coffee,' I realised she was frightened to go back into the kitchen. She would change the subject immediately, explaining, 'No matter how much coffee I drink, my throat is always dry. It's all that smoking;' or: 'I hate the dark afternoons.'

She returned often to the theme of age. She had always hated to feel old.

'You comb your hair in the mornings and it's just another ten years gone, every loose hair, every bit of dandruff, like a lot of old snapshots showering down. We moved around such a lot,' she went on, as if the connection would be clear to me: 'after university. It wasn't that I couldn't settle, more that I had to leave something behind every so often, as a sort of sacrifice.

'If I liked a job I was in, I would always give it up. Poor old Lucas!'

She laughed.

'Do you ever feel like that?'

She made a face.

'I don't suppose you ever do,' she said. 'I remember that first house we lived in, over near Dunford Bridge. It was so huge, and falling apart inside! And always on the market until Lucas and I bought it. Everyone who had it tried some new way of dividing it to make it livable. People would put in a new staircase or knock two rooms together. They'd abandon parts of it because they couldn't afford to heat it all. Then they'd bugger off before anything was finished and leave it to the next lot—'

She broke off suddenly.

'I could never keep it tidy,' she said.

'Lucas always loved it.'

'Does he say that? You don't want to pay too much attention

to him,' she warned me. 'The garden was so full of builders' rubbish we could never grow anything. And the winters!' She shivered. 'Well, you know what it's like out there. The rooms reeked of Calor gas. Before we'd been there a week Lucas had every kind of portable heater you could think of. I hated the cold, but never as much as he did.' With an amused tenderness she chided him – 'Lucas, Lucas, Lucas' – as if he were in the room there with us. 'How you hated it and how untidy you were!'

By now it was dark outside, but the younger cat was still staring out into the greyish, sleety well of the garden, beyond which you could just make out – as a swelling line of shadow with low clouds racing over it – the edge of the moor. Pam kept asking the cat what it could see. 'Nothing but old crimes out there,' she told it. 'Children buried all over the moor.'

Eventually she got up with a sigh and pushed it on to the floor. 'That's where cats belong. Cats belong on the floor.'

Some paper flowers were knocked down. Stooping to gather them up she said, 'If there is a God, a real one, He gave up long ago. He isn't so much bitter as apathetic.'

She winced; held her hands up to her eyes.

'You don't mind if I turn the main light off?'

And then:

'He's filtered away into everything, so that now there's only this infinitely thin, stretched thing, presenting itself in every atom, so tired it can't go on, so haggard you can only feel sorry for its mistakes. That's the real God. What we saw is something that's taken its place.'

'What did we see, Pam?'

She stared at me.

'You know, I was never sure what Lucas thought he wanted from me,' she said.

The dull yellow light of a table lamp fell across the side of her face. She was lighting cigarettes almost constantly, stubbing them out half-smoked into the nest of old ends that had accumulated in the saucer of her cup.

'Can you imagine? In all those years I never knew what he wanted from me.'

She seemed to consider this for a moment or two.

She said puzzledly, 'I don't feel he ever loved me.'

She buried her face in her hands.

I got up, with some idea of comforting her. Without warning, she lurched out of her chair and in a groping, desperately confused manner took a few steps towards me. There in the middle of the room she stumbled into a low fretwork table someone had brought back from a visit to Kashmir twenty years before. Two or three paperback books and a vase of anemones went flying. The anemones were blowsy, past their best. Pam looked down at *Love for Lydia* and *The Death of the Heart*, strewn with great blue and red petals like dirty tissue paper; she touched them thoughtfully with her toe. The smell of the foetid flower water made her retch.

'Oh dear,' she murmured. 'Whatever shall we do, Lucas?'

'I'm not Lucas,' I said gently.

While I was gathering up the books and wiping their covers, she must have overcome her fear of the kitchen – or, I thought later, simply forgotten it – because I heard her rummaging about for the dustpan and brush she kept under the sink. By now, I imagined, she could hardly see for the migraine. 'Let me do that, Pam,' I called impatiently. 'Go and sit down.' There was a gasp, a clatter, my name repeated twice.

'Pam, are you all right?'

No one answered.

'Hello? Pam?'

I found her by the sink. She had let go of the brush and pan and was twisting the damp floor cloth so tightly in her hands that the muscles of her short forearms stood out like a carpenter's. Water had dribbled down her skirt.

'Pam?'

She was looking out of the window into the narrow passage where, clearly illuminated by the fluorescent tube in the kitchen, something big and white hung in the air, turning to and fro like a chrysalis in a privet hedge.

'Christ!' I said.

It wriggled and was still, as though whatever it contained was tired of the effort to get out. After a moment it curled up from its tapered base, seemed to split, welded itself together again. All at once I saw that these movements were actually those of two organisms, two human figures hanging in the air, unsupported, quite naked, writhing and embracing and parting and writhing together again, never presenting the same angle twice, so that now you viewed the man from the back, now the woman, now both of them from one side or the other. When I first saw them, the woman's mouth was fastened on the man's. Her eyes were closed; later she rested her head on his shoulder. Later still, they both turned their attention to Pam. They had very pale skin, with the dusty bloom of white chocolate; but that might have been an effect of the light. Sleet blew between us and them in eddies, but never obscured them.

'What are they, Pam?'

'There's no limit to suffering,' she said. Her voice was slurred and thick. 'They follow me wherever I go.'

I found it hard to look away from them.

'What are they?'

They were locked together in something that – had their attention been on each other – might have been described as love. They swung and turned slowly against the black wet wall like fish in a tank. I held Pam's shoulders. 'Get them away,' she said indistinctly. 'Why do they always look at me?' She coughed, wiped her mouth, ran the cold tap. She had begun to shiver, in powerful disconnected spasms. 'Get them away.'

Though I knew quite well they were there, it was my mistake that I never believed them to be real. I thought she might calm down if she couldn't see them. But she wouldn't let me turn the light out or close the curtains; and when I tried to encourage her to let go of the edge of the sink and come into the living room with me, she only shook her head and retched miserably. 'No, leave me,' she said. 'I don't want you now.' Her body had gone rigid, as awkward as a child's. She was very strong. 'Just try to come away, Pam, please.' She looked at me helplessly and said, 'I've got nothing to wipe my nose with.' I pulled at her angrily, and we fell down. My shoulder was on the dustpan, my mouth full of her hair, which smelled of cigarette ash. I felt her hands move over me.

'Pam! Pam!' I shouted.

I dragged myself from under her – she had begun to groan and vomit again – and, staring back over my shoulder at the smiling creatures in the passage, ran out of the kitchen and out of the house. I could hear myself sobbing with panic – 'I'm phoning Lucas, I can't stand this, I'm going to phone Lucas!' – as if I were still talking to her. I blundered about the village until I found the telephone box opposite the church.

I remember someone – perhaps Yaxley, though on reflection it seems too well-put to have been him – once saying, 'It's no triumph to feel you've given life the slip.' We were talking about Lucas Medlar. 'You can't live intensely except at the cost of the self. In the end, Lucas's reluctance to give himself wholeheartedly will make him shabby and unreal. He'll end up walking the streets at night staring into lighted shop windows. He'll always save himself, and always wonder if it was worth it.' At the time I thought this harsh. I still do. With Lucas it was a matter of energy rather than will, of the lows and undependable zones of a cyclic personality than any deliberate reservation of powers.

When I told him, 'Something's gone badly wrong here,' he was silent. After a moment or two I prompted him, 'Lucas?'

I thought I heard him say:

'For God's sake put that down and leave me alone.'

'This line must be bad,' I said. 'You sound a long way off. Is there someone with you?'

He was silent again – 'Lucas? Can you hear me?' – and then he asked, 'How is Pam? I mean in herself?'

'Not well,' I said. 'She's having some sort of attack. You don't know how relieved I am to talk to someone. Lucas, there are two completely hallucinatory figures in that passage outside her kitchen. What they're doing to one another is . . . Look, they're a kind of dead white colour, and they're smiling at her all the time. It's the most appalling thing—'

He said, 'Wait a minute. Do you mean that you can see them too?'

'That's what I'm trying to say. The thing is that I don't know how to help her. Lucas?'

The line had gone dead.

I put the receiver down and dialled his number again. The engaged signal went on and on. Afterwards I would tell Pam, 'Someone else must have called him,' but I knew he had simply taken his phone off the hook. I stood there for some time anyway, shivering in the wind that blustered down off the moor, in the hope that he would change his mind. In the end I got so cold I had to give up and go back. Sleet blew into my face all the way through the village. The church clock said half past six, but everything was dark and untenanted. All I could hear was the wind rustling the black plastic bags of rubbish piled round the dustbins.

Civilisation – if it could be called that – made its bench-mark on the Pennine moors with water and railways, the great civil engineering projects of the nineteenth century. Things have been at ebb since. Over in Longdendale and the Chew Valley, the dams and chains of reservoirs endure, but their architecture is monolithic and not to scale. The human remains of these sites of obsession – handfuls of houses, some quarry workings, a graveyard – are scattered. There is nothing left for people. A few farmers hang on. Myra Hindley and Ian Brady, the 'Moors Murderers' of the 1960s, had buried their victims not far from Pam's cottage. Otherwise the spoil heaps and derelict shooting boxes have nothing to guard but an emptiness. I felt pursued despite that.

'Fuck you, Lucas,' I whispered. 'Fuck you then.'

*

Pam's house was as silent as the rest.

I went into the front garden and pressed my face up to the window, in case I could see into the kitchen through the open living-room door. But from that angle the only thing visible was a wall calendar with a colour photograph of a Persian cat: October.

I couldn't see Pam.

I stood in the flower bed. The sleet turned to snow. Eventually I made myself go in.

The kitchen was filled less with the smell of vomit than a sourness you felt somewhere in the back of your throat. Outside, the passage lay deserted under the bright suicidal wash of fluorescent light. It was hard to imagine anything had happened out there. At the same time nothing looked comfortable, not the disposition of the old roof slates, or the clumps of fern growing out of the revetment, or even the way the snow was settling in the gaps between the flagstones. I found that I didn't want to turn my back on the window. If I closed my eyes and tried to visualise the white couple, all I could remember was the way they had smiled. A still, cold air seeped in above the sink, and the cats came to rub against my legs and get underfoot; the taps were still running.

In her confusion Pam had opened all the kitchen cupboards and strewn their contents on the floor. Saucepans, cutlery and packets of dried food had been mixed up with a polythene bucket and some yellow J-cloths. She had upset a bottle of household detergent among several tins of cat food, some of which had been half opened, some merely pierced, before she dropped them or forgot where she had put the opener. It was hard to see what she had been trying to do. I picked it all up and put it away. To make them leave me alone, I fed the cats. Once or twice I heard her moving about on the floor above.

She was in the bathroom, slumped on the old-fashioned pink lino by the sink, trying to get her clothes off.

'For God's sake go away,' she said. 'I can do it.'

'Oh, Pam.'

'Put some disinfectant in the blue bucket then.'

'Who are they, Pam?' I asked.

That was later, when I had put her to bed. She answered:

'Once it starts you never get free.'

I was annoyed.

'Free from what, Pam?'

'You know,' she said. 'Lucas said you had hallucinations for weeks afterwards.'

'Lucas had no right to say that!'

This sounded absurd, so I added as lightly as I could, 'It was a long time ago. I'm not sure any more.'

The migraine had left her exhausted, though much more relaxed. She had washed her hair, and between us we had found her a fresh nightdress to wear. Sitting up in the cheerful little bedroom with its cheap ornaments and modern wallpaper, she looked vague and young, free of pain. She kept apologising for the design on her continental quilt, some bold diagrammatic flowers in black and red, the intertwined stems of which she traced with the index finger of her right hand across a clean white background. 'Do you like this? I don't really know why I bought it. Things look so bright and energetic in the shops,' she said wistfully, 'but as soon as you get them home, they just seem crude.' The older cat had jumped up on to the bed; whenever Pam spoke it purred loudly. 'He shouldn't be in here and he knows it.' She wouldn't eat or drink, but I had persuaded her to take some more propranolol, and so far she had kept it down.

'Once it starts you never get free,' she repeated.

Following the pattern of the quilt with one finger, she touched inadvertently the cat's dry, greying fur; stared, as if her own hand had misled her.

'It was some sort of smell that followed you about, Lucas seemed to think.'

'Some sort,' I agreed.

'You won't get rid of it by ignoring it. We both tried that to begin with. A scent of roses, Lucas said.' She laughed and took my hand in both of hers. 'Very romantic! I've no sense of smell – I lost it years ago, luckily!'

This reminded her of something else.

'The first time I had a fit,' she said, 'I kept it from my mother because I saw a vision with it. I was only a child, really. The vision was very dear: a seashore, steep and with no sand, and men and women lying on some rocks in the sunshine like lizards, staring quite blankly at the spray as it exploded up in front of them; huge waves that might have been on a cinema screen for all the notice they took of them.'

She narrowed her eyes, puzzled.

'You wondered why they had so little common sense.'

She tried to push the cat off her bed, but it only bent its body in a rubbery way and avoided her hand. She yawned suddenly.

'At the same time,' she went on, after a pause, 'I could see that some spiders had made their webs between the rocks, just a foot or two above the tideline.' Though they trembled and were sometimes filled with spray like dewdrops so that they glittered in the sun, the webs remained unbroken. She couldn't describe, she said, the sense of frailty and anxiety with which this filled her. 'So close to all that violence. You wondered why they had so little common sense,' she repeated. 'The last thing I heard was someone warning me, "On your own you really can hear voices in the tide—"'

She smiled.

'Will you come in with me?' she said, holding back the top of the continental quilt. 'Just for a moment? After all, Lucas can't mind any more, can he?'

'Pam, you're not—'

'Take your clothes off. Come in and hug me, if nothing else.' She made room. She said, 'You've stayed young while I got old.' And then: 'There, touch. Yes.' I held her until she fell asleep. All night the old cat moved about uncomplainingly but restlessly on the continental quilt, as if it could no longer be comfortable anywhere. I smoothed the fur on its bony head. Its huge purr filled the room. Once, Pam seemed to wake up suddenly: finding that I had rolled away from her, she murmured:

'I'm glad you got something out of it. Lucas and I never did. Roses! It was worth it for that.'

And, after a moment:

'Hug me. Come inside me again.'

I thought of us as we had been twenty years before. I woke quite early in the morning. I didn't know where I was until I walked in a drugged way to the window and saw the village street full of snow. I fed the cats again. As I left the house Pam was still asleep, with the expression people have on their faces when they can't believe what they remember about themselves. It was the last time I saw her before her illness took hold.

'On your own, you really can hear voices in the tide,' she had said. 'I started to menstruate the same day. For years I was convinced that's why my fits had begun: menstruation.'

For a long time after that inconclusive meeting with Yaxley, I had a recurrent dream of him. His hands were clasped tightly across his chest, the left hand holding the wrist of the right, and he was going quickly from room to room of the British Museum. Whenever he came to a corner or a junction of corridors, he stopped abruptly and stared at the wall in front of him for thirty seconds before turning very precisely to face in the right direction before he moved on. He did this with the air of a man who has for some reason taught himself to walk with his eyes closed through a perfectly familiar building; but there was also, in the way he stared at the walls – and particularly in the way he held himself so upright and rigid – a profoundly hierarchical air, an air of premeditation and ritual. His shoes, and the bottoms of his faded corduroy trousers, were soaking wet, just as they had been the morning after the rite, when the four of us had walked back through the damp fields in the bright sunshine. He wore no socks.

In the dream I was always hurrying to catch up with him. I was stopping every so often to write something in a notebook, hoping he wouldn't see me. He strode purposefully through the Museum, from cabinet to cabinet of twelfth-century illuminated manuscripts. Suddenly he stopped, looked back at me, and said:

'There are sperms in this picture. You can see them quite plainly. What are sperms doing in a religious picture?'

He smiled, opened his eyes very wide.

Pointing to the side of his own head with one finger, he began to shout and laugh incoherently.

When he had gone, I saw that he had been examining a New Testament miniature from Queen Melisande's Psalter, depicting 'The Women at the Sepulchre'. In it an angel was drawing Mary Magdalene's attention to some strange luminous shapes that hovered in the air in front of her. They did, in fact, look something like the spermatozoa which often border the tormented Paris paintings of Edvard Munch.

I would wake up abruptly from this dream, to find that it was morning and that I had been crying.

'On your own, you really can hear voices in the tide, cries for help or attention.'

A warm front had moved in from the south-west during the night. The snow had already begun to soften and melt, the Pennine stations looked like leaky downspouts, the moors were locked beneath grey clouds. Two little boys sat opposite me on the train until Stalybridge, holding their Day Rover tickets thoughtfully in their laps. They might have been eight or nine years old. They were dressed in tiny, perfect donkey jackets, tight trousers, Dr Marten's boots. Close up, their shaven skulls were bluish and vulnerable, perfectly shaped. They looked like acolytes in a Buddhist temple: grave, wide-eyed, compliant. By the time I got to Manchester, a fine rain was falling. The wind blew it the full length of Market Street and through the doors of the Kardomah Café, where I had arranged to meet Lucas Medlar.

The first thing he said was, 'Look at these pies! They aren't plastic, you know, like a modern pie. These are from the plaster era of café pies, the earthenware era. Terracotta pies, realistically painted, glazed in places to have exactly the cracks and imperfections any real pie would have! Aren't they wonderful? I'm going to eat one.'

I sat down next to him.

'What happened to you last night, Lucas? It was a bloody nightmare.'

He looked away.

'How is Pam?' he asked. I could feel him trembling.

'Fuck off, Lucas.'

He smiled over at a toddler in an appalling yellow suit. The child stared back vacantly, upset, knowing full well they were from competing species.

A woman near us said to the two children with her, 'I hear you're going to your grandmother's for dinner on Sunday. Something special I expect?' Lucas glared at her, as if she had been speaking to him. She added: 'If you're going to buy toys this afternoon, remember to look at them where they are, so that no one can accuse you of stealing. Don't take them off the shelf.'

From somewhere near the kitchens came a noise like a tray of crockery falling down a short flight of stairs.

Lucas seemed to hate this. He shuddered.

'I feel it as badly as Pam,' he said. He accused me: 'You never think of that.' He looked over at the toddler again. 'Spend long enough in places like this and your spirit will heave itself inside out.'

'Come on, Lucas, don't be spoilt. I thought you liked the pies here.'

Eventually he admitted:

'I'm sorry.'

Even so, I got nothing from him. We left the Kardomah in case his spirit heaved itself inside out; but then all he did was walk urgently about the streets, as if he were on his own. The city centre was full of wheelchairs, old women slumped in them with impatient, collapsed faces, partially bald, done up in crisp white raincoats. Lucas had turned up the collar of his grey cashmere jacket against the rain but left the jacket itself hanging open, its sleeves rolled untidily back above his bare wrists. He left me breathless. He was forty years old, but he still had the ravenous face of an adolescent. Halfway through the afternoon the lights went on in the lower floors of the office blocks; neon signs turned and signalled against the sky. Lucas stopped and gazed down at the rain-pocked surface of the old canal, where it appears suddenly from beneath the road near Piccadilly Station. It was dim and oily, scattered with lumps of floating styrofoam like seagulls in the fading light.

'You often see fires on the bank down there,' he said. 'They live a whole life down there, people with nowhere else to go. You can hear them singing and shouting on the towpath.'

He looked at me wonderingly:

'We aren't much different, are we? We never came to anything, either.'

I couldn't think of what to say.

'It's not so much that Yaxley encouraged us to ruin something in ourselves, as that we never got anything in return for it.'

'Look, Lucas,' I explained, 'I don't see it that way. I'm never doing this again. I was frightened last night.'

'I'm sorry.'

'Lucas, you always are.'

'It isn't one of my better days today.'

'For God's sake fasten your coat.'

'I can't seem to get cold.'

He gazed dreamily down at the water – it had darkened into a bottomless opal-coloured trench between the buildings – perhaps seeing goats, fires, people who had nowhere to go. ' "We worked but we were not paid," ' he quoted. Something forced him to ask shyly:

'You haven't heard from Yaxley?'

I felt sick with patience. I seemed to be filled up with it.

'I haven't seen Yaxley for twenty years, Lucas. You know that. I haven't seen him for twenty years.'

'I understand. It's just that I can't bear to think of Pam on her own in a place like that. I wouldn't have mentioned it otherwise. We said we'd always stick together, but—'

'Then why didn't you?' I said.

He stared at me.

'Go home, Lucas. Go home now.'

He turned away miserably, walked off, and disappeared into that unredeemed maze between Piccadilly and Victoria – alleys full of wet cardboard boxes, failing pornography and pet shops, weed-grown car parks, everything which lies in the shadow of the yellow-tiled hulk of the Arndale Centre. I meant to leave him there, but in the end I went after him to apologise. The streets were empty and quiet: by now it was almost dark. Although I couldn't see him, I could sense Lucas ahead of me. He would be walking very quickly, head thrust forward, hands in pockets. I had almost caught up with him near the Tib Street fruit market when I heard a terrific clattering noise, like an old zinc dustbin rolling about in the middle of the road.

'Lucas!' I called.

When I rounded the corner, the street was full of smashed fruit boxes and crates, rotten vegetables were scattered everywhere. A barrow lay as if it had been thrown along the pavement. There was such a sense of violence and disorder and idiocy that I couldn't express it to myself. But Lucas Medlar wasn't there; and though I walked about for an hour afterwards, looking down alleys and into doorways, I saw nobody at all.

I had lied to him about Yaxley, of course. For what motives I wasn't sure, though they had less to do with guilt than a kind of shyness. Even after so many years I had no idea how to proceed. Nothing would have been achieved by telling Pam and Lucas the truth, which was that my dealings with Yaxley began again at their wedding—

3
'Michael Ashman'

Pam's parents insisted on a marquee. They could, they said, afford it.

'And we've a big enough lawn, after all!'

Mr Stuyvesant's family, four generations in the Longdendale Valley, had owned Manchester's favourite department store. Finding themselves, late in middle age, in sole charge of this lumber room – scrolled iron lift gates, revolving doors 'and all' – he and his wife had sold it. Convinced they'd never settle out of England, they bit the tax bullet; and instead of retreating to Marbella let themselves be guided by Mrs Stuyvesant's lively childhood memories to one of the old stone houses in the woods behind Jenny Brown Point, jewel of Morecambe Bay's retirement coast. This they bought. They were a surprise to Silverdale village, with its view of Humphrey Head across the bay, its pretty coves and little limestone cliffs, its gardens full of tranquil yellow laburnum. Restless only a month after she arrived, Mrs Stuyvesant renamed the house 'Castle Rock'. She bought a souvenir shop from which she sold Indian silk scarves. At sixty she still wore an orange leather suit. Pam, her late child, reaching maturity then Cambridge from within a stone's throw of the sea, flowering only to books and epilepsy despite red hair and a Pre-Raphaelite calm, had always puzzled her. 'We're that relieved to have her wed at all,' joked Mr Stuyvesant. Nothing could dispirit him, not even Lucas Medlar, a novice English teacher with a poor degree planning to live near Manchester, refusing first to be married in church at all, then – after Pam had persuaded him it wouldn't matter – coming to the ceremony thin and hostile in a rented morning suit.

My train was late. By the time I arrived, Mr Stuyvesant was on his feet. He wanted to say a few words.

'Ladies and gentlemen, as father of the bride—'

Sitting next to him, Pam was dwarfed by the flounced white satin shoulders of her own dress. She smiled and waved when she saw me, but events seemed to have piled up against her even here, where they were of her own instigation.

The marquee was warm enough, but its floor tilted sharply to the left, so that everyone sitting at that side felt as if they were sliding out of it. The supporting poles, dressed with yellow and white ribbon, creaked uneasily in an offshore wind which that evening had brought mist and rain in from the bay. The air smelt of salt; the canvas bulged and slackened rhythmically; the electric chandeliers swayed. Halfway through the meal, the tennis court had begun to squeeze itself up through the coconut matting. Apart from Lucas and Pam, I didn't know anyone there. I sat on my own with my back against the tent, drank some champagne and stared up into the roof where, far above the central tables on which the ruins of the buffet lay scattered among yellow bows and sprigs of artificial flowers, a bright red helium balloon was trapped. Four or five children were staring up at it too, heads tilted back at an identical angle. Events seemed to have piled up against all of us.

'And so it is that we all wish you well,' Pam's father was repeating. 'To share a life with a young one is a tremendous blessing. Most of all we wish you lasting love.' He pronounced this in such a way as to sound like 'lust and love', sat down suddenly looking surprised, and felt for his handkerchief.

Everyone cheered. The cake was cut. Toasts followed, running into one another:

'Moments like this—'

'—the Reverend, with whom I had the pleasure of sitting a moment ago—'

'It is usual to say a few words—'

'—like to thank my great friends Alec and Katie, the sort of hospitality we've come to expect from them—'

'Brother Simon, for one, had jetted in from Australia "for a couple of days" or so he says, so things aren't very parochial at all!'

Throughout these inane or incompetent speeches – which gave me feelings of nightmare, disorder, the certain failure of everything the ceremony was supposed to represent – the children laughed at every pause, as if they were trying to understand less what to laugh at than when, so that in later life they could measure their responses as accurately by the rhythms of an occasion as by its content.

'I can only say,' someone finished, 'that if I had a pound for every time I've found this beautiful girl literally with her head buried in a book . . . Well, Lucas, I hope you know what you've taken on!'

At this Lucas, whose own speech had been inaudible, tentative, full of failed allusions, stared miserably ahead and tried to smile. Pam leaned across to touch his hand. By now the fabric of the marquee was in constant motion, an enormous muscle rippling and tensing over their heads. Pam's father, who lay like a log of wood in his chair between them, stirred. 'Now then!' shouted the young man who had got up to present a cellophane-wrapped bouquet to the bride's mother and aunt – in case, perhaps, they felt left out – 'None of that!' The plumbing, he had to inform us, 'on a more serious note', was broken. 'Could everyone go downstairs until gravity has caused the upstairs to flush.' While they were laughing at this I heard a voice close to me say quietly and very distinctly:

'The Upper World empties itself of everything which has previously choked it.'

It seemed to come from the canvas next to my shoulder; but there was no one there. Eventually, I looked down near my feet. There, I saw Yaxley's face, craning up at me from where the tent fabric met the floor. He must have been lying full length in the mud outside. Visible eye as blue as a bird's egg, stubbled jaw wrenched to one side, his head was at such an odd angle he looked as if he had deliberately dislocated his neck.

'Christ!'

'Something's going on in the Pleroma,' he said.

No one else had seen him. I pushed my way out of the marquee in time to catch sight of his overcoat flapping away across the lawns towards the woods and the sea in the dark. I ran after him.

'Yaxley!'

'It's something big!' he shouted back over his shoulder. 'All the signs point to something on a scale we can't imagine!'

'Yaxley!'

'It's trying to pull me in.'

I caught up with him and grabbed his wrist. Pulpy with new cuts, it twisted under my hand and he was off again into the stinging rain, heading for the beach. 'Yaxley!' I blundered about in the woods, then burst out on to a low headland dark with gorse, from which I could hear the thin rim of the sea breathing tiredly over the sand a hundred yards away. 'Yaxley! Yaxley! Leave them alone!' I called. But this time I had lost him, and my voice went away over the bay without effect. I stood awkwardly on the edge of the headland, certain suddenly that he had wormed his way into the gorse at my feet and would lie there grinning upwards with accumulated lunacy until I went away. Had he been trying to get into the tent? If he had come to warn us, why had he run off? I began to sense that he was as frightened as Pam or Lucas; of what, I couldn't then imagine.

When I got back to the marquee the dancing had begun, and there was only white wine left to drink. Pam and Lucas shuffled round on the muddy coconut matting. Soaked to the skin, I watched them from a table near the back. I had cut my face in the woods, the knees and elbows of my suit were stiff with wet sand. Though they avoided me, no one mentioned this, even obliquely, until I was leaving. By then the party had moved out of the marquee and into 'Castle Rock' itself. Pam's father came up to me in the hall, where I was waiting for a taxi, and asked,

'Have you been in the house before?' It was two or three o'clock in the morning by then, and he was slightly unsteady on his feet, a short man in preposterous clothes who said 'the house' as if this was the only one in the world.

I told him I hadn't.

'I'm one of the bridegroom's friends,' I added. 'Lucas's. One of Lucas's friends.'

He stared at me for a few seconds.

'Ah,' he said. 'It's just that someone rather like you came to the house a few years ago. About seven years ago.'

As far as he was concerned, his probably was the only house in the world. It occurred to me that I must look to him much as Yaxley had looked to me: something forcing its way in from outside, or up from inside, as deranging and unwelcome as his daughter's epilepsy. In his mild, hospitable way he was trying to tell me so. I had drunk so much by then that I rather admired him.

'I think my taxi's here,' I said.

Shortly after the wedding Pam and Lucas moved to West Yorkshire, where they lived in a large square unimaginative place, local stone, with one or two deteriorating outbuildings. Extensive gardens lay behind it, then the moors; at the front, on the other side of a quiet lane, the land droped abruptly into the narrow valley below the reservoir. The view from its upper windows was gloomy and bare, even in summer when a hot brownish haze spread like a cloudy lacquer over the moors, so that you never knew whether to expect rain, an electric storm, or some property of the atmosphere which had never demonstrated itself before. That winter, though it was so raw and cold, no snow fell, only steady drenching rain. Mist hung above the scrub oaks or clamped down motionless along the sides of the valley. During the school holidays Lucas could be seen at all times of day trying to keep warm by digging over the unproductive garden, clearing undergrowth, lighting rubbish-fires, obsessed with his own thoughts. He was teaching just across the county boundary, in a Thameside comprehensive. He drove there and back along the Woodhead Road in a small Renault he called 'the Tub'.

Pam, though she was uneasy on her own, had soon found how unbearably untidy he could be, and claimed, 'I'm glad he's out all day!'

It gave her a chance to clear up.

'Papers thrown everywhere,' she wrote to me. 'The place always looks as if a bomb has hit it!'

The drugs caused her to sleep late and wake exhausted: loaded with propranolol she would come down at eleven in the morning to find that Lucas, up late the previous night, had thrown everything around in a fit of rage. 'Even the furniture, even his precious bloody books!'

Sometimes at weekends, though she had only left the room for a moment or two, she would return to find him shamefacedly putting records back on the shelves, picking up the sofa cushions, righting a chair. She suspected him of a deep frustration (unable to sound it, grew afraid; unable to absorb or assuage it, blamed herself) but never drew it to his attention. And if in his turn Lucas caught Pam fey and scared, staring with a drowsy helplessness out of the kitchen window into the drizzle at the end of the day, he said nothing either: though he may for all I know have offered comfort. They were twenty-two years old. Already their skills were those of avoidance. They let each encounter slide past them. Off it rumbled, at the last moment, top-heavy with its emotional freight like a train swaying away down a tunnel. As a result, Pam's attacks became more frequent.

'I can't help it,' she would tell herself: 'I can't.'

While Lucas, halfway across the Woodhead Pass in 'the Tub' in the morning, banged the palms of his hands on the steering wheel and repeated savagely, 'I can't help her! I can't!' He hated his heart for lifting when he got out of the house; himself for noticing the way the early sunshine fell across the broad heathery slopes of Longdendale.

To me he wrote, 'It can tire you out, never being allowed to be miserable, or vague, or preoccupied.'

It was in the face of this, I think, that they began constructing between them the fairy-tale of the Pleroma which was to cheer them up in the years when Yaxley and I seemed to have abandoned them. Going through a shoebox of old postcards one lunchtime in an Oxfam shop in Hyde or Stalybridge, Lucas came across a photograph of the Cuxa Cloister in the Metropolitan Museum of Art, New York. 'This cloister contains important architectural elements from Saint-Michel-de-Cuxa,' he read, when he turned it over, 'one of the most important Romanesque abbeys of the XII Century.' No one had ever sent it to anyone. Struck by the enormous tranquillity of the scene, amused at the idea of sending her a card from only ten miles away, he put a stamp on it and posted it to Pam. Half dressed in the hall the next morning, she stared at it. 'Let your heart beat/Over my heart,' he had written on the back. She was so delighted this soon became a habit. He chose only exotic or medieval cards, 'The Creation and the Fall' from the British Library's collection, or Altdorfer's 'Battle on the Issus'; and on the back of them he would always scribble something from one of his favourite writers or painters. 'Every discovery is a rediscovery of something latent,' he informed her owlishly one day, only to advise the next: 'Carnation, Lily, Lily, Rose.'

He often read to her when she felt ill. A few days after he had sent the Cuxa postcard, he read her some chapters from the autobiography of Michael Ashman, a minor travel writer who had walked across Europe in the late Thirties, which began: 'Concrete only yields more concrete. Since the war the cities of the Danube all look like Birmingham.' Ashman, who – as the professional successor of Freya Stark rather than, say, Robert Byron or Christopher Isherwood – had travelled culturally rather than morally, and on behalf of his audience rather than himself, now found he was able to write a more truthful or at any rate a more intimate history of his formative trip—

*

When I was a boy (he went on) you could still see how they had once been the dark core of Europe. If you travelled south and east, the new Austria went behind you like a Secession cakestand full of the same old stale Viennese Whirls, and you were lost in the steep cobbled streets which smelt of charcoal smoke and paprika, fresh leather from the saddler's. The children were throwing buttons against the walls as you passed, staring intently at them where they lay, as if trying to read the future from a stone. You could hear Magyar and Slovak spoken not just as languages but as incitements. There in the toe of Austria, at that three-way confluence of borders, you could see a dancing bear; and though the dance was rarely more than a kind of sore lumbering, with the feet turned in, to a few slaps on a tambourine, it was still impressive to see one of these big bemused animals appear among the gypsy girls on the pavement. They would take turns to dance in front of it; stare comically into its small eyes to make it notice them; then pirouette away. As performers themselves, they regarded it with grave affection and delight.

I loved sights like this and sought them out. I had some money. Being English gave me a sense of having escaped. I was free to watch, and conceive there and then the Search for the Heart.

By day the girls often told fortunes with cards, favouring a discredited but popular Etteilla. (I don't know how old it was. Among its major arcana it included a symbol I have never seen in any traditional pack, but its langue was that of post-Napoleonic France: 'Within a year your case will come up and you will acquire money'; 'You will suffer an illness which will cost considerable money without efficacy. Finally a faith-healer will restore your health with a cheap remedy'; 'Upside down, this card signifies payment of a debt you thought completely lost'; and so on. It was like having bits of Balzac, or Balzac's letters, read out to you.) They would stand curiously immobile in the street, with its seventy-odd unwieldy cards displayed in a beautiful fan. While the crowds whirled round them head down into the cold wind of early spring. By night many of them were prostitutes. This other duty encouraged them to exchange their earrings and astonishing tiered skirts for an overcoat and a poor satin slip, but they were in no way diminished by it.

To me, anyway, the services seemed complementary, and I saw in the needs they filled a symmetry the excitement of which, though it escapes me now, I could hardly contain. Huts and caravans amid the rubbish at the edge of a town or under the arches of some huge bleak railway viaduct, fires which made the night ambiguous, musical instruments which hardly belonged in Europe at all: increasingly I was drawn to the gypsy encampments, as stations of the Search. It was in one of them I first heard the word 'Coeur'.

Was I more than eighteen years old? It seems unlikely. Nevertheless I could tell, by the way the dim light pooled in the hollow of her collar-bones, that the girl was less. She raised one arm in a quick ungainly motion to slide the curtain shut across the doorway; the satin lifted across her ribby sides. I thought her eyes vague, short-sighted. When she discovered I was English she showed me a newspaper clipping, a photograph of Thomas Maszaryk, pinned to the wall above the bed. 'Good,' she said sadly. She shook her head then nodded it immediately, as if she wasn't sure which gesture was appropriate. We laughed. It was February: you could hear the dogs barking in the night forty miles up and down the river, where the floodwater was frozen in mile-wide lakes. She lay down and opened her legs and they made the same shape as a fan of cards when it first begins to spread in the hand. I shivered and looked away.

'Tell our fortunes first.'

When I drew the heterodox card, she placed the tip of her right index finger on its picture of a deserted Romanesque cloister and whispered, 'Ici le Coeur.'

Her accent was so thick I thought she had said 'Court'.

Maszaryk had died not long before; the war was rehearsing itself with increasing confidence. Like many European gypsies, I suppose, she ended up in some camp or oven. Birkenau was in the room with us even then. A burial kommando drunk on petrol and formalin was already waiting rowdily outside like the relatives at the door of the bridal suite, as she closed the curtain, spread the cards, then knelt over me thoughtfully to bring me off in the glum light with a quick, limping flick of the pelvis. However often I traced the line of her breastbone with my fingers, however much she smiled, the death camp was in there with us. Any child we might have had would have lived out its time not in Theresienstadt, the family camp, but in Mengele's block. Its number would have been prefaced with a Z.

The Heart!

The war ended. The cold war began. It was clear that Europe would continue to settle elastically for some time, shedding the energy of its new politial shapes as they jostled against one another. Then, not long after the Communist seizure of power in Czechoslovakia, Thomas Maszaryk's son Jan, Czech foreign minister, was found dead in the courtyard beneath an open window in the ministry. I remembered the young prostitute, and the faith she had placed in his father. We don't so much impose our concerns on others as bequeath them, like small heirlooms. They lose one significance then, rediscovered in a drawer years after, suddenly gain another. I saw that the Search grounds itself – that perhaps the Heart itself speaks to us! – in such short-circuits of history. I spent the days in a fever of suppressed excitement: correspondence with European, Mediterranean and near-Eastern exiles had convinced me that their search and mine were the same. Many of us, remembering how the restless, apparently aimless overlapping of boundaries during the early and high Middle Ages had occasionally exposed the Coeur – wavering, equivocal, interstitial, but never less than a kingdom in its own right – felt that in these conditions it might surface again. It never did. And though I may have hoped for this myself in the bitter winters of the late forties and early fifties, by then I knew as well as anyone how final had been its downfall: a Czechoslovakian prostitute had shown me how to listen for it along the sounding board of history.

*

With its low ceiling, panelled walls and red velvet sofa, the lounge at Dunford Bridge was like the lounge of some comfortable 'country' hotel. It was full of indoor plants which Pam had planted in brass jugs, casseroles, bits of terracotta balanced on tall awkward wooden stands, even a coal scuttle made of some orange-blond wood – 'Anything,' Lucas pretended to complain, 'but proper pots.' Every evening Pam's footsteps would go tap-tapping restlessly across the polished wood-block floor, as, increasingly nervous, she looked for something to do. She rustled the newspapers and magazines they kept in a wicker basket by the fireplace; went from picture to picture on the wall – a head in pencil, turned at an odd angle away from the artist; a still life with two lutes more real than the room; a bridge. In the end she would flick the ash off her cigarette and sit down with a copy of *The Swan in the Evening* or *A View of the Harbour*, each of which she had read half a dozen times before.

She could not put away a feeling of dread, even with the doors closed, a life settled.

'Was that a noise in the garden?'

And she was up again, tap-tapping in and out of the shadows among the bulky old furniture she had chosen at some auction in Halifax.

'It's the cat,' Lucas would tell her.

'I must have a cat!' she had said when they were married.

But she showed no interest in the kittens her neighbours offered, or anything Lucas could find in a Manchester pet shop, and in the end adopted an old, blind-looking tom; brindled and slow. In the summer evenings this animal would move thoughtfully round the garden, marking each station of its reduced territory with a copious greenish spray. Suddenly it became bored and jumped in through the open French window. All evening it weaved about in the open spaces of the wood-block as if it were pushing its way through a thicket of long entangled grass. It smelled strongly, and its ears were full of mites. Pam put down her book. In a flash the old cat had jumped lightly on to her lap!

'Do you think he's in pain?' she would ask Lucas.

'He's not in pain. He only wants attention.'

'Because I couldn't bear that.'

And to divert her, Lucas would take down Michael Ashman's autobiography, *Beautiful Swimmers*, again. It was a strange book. Every so often you found interrupting the slow powerful stream of his journey from Cuxhaven at the mouth of the Elbe to Constanta on the Black Sea, weirs, rapids, passages so strange and personal they belonged in another kind of book entirely.

'The Expressionists chained to their mirrors – Rilke and Munch, Schiele and Kafka – never able to turn away or look anywhere else. A column of doomed and disintegrating soldiers in the long war against the father and the society he has created to imprison them. The mirror is not a simple weapon. It is their only means of defence, their plan of attack. In it they are allowed to reassure themselves: their nightmare is always of an identity so subsumed under the father's that it becomes invisible to normal light, causing them to vanish as they watch.'

At one moment he was full of the direct human details of the trip – 'I started walking again as soon as the rain eased off, then sat through the next shower in the doorway of an empty church, eating cheese and watching the clouds cross Augsburg' – the next, stimulated by the miraculous westwork of Aachen chapel, 'font of the German Romanesque', he would be speculating again about the nature of the Heart:

'We must sound the historical topboard, then, like someone testing a musical instrument, if we wish to hear the fading resonances of the Coeur – its convulsion, its fall, its disappearance as a kingdom of the World. Less acute researchers allow themselves to be deafened by a catastrophe which, they reason, goes through the fabric like the explosion of a bomb: but we know that by now it is only a whisper, an event implicit in the way other events are organised; less an event, in fact, than what rhetoricians might call a "gap". We can never be sure we have found the Coeur except by its absence!

'Falling into the gap we may glimpse that great light – which, though it takes a million years to fade, would otherwise remain invisible to us even if we knew where to look – in the shape of a ripple in the sand, the position of an empty cardboard box on a building site, the angle of a woman's head as she turns joyfully to listen to three notes of music, a playing-card King seen in a sidelong light.'

'How beautiful,' Pam said. She blinked hard; buried her face in the old cat's fur. 'Do you think it could ever really be like that?'

The point of everything they did was to hide.

Every morning, Lucas drove off into Longdendale. Unnerved by the tight bends and fast local traffic, he would peer anxiously into the sunshine or rain for the spire of Mottram church (known since the fifteenth century as 'the Cathedral of East Cheshire'), which signalled that his journey was almost over. At night the moon's reflection raced him home under the rusty pylons, across the chains of reservoirs. Meanwhile – even if the plans of previous owners had left its walls a confusing patchwork of filled-in doorways, bare stone alcoves, and sections of stripped-pine panelling which didn't quite come down to the floor; even if the connecting doors almost always opened into some odd corner of a room, behind the oak sideboard – Pam waited for him as if theirs was the only house in the world. She would have her own modifications in hand as soon as the builders could be bothered to arrive.

When did it become clear to her that 'Michael Ashman', as Lucas presented him, did not exist?

We can imagine her coming down one morning late. She stares helplessly at the reference books and concertina-files spilled across the living-room carpet, a standard lamp tipped over with its pink silk shade crushed out of shape, the pictures awry on the walls. Before leaving for work, Lucas – who often types on the Lettera portable they keep in a bulky old roll-top desk opposite the French windows – has crumpled up a lot of typing paper and thrown that around too. She smoothes out a sheet of it and finds the draft version of a paragraph from *Beautiful Swimmers*, a version without Michael Ashman's deftness:

'The Expressionists chained to their mirrors – Rilke and Munch, Schiele and Kafka – never able to turn away or look anywhere else. A column of doomed and disintegrating soldiers in the long war against the father and the society he has created. Like the assault rifle or the rocket launcher, the mirror is not a simple burden. It is their only method of defence. It is their only means of attack. In it they are able to reassure themselves of their own continuing existence; their fear is of an identity fragmenting, dissolving, fading to a wisp. The mirror assures them – or seems to – that they are still more than a twist of light at its heart. Those faces ravaged by egotism and insecurity still exist, modified by what is expected of them but not yet quite absorbed or transformed. Rilke and Schiele, glue on to what you can prove! – the bent light, the hard glass. Narcissism was hardly in it for you, your survival was so at stake! (By the same token there is endless despair at the centre of every narcissistic self-portrait.)'

The phone starts to ring, then stops before she can answer it. She stands indecisively in the hallway, barefoot on the cold quarry-tiled floor. The old cat runs up and rubs its smelly head on her ankles. Having seen their furniture moved in, everyone else in the village believes she and Lucas are antique dealers. A rumour is already growing up that they have another house just like this one, in Ireland, piled up with valuable sofas and Japanese firescreens. Staring first at the paper in her hand and then out of the window at the mist on the other side of the valley, Pam tells herself aloud, 'I must make a start.'

Shyly at first, each of them demarcated areas of interest: established a personality. Lucas was the creative one. From the start, his intention had been magical, calming. Pam was the critic. This enabled her to pretend for a long time that her interest in the Heart was archaeological, practical, cynical; she would, had she ever spoken openly, have claimed to be testing the theories of 'Michael Ashman' rather than swallowing them. But they never spoke openly, Pam Stuyvesant and Lucas Medlar. Instead, they sat in that huge front room of theirs, plaiting the quotes on one side of Lucas's postcards into the pictures on the other, until, by degrees, over the next year, perhaps two, they had extended Ashman's researches and woven between them, while pretending it was someone else's, a whole world. By two o'clock each afternoon, whatever time of year, twilight was already in the massive old sideboards and bits of pseudo-medieval art. Her prints of 'Ophelia' and 'The Scapegoat' glowed from the wall. He often looked across at his shelves of books by Alfred Kubin, Rilke and Alain-Fournier. The old cat sat first on his lap, then, yawning and straightening its arthritic legs, stepped cautiously over to hers.

What they believed separately about the Coeur when they began – to what extent, for instance, Lucas saw it as a useful fiction – I can't say. But what they came to agree later, by a sort of sign language, seems to have been this: that somehow, and in special circumstances, the Pleroma breaks into ordinary existence, into political, social and religious life, and becomes a country of its own, a country of the heart.

For a time it blesses us all, then fades away again, corrupted or diluted by its contact with the World. Consequently we can detect its presence as a kind of historical ghost.

The myth of the Coeur was centred on its Fall:

4
Dark Rapture

'In the beginning of course,' Lucas used to say, with a smile across the room at Pam, 'it must still have been perceptible as a catastrophe, the World and the Coeur a great wreck burning in the fabric of the Pleroma like two lovers in the glorious wreck of desire, a funeral done in Byzantine colours on cloth-of-gold – blazing ships, breached walls, smoke towering over everything! If only one had been close enough to hear that huge cry of love and loss, echoing and re-echoing across Europe through the remainder of the fifteenth century (so that, for instance, even the wars of York and Lancaster must be seen as a response – however characteristically cold and sluggish – an unconsciously constructed metaphor not so much of the politics of the Coeur as of its inmost griefs) and well into the sixteenth. We should know much more!'

'We know nothing,' Pam would remind him shortly, opening another packet of cigarettes.

Lucas tried to teach her to be willing to guess instead, taking the whole of the Middle Ages as his resource and ranging in his analogies from the Field of Blackbirds to Duns Scotus and the pursuit of Nominalism; from Courtly Love to the ecstasies of le roi Tafur, that shadowy European knight who relinquished armour and horse to fight on foot in sackcloth, and led the plebs pauperum to the Holy City ('What do I care if I die, since I am doing what I want to do?'). 'On one hand,' he said, 'We have the heresy of the Free Spirit, with its emphasis on the singularity and self-possession of the soul, on the other the beautiful staggered

Anima

apses *en echelon* of the Romanesque cathedral. Love and order: the very polarity of these visions demands the Coeur as a higher level of appeal, which will reconcile them by containing them as elements of its own structure, just as the Pleroma reconciles the World and the Coeur.'

But this only made Pam laugh.

'What was it like to live there, Lucas? What did they eat? What sort of pottery did they piss in?'

'We don't know.'

'No.' She smiled. 'We don't, do we?'

'For two nights and a day the harbour had been in flames. In any case, there is no escape from inside the meaning of things. The Empress Gallica XII Hierodule, mounted and wearing polished plate armour but – in response some thought to a dream she had had as a child at the court of Charles VII of France – carrying no weapons, waited with her captains, Theodore Lascaris and the twenty-three-year-old English adventurer Michael Neville (later "Michael of Anjou"), for the last assault on the citadel. The outer walls were already weakened by three weeks of bombardment from landward. The labyrinthine powder magazines were exhausted. Smoke from the besieging cannon drifted here and there in the sunlight, sometimes like strips of rag, sometimes like a thick black fog.

'At ten in the morning a force of Serbs and Albanians, on ladders of their own dead, breached the inner defences; by noon they were still only halfway across the citadel, fighting grimly uphill street by street.

'Lascaris was killed there early in the afternoon. Neville, trying wildly to come to his aid with the remains of the small English contingent, seems to have been ambushed and awfully wounded, and it is possible the Empress thought both of them dead. She was last seen on foot at four o'clock, near one of the gates. By then, someone said, she was weeping openly and had picked up a sword. Her armour, though spattered with blood, remained so bright that when the smoke cleared you could not bear to look directly at her. Several people saw her fall. Not content with killing her the Serbs trampled her unrecognisable.

'The invading kings — it seems hardly worth our while at this distance to know who they were — allowed their followers three days in the sacred city before they took possession of it. When at last they rode through the great arch they received into their care a city which seemed to have been in ruins for a thousand years. They wept to see that birds were nesting in the fallen basilicas, weeds growing up between the paving stones.'

Lucas told this story a number of times. At this point he would always pause and look at Pam before finishing.

'What had happened? The Coeur would no longer let itself be known, though it did not perhaps breathe its final breath in the world until they identified Gallica by her beautiful armour, and displayed the mutilated head.'

There was a silence.

Into it Pam said. 'That's all very well. We read "death" where we should read "transformation". But when will it allow itself to be known by us?' And she lit one Churchman's from another, looking steadily at Lucas until he lifted his hands, palms upwards, in a gesture of puzzlement as if she had asked the wrong question.

They were married for a year, then five. During that time Lucas was promoted, but grew no tidier. Pam continued to rise late, take her medication carefully, and stare out of the kitchen window at the trees on the other side of the valley. Lucas replaced his Renault with a more expensive one. The old cat died, and Pam, who had begun to call it 'Michael', buried it quietly in the garden before Lucas came home. Like any childless couple, they seemed a bit aimless, a bit clinging. Neither of them wanted to risk children. 'I wouldn't visit this on anyone,' Pam repeated often, meaning epilepsy. But their real fear was the entrance of some new and uncontrollable factor into a stabilised situation. While the fiction of the Coeur was central to their lives, it wasn't, to begin with at least, their only relief: Pam kept trying to make something of the house, though its size was always to defeat her; and during Lucas's school holidays, they often went to see her parents in Silverdale.

There the tide crept in and out unnoticeably behind 'Castle Rock'. While Pam's father stood on his lawn in the moist afternoons, looking out as thoughtfully towards the bay as he had done the morning after her wedding; and her mother sat patiently behind the till of the souvenir shop like a lifesize novelty made of leather, fake fur and red paint. They always seemed glad to see Lucas, and were industrious in making him welcome. Privately, he thought they drank too much in the evenings. Lucas rarely drank anything. When he did, he became a clinical parody of himself, swinging helplessly between elation and depression.

For Pam, this was a warm coast, full of geological faults which cut down obliquely through her life, where the blackthorn flowered early above the little limestone coves. Winter felt like spring. After her first fits she had stayed for a few weeks at a convalescent home above the thick mixed woods that come down to the sea at Arnside. She still loved to walk the coastal path there. 'It was so different then,' she promised Lucas repeatedly, as they slithered along tracks of blackish earth trodden aimlessly between caravan parks.

'It all seemed more private: the woods were more mysterious, more like woods.'

Lucas had his doubts. The caravans were old, often without wheels. Towed long ago into stamped-down clearings in the woods and painted green, they had quickly surrounded themselves with plastic gnomes which stared implacably out into the undergrowth from railed-off gardens; while inside at night retired couples from Salford wished, 'If only we could have TV.' There were more modern sites at Far Arnside and Gibraltar Farm – great bare strips of dirty grass in the twilight, dogs nosing about the rubbish bins as it got dark. Lucas bought a map – the current OS 1:25000 sheet – only to find parts of the woods marked an empty white. He studied the legend:

' "Information not available in uncoloured areas." You don't often see that.'

Pam found him an old snapshot of herself, in the grounds of the home.

'Who took it?'

'One of the other patients I suppose.'

There she sat, squinting into the sun: thin, eyes blackened with convalescence, one leg crossed over the other, smiling out at someone she had never seen since.

'Didn't I look awful?'

One summer weekend she arrived alone, by train. Two o'clock in the afternoon: Silverdale was deserted, awash with sunlight so brilliant it made her hood her eyes and look down, as if modestly, at her own arms. Outside the station, birch trees moved uneasily in a baking wind. That morning Lucas had driven her to Manchester Victoria in the Renault, settled her with a styrofoam cup of coffee in the tuffet with its luxurious old tiled walls, and then gone back to Dunford to mark third-year essays, promising, 'I'll come up tomorrow if I get finished.' From Preston onwards, she had entertained herself with the fantasy that he would change his mind, race the train north, and be waiting for her when she arrived. When he wasn't, she began to feel as if she was between lives for a moment – naked to whatever might happen, yet able to have some peace. She shivered with the danger of this, stared out over Leighton Moss, then picked up her suitcase. A crumpled white serviette blew along the up-platform.

Eventually she left the station and walked slowly down the road through the woods towards Jenny Brown Point, where she sat on some rocks in a stupor of delight in the sunshine, looking out over the sea-hardened grass at the distant water of the Kent Channel. Holiday-makers came and went along the shore, laughing and shouting. The tide rose, rearranged the sand and glazed it carefully, and then receded again. All afternoon Pam tried to remember her first fit, the hallucination which had accompanied it, her subsequent appalled dreams of that other seashore, with its rocky platforms shaken by the waves.

The evening was warm, night came: before she knew it the lights of Morecambe hung in the air to the south. She fell asleep, to be woken freezing at 5 a.m. by the astonishing racket of the seabirds on the sand. By then Lucas had arrived and was combing the shore for her; the police were out. 'I didn't remember anything after all,' she told Lucas. 'I only got a very strong sense that I might.' She touched his arm and smiled tiredly up at him. 'I'm sorry.' She seemed happy but dazed for the rest of that day, and kept asking her mother, 'Do you remember someone taking a picture of me, at the convalescent home? What was he like?', to which the old woman could only reply:

'He was a black man. Very interesting to talk to, very educated. You didn't get that much in those days.'

'I knew everyone would be worried about me,' Pam admitted. 'But I felt so lazy.' She laughed. 'Fancy falling asleep on the beach!' Then, in a panic: 'My suitcase! Did anyone get my suitcase?'

Pam was certain the woods and sands were benign. But the very nebulosity of the incident had frightened Lucas. Thereafter, he always tried to be at 'Castle Rock' with her.

'Better the devil you know,' he wrote to me: meaning perhaps epilepsy.

Remembering Yaxley's demented face thrust under the edge of the wedding marquee in the mud, I had my own doubts. But as far as Pam and Lucas were concerned, Yaxley had vanished. They seemed to have healed the old wound, and I wasn't anxious to reopen it. Besides, by then I had a life of my own. So I said nothing and, motives aside, this turned out to be a good decision.

As a way of diverting her attention from Park Point and Jack Scout Cove, Lucas organised trips to local towns. There, inevitably, Pam became bad-tempered. Morecambe had good fish and chips, but it was too crowded; Carnforth (though for obvious reasons they were drawn repeatedly to its vast secondhand bookshop) bored her; she was driven to distraction, she complained, by Lancaster's university-town smugness. All of them were needlessly expensive. Oddly enough she liked Grange-over-Sands: she had been there often as a child. It was middle-class, but it seemed to be in the grip of an endless bank holiday, which a real seaside town should be. She was quite happy to sit in the sunshine at the foot of the sea wall with her sandals off, eat ginger biscuits, drink 7-Up and gaze dreamily across the Kent Channel. Lucas was relieved until in September that year he realised she had been staring all summer at the hill above Arnside, where the convalescent home was situated. He shaded his eyes, consulted the now dog-eared OS map. Arnside Knott, 159m. From this distance the woods, wrapped in dusty gold afternoon light and showing no signs of habitation, seemed even more threatening and enigmatic. If he closed his eyes, black, aimless, muddy paths ran back into his memory. (All he could see were plastic gnomes, and then he was finding Pam again, newly awake and shivering on the shore at Jenny Brown Point, her mouth shocked and her soul as visible as a bruise.) When he opened them again and looked sidelong at her, her head was tilted back and she was laughing. Dazzled by her white cotton dress, which he had glimpsed suddenly from the water's edge, a little boy perhaps two years old had screwed up his eyes against the glare, abandoned his parents to the water, and trudged all the way up through the soft dry sand to stand wonderingly in front of her for some moments before he said in a loud voice:

'Shoes.'

Across his bare skin fell sunshine such a thick, sleepy yellow it was almost ochre. Pam opened her arms wide, as if to embrace him, then wider to take in the whole scene behind him: the clear air rippling with heat; the tide, slack and warm; the red setter running in delighted circles over the beach, snapping up at the gulls twenty feet above its head as if they were butterflies.

'Isn't it lovely?' she said.

She smiled.

'Why don't we walk back through the woods?'

Years of hiding had made them adept at manipulating each other's silences. Lucas was unable to refuse so direct a request. Too much else would have to be confronted.

Whatever he expected, the woods turned out to be cool, speckled with sun, smelling of wild garlic. Even the caravan parks seemed transfigured. But when they got home they found that Pam's mother had choked to death on half a Mars bar, thrashing about like a poisoned chicken behind the counter of the souvenir shop while retired couples from Burnley walked slowly past outside, intent on finding somewhere nice to have lunch, too stupefied by the sunshine to notice anything going on behind the festoons of silk scarves, printed tea towels and decorated leather handbags which cluttered the display window. Lucas Medlar was less appalled by the death than by its circumstances.

'I can't get that picture of her out of my mind,' he wrote to me.

How Pam felt was less clear. 'She doesn't want to talk about it, and I don't press her. People have their own ways of dealing with things.'

Her father didn't want to talk either. He passed his time between the bar and the big bay window at the side of the house, out of which he stared seawards. Or Lucas would find him on the lawn in the mist and rain. Every blade of grass was covered with drops of water, so that it looked as if a hard frost had clamped down in the night. He would be tilting his head as if listening for something. A few days after the funeral they left him to it. He needed help, you could see: but Lucas wouldn't risk leaving Pam there on her own. 'When we talk about the Fall of the Heart,' Lucas was always careful to point out, 'we are actually using a figure of speech. Further, this "fall" has two opposing trajectories: even as we watch the City recoil from the world and back into the Pleroma – a swooning away from us "into the mirror to die in root and flower" – we interpret this movement as its precise opposite, as a fall into experience of the world, which we read as the loss of ontological purity. It is this aspect which must interest the historian and the genealogist.

'For the Empress there was no escape from "inside the meaning of things"; and by definition we can know nothing of those who survived within the Coeur as it snapped back along that first trajectory, and who were thus withdrawn from the world along with it. But if Neville escaped the revenge of the Albanians, so must others have done, and it is their subsesquent history – not as a series of events so much as the clue to a direction of movement – which allows us to plot that second trajectory.

'In this sense, the pedigree of the Heirs of the Coeur is, literally, a fall from Grace.'

The Empress Gallica XII Hierodule, he claimed, had at least three children. Of a shadowy daughter whose name may have been Phoenissa, least is known. 'She was beautiful. She may not have escaped the wreck. You can still hear in the Pleroma a faint fading cry of rage and sadness which may have been hers. The older of the two sons was popularly supposed to have been the son also of Theodore Lascaris, but this seems like a late slander. His name was Alexius and he died in Ragusa in 1460, where, ironically, he had a reputation as one of the secret advisers of George Kastriotis, the national hero of Albania.

'It was his brother, John, who fled to Rome after the Fall, and took with him something described as a "precious relic".'

What this might have been, Lucas was forced to confess, was a matter of speculation. It had been variously referred to as 'the head of Saint Andrew', which when stuffed with chemicals would speak; a rose, perhaps the centifolia brought back to England from the Low Countries over a century later by John Tradescant the Elder, gardener to the first Earl of Salisbury; 'a magic book of which certain pages open only when a great variety of conditions are fulfilled' (this Lucas saw as a parable of overdetermination); and 'a mirror'.

'One description,' Lucas said, 'has it all or most of these things at once. Whether it was head, mirror or cup, book or flower, it continually "extended its own boundaries through the medium of rays". It was known as the Plan, and was thought also to contain within itself an explanation of the ontological relationships between the Coeur, the World and the Pleroma which continuously gives birth to them both. Whatever it was, it was enough to secure a pension from Pope Pius II; and John remained in Rome until his death, fathering three sons. Yaxley, who believes the Plan is still in the world, would dearly love to get a sight of it, but he's barking up the wrong tree – you could learn more from a pair of little girl's shoes left in a ditch.

'It was stolen some years after John sold it to the Church, in the reign of Clement VII; reappeared briefly in the possession of "an Englishman" during the Sacco di Roma in 1527; and has not been seen since.'

By now the age of religious discord was beginning, and with it the Decline of the Heart. Of John's three sons, two died without issue. Mathaeus married a Roman prostitute whose name he changed to the imperial Eudoxia. He made a secret journey in the late 1470s to try to sell succession rights in the Coeur to Vladimir of Bohemia. (Vladimir is said to have asked, 'Where?'; but clearly he knew.) Nothing is known about Stephen except that he was a follower of Contarini, who in the teeth of the historical wind tried to reconcile the old and new faiths of Europe. Did Stephen see in this conflict of simple minds a parody of the Pleroma's dialectic of love and order?

'We can't know,' Lucas would admit with a smile, while Pam looked away at something in the garden, shaking her head and blowing cigarette smoke out of her mouth.

('He was a child,' she became fond of saying later. 'You couldn't reason with him.' But her own desire was deeply passionate and impatient. She was chafed by the closeness of the Coeur, and perhaps she was less frustrated by Lucas's rhetoric of the imagination than by the painstaking way he constructed it. 'Phoenissa didn't die,' she interrupted him one day. 'Or if she did, she died into the World, and a bit of her is in all women.' And Lucas could not convince her of anything else.)

*

The third son, Theodore, had a son of his own when he was fifty. Beyond this his significance is slight. He took the family to Pesara or Pesaro in the provinces and began the Romanisation of it which could be seen over the next two generations until with the birth of Andrew John Hierodule in 1575 the Coeur flared up again like a firework in the genetic material of its heirs. Andrew, Lucas's researches led him to believe, was employed by the House of Orange, 'perhaps as a soldier of fortune, perhaps as diplomat or spy', in 1600. He must have travelled habitually, because he married in Tuscany a year later: the wife died giving birth to a daughter he called, with some irony and an acute sense of his historical position, Eudoxia.

'He disappears quite suddenly after that,' said Lucas, 'but the Coeur is on fire in him, and our next sight of him is at the Hradschin Palace, where the Emperor Rudolph – a solitary and helpless figure more attached to his pet lion Ottokar than any human being – relies in his dealings with Spain on an adviser called "John Cleves" or sometimes "Orange John", who in all respects fits the descriptions we have of Andrew Hierodule. Later he witnessed the Defenestration of Prague. It was Orange John who shouted as Jaroslav Martinez and William Slavata fell fifty feet into the courtyard of the palace, "Let your Mary save you now if she can!" – and then, when Martinez actually began to crawl away: "By God, she has!" Had he gone to Bohemia to hawk the rights of succession in imitation of Mathaeus a hundred and twenty years before? If so, he had been equally unlucky in his choice of Emperor; and he next turns up, still calling himself John Cleves, in England, where he seems to have served the notorious Earl of Lincoln.

'He died in 1638. His sons Leo and Theodore fought on opposite sides during the Civil War. With them – though Theodore, falling among the Royalists at Naseby, was said to have cried out, "Oh, the shiny armour!" – the Coeur withdraws itself again. Leo, less of a lion than his brother, became a pineapple planter in Barbados. Towards the end of his life he was warden of his parish church, and you can see his grave there as

Michael Ashman claims to have done. Of his son Constantine we know nothing at all except that he came back to live near Bristol, where he changed his name to St Ives, married twice, and left a daughter to whom he gave the eerie name of Godscall: this little girl, traditionally, is the last of them.

'Whatever happened to her, she carried in her bones the cup, the map, the mirror – the real heritage of the Empress, the real Clue to the Heart.'

PART TWO
The Poor Heart

5
China's in the Heart

Letters arrived from them at irregular intervals. I remembered them guiltily when I was tired or depressed. Though I never had much faith in their solution, which made me think of two monkeys huddled together at the back of a cage on a cold day, I allowed myself to be lulled by it. It was easier to assume they were happy. Of course I knew nothing about the story they had begun to tell one another; it would be nearly twenty years before I found out about 'Michael Ashman' and the Search for the Heart. About a year after the wedding I moved to London, which I'd always wanted to do. Work – in the editorial department of an independent company specialising in reprints from American academic presses – kept me busy. For five or six years after that my life was my own. Then it all came to bits again.

Late May, Westminster Bridge, sudden gusts of wind like bad predictions from the City. A northbound Number 12 stopped briefly at St Thomas's Hospital to let an old man get on. He hesitated at the kerb and looked up briefly, his face a blur. Despite the wind he wore only a pair of dirty white shorts and a singlet. I was on my way back from the London College of Printing, where I had spent most of the morning, I forget why. I was sitting upstairs at the front of the bus. He settled himself next to me, though there were plenty of empty seats, and – as the Number 12 pulled out on to the bridge and began to cross it – put his feet up companionably on the windowsill in front of us. He smelt rank and lively, like a small animal in straw.

'China's in the heart, Jack,' he said, and laughed.

Careful not to answer, in case he was encouraged, I looked out over the river towards Hungerford Bridge. The tide was high. Light came up from the water, filling the space between Westminster Pier and Riverside Walk.

'That's what they say. China's in the heart!'

The bus edged past Parliament in fits and starts, eased itself through an orange light and turned up towards Trafalgar Square. From the corner of my eye I could see the backs of the old man's hands with their prominent ropy veins, his ankles white and dirty above his old suede shoes. Suddenly he put his hand into the pocket of his shorts and brought out a handful of thorns and crumpled leaves. I thought he was going to roll a cigarette with this stuff: instead, palm out flat, he offered it for my inspection. At that moment the bus driver found a clear patch in the traffic and accelerated the length of Whitehall. I heard a familiar voice intone, 'The burnet rose—' (or perhaps it was 'the burnt rose') '—five white petals with the light shining through to make a cup for its pale yellow stamens.' I jumped to my feet.

'Yaxley!'

I lurched down the gangway, down the stairs, waited trembling on the platform for the lights to stop the bus at Trafalgar Square.

Yaxley followed me more slowly.

'I'm getting off here too,' he said, showing me his handful of rose leaves again before he crumpled them up with a vague, distributory gesture, as though to scatter them over the stone lions, the dry boarded-up fountains, at the base of Nelson's Column. They were blown under the wheels of a stationary taxi while I waited passively for whatever would happen next. I felt sick. What was I expecting? That he would perform some magical operation, there on the pavement outside the Whitehall Theatre? All he did was study me for a moment. 'Never waste an opportunity!' he advised, then set off rapidly towards the lower end of Charing Cross Road.

I followed him.

'Yaxley,' Pam Stuyvesant pointed out a long time later, 'never did anything to anybody. He always encouraged us to do it to ourselves.'

Up past the National Gallery, left across the toe of Chinatown by Gerrard Place, over Shaftesbury Avenue at the Queen's. He knew I was there. He would step out deliberately in front of a car then stare back at me with a triumphant grimace from the other side of the road; or bump into a woman shopper and shout, 'Fuck me! See that?' Under the tower of St Anne's Soho, with its skeins of dead ivy like a shrivelled venous system, he turned and made pushing motions at me – 'Go back. Go back.' Wardour Street was deserted. He turned left abruptly, to make a curious loop through the gut of the Berwick Street fruit market (where a stallholder's call of 'Twelve for a pahnd. Twelve for a pahnd 'ere!' prompted him to look up and shake his fist at the signboard of the King of Corsica, with its collage of brooding faces), along Broadwick Street, and back on to Wardour Street again. His gait was shambling and agitated. He wavered at the entrance to Flaxman Court. On Meard Street a few blackened pigeons scattered across the cobbles in front of him: he stopped on the corner in front of the old, boarded-up clockmaker's shop – with its faded sign, dusty pillared doorway and stucco rosettes – to stare into a basement area as if he had forgotten something. It was a strange, illogical tour, which ended suddenly when he dodged into the Pizza Express at the corner of Dean Street and Carlisle Street.

I caught up with him as he lurched and shoved his way between the crowded tables to a corner by the window. Disturbed by his smell, people looked up suddenly as he passed, only to look away again when they heard him say quietly but distinctly to himself, 'Cunt!' or 'Who's this nasty little animal then?' He sat down and emptied the plastic flowers out of the little vase in the centre of the table.

The waiters ignored us.

'Yaxley—' I began, but he had lost interest in me again.

All of a sudden rain began to stream down into the street, and with it a kind of sad, silvery, watery light, which splashed off the front of the pub opposite. Within seconds the road was empty. 'There's a parrot up there,' said Yaxley, in an inturned, empty voice. He was right. I could see it clearly through the upper windows of the pub, running up and down inside its cage like a little mechanical toy. There wasn't much else to look at: another restaurant, the 'TRUSNA' with its pink and purple façade, closed: the rain.

'Yaxley?'

'Just fuck off and leave me alone,' he said.

He seemed to be waiting for something.

After a moment two men appeared, pushing a car which wouldn't start. They went round the corner into Dean Street and only one of them came back. He stood in the doorway of the Pizza Express and shook out his umbrella. As he came into the restaurant, his gaze caught mine for a moment. It was absent and empty. I looked away.

Yaxley grinned and leaned over the table. He had torn his paper serviette into several thin strips, one of which he laid across my place mat. Its edges were fibrous and delicate in the washed-out light.

'Look at that!' he said.

I stared at him. I realised that he meant not the torn serviette, but the man who had just come in.

'No, be careful not to let him see you! His name is Lawson.'

The Pizza Express was full of middle management from the advertising and TV industries, lunching each other on the cheap. 'The only reason you go to Germany for two years is to make more money than you do here,' said someone a few tables away. After that I heard only, 'BBC.' There was some laughter. Lawson looked no different to the rest of them. He had furled his umbrella and taken off his raincoat, and was now sitting two or three tables away from us, with people he knew. He wore a gold watch, a striped shirt, one of those pale blue ties with the small white spots you see in the shop next to the men's lavatories at Euston Station. His hair was grey and curly, the curls tiny, tight and wiry: he had on a blue suit.

'Listen to him!' urged Yaxley.

I could see that Lawson was speaking, but in the lunchtime hubbub it was hard to separate his voice from all the others. He talked with his mouth open all the time: the lips moved in a jerky rhythm unrelated to speech, like those of a puppet, so that you imagined left to themselves they would make a constant 'wah wah wah' noise, not loud but penetrating. For a moment I thought I could hear this noise. I was wrong. Then suddenly he said, and I heard him clearly even at that distance:

'Ba-luddy woman. Ba-luddy woman! My God!'

He moved his mouth down to his fork to eat.

Yaxley seemed delighted.

'That man knows four things about the Pleroma,' he said. 'Three of them he learned from me.' He shrugged, and as if to justify himself went on, 'So what. Everyone knows them. But the fourth is important. He is unaware that he knows the fourth, or that he is keeping it from me.'

'I thought you knew everything,' I said.

Yaxley gazed across the junction at the baskets of flowers above the appalling façade of the 'TRUSNA'. The rain had eased off and people were walking past again.

'How are Pam Stuyvesant and Lucas Medlar?' he asked me distantly.

Before I could answer, he went on:

'Let me tell you what Lawson will do this afternoon, when he leaves here. He'll go down to the Thames at Charing Cross Pier, wait in the Victoria Gardens for a very young woman to get off a pleasure boat, and follow her to a house in West Kilburn. She will go inside and shut the door. Then he'll stand outside for an hour, willing her to cross an uncurtained window; while she sits on the bed with her hands in her lap, staring at the wall in front of her. After an hour or two, Lawson will turn away and go home.

'He thinks this girl is his daughter, but she is not. She is a daughter of mine.' He laughed. 'One of my daughters.'

'I don't want to know any of this,' I said.

'Yes you do,' said Yaxley. 'Because if you help me with Lawson I will help you with Pam and Lucas. Would you like me to help them? Things will get worse for them even if I try.'

'What things, Yaxley? What things will get worse?'

He only shrugged.

'If I don't try, they haven't a chance,' he said. 'Look—'

He pushed a Polaroid photograph across the table to me. It showed quite a pretty teenage girl in the white blouse, royal blue V-neck and pleated grey skirt of some private school. Failures of the developing chemicals had drained colour out of her face, so that it had a blank, unformed look. I couldn't see any resemblance to Lawson. She was sitting on a garden bench, leaning forward with her clasped hands resting on her lap. Behind her it was possible to make out a neo-Georgian door; some standard rose bushes in grey, loose, heavily weeded earth; a black BMW. Something about the curve of her back, the clasped hands, the way she seemed to be staring straight ahead into the air, reminded me of a painting. I couldn't think who it was by.

'Lawson wants to fuck his own daughter. Do you understand? He wants to fuck her, but he hasn't the courage or the determination to do it. She lives in Cheshire with his first wife. He says she is fourteen years old, but I imagine she is younger. He is afraid of himself on her behalf. I've explained to him how he can deflect this stroke on to a substitute. I've made him an image of her. When I'm ready I'll allow him to use it in return for what he knows.'

'I won't be involved, Yaxley.'

'Yes you will,' he said.

I stared at him across the table. He pushed his chair back and stood up. 'Keep that,' he said, indicating the Polaroid. 'You'll need it.' He arranged the rest of the torn serviette around my place mat, then as an afterthought added the plastic flowers.

'There,' he said.

*

For Yaxley, everything had to be clouded, discerned with difficulty, operated at several removes. Even the simplest journey was only the superficial evidence – the diagram – of another, more difficult one. I had seen this clearly, even at Cambridge. It was not so much a 'belief' or a method as a tendency, an intuition about the world. All along he had been trying to pass it on to us. Had he abandoned Pam and Lucas because they learned it too quickly and superficially? I was less in Soho that afternoon, I guessed, than in some scene of instruction, some teaching space of his. Later I would be able to understand the feeling that all of it had been mimed for my benefit. I would recognise St Anne's church, the signboard of the King of Corsica, the front door of 68 Dean Street, a few feathery strips of paper, as the furniture of an initiation. For now I could only sit looking furiously at the torn-up serviette while he left the restaurant, crossed the junction and hid himself in the side doorway of the Nellie Dean. The pub parrot ran nimbly to and fro in its cage above him. The sun broke through.

When Lawson finished his lunch a few minutes later and went off east along Carlisle Street, Yaxley allowed him fifteen yards' start then slipped after him. I followed them in my turn, through Soho Square and into Sutton Row. It was a useless gesture. They were still ahead of me as I went past the dustbins outside the 'Society of Our Lady of Lourdes, but by the time I had emerged at the top end of Charing Cross Road they were nowhere to be seen. I wandered about in the shadow of Centrepoint, thinking of Pam and Lucas, and didn't come back to myself until I saw the tower of St Giles-in-the-Fields, with its eight white pillars and white spire, against a very blue spring sky. Four in the afternoon. The clock was a minute or two fast. I had been walking in aimless overlapping loops, like a fly on a television screen. 'Ordinary destinations,' I remembered Yaxley telling us at Cambridge, 'are unearned.' Around me, people were hurrying northwards into the wind, faces set for an hour's commuting home. Even though the traffic was light they still looked suspiciously up and down the street before they crossed.

By then I was married, too.

My wife's name was Katherine. She owned a house which backed on to the canal where it runs between Camden High Street and Regent's Park.

An overgrown garden, with terracotta pots and little figurines, sloped down to the cut: from the upper windows you could look down across it to the surface of the water, green and gold, as solid in some lights as a polished floor, shadowed by trees in the summer, strewn with leaves in the autumn. That was some years before they cleaned up the locks, extended the markets and brought Disneyland to North London in the shape of TV-AM. I had often teased her when I first moved in:

'I can't tell you and your house apart.'

'Touch me here, then.'

Her parents were dead, but remained embedded in the stories she told, like a fossil record in stone. A fortnight after their marriage, her mother had driven a milk float into a ditch. It was a manifesto, or tremor of intent. Later, sleepless in a Cambridge hotel, her father heard knocking late at night behind a bricked-up door. 'That whole family were psychic.' In some way the house still belonged to them. I loved its high, elegantly proportioned windows and polished wooden floors. Every room was full of light, which she encouraged inside – like someone encouraging a shy cat – with white walls, pale eggshell colours.

'Now touch me here.'

She would take my hand, lead me from room to room, and pretend that by touching a cushion, a picture in its frame, the stem of a silk rose woven between the spokes of a dining chair, I was arousing her.

So we exhausted ourselves, dissolving into one another and then further, into a reflection from the bookcases in the lamp-light, the smell of a perfume called Anaïs Anaïs. I dreamed of the fold of a velvet curtain, the inside of a cup, the long white curve of her back as she knelt in front of me. A bird sang confusedly in the middle of the night. Everything ran together. On my way downstairs to collect the post the next morning, I would stand still suddenly and say 'Katherine' to myself, just to feel that quick lurch of excitement, like something alive inside, you get when you know that in the next instant you are going to be happy.

6
The Facsimile

'What do you want me to do?' I had asked Yaxley at the Pizza Express.

When his instructions arrived a week later they were scrawled, along with a telephone number, on the back of a postcard. He had sent it from Kensal Rise. Some other project was occupying his time there, but the card, which depicted a street in Meudon in 1928, offered no clue to what it might be.

I rang the number and said: 'I can't drive.'

'Find someone who can then,' Yaxley said, and put the phone down.

I rang him again. 'Be reasonable, Yaxley.'

There was a kind of scraping noise on the line.

'I'll send someone,' he said.

He sent David.

David, a tall lad perhaps twenty-two or twenty-three years old, who wore jeans and a donkey jacket over faded T-shirts and frayed pullovers, lived with his mother in Peckham. He had worked only once or twice since he left school. His face was thin, already muscular about the mouth from the effort of suppressing some internal tension. His eyes, though, remained clear and childish, and he had a habit of staring at you after he had spoken, as if anticipating some response you could never make. He knew you could never make it, never guess what he wanted. Disconcerted, you stared back.

When I asked him what he did with his time, he said,

'Oh, read a lot mostly.'

He enjoyed science fiction, of which he had gathered quite a large collection; or books about concentration camps bought from the non-fiction shelves of W. H. Smith's. He had read Primo Levi, but preferred Wieslaw Kielar. Growing up on this stuff in his mother's one-bedroom flat – the third of four in a gloomy Victorian house with gabled upper storeys – he had failed to notice the gas water-heater above the bath, the loose floorboards, the doorframes which changed shape every summer as the London clay dried out. His mother, who tended to doze off during *News at Ten* or earlier, had the bedroom. This left David to sleep on the convertible sofa in the lounge; more often than not he kept the television buzzing instead and drank Harp lager out of a tin in the wavering half-light.

Two young Asian women lived on the floor below. One of them was a paranoid schizophrenic on community release, who often shouted and screamed deep in the night.

'Get that filth out of here!' David would hear her call suddenly after a long silence.

'The People next door,' he told me, 'had to get rid of their dogs. They used to join in when she started. They'd howl until it got light.' She wasn't too bad at the moment, he believed, because he played his stereo loudly during the day. 'That keeps her awake, so she sleeps more at night.' He was solicitous about her, despite the trouble she caused. 'We keep an eye on her when we can,' he said. 'Her friend has to go out to work.'

The flat above was empty. In that lay much of David's usefulness to Yaxley and Lawson. Sometimes I can still smell the fire that ended all this, and hear the crash of air brakes as the fire-engines sawed back and forth across the street. Eventually they blocked their own access. You could read by the blue lights. David ran aimlessly about until he was exhausted. Because I was careful never to go into his relationship with those two, I have no idea what he owed them. As for his mother, they didn't even know her, although Lawson – who believed in what he called 'family values' – once said:

'God knows what she cooks all day down there. It smells like somebody's bad breath.'

That was typical of the way Lawson spoke. If you rendered his pronunciation of 'car park' as 'caw pawk', you would be close but not quite there. The initials BMW weren't short enough for him – he was always comparing his 'BM' with someone else's 'Jag'. He said 'on the drip' to mean hire purchase. Sensitised to his voice by half an hour in the Pizza Express, I heard it, or thought I did, every lunchtime thereafter. A glimpse of his shoulders and the back of his neck, two or three places in front of me on the escalators at Tottenham Court Road underground, the sight of a suit I thought was his, in a crowd trying to cross Oxford Street opposite Marks & Spencer's, would be enough to send me hurrying in another direction. He always seemed to be eating something. Once, in the restaurant at Smith's Gallery in Covent Garden, he actually spoke to me.

I came in from Neal Street, hung my coat on the rack by the bar, and realised he was sitting with his back to me at one of the tables near the bottom of the steps, less than ten feet away.

Like David, Lawson was never more than a victim: even so, he had appalling energy. Perhaps in the end this is what attracted Yaxley to him. He was never still. Some barely contained greed caused him to rock about in his seat as he ate, touch his hair and face with his hands, move the chair next to his, move it back to its original position. He called for pepper: let the waiter go: immediately called him back for more.

'Most people want to be pastry,' I heard him say to the woman he was with. 'Don't you think?' Instead of answering, she looked up and saw me standing there helplessly.

'Do I recognise you?' Lawson said loudly, turning to face me. I shook my head.

'Well then can I do anything for you?'

'I—'

'It's just that when I catch people staring at me like that, I wonder if I can do something for them,' he said. 'But if I can't—'

As I walked away he was leaning across the table to whisper something to his companion – or at any rate to thrust his face into hers – and laugh.

'Because if I can't do anything for you,' he called after me, 'perhaps you could stare at somebody else.'

Smith's was full of people from design agencies, brand new PR firms. I felt them watching amusedly as I followed the waitress between the pillars, through the heat and buzz and the smell of food. I had been expecting to meet a friend of mine who worked in the academic division of Allen & Unwin. I sat down and stared hard at the tablecloth, then the menu; the pictures on the walls. Lawson's voice was clearly audible from across the room. 'Ba-luddy caw pawk attendants,' I heard him say. 'Ba-luddy little Stalinists!' It was easy to imagine him, still implacable with greed, following his 'daughter' home every afternoon in the rain. How accurate, how sustainable, was the facsimile? Perhaps, when Yaxley's attention was elsewhere, it ran like watercolour, grew blurred and unsatisfying, failed to nourish. And did the real daughter feel any of this, staring out of a stockbroker-Georgian window across the darkening Wirral at the end of the school week? Waiting to hear the low-profile tyres of the BMW crackle up the gravel drive, she would be sticking pictures of ponies and Barbour jackets into a book. 'Term is over. Today the holidays begin.' Did she feel her danger?

When the waitress asked me, 'What would you like with that, sir?' I realised that I couldn't remember what I'd ordered.

That afternoon I rang Yaxley.

'Oughtn't we to move soon?' I suggested. 'He saw me. He may have recognised me from the Pizza Express.'

But although Yaxley had finished his business in Kensal Rise, he still seemed indecisive. The instant he picked up the phone I had received a clear impression of him, sitting in his room above the Atlantis Bookshop, staring straight ahead of himself while the clock of St George's Bloomsbury struck twenty-one and the light fell across his furniture like a kind of yellow varnish that would never set.

'Yaxley?'

I wanted him to succeed with Lawson. By now I was frightened of what might happen if he didn't.

'Don't bother me now,' he said vaguely.

Thirty or forty seconds passed. He still had the phone to his ear.

'Yaxley? Hello?'

David owned an old Hillman Avenger. It was a fawn colour, patched with maroon where he had sanded and primed it for respraying. Inside, it smelled of oil, Halford's air-freshener and foreign food, like a Peckham minicab. His mother, as undeterred by this as by its scabbed chrome and deteriorating wheel-arches, redeemed it every week with a new soft toy. She bought him a sticker which warned, 'You toucha my car, I smasha your face.' On Saturdays in the summer they Blu-Tacked a crocheted blanket to the inside of the glass to keep the sun off the back seat, and David drove her slowly round the Rye into Dulwich Village, so that she could enjoy the posh houses with their oriel windows and hundred-year-old trees. David was her youngest child. He had arrived late and learned slowly. Prone, especially after his father died, to obsessions and enthusiasms – model fighter aircraft, weekly encyclopaedias of military history, anything you could collect or assemble – he had puzzled her by becoming self-contained. 'Very much his own person,' she told people. 'Not like the other three.' That innocent obsessiveness lay curled inside him, waiting until Yaxley – surfacing from dreams of the Pleroma to take a few long ragged breaths – eventually found a use for it. Three days after I had run into Lawson, David arrived at my office, where he undid his coat nervously, gawping like a tourist at the rows of books.

'I'm ready if you are,' he said. 'Where we going?'

Yaxley had told him nothing.

'It's half past three,' I complained. 'I haven't finished work.'

He sat down. 'I can give you another ten minutes or so,' he offered, 'but I'd prefer to be there before it gets dark.' The car had developed an electrical fault: once he turned its headlights on, we wouldn't be able to stop. 'Electrics can be complicated.' Parking had been a problem, too. 'I've left it over in Poland Street.'

He thought for a moment. 'It's probably not what you're used to.'

'We'll go up the M1,' I said.

On the motorway he turned out to be an impatient driver, pushing aggressively through the Friday afternoon traffic with the speedometer up against the stop, where he kept it until near Luton all three lanes began to back up.

'Nice to be out, anyway,' he said.

'Nothing wrong with this engine,' he boasted. 'As long as you stay on top of it.'

Then:

'Look at him. No, him, him over there! Is he a wanker, or what? Three litres, fuel injection, antilock brakes. What's he doing? Fifty miles an hour.

'Fifty fucking miles an hour!'

When there was no one to overtake he became restless, switching the radio on and off, opening and closing the ventilators. He had a trick of swapping his left foot to the accelerator pedal, tucking his right foot up between the seat and the door. He could do this with hardly a blip in the engine revs; although sometimes while his attention was diverted the car itself lurched disconcertingly through the slipstream of a sixteen-wheeler. Spray shattered the light on the windscreen, blowing in all directions through a haze of sunshine and exhaust smoke. We watched two crows flopping heavily away from the hard shoulder, reluctant to leave something they had been eating there.

'I used to drive a van,' he volunteered suddenly. 'Rented van, for a firm of builders. We took it back to the rental place and said, "It's overheating if you do a hundred for any length of time." '

He chuckled.

'The bloke said, "A van like this won't do a hundred." Fuck that, mate!' He looked sideways at me to see if I believed him. 'I had that job a month.'

'Why don't we try the A5 for a few miles, then join the M6 near Rugby?'

'Why not.'

As we turned off the motorway, a Ford Sierra station wagon, logy with children, spare bedding and pushchairs, wallowed past us in the middle lane.

'Can you believe that?'

By the time we got to Cheshire, he had worn himself out. 'I could do with a cup of tea.' He put his feet up on the dashboard, rubbed his eyes, stared emptily out across the Little Chef car park at a strip of bleak grass rising to newly planted trees, where, in the gathering twilight, some children were running around the base of a pink fibreglass dragon fifteen feet high. 'Who would build a thing like that for kids?' he asked me, wriggling about behind the wheel until he could get one arm into his donkey jacket and pull it awkwardly over his shoulders. He looked genuinely puzzled. 'Who would want their kids playing in that?'

'Stay here,' I told him. 'I'll fetch you the tea.'

'Fucking hell.'

The Little Chef franchise includes a carpet with a repeating pattern of swastikas, each arm of the symbol a tiny chef who smiles all day while he holds up a dish. Inside, three sales reps were eating cheeseburgers, fries, a garnish of lettuce shiny with fat. Every so often one of them would read out a paragraph from *Today*; the other would laugh. I found Lawson's daughter waiting quietly in the No Smoking section. 'Be certain it's her,' Yaxley had warned me, as if he expected his substitution to be trumped before he could make it. When she saw me comparing her to the Polaroid, she pretended to be looking out of the window, from which, if she moved her head slightly, she could see the parked cars; the line of the Derbyshire hills a long way in the distance south and east; and against them the fibreglass dragon with its slack, Disney Studio jaw signifying helpless good humour. She had on the identical pleated skirt, with a white blouse; but her hair was in a plait. Close to, she smelled of Wright's soap.

'Your father sent me to fetch you,' I said. Yaxley had schooled me: 'Be certain to say that first. "Your father sent me." ' A waitress arrived at the table. I ordered a pot of coffee and sat down while she brought it. Then I added – because what else could I say? –

'He's looking forward to seeing you.'

David came to the door to find out if his tea was ready. 'For God's sake!' I called. 'I'm bringing it!' He ducked away, and I saw him walking quickly back to the car, his shoulders hunched under the leatherette yoke of the donkey jacket. I got Lawson's daughter and her things together and went up to pay.

'Everythink all right for you, sir?' asked the woman at the cash desk.

'Yes thanks,' I said.

'Want anythink else?'

I could see her looking worriedly at the girl.

'No thanks,' I said.

The M6 was deserted. From the moment David launched us down the access ramp into a rushing darkness broken only by the occasional oncoming light, someone else's will clung round us like the smell of the car. Despite our speed we were in a kind of glue. David wouldn't speak to me. If Lawson's daughter had isolated me from him, what I knew about her seemed to detach all three of us from our common humanity. 'The sacrifice,' Yaxley had taught me at Cambridge, 'has its own powers.' She made herself comfortable in the back, and sat so quietly at first that after a few minutes I asked:

'Are you all right?'

'I quite like this grey fur,' she said, touching the seat covers. 'It's soft as a cat.'

Then: 'I'm not often car sick.'

'Are you warm enough?'

'The last time we went on a motorway with Daddy, there were three dead cats,' she said suddenly.

'When we got home we found our own cat had been hurt by a lawnmower and had all the flesh stripped off one front leg. You could see all the lines under the skin. You never know whether it's bones or tendons, or what, do you? He kept pawing us and howling, there was blood all over the kitchen top. Mummy was funny after that. Every time she saw something in the hedge or in the gutter, she made us stop the car.'

She laughed.

'"Is that a dead bird?"' she mimicked.

'"Is that somebody's walking stick, or just a broken umbrella?"'

Unnerved perhaps, David began to talk too—

He had seen the most brilliant film when he was small. '*Flying Tigers*, fucking amazing!'

He was reading a book about the Auschwitz museum.

'In Birkenau,' he said, 'they cut the hair off the women prisoners before they gassed them. It was sold to manufactures for mattress stuffing. Can you believe that?'

I admitted I could. He added:

'But the worst thing is, tell me if I'm wrong, some of those mattresses could still be on beds. Couldn't they?'

He was worried about his mother.

'She's due to go into the Maudsley for a couple of days soon.' It turned out that she had some kind of bone disease. A broken wrist had failed to heal after two months in plaster, and would have to be pinned. 'It always happens to someone else, doesn't it? Cancer, air crashes, drink-driving, it's never you it happens to.'

He stared ahead for a moment.

'It always happens to someone else.'

He meant to be ironic, but only wound up sounding wistful.

'Look!'

Our shadows had been thrown on to an enormous exit sign by the headlights of the car behind. Briefly we became monumental and cinematic – yet somehow as domestic as the silhouettes of a married couple caught watching TV in their front room – then the journey resumed itself as a series of long, gluey moments lurching disconnectedly one into the next until we reached the outskirts of London, where the traffic, inching along under a thick orange light, filled the steep cuttings with exhaust smoke. Two men fought on the pavement outside the Odeon cinema, Holloway. Lawson's daughter had gone to sleep, her face vacant, her head resting loosely against the window, where every movement of the car made it slide about uncomfortably. She didn't seem to notice when I reached back and tucked a folded pullover under it. Later – or it might have been in the same moment – I looked up and thought I saw roses blooming in a garden on top of the Polytechnic of North London. Between the lawns were broad formal beds of 'ballerinas' grafted on to standard stock, with lilies planted between them. Dog-rose and guelder spilled faint pink and thick cream over old brick walls and paths velvety with bright green moss. White climbing roses weighed down the apple trees. Two or three willows streamed, like yellow hair in strong winter sunshine, over the parapets of the building; briars hung there in a tangle. A white leopard was couched among the roses. It was four times the size it would have been in life, and its tail whipped to and fro like a domestic cat's. Other buildings had put forth great suffocating masses of flowers; other animals were at rest there or pacing cagily about among the service gantries and central heating machinery – baboons, huge birds, a snake turning slowly on itself. 'The Rose of Earth is the Lily of Heaven.' The scent of attar was so strong and heavy it filled the street below: through it like flashes of light through a veil came the piercing human smells of fried food, beer, petrol.

David braked suddenly.

'Jesus!' he said.

The back of a refrigerated truck filled the windscreen,

TRASFIGURANTE painted across it in huge white letters. I jumped out of the car in the middle of the road and shouted back through the open door, into the heat and smell and David's surprised white face:

'I'll walk home from here.'

'What?'

I slammed the door.

'I'll walk.'

That night at home I had a nightmare about hiding from people. I was rushing about trying to keep trees, buildings, cars, anything between me and them. I heard a voice say, 'The double paradox. Life is not death, and neither is death,' and woke up to an empty bedroom. It was three o'clock, pitch dark. A rhythmical thudding, with the muffled but determined quality of someone banging nails into a cellar wall or knocking on a heavy door two or three houses further down the street, had carried over from the dream. When it failed to diminish I got up unsteadily. The bedroom door was open, the stairwell dark.

'Katherine?'

Pounding, as distant as before.

'Katherine? Are you there? Are you all right?'

I went from room to room looking for her. All the internal doors were open. Orange street light had established itself everywhere, lodging within the mirrors, slicking along each mantelpiece, discovering something in every room. In the lounge that evening a book, *Painting and the Novel*, had been pulled partly off a shelf – the shadow of its spine fell obliquely across five or six others. In the kitchen, a knife, a breadboard and a loaf of bread lay next to a Braun coffee-grinder like a little white idol. Up in the studio, near the top of the house, something had fallen and broken in the empty grate. 'Katherine?'

She wasn't there. Outside, St Mark's Crescent was full of parked cars; behind the house, the Regent's Canal lay exhausted and motionless. Though I was naked I felt languorous and comfortable, as if I was surrounded by some warm fluid; I had a partial erection which hardened briefly when it touched the fabric of the living-room curtains. At the same time I was filled with anxiety. Its cause was hidden from me, but like that noise it never stopped.

'Katherine?'

Eventually I went back to bed and found her lying there awake in the dark.

'What's the matter?' she whispered,

'I—'

'What is it?'

'I thought you'd got up,' I said. 'That noise—'

'I can't hear anything.'

'Didn't you get up?' I said. And: 'There! Listen!'

'I can't hear anything.'

I had begun to shiver. 'I went all round the house,' I said. 'I can't get warm.'

Katherine put her arms round me.

'What have you been doing to get so upset?'

'Listen!'

Some dreams, I know, detach themselves from you only reluctantly, amid residual flickers of light, sensations of entrapment, effects which disperse quite slowly. Everything is trance-like. You wait to understand the world again and, as you wait, fall back into the dream with no more fear. But there was something awful about that thudding noise, its remoteness, its persistence.

'How do you feel?' Katherine asked next morning.

'Oh fine, fine,' I told her.

But I knew that something had been knocking. Something had come into the house.

'I hope you are,' she said.

She was a painter. We had met one night two or three years before, at an exhibition at Goldsmith's. Somewhat older than me, she had been recovering from an affair I never asked about. At first she was unwilling to commit herself. But soon we couldn't be away from each other for a day, or even pretend to be: so she woke one morning in her perfect house to find me propped on one elbow, staring down at her with a kind of slow delight, and smiled and said, 'I can always feel you near me, even when I'm asleep;' and that was that for both of us. We were married almost immediately. I loved to look at her, in those first few weeks. I would hold her head gently between my hands and stare down into her face and think: She's in there.

'I'm fine.'

Later that morning I went up to her studio. There, a ghost of the canal-light, reflective and mobile, lived like a quiver at the edge of vision in the matte white ceiling and walls. I don't know whether she ever noticed it, any more than the smell of the turpentine she kept in a Victorian glass inkwell; but it resides in her paintings too, whatever their subject – the flicker of summer sun off water and green trees.

For Katherine, painting was about space. 'You should always sit,' she had told me the first time I visited her, 'in the middle of a studio, not along the edges of it.' I wandered about now as I had then, leafing through a shoebox in which she kept small sketches on French watercolour paper – wavering pencil lines and little dabs of paint, clues to her inner life; inspecting the brushes – dull orange, blue and brown – laid out on the varnished floorboards beside her on a sheet of corrugated paper to stop them rolling about; or turning over the tubes of oil paint in their wire basket. Vandyke brown, Indian red, crumpled tubes leaden in the dull light. Their names will always delight me. Oxide of Chromium. Monestial green. Speedball oils from America. I still own the picture she was working on that morning. In it a woman stares out at the viewer. Behind her are some other people, and an unfinished, ghostly background of desks in a school or typing pool.

A kind of hypnotic tranquillity always seemed to issue from Katherine as she worked. She had an extraordinary calming effect. You could hear the dab and whisper of the brush on canvas; and behind that, so faint as to be an illusion, the sound of her breathing. It was like watching my mother, ironing in the kitchen on a September evening. I touched the place where the nape of her neck made its soft but powerful transition into the muscles of her freckled upper back. After a moment she turned her face up to me and said, 'Kiss me then.'

We stared companionably at one another. She put her brush down and took my hand.

'Are you sure you feel OK?'

'I'm sure,' I said.

She picked the brush up again.

'I wonder about you,' she said. 'What a lot you keep to yourself!'

7
Number 17, Hill Park

William Blake experienced his first vision during the course of a family outing to Peckham Rye, which was at that time a village of quiet, largely agricultural character in the Parish of Camberwell. Eight or nine years old, his biographers report, William hallucinated (what else can we think?) a tree full of angels, 'bright angelic wings bespangling every bough like stars'. He escaped a thrashing, though his father wanted to give him one. More importantly, his foot was on the path. He had his idea. It wasn't yet a burning spear, but it was never to let him down.

Whether Lawson's daughter saw anything after David installed her in Peckham, I can't say.

17, Hill Park lay on the left of the Rye as you looked south, caught between some bleak low-rise flats and two or three pointblocks built on a hill. A burned-out Vauxhall had sagged on to its brake drums in the street outside; the basement area was full of broken furniture – chipboard, Formica, warped and lifted veneers. If you stood on the doorstep and looked up and down the road, it was nothing but a line of skips heaped with builders' rubbish. Inside, I never saw much more than the staircase – grimy lino, spent matches, missing banisters, a corroded sisal mat outside each door: At night the stairwell was lit by bare forty-watt bulbs, one on each landing. By day a kind of grey illumination leaked in through the skylight, high up in its shaft. You could hear the sound of rain on the glass. When you walked through the front door of the upper flat, you were faced with two or three carpeted steps then a little passage with white plasterboard walls and chocolate brown woodwork. It was like finding your way to the toilets of a tea shop in some bleak tourist town at the top of a cliff.

The morning after Lawson's daughter arrived there, I had a call from Yaxley.

'I want you to fetch some things for me,' he said. 'A few things.'

Prominent among these was a shoebox of Polaroid photographs he had taken himself, but which he never kept by him, I suspect out of fear. Magic had exhausted him sexually long before Pam, Lucas and I met him. He found it difficult to reach the levels of arousal necessary for a demanding operation. Neither was ordinary pornography of any use. One of the first tasks of my apprenticeship to him – though at the time I didn't think of it in that light – had been to accompany him on a round of the Cambridge public lavatories once a week. He preferred the older ones, seeping and cracked, reeking of piss, which you approached down a dozen greasy stone steps. There would be a soaked uneven floor in the gloom; three stalls with shiny black doors; blue distemper flaking away above the chipped white tiling. Homosexual graffiti covered the walls, done in straight lines and little boxes, in careful expressive designer handwriting. Heterosexual commentary blundered over and around it, in a vigorous but barely legible scrawl. Where Howard had articulately written that he owned his own place and would be happy to try you out any Friday evening – including for your information a hyper-realist illustration of what he claimed to be his penis in an erect state – some drunken boy had added:

YOU POOF.

'These simple endearments,' Yaxley said. He photographed them all. 'See that no one comes in for a moment.'

It was an unnecessary precaution. Places like that are always empty when you go in. A sound in the cubicles turns out to be the trickle of the cistern. Nevertheless, unwilling to be blinded however briefly in such circumstances, I was grateful to establish myself in the doorway and stare across the road – at the rain, the railway station, the woman with the dog – while Polaroid flashbulbs etched at the gloom behind me, and panel by panel Yaxley built his reredos and altarpiece.

'That man,' he had told me the day I first saw Lawson, 'knows four things about the Pleroma. Three of them he learned from me. He is unaware that he knows the fourth, or that he is keeping it from me.' In some sense I couldn't comprehend, Lawson himself was to be made to stand, by metonymy, for that fourth item of knowledge, so that its resources could be drawn upon without it being present in the world. Yaxley called this metaphysical sleight of hand an 'infolding'. I pondered it as I bought or collected objects and artefacts from all over London – books from dealers in Shepherd's Bush and Camden; secondhand garden statuary from Kent; dusty artificial flowers, hanks of hair and a jar of something which looked like preserved ginger from a woman in Golders Green – and delivered them, over the next week, to Peckham.

The upstairs flat at Number 17 could not simply receive these things. First, David must strip it bare. The furniture and carpets came out. The floorboards were scrubbed. In certain places, to erase some stain Yaxley thought might interfere with the operation, they were sanded down to reveal pinkish new wood. All stains, spills, dirty marks, carry an energy of their own. Particular attention was paid to the walls. To ensure success, all the old paper had to be taken off: above the fireplace and near the windows, Yaxley had got down through the old plaster and into the brick. Another kind of magician might have wished to preserve the resonances of Number 17; in other circumstances Yaxley himself would have valued them. But recourse to pornography is by definition a loss of confidence. Where previously he had conceived and assembled the details of such an operation on impulse, holding them together by sheer force of will, he now let caution undercut insight. He made David hire a steamer from a DIY store in Nunhead, and watched thoughtfully as twenty or thirty years of interior decoration bagged and blistered away from the yellowed, sugary plaster in front of his eyes.

'The stuff underneath's not much better,' David told me one evening, when we met on the stairs outside his mother's door. 'These old places are rotten to the core.'

He was sweating. His clothes were covered in dust from the plastic bags of lino, plaster and broken furniture he had been carting down to the bins in the street. Clearly though, it was an effort he enjoyed: something to do. He pushed his hair out of his eyes and had a look at the parcel under my arm.

'What you got there?'

'Gethsemane.'

'You what?'

Gethsemane, in a plastic frame the colour of bone. Painted in greens and golds by someone with no sense of perspective, nevertheless it had in some lights a strange stereoscopic quality. Christ swam out past the picture-plane with his arms spread wide in a gesture of welcome difficult to understand, while the trees and rocks of the Garden, laid on with a palette knife, roiled and eddied behind him like bad weather. It had been much stocked by Catholic outlets a decade before, but after scouring the secondhand shops for two or three days without result, I had taken Yaxley's advice and tried boarded-up premises on the Old Kent Road, under the sign 'ICTURE, Sean Kelly'. Icture, I thought, would resemble ichor, that fluid which runs in the veins of angels as well as kitchen beetles. Or perhaps it was a service, like acupuncture. Anyway, there the picture was, not even dusty, hanging up in a smell of old men and milk bottles, while in the back room an American pit-bull terrier fought with silent determination against its tether to get at me.

'Somethink else for His Nibs, eh?' said David.

He winked.

'Is he mad, or what?'

'Make your own mind up,' I said. 'How's the girl?'

'Hardly a peep out of her. She's with Mum most of the time.' In the day, she stuck pictures in a book, or helped with the housework. 'Watches telly a lot.' It made you wonder what she did at home. You had to give her full marks for quietness, though.

'Mum's teaching her to knit.'

I knew Lawson was in the house with us. I had passed his BMW in the street, black and shiny among the rubbish skips. I could hear his voice, ba-luddy caw-pawking away in the flat upstairs. Somehow this magnified David's good will and made it all the harder to bear. I wanted to shock him out of it. I wanted him to feel the girl's danger. Most of all, perhaps, I wanted him to feel guilty. I pushed him into the corner of the landing and said urgently:

'This is the real daughter.'

He gave me a puzzled look.

'Yaxley's substituting the real daughter,' I said.

'What?'

'He's going to use Lawson's real daughter for the operation! You must have known that!'

'Operation? I don't—'

'Hasn't he told you anything?' I shouted. 'For Christ's sake, David!'

He stared at me.

'I'm just helping him out,' he said eventually.

'Shit.'

The door to the top flat banged open, and down came Lawson. He was in a hurry. He had on a beautifully tailored overcoat in grey wool, which somehow accentuated the breadth of his shoulders, the thickness of his neck, the forward thrust of his head; and he was carrying a bottle of Louis Roederer champagne as shiny and incongruous under the yellow forty-watt light as the car outside at the kerb. 'I can't be bothered with that now,' he called back up to Yaxley. 'Get someone of yours to do it.' There was no answer. When he reached the landing, he inspected David, as if he had never seen him before.

'Just as a matter of interest,' he said. 'What *does* your bloody mother cook all day in there?'

I don't think he once suspected his daughter was behind the same door, watching *Game for a Laugh* and *Celebrity Squares* every evening when he went past.

David, who had never understood Lawson well enough to defend himself, could only laugh and shrug. Lawson laughed too. 'Well, best be off, eh?' he said. I was in his way: he started to shove me aside, then stopped abruptly and, his hand still resting on my arm, eyed me with hatred. Yaxley appeared at the top of the stairs and smiled weakly down on all three of us, his face damp and indescribably vacant in the yellow light. Leaning forward, he looked as if he might launch himself off the top step and float out over us; or else cover us with vomit.

'I'll remember you,' Lawson promised me softly, as if he had only now understood something.

'Oh, I'll remember you.'

The infolding took place two or three evenings later, in the main room of the upper flat, at about nine o'clock. I arrived late and, in the end, saw very little of it.

The room was cold. On the wall surrounding the empty fireplace, Yaxley had pinned a dense mass of overlapping Polaroid photographs. From a distance, these tiny, often blurred images seemed to condense into a single sign from some randomly devised but powerful magical alphabet. Above them, like a lock to keep their meanings under control, he had hung the Gethsemane I had found on the Old Kent Road. Its central figure swam out of the cheap frame with motions of despair. In front of the fire had been placed a stripped-pine table with short bulbous legs, which in any other ritual would have taken the part of the altar. Since no actual sacrifice was to occur here, I wondered how Yaxley would use it. For a moment I had a clear vision of Lawson with his trousers down round his ankles, trying to mount his own daughter as she clung pale and goosefleshed to this object, with its cigarette burns and whitish ring-shaped stains. Then I caught a glimpse of the girl, and saw what they had done to her.

She was sprawled legs apart in a corner, naked but for a pair of white briefs designed for someone twice her age, with lace detail and legs cut very high to accentuate the pubic mound. Her ribcage and immature nipples stood out in the forty-watt light. Shadows pooled in the hollow of her collar-bone. A musing, inturned expression was on her face; but every so often she laughed inappropriately at something Yaxley or her father said. They had got her drunk on some kind of cherry liqueur, which I could smell from where I stood in the doorway at the end of the passage.

Yaxley and Lawson were occupied burning something in the grate. Yaxley's wrists were covered in new scabs; Lawson blew on the pale blue flames until his cheeks were red. I could hear them murmuring excitedly, but I couldn't quite see what they had set on fire – glossy paper, I thought, of the sort used for soft pornography: I could see it, wadded, reluctant to catch, curling at the edges. But its thick, stale odour was of something else entirely, wood, hair, kitchen waste. The fourth person in the room was David. David seemed drunk too. He had propped himself up against the wall near Lawson's daughter and was staring at her small white shoulders and arms. Every so often his gaze would fix with a kind of wonder on the place between her unformed thighs where the lips of her sex were quite discernible beneath the thin white fabric.

Apart from the girl they were all fully dressed.

I watched for a minute or two in silence. Lawson was the first to notice me standing there.

'I told you he'd turn up in the end,' he said to Yaxley; and then to me: 'Traffic bad, was it?'

His daughter laughed.

'See any dead cats?' she asked me.

'Christ, Yaxley!' I appealed.

He turned away from whatever he was doing. His eyes were yellow and empty, his face grey. He looked like a cancer patient.

'I'm not going to be involved in this,' I told him.

'Yes you are,' he said.

David laughed suddenly.

'Fucking hell,' he said. 'Eh?'

'Yes you are,' Yaxley repeated.

'Come here, lovey,' Lawson said absently to the girl.

She pulled herself to her feet, then clutched at herself with both hands.

'Daddy, I've wet my knickers.'

I took a pace into the room, said, 'Lawson, this is your *daughter*,' then when I saw the expression on his face, turned round and walked straight out down the stairs and into the street. Rain was falling through the sodium light, pattering on the leaves of the sycamore trees. It would have been easy enough to walk into Peckham and catch a train into London Bridge. I meant to go home to St Mark's Crescent and tell Katherine everything. I knew she would help me. Instead I crossed the road, positioned myself in a doorway with the collar of my coat turned up, and stared numbly at the lighted upper windows of 17, Hill Park.

At about a quarter past ten, the glass blew out of them and tumbled into the basement area beneath. Smoke poured into the air, grey at first then thick black then back to grey again. Shortly afterwards, amid cries of fear and pain, the front door slammed open; Lawson, David and the girl appeared at the top of the steps. Lawson and his daughter were naked, but David still had on his Union Jack underpants. The girl ran off immediately, zigzagging away into the uncertain light of the sodium lamps like some quite new city animal, a vulnerable slip of flesh with a face pale and streamlined to featurelessness – frightened yet touched with all the triumph of the victim. I expected Lawson to follow. Instead he stared after her; said something incoherent; then, suddenly aware that he was being watched, stormed across the road towards me. The whole left side of his body was scorched and reddened, so that he looked as if he had been dyed. His genitals hung shrivelled and vestigial-looking beneath a belly larded with middle age. He thrust his face very close to mine. Expecting him to hit me, I stepped back into the doorway:

but all he did in the end was shake the keys of his car under my nose and shout:

'I've still got these, you bastard!'

And then:

'I remembered you. Don't think I didn't!'

He ripped open the driver's door of the BMW, made one or two hasty attempts to start it, then drove away at high speed.

This left only David, running helplessly about in the street in front of me, trying to say one word over and over again, as if it might describe what had happened in the upper room.

'Ungestalten, Ungestalten, Ungestalten—'

Ungestalten: the shapeless. The pain of being without shape. Some days before, prowling restlessly round the High Street Smith's in search of – as he put it to the assistant – 'Anything about concentration camps,' he had bought the newest Primo Levi. At home, sitting with a can of Harp in the television half-light, he had foundered immediately on this reference to Nietzsche and the suffering of the underclass. It was a strange idea to have encountered between biographies of Myra Hindley and David Niven. I had tried to explain to him the 'price that must be paid for the advent of the reign of the elect'. From the beginning, though, David had understood it all literally and personally. *The pain of being without shape.* It was not the idea that frightened him, so much as the question of who – or what – might suffer this pain.

'Ungestalten, Ungestalten—'

As Lawson turned the BMW out on to the main road at the bottom of Rye Hill, the fire brigade was turning in. They crowded into the narrow street in front of Number 17, the back of one appliance lit up silver by the headlights of the next. The heavy grinding sound of pump engines filled the night. David seemed not to notice them. He ran up and down between the engines, repeating 'Ungestalten, Ungestalten,' in a kind of formless whine; then fell over suddenly. When he got up again, his mouth was slack. Blood and mucus ran out of his nose.

Eventually one of the firemen captured him and he was put into an ambulance. His mother was still inside the house.

'Ungestalten.'

Unable to act, I remained in the doorway for some time after he had been taken away. Yaxley's will was like glue: it was all round me still. Brought steadily under control, the fire began to smell like burning rubbish in the distance on a clear day; a human, domestic smell, rather more frightening because of that. They had illuminated the front of Number 17 with a powerful floodlamp, but its white glare revealed nothing. How Yaxley had escaped, I don't know. I hoped at the time he was dead, but I knew it was unlikely. Everyone who lived in the street came out on the pavement to watch the firemen at work – there were frail but cheerful old men and women from the flats, families with children not much younger than Lawson's daughter, a woman who brought her baby with her as if to accustom it early to tragedies and occasions. Someone said:

'They've burnt the dinner again, then.'

Firemen were in and out of the house now. Much of their activity seemed aimless. Blue lights flickered down the hallway, reflected from the pictures on the walls. ('There!' they said in the street: 'Look there!') The smoke abated briefly, the beam of a torch struck out through it: a fireman was in the upper room! Flashes, as the torch moved about. I wondered what he could possibly be seeing, there in that exhausted, sticky zone of Yaxley's will. Finally, a figure in a yellow helmet leaned out of the window and, framed against faint grey smoke, looked down, shrugged. Two hours from the first appearance of the engines, it was all over. People went back to their own houses, a little subdued, whispering, 'Doesn't a woman with kids live there? Ain't that a family with kids?'

'I don't think anyone was in there.'

'There must have been someone.'

I was left in the rain, soaked to the skin, still looking upwards.

What happened that night? It would be naive to think that

Lawson's sexual satisfaction was at issue. A facsimile would have done for that. Yaxley had planned all along that real incest should be committed in the upper room at 17, Hill Park. He had planned all along to reveal this to Lawson as soon as it was too late to withdraw. But though he enjoyed these layers of deception for themselves – it was the mark of his increasing impotence – he must also have had a clear magical purpose, some assumption upon which was predicated the whole ritual of 'infolding'. What this purpose was never really became clear. Neither was any help forthcoming for Pam Stuyvesant or Lucas Medlar. I don't think he had ever meant to keep his word on that. Along with the two Asian women, David's mother died of smoke inhalation. I'm not clear why David had to lose so much.

8
On the White Downs

After the fire nothing seemed to lift me. I was unable to convince myself I had lost nothing by being involved with Yaxley. Each attempt to get him to help Pam and Lucas had only intricated my motives fatally with his. Every night I dreamed of a Pleroma screaming and convulsed by his attempts simultaneously to penetrate it and escape it; meanwhile, Lawson telephoned daily to harangue me, or offer me his daughter, or abuse me incoherently for having taken her already thus reducing her value in any further operation. He didn't seem to understand that Yaxley had abandoned us all again. At first he promised scandal, public exposure, legal action: but he knew quite well the extent of his own involvement. Even now I'm not clear what he thought he wanted, unless it was to retain somehow his links with the magician; to express somehow that dim sense he had of the Pleroma as a power – an immanence, a closeness – he had failed to share.

By then I was bone-tired from morning until night. I wept easily at Japanese films.

At the office I found myself unable to work, staring puzzledly instead at the shelves of paperbacks while my assistant fetched me cups of lukewarm instant coffee the surface of which was always covered with undissolved powder. February came and went. The winter dragged into March and then early April, driving a fine cold penetrative rain across the junctions of Tottenham Court Road. Eventually I caught myself staring at my own deformed reflection in the window of a tube train between

Goodge Street, where I worked, and Camden Town, repeating, 'Was that all? Was that all?' Perhaps the agony of the Pleroma was fading. Soon after that Lawson seemed to become less of a nuisance. His threats were replaced increasingly by bursts of uncontrollable weeping, until the calls ceased altogether.

'Why don't you go down to Cornwall for a month?' Katherine suggested. She owned a cottage there, between the road and the sea perhaps two miles north of St Just. Originally she had intended to use it in the winter, rent it out between April and October. 'Have a holiday!'

'I think I might. Everyone in publishing suddenly looks like Anthony Blunt.'

'Have a holiday,' she repeated. 'Recover yourself.'

'I wish I could find a self to recover.'

She stared at me.

'I don't suppose you'd like to come?' I said.

The cottage was one of a neat terrace, built in Penwith granite. While she was waiting for the conversions grants to come through Katherine had filled it with old furniture: a good suite of her mother's with one chair missing, divan beds, one-bar electric fires with perished rubber flexes fitted in 1958, all that detritus which accumulates in houses whose use the middle class have temporarily failed to define, or which they have furnished for the use of others. But you could smell the sea – though you couldn't see it – and hear it, and even at night feel that vast emptying-away of the sky to the west where the headlands fall into the Atlantic like folds in a velours cardigan.

I arrived late and went straight to bed.

There, unused to the silence, I slept fitfully and dreamed I was walking down the coast road towards Zennor Head in the dark:

The air had veiled, brown qualities, draining the colour from the stands of gorse which sometimes appeared at the landward side of the road. Every so often the white finger of an old signpost came into view – not the yellowish white of bone or ivory, but the hard chemical white of typewriter correction fluid: Penzance 5 miles. The figures of Yaxley and Lawson jumped out at me from the gorse, their faces drawn and self-concerned. Lawson's daughter in her white knickers opened her legs – Yaxley mopped his forehead, breathing stertorously. 'Sperms!' he cried. 'Sperms in this picture!' – while Pam and Lucas looked on in sorrow. Something was wrong, clearly, and it seemed important to do what they wanted. But I couldn't make out more than a word or two of what it was. In the dream I was worn out but I couldn't go to sleep: I knew I was too tired to move my limbs, even though I was walking.

This prostration of the will seemed to flow smoothly out of the dream and into the days that followed.

Each morning I would walk into St Just, buy bread at Warren's, milk or groceries from the Co-op in the square, then make my way back exhaustedly to the cottage, where I sprawled in a chair – head thrown back, legs stuck out in front of me – like an old man, so worn out I felt as if I was being pushed firmly down into a hole.

There was no telephone.

I began a letter to Pam and Lucas. 'Katherine Mansfield lived along this coast,' I wrote. Then: 'When I look forward I can only see it getting worse: middle age, apathy, death.' I couldn't post that to them of course. I let it stay on the table while I stood helplessly in the middle of the room wondering what on earth I could say. 'Arthur Symons lived here too.' The next day a cat lay like a splatter of black ink on the concrete path under the window; when I spoke to it, it looked up deliberately, stretched, and walked away. I laughed. I was released. I would probably feel fragile for some time: but the crisis, I believed, had passed. Suddenly I screwed the letter up into a ball, which I squeezed until it was packed and hard.

The downs with their granite outcrops and hut-circles overshadow everything. They squeeze everything seawards, into narrow bands: the coast road, the linear villages, a little grazing.

Long bracken-covered salients fling themselves down between the pasture and the sea, the boggy re-entrants that separate them full of low-lying elder pruned by the wind into a dense, tangled scrub. Old cinder lanes wind over them, linking the abandoned mine workings and empty hamlets from Kenidjack and Pendeen up to Gurnard's Head. Kittiwakes wheel above them in the blustery air and sunshine.

I was grateful for this abrupt falling-away of the coast, the luxurious feeling of light and distance it gave. Half a mile below the cottage, I discovered one morning an unworked quarry, warm and sheltered, from which I could look out at the sea. I sat down and unbuttoned my shirt. Shortly afterwards I took it off altogether. I feel asleep, and woke with a start of surprise in a burning blue space. The curve of the workings drew the skyline away out of my field of vision: above that, nothing but sky, alive and glittering as if it somehow reflected the sea beneath, yet heavy and reverberant with heat. I went back to the house and found a faded woollen blanket; a cold drink.

'After all,' I wrote to Pam and Lucas that evening, 'I'm here to get better, just to lie in the sun and get better—'

The next morning I took a book with me, and by the end of the week I had read *Tristes Tropiques*, *The Gypsy's Baby*, *Mr Beluncle*. In the afternoons I would close my eyes against the glare and let the heat press insistently on their lids. Opening them again suddenly, I saw that my feet were white, blue-veined, delicate-looking. I couldn't remember ever having looked at my feet before.

There at the end of a long sleeve of land, the quarry held its contents gently, miraculously, like a hand opened wrist upwards to face south-west. The leaning walls of dark Killas slate, low at first, with thick green and white masses of vegetation piled up against them in an arrested wave, rose steadily to a height of eighty or ninety feet where they overhung a shallow pool. Here, towards the back of the workings, the rock was always damp and streaked with lichen. Hybrid willow, purple and white foxglove, contorted dwarf oak grew profusely on the collapsing terraces amid colonies of wild roses. A thin perpetual trickle of water ran down through dripping mats of moss and fern to fill the pool. In the oblique gold evening light that wall dominated the quarry: and even during the day, when I lay among the mysterious knolls and reefs of the quarry floor – where the heather was mottled with the bright green of new bilberry, and children had scratched narrow, aimless, sandy paths up and down the blunt salients of old spoil – I sometimes found myself looking up at it in surprise. Then I would smile, bury my face in the aromatic turf, and listen to the sound of the water dripping down behind the foliage. It had become a voice. A gull screamed overhead. The tide poured out of the zawn below the headland, and back again with a muffled thud. With my eyes closed I felt as if I were hanging unsupported in the air – burned, clarified, renewed by the summer light,

I knew that if I stayed there long enough I would be let into a secret.

During the week people used the quarry as a car park, especially at lunch time. Most seemed content to roll down the driver's window and read the *Western Morning News* with one elbow stuck out into the sunshine; but one or two locked up the car and walked off to look at the sea or wade into the montbretia which, escaping for a hundred years from the village gardens, now roared over the headland like a heath fire. They were gone by one o'clock.

Every afternoon when the quarry was most likely to be deserted, a handicapped couple arrived.

They were shy and strange, easily put off. The woman was blind, the man could not walk. I watched them. This is how, together, they made up a kind of organism:

At three o'clock their little fawn Reliant van, whining in first gear, would bounce down the track from the village; turn into the quarry with exaggerated care; then, chrome winking in the glassy light, roll uncertainly to a stop. The woman expected rain, so she always wore a white raincoat buttoned to the neck. She talked to the driver in a loud, animated voice. He replied in monosyllables. She got out, and a black labrador guide dog jumped out after her and ran about barking. Every afternoon before allowing it to lead her round the quarry she made it stand still for a few moments.

'Can't you behave, you daft old dog?'

Her left leg was twisted so as to point the foot inwards instead of forwards, which gave her a rolling and limited gait. Nevertheless the dog wasn't always quick enough for her. It blinked up at her and sneezed. She laughed with delight, turning her round, perspiring face up to the sun. After a circuit or two like this she let the dog off the lead. While it raised its leg among the nettles, she would feel her way along the side of the van to the rear doors and fetch out a folding wheelchair. This had to be assembled by touch, which took several minutes. By then the driver had got his own door open and was waiting for her to help him out. He was impatient, unhelpful, gesticulatory; she laughed and groaned at his weight. The dog watched them indulgently, hanging out its long red tongue. In the end the driver fell into the chair and lay there breathing hard and staring into the sky.

'Can I help at all?' I asked, the first afternoon I saw them.

The paraplegic, slumped white-faced in his chair, tried to ignore me. He was still in his twenties, with muscular shoulders, black hair and deep-set angry eyes; he had been a swimmer or a cyclist, perhaps: a runner. Suddenly he pulled his mouth into a sweet, extraordinary, practised smile and said,

'We'll manage, thanks.'

'It's easier in the end,' the woman agreed quickly in her loud voice. 'Really.'

They had their own way of doing things, habits long-formed. They had their independence.

'I'm sorry,' I said. 'If there's anything—'

'Thank you anyway,' she said.

She offered me the ghost of her sight: a faint discoloration of the whites of her eyes. She had buttoned her coat unevenly that morning, so that one side was higher than the other.

Every afternoon she hobbled round the quarry then wheeled the man in his turn, while he guided her with curt rights and lefts, his head tilted to one side as if it were too heavy for his neck, his body held with the legs stuck stiffly out in front. Every afternoon he made her stop so he could look across the pool at the tangled roses, the cushions of moss, the waterfall, the tottering ribs of Killas slate. He clutched her arm: pointed here and there: followed with his head the sudden zigzag flight of a bird. Every afternoon she wheeled him back to the van and with a lot of grunting and straining forced him back into the driving seat like someone trying to force a snail back into its shell, whereupon he took charge again, revving the engine on its hand-throttle, calling to her to hurry the dog up.

They were like the parts of the jellyfish, a million years ago, coming together for the sake of convenience and never being able to go back on the arrangement.

At what point do you recover your self?

I wanted to do things, but not the things I had always done.

A barely suppressed excitement drove me out, on to the headlands, into the abandoned tin-streamers' cottages at Nineveh, along sunken lanes, in the mornings before I had time to eat anything.

By eight the tracks were already warm and airless. Bees wavered past on long curving courses. In the grass grew bird's-foot trefoil as yellow as the inside of an egg, tangled up with wild violets and cinquefoil. Great spear-thistles commanded the sagging walls and ruined gardens, thrusting up out of patches of fuchsia. The bramble-covered banks were alive with butterflies like new, complicated kinds of petals. Emerging suddenly on the upland lawn above the cliffs at Porthmoina Cove or Cam Clough, I would stare out at the Atlantic framed violet and silver between blunt brown headlands, and, astonished by the landscape, feel my imagination reach out vainly to touch its essence. The sea! A vigorous wind blew between the white boulders; the cliffs fell away; behind me, waves of gorse and bell-heather broke on the gentle slopes. All around was blue and unrelenting air!

I was elated one minute, tired out again the next.

I felt as if I was listening for something, but that it would never speak.

Subsidiary workings opened off the quarry, two or three interconnected troughs full of dust and flies, used by the local farmers as a rubbish dump. Hanks of last year's fern stuck out of the sandy walls, which nowhere rose higher than ten feet. A dry whirring, the sound of grasshoppers, came and went with the sun.

Crouched listlessly in one of these pits, knees drawn up to chin, arms hanging at my sides, I fell asleep and dreamed of a green woman who led me a dance over the downs:

It was the middle of the day.

All morning a hot enervating wind had scoured the village, bringing with it unidentifiable, tarry smells. Among the quarries it was even hotter. Suddenly there was a movement deep in the shadowy crevice between two walls, and the green woman walked out into the sunlight, relaxed and naked. I watched her carefully, from a distance. While her outline was perfectly sharp, it seemed to have no surfaces, and flowers came and went within it as she turned her head deliberately this way and that. She was like a window opened on to a mass of leafage after rain, branches of blackthorn, aglet and elder interwoven, plaits of grass and fern, all held together with rose briars, over and between which went a constant trickle of water. She knew I was there.

'We are never simply ourselves,' she said.

She stretched her arms, standing with one leg bent and the other stiffened to take her weight.

Now she passed landwards in a stately way, striding between the great rays of light which fell upon Morvah, Rosemergy and the White Downs, to places even beyond that where I stumbled naked after her along the windy edges among the broken stones and earth. Soon she stood in a steep, hidden ashwood, where a stream descended a series of mossy steps and pools. I straddled this and masturbated convulsively, standing up. 'Don't look at her,' I told myself. 'Don't look.' I came again and again until I was exhausted and out of breath. I thought of Pam Stuyvesant, and my wife, and Lawson's daughter, each sprawled and spread open on to the same pink wet rose, and came again. Then the green woman led me back to the quarry, where I felt no fear of the unknown: here she climbed up behind the mat of vegetation on the back wall. She turned and looked at me directly! Her eyes were a pitiless chalky blue, without white or pupil. They were flowers, too. When I knew I could no longer avoid their gaze I ran about waving my arms and shouting, filled with a mixture of terror and happiness.

Hundreds of elder flowers, tiny cream stars with five blunt, points, showered down on me in a cold wind. When I woke up it was because clouds had covered the sun and great splatters of rain were falling on my bare arms.

For the rest of that week the weather was bad. Offshore winds packed the clouds down tightly round the cottage, where I sat by myself listening to a length of washing line tap-tapping against its metal pole in the garden, while the foghorn at Pendeen Watch boomed morosely out into the grey Atlantic spaces. The flower-beds were black with something between mist and rain, and water hung in beads along the power cables. Each evening, just before it got dark, the clouds seemed to lift for a moment: one or two wallflowers, already past their best, glowed in the thin flat light. Inside, a little of this light collected about the spines of the paperbacks; and you could hear a petal fall in the bowl of dog-roses on the bookcase. I had been in the cottage for a month. Neither Pam nor Lucas had answered my letters.

All the telephone boxes on the coast road were damaged. I began catching the ten o'clock bus into St Ives every morning. There I watched people driven into the arcades and surf shacks by the rain; picking over heaps of souvenirs at the indoor market, avid, bored and helpless by turns. 'Esperdrilles,' advertised the handwritten signs on the stalls: 'Plimpsoles.' Plump young couples, their faces as unblemished as their brand new windbreakers, linked hands by the lifeboat station and looked across at the hundreds of houses of Mount Zion, roofs and walls of all colours tumbling up the hill in stacked planes like an amateur post-Impressionist landscape. The tide was out. The moored boats canted in disorder against their weedy strands of rope, a box of sweets tipped out on wet sand the exact colour of the coffee served in the Tudor Rooms; while a hundred yards away the sea lapped like a kitten and the young herring gulls walked awkwardly about trying to eat pieces of paper. I telephoned Pam and Lucas anxiously from a fish and chip café on the front. The phone rang at their end but no one picked it up. All I could hear was the woman behind the counter:

'Yes, love?'
'Coffee, please.'
'Thank you, love. Anything else, love?'
'No thank you.'
'Twenty pence then thank you, love, eighty pence change.'
'Thank you.'
'Next please, yes, love?'
Yes, love (I thought): Love.

I tried the phone again. This time no one could connect me. All the lines were engaged.

Pressing the receiver as tightly to my ear as someone trying to hear the sea in a shell, I stared at the back wall of the café where a few greasy-looking landscapes hung, 'original' but unsold. One or two of them showed the cottages and breakwater of a fishing village in some less well-designed world than ours. There was a sunset of suety ochre bands. The boats with their crude triangular sails, you imagined, would shortly go out and fish for something more amorphous, less evolved, than haddock. Someone there would be looking out of a window, writing in a letter, 'We must not judge God by this. It's just a study that didn't come off.' This Platonic reversal, the suggestion that ours is not perhaps after all the shadow but the thing – the Pleroma, not its imperfect index – attracted me obscurely. Outside, a black dog ran in circles on the sand in the rain, snapping up at the gulls twenty feet above its head as if they were butterflies.

'Pam?' I said. 'Lucas? Hello?'

I thought about the handicapped couple, who were often to be seen in St Ives, separately and together. They were ill-adapted to it. They were without routine to help them. The blind woman waited at the High Street kerb in the rain, her hair plastered to her scalp, her head directed madly at the traffic. She could not cross; I saw her reach down deliberately and slap the dog. Down by the lifeboat station, the paraplegic lay back blasted in his wheelchair under an afternoon sky so dark it might have been November, ignoring everything that was said to him, his mouth open in boredom or pain. Forced into the same troglodytic existence, I was sympathetic: I stood under a butcher's awning as they blundered along the pavement, their faces showing no animation, thinking, 'How much happier they'd be in the quarry!' I followed them up the steep streets to the car park and watched them drive away.

Eventually the bad weather blew itself out in three spectacular storms. Chocolate brown water raced down the hillsides above the coast road and whirled along the village street. The women ran squealing into one another's houses to borrow buckets. I left the flood to subside and went for long walks across the sodden moorland. I thought I would stay another week, perhaps two. On Cam Down the sun was already boiling the moisture out of the peat. From Boswens Common I went down to the sea. Over everything inland hung a warm haze like watered milk. I could walk all day without tiring myself, along the steep, narrow valleys where streams ran in beds of roseate granite like formal paving; as long as I avoided the White Downs, I could sleep when it got dark. I was well again.

At night, the quarry's pillars and terraces had something of the same soapy, veiled quality as my dreams when I had first arrived at the cottage. Lovers used it then. You would hear them moan or laugh from their car, or see it rock gently on its springs. The waterfall made an uneven spattering sound, like a tap left running all night in a concrete yard. One night I found a car parked in front of it, silent, with the filtered moonlight reflected from its windscreen. I decided it was empty. Just as I got close enough to see inside, its engine started up. The headlights came on full in my face. I flung up my hand. With a roar and a scrape of gears it raced past me. I had the impression of two excited faces staring out: music from a radio. Its rear lights bumped hurriedly up the track. Later a light breeze moved the vegetation on the back wall.

I gave up trying to telephone Pam and Lucas. 'People change,' I told them in a letter. 'You build up opinions like layers of sediment in the bottom of a jam jar. Suddenly someone tips over the jar by accident. Or you get bored and shake it up to see what will happen. Or perhaps you just throw it all away and start again with clean water.' Was I making myself ridiculous? 'You should never assume you're talking to the person you knew five years ago,' I ended lamely. 'All the best.' I looked at the envelope for a moment or two before I put it in the post.

If anyone had come to visit, they would have found me dressed for most of the day in an old pair of shorts. Reading had begun to bore me. Instead I ran about in the lanes below the village, or took the bus to Sennen Cove, where I scrambled down the cliffs to stand grinning on the wave-washed rock platform in the glittering spray, dazzled by the sun and rendered speechless by the salt smell and roaring edge of the sea. When I looked in the mirror, I thought of myself as a castaway, with the thin, sunburnt, muscular look by which all castaways can be recognised.

The quarry stood bleached and empty in the sun. Heat clanged soundlessly from its walls until the air began to shiver and dance. I slept with my hands behind my head in a hollow between some boulders, dreaming vaguely. People parked their cars without ever knowing I was there, and went away again without my ever knowing they had been.

One afternoon I woke with a sense of confusion I couldn't attribute directly, to a change in the light, for instance, or the sound from the baling machine which had been chugging to and fro all day in the fields above the headland, leaving a brown stain of exhaust smoke in the clear air. I lifted myself on one elbow and saw the blind woman hobbling round the quarry with her dog; or standing still, rather – as if something had caught her attention in the middle of her walk – and staring up at the spongy green pillows of moss, her head tilted to one side. A light wind animated the willow branches and rustled stealthily along the rose terraces; it stirred the dust round the woman's feet in their square ungainly shoes. She smiled. The man in the car called out to her. Still smiling, she went back to get him into his wheelchair. I watched them for a few minutes then dozed off again, closing my eyes on an image of the wheelchair parked by the pool beneath the wall, so that drops from the waterfall spattered man, woman and dog as they looked up.

When I woke next it was to a coarse and screaming cry like a herring gull's. Filled with panic, surfacing from dreams in which great masses moved against one another in a confused space, I could only imagine that the wheelchair had fallen into the pool. Still half asleep, I went running to see if I could help.

Nothing so simple.

The blind woman and the paraplegic had quarrelled at last.

They were at one another with a frightening muddled ferocity, pushing and shoving and panting while the wheelchair rocked precariously this way and that. Every so often one of them, I couldn't tell which, let out that inarticulate animal cry. Then the woman knocked the chair over, spilling the man out and falling on top of him. He went down slowly and reluctantly, making a noise like a laugh and waving his arms. They struggled there, while the dog first rushed round them in circles then turned yelping and growling to attack me. Fending it off, I shouted:

'Are you all right? Can I do anything?' and 'Stop it. Stop it!'

I was too disgusted and frightened to get close enough to separate them. They were murdering one another. Sick to death of its dependency on the dog, the wheelchair and the van, the violent, miserable half-creature they made had pulled itself apart.

'Stop!'

Neither of them even looked up. Their faces were drawn into snarls of concentration; they were grunting and sobbing frustratedly. Suddenly I saw my mistake. I put my hands up to my face and laughed. Not murder, then. They were fumbling and ripping at each other's clothes. In a moment they would be down to the pale, starved flesh. The dog was only defending their privacy.

I retrieved my things later: two days after that I was back in London.

9
The Place of the Cure of the Soul

We are so quick to look for closure, for the clear termination of sections of our life, that we often invent it. After the debacle at 17, Hill Park I had assumed I would never be caught up with Yaxley again. Indeed, obsessed with the Pleroma, he did leave me alone for two or three years. But after his failure with the infolding, everything failed. The fear that he would be absorbed grew daily, until his whole position was undercut by it. Associated phobias developed to include a horror of dirt. That, and the residue of one too many magical operations, drove him out of the rooms above the Atlantis Bookshop and into a spacious modern block on the north side of Upper Richmond Road, close to East Putney tube station. There I found him, on a rainy, morning in June. He needed me again.

I walked past the building twice. It reminded me less of Yaxley than Lawson, and perhaps it was in fact some fossil of their brief partnership, prepayment for a sleight of hand which never came off. The people who lived there worked in property or investment banking. Traffic laboured under their windows all day, but double glazing muted the noise to a comfortable hum. By night their black European executive saloons lined up outside in rows. I went through a cold well-kept entrance hall, unrelieved by two shallow brick structures like small municipal flowerbeds filled with decorative gravel, and took the stairs to the top floor. Between landings I wavered; touched for reassurance the white painted metal handrail. Had I heard someone coming up behind me?

'Yaxley?'

Modern flats have a precision, a bleak openness to their angles, which encourages hygiene. Yaxley's was painted off-white throughout, with white woodwork. Every wall, every wainscot, was spotless. There were some rather nice carpets in a kind of flushed pink. Furnished properly, it might have been comfortable if rather affectless. But all I could find was a telephone on a table and, in the middle of the lounge floor, a state-of-the-art VTR. (When I switched it on, an unlabelled tape began to play. I switched it off again immediately.) The kitchen was fitted expensively enough, with oak units, Creda Solarspeed hob, butcher-striped roller blinds. Under the immaculate stainless-steel double sink I found Flash, Jif, sponge floor-mops, plastic buckets and Marigold rubber gloves – several of everything, all brand new, as if he had cached them against a siege; or agoraphobia.

The night before I had received a telephone call, I don't believe from Yaxley himself. After I picked up the receiver there was a prolonged silence, into which I prompted—

'Hello? Hello?'

Nothing. Then someone said softly:

'Go to this address—'

Other instructions followed, some infantile, some meaningless. I did not recognise the magical operation to which they referred. The voice was hard to hear, let alone to identify. It paused, failed, picked up again. Once or twice it laughed. 'Two fucks and a pig,' it said. It seemed to come from a long way away, and there were other voices behind it. 'Two fine fucks and a pig. Go to this address.'

Yaxley was in the bedroom.

He lay naked on his side in the middle of the uncarpeted floor, knees drawn up slightly. One hand was curled gently under the side of his head to support it. The other cupped his genitals. Death had aged him. With his long deceitful face, grey stubbled jaw, and lips drawn back over blackened or yellowish teeth, he might have been seventy or eighty. He looked like an old untrustworthy dog, shrunk, famished, reduced. Before he died, he had been trying to make something with two sticks. Above him on the wall was pinned a postcard reproduction of the steps of the British Museum. Under this he had scrawled in soft pencil the words 'The Place of the Cure of the Soul', a description reputed to have been carved over the doors of the Library at Alexandria. Otherwise the room was empty. There was no furniture, not even a bed. It stank. Yaxley hadn't washed since I last saw him. The dirt was glazed on, as if he had spent the intervening years living in a doorway off the Charing Cross Road. In addition some sort of fat was smeared all over his emaciated upper body, perhaps as lubrication. He had been frightened the Pleroma would invaginate him. In the event though he seemed to have been not so much sucked in as sucked.

Behind him on the floor I found an envelope; inside that the key to a safety deposit box in the City. In the box, I knew, there would be two thick black notebooks. I had seen them before. I collected them that afternoon, and over the next two days, coming and going under Yaxley's dead ironic eye, fetched his papers, his pictures and other magical paraphernalia from locations to which the notebooks gave access. Some of the larger items – an old-fashioned Dansette record player, a wooden chair with awkwardly curved arms, two crates of books – I was forced to move by taxi. Decaying ring-binders burst and gave forth yellow papers, upon which I read in a scrawled hand:

'The door! The rosy door!'

Or:

'. . . two distinct and irreconcilable worlds, *pleroma* or fullness – which has come down to us as the muddled Christian promise of "Heaven"; and *hysterema* or *kenoma*, pain, illusion, emptiness – the life we must actually live. Between them, it used to be said, lies the paradox or boundary-state *horos*. But the great discovery of this century has been to knock at the door of *horos* and find no one at home. *Horos* is the wish-fulfilment dream, the treachery of the mirror . . .'

Eventually I had assembled it all in the stinking bedroom. The rest of the instructions proved harder to follow. I was required to set certain small objects – including a stoppered bottle half full of rose-water and a Polaroid photograph of someone's left hand – in precise relationships to one another on a small wooden table, about five feet in front of the corpse. The table itself must stand at the apex of a precise triangle, the other two points of which were represented by a burned-out electric kettle from some Tufnell Park bedsitter; and a split PVC bucket. I was to turn on the old Dansette in its peeled grey leatherette case, play a certain record, then to undress and masturbate. That was the difficulty. At that time I rarely needed manual relief. If I did, I would think automatically of Katherine, and one of her favourite ways of making love—

How she would lie on her side with her legs drawn a little way up and encourage me to enter her from behind, then move one leg gently and rhythmically over the other, so that her body rocked while I remained still. How after a minute or so she would moan and stop – the signal for me to begin moving inside her until her breathing became ragged and harsh, she sighed and began to rub one leg against the other again so that her body rocked and rocked on the pivot of the lower hip.

'Is that good? Is that good?' – turning her head to look at me over her shoulder, sometimes reaching round to draw my face down to kiss it.

'Is that good?'

'Yes.'

How, after a few minutes of this, I would reach round to where the base of my penis emerged from her and dabble my hands there until they were wet. Then, with this lubrication, gently insert the middle finger of my right hand into her anus, slipping it in and out in a counter rhythm to hers. How this drove her quickly to orgasm, at the approach of which she would whisper:

'Do you want to fuck me?'

'Yes.'

'Do you want *to fuck* me?'

'Yes.'

'Are you fucking me?'

'Yes.'

'Oh, fuck me then, come inside me. Fuck me, come inside me. Fuck me, *come* inside me. Fuck me, *come* inside me . . .' – until the words lost their meanings and became an intense, moaning, rhythmic incantation. How a deep pink flush spread across her shoulder-blades. How just before her orgasm I would straddle her with my right leg, press her half over on to her front, she would groan in anticipation and push my hand away from her anus. 'Oh God Oh God Oh God. Yes. Oh *yes*. Oh God oh fuck me yes I'm coming I'm coming oh yes oh fuck me.' How, clutching her breast or hip I would drive into her as hard as I could until we both shouted and stiffened and groaned and relaxed, panting and smiling and beginning to laugh—

All men keep to themselves some image like this of love, exciting but at the same time valued, full of sentiment, even if it is only a memory of someone whispering 'Make me wet,' at the beginning of the night. But when in Putney I set out to remember mine, I could see nothing. I took my clothes off and folded them up in the corner of the room. I knelt down before the table, with its burden of futile or malign objects. I pulled bleakly and unhappily at myself for perhaps ten minutes, but every time I felt the drowsy approach of orgasm, I seemed to snap back into a self-awareness, and feel upon me the dead magician's amused, dispassionate gaze.

'Fuck me, come inside me—' whispered Katherine.

'Yaxley never did anything to anybody,' Pam Stuyvesant reminded me. 'He encourages you to do it to yourself.'

From the cloth-covered speaker of the Dansette, to a background of crackles and distant music, some chirpy pre-war entertainer sang:

> Who's been polishing the sun,
> Sprucing up the clouds so grey?
> Does she know that's how I like it?
> I hope she's going my way!

Suddenly I felt exhausted and ill. I gave up the attempt and instead was violently sick into the plastic bucket. Yaxley, I suppose, may have allowed for this. It was hard to see whether the act had been designed to free or redeem him; or as a last meaningless sneer. Anyway, nothing seemed to happen, so after a bit I left. I closed and locked the door behind me, and later threw the key and the notebooks off Putney Bridge and into the river.

As far as I know, Yaxley's corpse is still there now.

When I got home that evening I found letters from Pam and Lucas. They had written separately: they were going to get divorced. They were never quite able to say how it had come about.

Lucas claimed they had grown out of one another, and raged with guilt:

'I always knew you couldn't cure other people of their character. Now I see you can't even change yourself. Anything in that direction is just thrashing around, a kind of panic. You haul yourself over the wall, you glimpse new country: good! You can never again be what you were! Just as you're patting yourself on the back you see this string of stuff tied to your leg like the tail of a kite, and it's all the fucking Christmas cards you ever sent. All the gas bills you ever paid. All the family snaps which will never, ever allow you to be anybody else: there you are, goggling out, nosing against the glass – your own pet fish.'

He had moved into a flat in Manchester, he said. 'I'm getting a lot of work done.' He asked me to make sure that Pam was all right.

Pam wrote:

'I don't feel as if Lucas knows what he wants.' What had upset her most was that he had left most of his things with her. 'He said he was sick of the clutter, but he must need his books.' She asked me to make sure that Lucas was all right. 'I don't quite know what went wrong,' she added puzzledly.

Neither of them knew, in fact.

'That's why you're being so silly,' I told them. But Lucas would only repeat that he had suddenly felt suffocated under a weight of objects he had never meant to own; while Pam, though desperately miserable, repeated, 'We fell out such a lot,' maintained that Lucas must do what he thought fit, because she only wanted him to be happy; and claimed that she had often wondered what it would be like to try being on your own. And so it all went ahead later that year.

They seemed in such bewilderment, afterwards, to find themselves apart from one another. Lucas kept trying to explain his rage, which was in the end directed less at Pam – or even himself – than at some incurable state of the world. 'A thirty-five-year-old woman,' he wrote to me that winter, 'holds up a doll she has kept in a cardboard box under a bed since she was a child. She touches its clothes, which are falling to pieces, works tenderly its loose arm. The expression which trembles on the verge of realising itself in the slackening muscles of her lips and jaw is indescribably sad. How are you to explain to her that she has lost nothing by living the intervening years of her life? How is she to explain this to you?' Meanwhile Pam fell full length into herself, hour by hour, and was chronically hurt. 'He always used to love the north. That's why we came here.'

They had been not so much divorced, I suspect now, as wrenched apart by some metaphysical event none of us could imagine, precipitated by Yaxley's death. Whatever the meaning of his intrusion into the Pleroma – however he had distorted its shape, however it had vomited itself inside out – one of its effects here had been to cause similar convulsions in all our lives. Pam and Lucas blamed themselves increasingly for living apart. They were bemused. But in the end the very inexplicability of the experience became something they could share. If nothing else, they had been given the fiction of the Coeur, to which they soon returned, developing it by letter.

Yaxley's death, which I believed then would free us all, had filled me with a kind of excitement, to which the divorce only seemed to add. Unable to sleep more than an hour or two at a time, I took to the canal, rowing down to the empty lock basin every morning before anyone else was awake, in an old boat with peeling blue paintwork Katherine had found tied up at the bottom of the garden the day she moved into St Mark's Crescent. An acre of water waited for me, flickering in the cool sunlight. It was very quiet. On the towpath side stood a crescent of Edwardian houses, each with a long thin wedge of overgrown garden. Brambles, willow herb, and some kind of red-leaved ornamental ivy had rioted over the walls to within a few feet of the water. On the other bank wrecked cars glittered in a repair-shop yard; beyond them were the silent arches of a railway bridge.

It was the longest summer, Katherine often said, that anyone could remember.

One morning I lay back in the boat, my eyes half-closed against the reflections from the water, wondering if I could make myself operate the lock. I was never sure of myself with locks. As soon as I looked into one it would bring back some childhood afternoon when, kneeling down to peer at a swarm of fish-fry eight or nine feet below in the narrow cleft, I first suspected the depth of the water. I decided that if I wanted to go any further it would mean dragging the boat out. I let the oars trail. A dog began to bark monotonously from its wired run in the garage yard. A milk-float rattled past on the main road. Tufted ducks were diving in the basin, vanishing unpretentiously under the surface to bob up some seconds later like cork toys, bright of eye and beaded momentarily with drops of water.

A faint breath of air moved the willow herb.

I heard a voice say to me quietly but distinctly: 'The woman that grows, and may be harvested for ever. 'The grown, not the natural woman.'

When I looked up I saw her watching me from the towpath, her outline filled with the leaves and stems of burnet roses, her eyes blind, intent, and speedwell blue. She raised her arm. Somebody in one of the houses behind her woke up and opened a window. The sun caught it and filled my eyes with light.

PART THREE
The Course

10
It Always Happens to Someone Else

After that my life seemed to settle down again. The publishing industry was expanding greedily to meet the 1980s. Never comfortable with authors, I moved on to the production side of things. Katherine, meanwhile, exhibited pictures in London and then New York. She renewed her membership of the Chelsea Arts Club, and I would find her there sometimes in the evening after work, watching the players nose quietly round the billiard tables like fish in a lighted tank. We had a daughter we called Kit. Kit learned to talk early, then encouraged us to sit her out under the willow in the garden at St Mark's Crescent, where she could whisper at the muted reflections of the water in the foliage. She loved the seaside. At Fowey or Caswell Bay she spent each hot afternoon crouched on the tideline, sorting bits of nacre from the gravel of tiny coloured stones and wave-polished glass. Once she called out in her sleep: 'The lights in the shells. Daddy! The lights in the shells!' Kit turned out to be a dreamy, equable little thing, sensual, patient, pleased with everything she found. As if to compensate for this, Pam and Lucas were as demanding as children. Pam continued to write letters full of vague regrets, Lucas telephoned me in the middle of the night.

'I don't like the sound of her voice,' he would say. 'You try her.'

And I would sigh and shrug and in the morning catch the Huddersfield train and visit whatever bleak village she had removed herself to this time.

'You try her. See what she says.'

What she said was always the same. She was lonely and ill. The Pleroma was aware of us, even after all those years. Lucas Medlar didn't love her any more. I would hug her – though I got into bed with her only that once – and telephone him. 'You should see more of one another,' I would tell them. 'We never see enough of you,' they always replied; and I would promise to write more often. Each time, some kind of balance of anxieties would have to reassert itself before I could go home again. Nevertheless it was a relationship which suited us, until I saw the White Couple in the snow outside Pam's kitchen window on the third anniversary of Yaxley's death. Even then, something might have been salvaged. I admit that the White Couple frightened me. How could they not, after everything else that had happened? I had hated the look on their faces as they hung in the air in front of Pam's kitchen window. I was angry with Lucas, and disappointed by his feeble attempt to avoid the issue. But whatever I told him the day after, in the Manchester Kardomah with the rain streaming into the crowded shopping streets outside, I would still have been happy to help (less out of guilt than he assumed, or at any rate, less out of – the guilt he knew about); and things would have gone on in the same way for ever if, in the following spring, Pam's illness hadn't flared up suddenly.

No one knew what was wrong. Migraines paralysed her. Epileptic incidents increased in frequency and scale. She fell asleep, sometimes for a day, two days, at a time; then ranged restlessly about the cottage for a week, reading, smoking and shouting at the cats late into the night, unable to sleep at all. Her weight fluctuated violently over quite short periods. To these metabolic disturbances were added outbreaks of ulcers, ringworm, colitis, abscessed teeth. She became allergic to increasingly exotic forms of penicillin. Finally her skin flared up bright red with erysipelas – St Anthony's Fire, often called simply 'the Rose'. (Afterwards, it would be easy to see this portfolio of symptoms as a secondary stage; a transition. It was as if the illness was searching for its own best expression. Her original symptoms, you will say, were so clearly hysterical – fits, headaches, a hallucination in a kitchen – that this must be a form of speech, the language of some quite common psychic disorder. I wouldn't deny that, even now.)

Then, in April, Lucas telephoned me from Manchester. He was panicky and fey, he didn't know what to do. Pam had been taken into Huddersfield General Hospital.

'She needs a heart bypass,' he said.

'Lucas, a week ago her heart was sounder than mine. It must be a mistake. What are they saying?'

'They don't know what's wrong with her!'

'Try and stay calm,' I advised.

'It's easy for you. She isn't just breaking to pieces in front of you.'

'I'll come when I can.'

But spring is a difficult season. We were publishing as many books as we could print. It took time to extricate myself, and by then Pam was already recovering. I found her propped up in bed in the front room of her cottage, wearing a Marks & Spencer's cotton nightdress and a blue woollen bedjacket with short puffy sleeves. Her hair was longer; she had tied it back with a piece of ribbon. Her face and arms were very white. Around mouth and eyes the skin had a soft, powdery, inflated look; the flesh was yielding, deeply cut with crowsfeet and lines of strain. She seemed to have gained weight in the hospital rather than lost it; despite this you could feel the presence of the bones beneath.

'How are you?'

'Sore!'

Lucas had manhandled the bed downstairs and arranged it by the window so she could look out at the great bars of sun and shadow chasing each other all day across the moors towards Holme. There was more light in the room than I remembered from my last visit, falling on the lively red and black design of the quilt-cover, where it found scattered an invalid's things: Kleenex, the *Guardian* folded tightly to display yesterday's half-completed crossword puzzle, a spectacle case, two or three paperbacks with predominantly pink-and-lavender covers and titles like *Sweet Dawn of Desire*.

'You can't be serious about this,' I complained. Knowing her taste, I had brought her Willa Cather's *A Lost Lady*.

'They belong to the woman next door,' she said. 'It was very kind of her to think of me. And look at all these flowers! You never know how nice people are until you're ill.' Everyone had been kinder than she had a right to expect: they fed the cats, they did the housework even though a home help came in twice a week; they went shopping for her. 'The old man two doors along offered to lend me his television.' She laughed. 'And it's cleaner in here than I ever managed to get it. So keep your literary pretensions to yourself! Here. Let me hug you. Oh, it's so nice to see you!'

She blinked, blew her nose.

'I cry very easily now. Make us some coffee, eh?'

'I'm not sure I want to be in that kitchen,' I said, trying to make a joke of it. 'Remembering the last time.'

There was a silence. To occupy herself, she moved her books about; smoothed the quilt with quick deft movements of her hands.

'Do you still see them, Pam?'

'The cats?'

'The White Couple.'

She lay back on the pillows and turned her head away from me.

'What do you think? What did you expect? That it would all go away like magic once you became involved?'

I couldn't think of an answer to this.

'Don't worry,' she reassured me tiredly. 'They're not out there now. I'd know.' Silence drew out again. She asked it, as if I wasn't there, 'Do you remember the Moors Murders? All those dead children buried up behind Saddleworth? They weren't the only ones.'

'A moor is only a moor,' I said.

She wiped her eyes again – 'I know. I know.' – then sat up suddenly and took both my hands in hers. 'Go into the kitchen and make some coffee,' she said. 'All that's changed is that we've admitted something to ourselves.'

'I hope you're right.'

In the event, there was a yellow roller-blind to pull down over the window.

'I haven't seen this before,' I called.

'No.'

Pam's neighbours, Yorkshirewomen with determined views, had scrubbed down the Formica surfaces and pine shelves. They liked order and optimism; they liked to see a place clean. New coffee-mugs, with cheap and cheerful artwork and optimistic slogans, had replaced her old chipped favourites. When I needed a tea towel, I found them all freshly laundered. Even the stainless steel cat-bowls had been polished until they shone. The kitchen was a kitchen. I filled the kettle. Nothing happened to me.

'You see?'

We drank the coffee. We talked about this and that. We tried to finish the crossword. The afternoon darkened towards evening. Eventually I asked her: 'Do you see Lucas much?' I meant something like: Does Lucas fulfil his responsibilities to you? Instead of answering directly, she showed me a pendant he had bought her nearly twenty years before. It was a teardrop of Iranian mother-of-pearl, about an inch by one and a half, mounted in a silver filigree of tiny roses and decorated with peacocks and flowers, in blues, oranges and greens which glowed in the darkening room like paint from Byzantium. God knows where Lucas had found it, or what he had paid.

'It's beautiful, Pam.'

'Isn't it? He bought me that when he was in London the first time.'

'Lucas?'

'Oh yes. He often went down during those first few years, to see if he could find Yaxley and make him help us. Poor Lucas!

He was frightened: he didn't know where to look. He wandered about, I expect, and then just came home again.'

'I had no idea.'

She smiled drowsily at me. 'Lucas does his best.' Then: 'It wasn't that we didn't trust you. Our own feelings let us down.'

I could see that she was tired. I got up to leave.

'Take care of yourself, Pam,' I said. 'I'll come again soon.'

'Do you know what I'd like?'

'What?'

But she was asleep.

I talked to Lucas a day or two later.

'She's much better,' we reassured each other: 'Isn't she? So much better.'

Within weeks she was back in Huddersfield General. A nagging discomfort in her left hip had migrated to her chest on that side, where it settled in the ribs previously broken for cardiac surgery. A consultant described this condition as 'arthritis', but kept her on hand anyway, for observation.

Lucas was frantic.

'They aren't being honest. She knows there's something else wrong with her.'

Pam drifted, ill in some unacknowledged way, assuaging her anxieties with *Love's Stormy Heights* and *Dark Music of Delight*: suddenly, breast cancer was confirmed, and the mastectomy carried out in early July.

'We've caught it in plenty of time,' the consultant assured her. But when Lucas went to see her the day after, all she could do was shake her head and say:

'Something's still not right.'

He was at the hospital as often as his work allowed, which was perhaps more often than he could cope with. I still have his letters of the time, addressed less to me than to himself, crammed foolscap pages typed out furiously at night on the old Lettera portable he had brought to his marriage like a statement of intent. Yellow with age, they break apart at the folds when you try to open them; but there inside are Pam and Lucas, as easily visible – and just as distant – as figures in a glass paperweight. He wavers between the appalled and the self-pitying. She is a woman already deeply ill, bemused by morphine (though as yet in quite light doses), uncertain of the future. Every time he sees her, she has grown thinner. The visiting hour breaks into her isolation; his appearance is always a relief. She clutches his hand so hard it hurts, but woe betide him if he should give her the wrong drink from the bedside table! Or if her back-rest needs adjusting, and Lucas, shy of seeing the amputation scar when she leans forward, makes a muddle of it—

'For God's sake leave me alone, Lucas. You were always so useless!'

She has become more demanding, he tells himself, 'only as a way of saying "We don't have time for this any more." Not just because she's in pain, but because these things are now the measure of our love for one another, our humanity.'

If he infuriates her, the doctors infuriate him.

'None of them will admit how ill she is,' he writes, after one of the endless courses of chemotherapy has come to nothing: 'It's always, "try this, try that". With these people there's always "hope" and never any progress!'

No one will tell Pam anything. No one will tell him anything. 'Worse,' he alleges, 'she isn't even given proper care. This morning she had a fall trying to use the lavatory on her own. At visiting time all she said to me was, "My knee's gone red. The doctor's going to come and paint it." Sometimes she has no idea what she's saying. But this time she was wide awake. She wouldn't let go of my hand. "Don't go yet, Lucas. Don't go." Those bastards had really allowed her to fall down and hurt herself!

'Why are they letting this happen?' he asks, and concludes wildly:

'Doctors need disease. It's the source of their power.'

The hospital was a maze, with every exit marked 'Oncology'. They were both trapped there. As a result they found themselves closer together than they had ever been. Whatever its source, Pam's distress upset Lucas too. Her pain hurt him. The letters go on, shocked, bitter, uncertain, more and more underscored for emphasis. But what they don't explain is how Lucas was trying to staunch the wound. Every evening after work in Manchester, he started up the Renault and edged it carefully into the dense eastbound traffic of the M62, leaning forward anxiously over the steering wheel to peer through the streaming rain for Junction 23: Outlane. An hour later Pam's hands would be held tightly between his, and he would be reminding her, in a low, persuasive voice—

'Always remember: what we mean when we talk about the Heart is that it is a real place.'

He knew he mustn't stop.

It was harder to catch her attention than it had been in Dunford Bridge, with the light going slowly out of the heavy old furniture and the brindled cat weaving about the woodblock floor. There he had only ever to ask 'What would you like tonight?' to be answered: *'Beautiful Swimmers!'* Here, nervous and agitated, unable to concentrate, she would look away from him restlessly at first, up at the clock or the other visitors trooping in and out, or the ward television where *Emmerdale Farm* or *All Creatures Great and Small* unwound episodically and in silence the stories of shrewd but likeable locals, faces skewed by poor colour-balance to a purplish red. Eventually, struck by a phrase – 'disillusioned with the actual'; 'bound in wood and velvet' – she would stare at Lucas as if he had only just begun to speak. From that moment the haunted look would gradually leave her face; and by the time the ward sister called cheerfully, 'Come on now. Nine o'clock. Throwing-out time,' she would be smiling drowsily and ready to sleep on the complex promises he had begun to make her—

'At the end of his life, Michael Ashman seems to have lost his way. It's hard to understand why. His own best explanation leaves us frustrated, wondering if he has quite deliberately left something out: "As a child I had often spent Christmas with my grandmother, who lived near Catesby in a biggish Victorian house of warm orange brick, to which fake Queen Anne chimneys and an overgrown garden lent an air of history I loved—"'

In that part of Northamptonshire (Lucas read on) the winter copses seem to hang for ever in the moment of darkening against a pale blue sky – as if it will take for ever for night to fall – in a gesture so perfect there will never need to be another day. Medieval strip-fields, Tudor gateposts; narrow lanes and banks choked with ivy awash in horizontal light; yew berries, waxy and tubular, somehow lit up from within so that they look like fairy lights in the gathering dusk: even without snow this is a landscape continually composing itself as a Christmas card. Even now, a chance configuration of cottages and bare elm trees will remind me how I trudged home across the cold ploughed fields at the close of an afternoon in late December: a boy thirteen or fourteen, composed only of the things he wanted at that moment – the warmth of a front room with its Christmas lights and strings of tinsel, the smell of toast.

I loved the holly that grew by my grandmother's door. Every spring, among its new leaves, you found clusters of small flowers as complicated as cyphers, four petals and four white stamens arranged to make up a sort of eight-pointed star. The petals had an almost hallucinatory touch of purple near the tips. Male and female holly flowers grow on separate trees; only the females bear berries. In winter, my grandmother's holly bore 'a berry as bright as any wound'.

The holly and the ivy! Every time you hear that carol, whatever its provenance, you take the full weight of the medieval experience, which was itself just like a childhood. To them, words seemed mysterious and valuable in their own right; the berries so bright against the dark foliage of the tree! But rowan and yew berries are just as bright. So are hawthorn berries, especially when they are new. Hips and haws are as bright. All are instrumental and have their magical and symbolic associations, but none as dark and childlike as this myth of conscious sacrifice, organised, performed, expressed, as the matrix of a culture!

When I came back to that house to live, I was forty-five years old. 'You can't understand the Middle Ages,' I had just written to a friend, 'until you begin to feel death treading on your own heels.' As for that 'elasticity of boundaries' I had once recognised as the necessary prelude to the return of the Coeur: it had quickly exhausted itself. Kennedy was in Berlin. Europe was frozen into the postures of the Cold War. *'Ich bin ein Berliner'*! I told myself that I had been born into a world which, despite its horrors, had always promised more than this.

'That poor man!'

Caught up despite herself, Pam began to look forward to Lucas's visits.

'Can't you come in the afternoons too?' she asked him.

He didn't see how he could.

'Because I get so bored here.'

Correctly reading 'middle age' for 'Middle Ages', she had identified in Ashman's despair the footprint of her own condition. But where Pam saw melancholia, fear, bewilderment (in some archaic sense of that word which implied lost bearings, night, tangled woods), Lucas saw only a failure of imagination.

'By this time Ashman could read the fifteenth century out of a damp cardboard box on a building site. He had built one of the most powerful metaphysical instruments in the history of European thought but he didn't know what to do with it next.'

'Read me some more anyway,' said Pam.

'Listen, then—'

The ward staff, a rich mixture of SENs, trainees, and unqualified 'helpers' in green overalls – heavy women with big feet and grown-up families, who came in by bus from as far away as Bradford and for whom lifting and carrying had been a life's work – were soon intrigued. Seven o'clock in the evening: Lucas would enter the ward carrying a plastic briefcase and a Sainsbury's carrier bag; sit on the side of the bed; and take out the round, steel-rimmed reading glasses he now affected. These made him seem vulnerable; or, as one of the women put it, 'too young for his age'. They liked him anyway. Pam wasn't much more now than a lot of bones and heat: they were impressed by the care with which he embraced her. And they grew used to his low, even reading voice. 'You two and your stories!' they would call. 'Whenever we come through here, you're telling her some story! Has it got any rude bits?'

Lucas could only give a shy smile.

'I'm afraid not.'

'Shame!'

He stared after them. Then he said:

'Ashman continued the research with a kind of wan intensity. After all, it represented the years of his life since that formative European journey; and sometimes brought back to him – with a shiver of delight now only the memory of a memory – images of a dancing bear, the frozen floodwater of the Danube, the legs of the Czechoslovakian girls as they spread their tiered skirts like a fan of Tarot cards. But he had begun to believe that the historical past of the Coeur was only a kind of involution of his own life, a way of twisting or folding the outside of his experience to imply an inside, a meaning.'

Lucas thought for a moment.

'It's not entirely clear what changed this,' he said. He took his spectacles off and rubbed his eyes.

'Don't tease me,' Pam warned him.

'Early one April morning, Ashman caught a train from Birmingham Central station and made his way first to Bath, then Weston-super-Mare on the Bristol Channel. From there he went ten or fifteen miles inland, to a small village near Burrington, on the northern edge of the Mendip Hills. What he found in the parish church there is important to us, and easy to understand. The rest is more difficult—'

'Lucas!'

Lucas took the point, and read on—

*

I left the church quickly.

There were two churchyards, the inner one well-kept and intimate, with trimmed squares of box hedge, little curving lawns and paths. Yew and elm surrounded it; lesser celandines edged each path; daisies and dandelions were already out in the grass. There I sat down for a few minutes, listening to the song of a thrush as it shaped and defended its spring territory among the ornamental shrubs. The church itself was Norman, small but massy: nave, choir and sanctuary quarried block by block, with all the enormous energy of that time, out of a rosy limestone which reminded me of Tintern and the Wye Valley. Faint shadows of the surrounding trees, cast by the light falling across its south flank, were like the shadows traced on a white cliff by a warm winter day. All this filled me with delight. When I got up to go, much of the excitement of my discovery had drained away into the thrush's song, the pale but warm sunshine on the grass: but it was replaced by an extraordinary happiness.

The outer churchyard was less secluded. In an acre of obscure untended sites among colonies of rhododendrons, masses of bramble, and thickets of sapling trees, it served a less favoured clientele. I looked for them as I made my way towards the gate. Some lay completely hidden under the coarse, tangled grass. Headstones were rare. Instead the graves had rusty ornamental chains, and over them a kind of iron cage, as if something were needed to hold in the dead. From the three or four stones I was able to find – all greenish, and with shoulders carved to represent a scroll – I read messages incomplete, ordinary, strange:

'. . . also his Beloved Wife.'

A little way in from the gates, attempts had been made to clear the vegetation. Here for some reason the graves were simply heaps of earth with unpainted wooden crosses at the head of them: an unaccustomed sight, shocking and yet somehow exciting in that it bared a process usually so well hidden under marble chippings, urns, angels standing on great pillars. Across this raw ground, you had a view into a long bleak sloping field, where not far from the churchyard wall some men were tending a fire, staring at it aimlessly but with a certain satisfaction as one of them turned it over with a rake. Going through the gate and out into the road, I wondered what they could be burning, on a Saturday afternoon in April.

The village smelled of furniture polish. A fat woman with red arms sat in her garden eating an apple. From inside the house behind her came the sound of a vacuum cleaner.

They were used to visitors. Someone had converted the old toll house into a bookshop. In the square, with its chestnut trees and limestone cross, I found three whitewashed cottages knocked together to make a café called the Naked Man, a popular starting place for parish outings to Burrington Combe, where, caught in the rain nearly two hundred years earlier, Augustus Toplady had taken shelter in the famous cave and been inspired to write 'Rock of Ages, cleft for me'. That morning a lot of old people had come down from Bristol: frail but lively men in braces, flannel trousers and straw hats with a black ribbon, who trooped in and out of the public lavatories; women with faces like buns, sailing along in their cotton print frocks only to stop and exclaim over a baby as if they had just found it. Now they were waiting for the bus to take them home. It would be another hour. Meanwhile they packed the Naked Man, where under the low ceiling beams and in front of a fireplace decorated with paper flowers and ears of corn dyed transparent green, they examined a sepia photograph entitled 'Washday *c*. 1900' (three or four sullen-looking women outside a stone building) and asked one another:

'Now do you like seafood, because they do a really nice seafood platter here, dear—'

'Seafood platter? Seafood platter?'

'Oh no, not for me, dear!'

When the food came they shovelled it down themselves vigorously, then chewed with inturned expressions as if they weren't quite sure what they were eating. Forty-five minutes passed. The sky darkened and a few spots of rain dashed against the windows. At this the men consulted their watches, while their wives smiled indulgently at a toddler. (It ate for them a cream cake, then banged its blue plastic cup repeatedly on the table.) They were less certain about the mother. She was chain-smoking Players Number Six and kept saying, 'I'm never satisfied with anything.' To this her companion, a woman of about forty with a deep, measured voice and pulled-back hair which made her face look like a bone on the shore, only replied:

'You should wait until you see something you really like, then buy it. You can always throw away something you don't like as much. You can pass on something you've grown tired of.'

She sniffed suddenly and added:

'Can you smell that?'

The child stopped banging its cup and stared at them both.

Suddenly, everyone was getting up agitatedly.

'That smell!'

'Is it the bus already? It's the bus!'

'I can't smell anything.'

'What is it?'

The old men gathered round the war memorial in the square, staring up at a huge plume of dark grey smoke which rose, out of proportion to any possible cause, from behind the houses. Rain streamed down their tilted faces, darkened the shoulders of their jackets. 'Oh dear, oh dear, what is it?' called the women anxiously from the café door, their expressions vague, loose, expectant.

We all ran down towards the church. Intense heat met us at the gate. The graveyard had caught fire.

A rake lay abandoned in the empty field next door, and two or three figures were running in and out of the edge of the smoke. I could hear them calling to one another, their voices distant and panicky beneath the roar and crackle of the fire. One of them toppled over; confused, the others took hold of his feet and pulled him inwards, towards the church. 'This way!' shouted the old men. They began to take off their coats, but nothing could be done. 'Over here!' Too late. However it had started, the blaze seemed to have seated itself everywhere at once, crackling and hissing in the saplings, racing through the grass between the railed and caged graves. (Through the heat mirage they seemed to bob like small boats on a burning sea, their ironwork glowing a dull plum colour. They remained unexpectedly afloat.) Tangle by tangle, the brambles quivered like red hot barbed wire and fell into ash. The elms nearest the church went up like bunches of straw: from where I stood, thirty or forty yards away, I could feel the heat on my skin.

The woman with the toddler held it up to see the flames. 'Look,' she urged. 'Timmy, look!' Her friend, who was occupied lighting a cigarette, said neutrally:

'It'll be the church next.'

This stopped the old men short. While they were considering it, the wind shifted a point or two and blew the flames towards us. Smoke roiled and eddied, alive with sparks. Eyes watering, I stepped back, expecting the acrid, powdery but reassuring smell you get from a garden bonfire on a wet day. Instead it stank of chlorine and putrefying bodies, then the crematorium chimney; and I heard a voice speaking as if from a great distance, in a middle-European accent so thick I could understand only a phrase or a sentence here and there. 'Ice,' it whispered. Then something that might have been, 'Our clothes.' And then, quite clear: 'They took us from Theresienstadt without warning at night.' I was in Birkenau. It was October. I could hear dogs barking somewhere a long way off across the river Sola, which had frozen early. The huts were dark, filled with the smell of exhausted women. 'All killed. Killed by injection.' Birkenau! How can I explain? History, not smoke, had enveloped me. Racked and nauseated, I stumbled across the road away from the church gate, knelt down, and vomited copiously into the grass verge. By the time I felt like standing up again, the fire in the churchyard had consumed itself. I thought: 'You're nearly fifty years old.'

It was the year of the Prague Spring. Dubček had yet to be defeated; Jan Palach had yet to make his appallingly confused gesture of hope and desolation in Wenceslas Square.

Were the borders beginning to move again?

The dead remain with us, passed down as the things that concerned them while they were alive. I recalled, suddenly and in succession: the prostitute in her booth above the Danube, light pooling in the hollow of a collar-bone; the orgasm of an eighteen-year-old boy, sad as an exhaled breath; the yellowed photograph of some old statesman who had meant so much to her. Had she died in Birkenau?

'I know you're here!' I shouted.

I knew she wasn't.

I wiped my mouth, raised my eyes, and found the toddler staring at me in bewilderment from his mother's arms. The rain poured down on us both.

Lucas closed his briefcase. The ward was quiet.

'What happened to Ashman that afternoon? He can only answer: "I'm not sure." It's almost as if he wants us to decide for him—'

Pam touched Lucas's arm tiredly.

'Lucas, what had he found in the church?'

'A cup, a map, a mirror. A rose. The real heritage of the Empress. The real clue to the Heart.'

'Lucas . . .'

'He had found the record of a marriage.'

'Will you come and see me in the afternoons?'

'I'll try.'

11
The Slave of God

However Pam had described Lucas to herself, however she had thought of him during their life together – as a demanding but perfect child; as the mirror of her own supernatural guilt; as the author 'Michael Ashman' – he had always been able to comfort and convince her. What he now achieved in this direction was as extraordinary as his original success with the Coeur. Folding her pain across itself repeatedly until it was so small she had no sensation of it, he placed it exactly at the heart of the Heart (that Romanesque cloister, he said, where whatever our anxiety we are always able to listen to the fountain playing in silence). There, though she could feel it once more, it was very distant; perhaps even a blessing.

'The first great echoes had died away,' he began. 'Yet visions and revelations were still possible. Put your ear to the cavity of history and you can still detect them – sighs, confused harmonies, ripples of ripples intersecting across the whole surface of a lake after some great significant object has submerged!

'1683:

'William Penn was founding Philadelphia. In Britain, Christopher Wren had abandoned astronomy for urban renewal. A bracing pragmatism seemed to rule. But while the modern world had its back turned, the Ottoman Empire besieged Vienna with scimitars, polished brass culverins, horsetail banners in gorgeous reds and yellows, and camels whose tulipwood saddles glowed in the sun less like earthly wood than some perfect Platonic material. And in the Low Countries, Christiaan

Huygens was intuiting his way towards a wave theory of light! As an approach to the day-by-day meaning of the world, the dream might have fallen into disfavour; but that great European bestseller *The Judgement of Dreams* had entered its fifteenth edition since 1518. Nicholas Coleman of Norwich experienced visions of "an army of men" whose beggar's rags disguised finery beneath, "burning the market towns of England at night". A tailor from Stamford was encouraged by dreams to try "the miraculous healing of the deaf and blind". And then, suddenly hallucinating a rose which opened "not in but somewhere behind" her sleep, a Bristol woman, christened in the year of the Great Fire with the extraordinary name Godscall St Ives, renounced her faith to marry a gardener named Joseph Winthrop.

'Winthrop was a man of his time. Commercial and scientific botany delighted him equally. He had corresponded with the younger Tradescant, and worked with Philip Miller on what they hoped would be a new centifolia rose. His Dutch connections balanced a distant relationship to the governor of Massachusetts: he was able to exploit both.

'Three of their children chose the New World. We know nothing of them. The fourth, Liselotte, prone to chlorosis, melancholy from an early age, married a Leiden pump-engineer called Boerhaave. At this, saddened perhaps by the whole charade of Enlightenment, Godscall fell prey quite suddenly to a quartan ague – of which Winthrop, plant-collecting in the Netherlands, learned only on his return – and died. "Something burns within me," she had written in her diary in 1695, "but I am never consumed."'

Pam loved this.

Lucas was delighted by her delight. It would be oversimplifying, whatever my opinion, to claim he had been disappointed by his life since the divorce. Nevertheless, an unfamiliar excitement now filled him whenever he thought about her. At first, surprised to find himself daydreaming in the school staff-room after lunch, he would shake his head and go back to marking books. Soon, though, the work itself began to bore him. The children seemed wilfully slow and uncooperative, the things he was trying to teach them rang with meaninglessness. Clearly, he was approaching the crux of things. He and Pam had been telling themselves the story of the Coeur for twenty years: its worth as an invention – never mind as solace – now depended as much on his ability to convince as on her desire to be convinced. This was the moment of greatest danger. Despite that, he wanted to be at the hospital as often as possible. He wanted to be next to her. Stuck in the classroom, he yawned; heard himself tell some twelve-year-old boy, 'For God's sake go, then. But don't ask me again this afternoon;' and stared out of the window.

He could see Pam, sitting up in bed reading a book!

Four in the afternoon. Time to be off. It was a momentary relief to throw his stuff into the back of the Renault, slam the door, start the engine: but predicating his whole day on this gesture solved nothing. An hour later he was as impatient as ever.

He loathed the drive out through Rochdale, with its debilitated public buildings and small businesses. 'The Pine Brunch Bar & Coffee Lounge' replaced 'Carol's Wools', to be replaced in its turn by 'A Maze of Pine & Roses'. These fantasias of transformation and escape – pursued with increasing anguish as they approached the depressed outskirts – chafed him into misreading familiar traffic signs, so that he missed a turning he always took. Or he would brake suddenly for an imaginary dog or child. Further east there was only moorland, successive arcs of waterlogged peat, elegant concrete bridges connecting nothing to nothing across the motorway. It was dark even in the afternoon, and the traffic was always bad. The aggression of the other drivers as they jostled nose to tail at eighty or ninety miles an hour through this desolate landscape made him nervous and contemptuous at once.

'They look so stupidly greedy,' he wrote to me, 'you wonder how they ever managed to learn to drive at all. I suppose none of us do more than the minimum necessary to get what we want.'

He would arrive at Huddersfield General in a mood impossible, he said, to describe; though he tried hard enough, and in fact it wasn't hard to recognise – 'Impatience, anger, elation, all at once: sometimes so intense I can feel myself draining away out of my own body, like water.' It made him look through the nurses as though they weren't there; and advise the hospital florist, always slow to calculate change from a five-pound note, 'Keep it!' The lifts had been full so often he no longer bothered with them but took the stairs instead, three at a time. Every evening there seemed to be more people in his way. New patients with sheaves of documents en route for Haematology, new visitors on timid quests for husbands in Cardiac or daughters in Maternity, they were easily snared in the web of primary-coloured lines painted on the corridor floors, which is where Lucas came upon them.

'Excuse me. We're looking for . . .'

He stared at them as if they were deranged.

'. . . X-rays.'

'I can't help. Sorry.'

He pushed open the door of Primrose Ward at last. 'Lucas,' Pam called: 'Here.' They had moved her bed again! For a moment he stood confused in the middle of the polished floor; then she waved and suddenly he could relax. She took the flowers from him. His heart was pounding. He had been walking so quickly, he found, that he was out of breath.

'Lucas, they're beautiful!'

'Listen,' he said—

' "Something burns within me, but I am never consumed!" But whatever it was, it clearly failed to kindle in Godscall's daughter. Boerhaave settled in East Anglia, where – encouraged by the success of the Haddenham Level project in 1727 – he planned to drain and farm. But his capital proved insufficient, Liselotte soon died of smallpox, and, its income fallen radically, its only issue daughters, the family followed her into oblivion.

'We have only glimpses of them after that.'

Liselotte's children, Lucas maintained, were to marry into the hand-looming industry which had grown up around Norwich. As for their descendants:

'For nearly a hundred years, they drift north. Norwich to Nottingham and then Manchester; flying shuttle to spinning jenny; figured cloth to stockings and lace. Their names have not survived the famines, wage cuts and migrations, the long slow tragedy of the eighteenth-century cottage industries. When they re-emerge, it is with the invention of the power loom, and the death of Paul Sturtevant, a middle-aged artisan from Horrocks' Stockport factory who walked all the way to Manchester one day in August 1819, because he wanted to hear the radical Henry Hunt speak in St Peter's Fields.'

Sturtevant fell under the hooves of the cavalry as they swept across Peterloo to break up the meeting. He survived hideous injuries to his head, only to die of an infection twelve days later. 'In his delirium,' Lucas told Pam, 'he dreamed of "the perfect time which will come to us all". He was able to describe it: but it was nothing like the life we have now. Six daughters huddled round the deathbed. The youngest, Alice, only seven years old, records:

"Before he died he cried out, 'What does it matter that I'm dying, since I am doing what I want?' "

'Anything we make of this glimpse depends on the quality of our intuition. Was the Heart waiting for something? (Nothing, surely, that could ever happen in Manchester!) We can only say that we feel it beating again before silence sets in. By the last quarter of the century, its heirs have passed through the Industrial Revolution as if through a fire. They will never retrieve Godscall's sense of something beyond and yet within herself. They will never prophesy like Sturtevant. They no longer allow themselves rage. They repress their fear, their sex, their dreams. The skills of the affect have been burned away from them. All they can do is seek advancement.

'They become shopkeepers.'

Outside in the corridor after each visit, Lucas took off his spectacles and rubbed his eyes.

'I'm tired out,' he told the ward staff.

'You're doing her the world of good,' they reassured him.

It was, he knew, too simple a diagram of the relationship.

One weekday afternoon had turned into two. By then, Rochdale no longer seemed such a labyrinth to him. He would stop off there at 'A Maze of Pine & Roses' to buy her a figured silver bracelet from Nepal, or a photograph of someone else's Victorian ancestors slipped naïvely into a small art deco frame because, the woman behind the counter said, they looked so nice together.

Pam responded with physical improvements like shy gifts of her own. She woke early and, with the blue bedjacket round her shoulders, sat up more often during the day. As a result she slept better at night. Though her skin was still very white, it lost the floury look which had so frightened Lucas at the outset of the illness. The pain was still there, of course, but easier to ignore. She entered into the life of the ward around her. Some days this was hardly more ambitious than a discussion of the events at Emmerdale Farm, but even that helped: where previously she had stared clueless and owlish at the TV, allowing the soaps to wash her as smooth as a stone in a stream, she now followed them with a kind of amused greed. The opposite of innocence is not irony but emptiness. Halfway through *Love's Gold Dream* she lent it to one of the nurses, who forgot to give it back.

'What do I look like with my hair like this?' she asked the other women tentatively.

She put on weight. She put on make-up.

It is easy to see that Lucas, who would have done or said anything to preserve the delight he saw on her face when he entered the ward, had rediscovered the excitement of being pivotal to someone else's happiness, a condition which promised to alleviate all his own wounds. But what Pam had rediscovered could only be inferred from her clear intention to get well. The ward staff thought they knew. Mistaking her smile, her intensity, the attentiveness that came back into her face when she looked up at Lucas, they often conspired to leave him there for half an hour after the rest of the afternoon visitors had gone. They knew, anyway, that left to his own devices he would only make his way back to the waiting area and write furiously with a cheap red ballpoint pen until visiting began again at seven o'clock.

'You've just got to look at her,' trainee nurses told one another delightedly, 'to see.'

'I can't fancy him myself.'

'Get on!'

It was too early to talk about remission, and they were careful never to use the word near her. Would Pam have heard them if they had? With Lucas constantly at her side offering the life-jacket, part of her at least was free to abandon Huddersfield General the way you abandon a ship. This she did with relief. At night, lapped in the faint fake radiance of morphine, she could remember herself as a little girl dancing on a low wall (though she couldn't remember whose hands caught her again and again when she jumped). Falling for ever, always being saved, she heard Lucas say—

'Alice Sturtevant grew up frail-looking and pretty, but more obstinate than she seemed. A photograph taken in middle life shows her in an amazing black bombazine dress. If her eyes are dark-ringed like all that family's, it is less from anxiety than determination. In 1835, she had married a milkman named John Duck. His surname amused her; but they wanted the same things, and he promised a life without visions.

'He came from Mottram, a village east of Manchester in the gape of the Longdendale Valley, and at the time of their marriage was poised to convert his milk profits into a small shop on the old saltway, close to the Packhorse Inn. There, in the shadow of the fifteenth-century church, 'the Cathedral of East Cheshire', Alice helped him sell groceries by weight (a piece of bacon was stuck with its own fat to the base of the scales to 'adjust' them); cough mixtures full of opium which went down like warm pitch; and boot laces from a card.

'Alice had seven children. Of five girls, one died at birth;

another, three years old, from diphtheria. The boys survived, which was a blessing. She was happy enough; and if she never liked the dark gape of Longdendale, she could always look back at the Altdorfer sunsets burning away above the chimneys of the city.

'John Duck, meanwhile, looked eastward. Under construction ten miles up the valley were railway lines, tunnels, a chain of dams and reservoirs intended to water the industries of Manchester. From 1838 until the end of the century, these obsessional works drew a massive labour force to the shanty villages of Rhodeswood, Woodhouse and Dunford Bridge. Conditions were bad. Men, women and children died in subsidences and premature explosions, of privation, overwork, bad housing, puzzlement, or grief; and were often buried on the moor with less ceremony than the victims of Ian Brady and Myra Hindley a hundred years later. Pictures of the time show them grouped outside their "homes" in New Yarmouth – blurred faces in the foreground, bleak oak woods behind, then the high black edge of the moor.

'John supplied groceries to the survivors. It was a good business, and – apart from the younger son, who seems to have registered as a quarryman at the age of thireen – all the Duck children went into it.

'By 1880, the oldest boy William was ready to branch out on his own. John bought him a milk round in Salford, and taught him to keep the product fresh by adding formalin. With the death of his parents within two months of one another in 1900, William brought his sisters to Manchester and liquidated all three enterprises, along with a Salford public house – the Junction – he had acquired in the meantime. This enabled him to buy a share in a modest but successful department store on Victoria Street.

'He began with three partners. Buying out the last of them twenty years later, he determined to give the store his own name. But by then it was the biggest in Manchester, and his wife – a publican's daughter from Burnley-persuaded him that

"Duck's" had no ring to it. Looking back through the family history, they chose his mother's maiden name, modifying it after some thought from Sturtevant to Stuyvesant. Stuyvesant! It was European yet transatlantic; it was American yet aristocratic. William loved it. He changed his name by deed poll.'

'St Ives to Sturtevant. Sturtevant to Stuyvesant. Godscall's descendants have found their way down to us. The Heart has its Heir.'

Thursday afternoon, Primose Ward.
Patients and visitors exchange desultory talk.
'We got toast this morning.'
'Move, Nina, move and let your grandma sit down. She's not been very well.'
'Thanks, flower: 'as your 'eadache gone?'
'In Ashton they were all dreaming of toast. It was all they ever thought of.'
'It's not time yet is it? It's not time. Do they come and check if the visitors have gone?'
'You had to have an operation to get toast. Or else be in the Maternity Unit—'
Laughter.
'Nina, love, it's not time yet.'
Only Pam and Lucas are silent. Lucas, having told his story, turns away for a minute or two as if out of shyness. Given this time to herself, Pam regards him thoughtfully. The afternoon, swinging round on its pivot, isolates in a kind of flat light one flower vase after another: tulips, asters, lilies, 'like a tart's boudoir'. On the TV a dog is running through rubbish by some docks, under the stern of a ship. An old woman's voice sings a few quavering notes. 'That's nice, isn't it?' And, to a passing nurse: 'I'm singing. Ha ha.' Rain scratches at the windows.
Eventually Pam says:
'Somehow that makes it even sadder.'
'Oh, Pam!'
Lucas laughs. They hug.

'Pam, Pam, remember Valentinus: "Do not be afraid. In death you shall not die." You were in the Pleroma all along without knowing it!'

'Less of that, you two,' orders the ward sister, coming in briskly to fuss with an empty bed. 'Throwing-out time now. Come on, it's four o'clock, you've had a good innings.'

Over the years Lucas too had wrung from the myth what comfort he could. By allowing him to experience the Coeur as if it came from outside himself, 'Michael Ashman' had relieved him of responsibility and salved his intellectual guilts. More importantly, 'Ashman' hid – or at least disguised – Lucas's own intuition, of which he had an almost comical fear. Pam understood much of this. It was, after all, a shared dream. But while she could accept Lucas's needs, they had always chafed her. As soon as he confirmed what she had somehow sensed all along – that the whole of this history aimed itself through her – she lost interest. Her sense of urgency prevailed. She laid the Search aside like a crossword puzzle faintly pencilled in with guesses and instead focused her attention on the dream itself.

Increasingly, it centred on the Empress's shadowy daughter Phoenissa, of whom Lucas had said, 'She may not have escaped the wreck. You can still hear in the Pleroma a faint fading cry of rage and sadness which may have been hers.'

The crux, Pam claimed, the absolute meaning of Phoenissa's 'death into the world', lay in its counter-trajectory to the Empress's.

'From the start Phoenissa was fucking her mother's general, Lascaris; he only had to be near her to drive her into a kind of delighted paralysis – she could feel herself tremble and moisten if he walked past fifty yards away not even looking in her direction.

'Things had begun to slide long before the siege began. Everyone knew that. The court was split, the Empress already fatally inattentive. Weeds sprang up between the stones. The wells faltered. In the afternoons the City baked silently in the heat.

Lascaris and Phoenissa met in the little deserted courtyards beneath the inner walls. At first he was brutal with her. He would bend her over a dry fountain, enter her, come suddenly with a groan. The sunlight illuminated them mercilessly in this moment: both helpless, half out of their fine clothes, weak with sex. Towards the end, when smoke from the besieging cannon hung above the City like strips of black rag, he seemed to relax. In some cool empty room with broken earthenware scattered over the tiled floor, he would cup the back of her head in his hands, and whisper "Don't be afraid," a kindness which disappointed her inexplicably.

'Then suddenly it was all over. For two nights and a day the harbour had been in flames. The outer walls, weakened by twenty days of bombardment from landward, went down. Lascaris was killed early in the afternoon, the Empress two hours later near one of the gates. She was weeping openly, they say, and had picked up a sword: but they never say why. No one could bear to look directly at her.

'In the moment of her mother's agony, as the Coeur snapped back away from the world and into the Pleroma, Phoenissa was given a choice. Alone all day in a deserted cloister, she had watched the air suffuse with a dusty glow the colour of rose petals. The sounds of battle faded. She could hear the nearby fountain; and behind that a thread of music, one phrase repeated over and over again on some stringed instrument. Eventually Lascaris, dressed in his beautiful armour, walked slowly across the courtyard in front of her. "Theodore!" she wept. The air smelled of attar, called the heart of the rose. "Theodore!" He turned back to face her and she saw his wound; she remembered the wounds he had given her. He was, of course, already dead. She had mistaken the tawdry glitter of the world for the light of the Pleroma! She fled towards it: her very desire for fullness led her to choose the world.'

Pam laughed.

'She's been whoring through it ever since, under the impression that it's Heaven.'

Lucas was rather shocked.

'We can't know that,' he said.

'The Empress knew. Oh, Lucas, Lucas! It's easy to talk about the World and the Coeur as "burning in the fabric of the Pleroma like two lovers in the glorious wreck of desire". But we can mean only one thing by that. All those years ago, you talked about "a huge cry of love and loss, echoing and re-echoing across Europe."'

'But who lost the most?'

'If the Coeur would no longer let itself be known, we mustn't blame the invading kings and their conspiracies. It had breathed its final breath long before they identified Gallica by her beautiful armour, and displayed the mutilated head.'

There was a silence.

Into it Lucas said, 'We can't know that, either.'

Pam smiled.

'We can't, can we?' she said.

And looking steadily at him she lifted her hands, palms upwards, in a gesture of weighing: as if he had asked the wrong question. But if he remained a bit unnerved by the energy and sensuality of her vision, Lucas was always willing to contribute what he could. There were days, too, when she seemed to falter. 'I'm tired, Lucas,' she would whisper, blinking back tears and staring at the bed opposite hers: 'I can't remember things which happened so long ago.'

To help, he told her a story of Richard Coeur de Lion which went like this:

'Traditionally, of course, Richard, returning to England incognito from the Third Crusade, is captured by Leopold of Austria who imprisons him at Durnstein. He is found and freed by the troubadour Blondel, who sings the first verse of a popular ballad outside every keep in Europe until Richard replies with the second. In fact by 1193 Richard's place had already been taken by a hostage called Hugo de Morville. Hugo, who had helped murder Thomas à Becket on behalf of Richard's father, is supposed to have died of guilt on a pilgrimage to the Holy Land. But a poet called Ulrich von Zatzikhoven saw and talked to him, there in the Durnstein keep. So there was no Richard. Was there ever a Blondel? Who knows. But there was certainly an exchange of songs. Hugo de Morville gave von Zatzikhoven a copy of the Anglo-Norman *The Legend of Lancelot*, Zatzikhoven's translation of which – though authorities regard it as both banal and dilute – must be seen as one of the late flowers of German chivalric poetry.

'The insoluble conflict between ideal and reality! Richard vanishes from his own story for a year. Where does he go while de Morville is impersonating him in Durnstein? Only the codes embedded in his name enable us to guess.

'Gallica carried the blood of the Lion.'

'Really, Lucas,' Pam interrupted suddenly, 'I don't care what fucking colour she bled.'

Soon she was laughing at him again.

' "Ideal and reality"!' she said.

In this way, turn and turn about, losing their confidence one day only to regain it the next, they steered the Course of the Heart. Pam's compass was hidden, glandular, difficult to read: less romantic than Lucas's. But she was equally determined; and perhaps in the end she had the truer sense of direction. Her health continued to improve, while Lucas watched in awe and Huddersfield General held its breath. The disease went into remission. Within a month – though she was a little too frail to fend for herself and would still need treatment as an out-patient – they had allowed her to go home.

From then on Lucas spent his free time at the cottage, although he always drove back to Manchester at night. No cook, he bought what he called 'middle-class convenience food' – filled pasta and tins of ratatouille – after school at Sainsbury's; and in the evenings did the housework (rarely to the standard of Pam's neighbours, who came in and did it again during the day). Pam slept a lot; Lucas sat by the bed and wrote letters to me, in red ball-point on lined paper. 'We try and get as much fresh air as we can.' At weekends he carried her out to the Renault and drove to one local beauty spot or another – anywhere she could look out over a reservoir and some woods without having to leave the car – or pushed her round the Huddersfield shopping arcades in a wheelchair. When he picked her up, he told me, she was just a lot of bones and heat that weighed nothing.

One Saturday in late August they drove through Dunford Bridge, past their old house.

'Look, Lucas!'

Lucas parked the car on the grass verge, where the road dipped northward into a valley with beech and dwarf oak. The valley was full of haze, the haze full of sun. A strange bronze light fell on the tangled grass in front of the house. From behind rose a plume of smoke so thick and perfectly detailed that it looked like a solid object.

'Wind your window down,' Lucas said.

He studied the house.

'Good God.'

Builders were at work on it again. They had opened one gable end, then sealed it temporarily with heavy-gauge polythene. The front windows were out, the stonework above them jacked into place until the lintels could be replaced. A yellow JCB lay hull-down among the muddy hawthorn stumps it had grubbed out of the gardens at the back, where two men were burning a dozen or so metal chairs. Only the frames remained, tangled together inextricably and outlined with fire.

Lucas wheeled Pam across the road and through the gates.

'Let's have a look round.'

'Your poor old garden!' Pam said. She studied the empty windows. 'I think I'll stay here.'

'What a warren!'

It had always been too large and complex for them; perhaps for anyone. The Local Authority had bought the building when they left, converting it into a home for disturbed children, a kind of halfway house for those bemused before they reached the age of consent. Now cutbacks had returned it to the private sector, where according to the builder's signboard it would become a small exclusive 'estate' of five or six houses round a courtyard. Lucas looked in through one of the windows and tried to imagine this. All he saw was an empty room, flowered wallpaper, dusty air across which slanted a bar of light. He mooched round for a bit among the demolished outbuildings, picking up pieces of broken lath, stooping over a pile of brand new yellow drainage pipes, then made his way back to the front garden, where he had left Pam. He found her trying to smile and cry at the same time. To cheer her up he said:

'I loved this view.'

'You didn't like the house much.'

'It was never very lucky for us,' he admitted.

She touched his hand.

'I'm glad they're doing something with it at last,' she said. 'Aren't you?'

He began to push the wheelchair back to the car.

'Do you know what I miss most, Lucas?'

'What?'

'A cigarette.'

'Wipe your nose now.'

All along they had known that the one word neither of them must ever pronounce was 'metastasis'. But in September, cancer was diagnosed in the remaining breast. From there it seemed to rage across her like a fire. As he said bitterly, there wasn't much left of her to burn. In case anything could be done, the consultant had her admitted to Christie's, the Manchester cancer-hospital, where she underwent state-of-the-art scanning, exploratory operations and then a second amputation; radiation treatment followed. It was too late. By November she was very ill indeed, and in December we knew she would die.

Lucas telephoned me a few days before Christmas.

'You'd better come up here,' he said.

He sobbed suddenly and put the phone down.

12
Trasfigurante

My train rolled slowly into Manchester Piccadilly the next morning just before twelve. I had an overnight bag with me, and a copy of *Roman Tales*. While I was waiting for the train to stop, I pushed the window down and had a look along the platform: there was Lucas, reading the travel posters outside the buffet while he warmed his hands round a styrofoam cup. His grey cashmere jacket hung open over a thin grey cotton T-shirt with the word 'Technique' printed on it in fluent red script like lipstick on a mirror. He had wrapped a long black scarf twice round his neck. The way he hunched his shoulders made him seem vulnerable as well as cold. I wondered how long he had been standing there. The train lurched twice and drew to a halt at last. I opened the door and got down, wincing in the raw air. Sleet had begun to fall as we crossed the south Staffordshire plain, only to turn to wet snow at Stockport. Piccadilly smelled of gas turbines, acetylene, diesel.

'Lucas!'

We shook hands.

'How are you?' I asked.

'I can't seem to get warm nowadays,' he said. 'Especially in the mornings.' He offered me the cup. 'Want some? It's hot chocolate. No? The cold seems brutal to me. I'm getting old, I suppose.' We were forty that year, I reminded him: if he was old, so was I. He had the grace to laugh. It wasn't far to the Christie Hospital, he told me: though at this time of day traffic would be heavy. 'Let's go straight there,' he said. 'I've got the car out the back.' He touched my upper arm shyly.

'Pam will be so glad to see you!'

'You don't wear enough,' I said. 'That's why you're always cold.' As we trudged across the car park through the snow I warned him, 'Lucas, I haven't got long.' It was important he didn't expect too much. 'A week at most. Kit and Katherine want me home at Christmas.'

For a moment I wondered if he understood.

Then he said: 'Oh, I see. You mean she'd better get it over with in the next couple of days.'

'It wouldn't be fair to them, Lucas.'

His face white and miserable, he unlocked the front passenger door of the Renault for me, then went round the other side to get in. 'I'm sorry,' he said, as soon as he had the bulk of the car between us. 'I shouldn't have said that. Of course you must go back.' He started the engine, put the heater on. The windscreen misted up. The windscreen wipers batted back and forth, making a soft thudding noise as they piled the melting snow against the glass. 'What's the weather like in London?'

'Bad,' I said. 'It's bad all over the country.' I felt emptied out by his distress. 'Lucas, why don't you come down to us, just for Christmas Day?'

He put the car into gear.

'Because she'd be alone,' he said.

Ward Three was long and narrow, with tall sash windows, a dozen beds along either side and a red sign at one end which said ZONE 3 WASHROOM. Later I would remember it as having a ghoulish air of fancy dress, like a concentration camp Christmas. Radiation and chemotherapy implants had slowed the women down. Their hair had fallen out. Despite this, morale was high, and morphine often left them as cheerful and vague as toddlers. White plastic strips fastened to each emaciated wrist – as a precaution against the wrong medication-reduced their responsibilities. Haggard yet childlike, they had a name, an age, an admission number. They needed no more unless it was to vomit: for that they were given a thing that looked like a papier-mâché bowler hat.

Pam's face was all bones, yellowy-white skin, eyes in deep black hollows not much larger than the eyeballs themselves. She hardly seemed to recognise us. Perhaps as a way of protecting herself from her memories, she had begun to keep the outside world at a distance. If she had to live, she would live inside her condition. Consequently, most of her talk was about the ward or the other patients. 'Mrs Eddy goes home tomorrow,' she told us. We had no idea which one Mrs Eddy was. 'We call her "Mary Baker". Everyone gets a name. That's her husband just come in.' She added, with a certain professional scorn: 'How they expect him to manage her on his own—!' Then something else caught her attention.

'See the old dear over there? No, there. Just going off to Radiology.

'We used to call her "Steve Ovett".'

To all intents and purposes cured, but needing exercise to build her up before they could discharge her, this old woman had dutifully pushed a walking frame round the ward for fifteen minutes twice a day, scraping it along the worn polished floor in front of her and telling everyone:

'I'm joining a marathon when I get out.'

'You'll win!'

Without warning, circulatory complications had made it necessary to amputate her left leg just beneath the knee, and after that, as Pam said, 'Steve Ovett' seemed a bit close to the bone. The old people were typically cheerful, 'But a thing like that would give anyone a shock.'

'So what do they call her now?'

' "Long John Silver".'

We watched as, with some care, two nurses knotted the old woman's stocking below the stump; helped her put on a dressing gown decorated like a running strip in different shades of blue; and finally manoeuvred her into a wheelchair. 'I must have a fag before I go!' she shouted. 'I must have a smoke.' The nurses tutted her. Amused by the baldness of the irony, the rest of the patients were prompted to call out 'Tarra, duck!' as she was wheeled away.

'Tarra!'

Suddenly Pam said:

'There are only two paces in this place, slow and dead stop.'

After that she seemed to go to sleep; but then as we were leaving she touched my arm and smiled. 'I'm glad you came,' she said—

'Look after Lucas.'

Stuck in traffic on Oxford Road, Lucas stared out of the Renault at slushy pavements, hurrying shoppers, the remains of a late December afternoon.

'This will be gone tomorrow,' he said. 'It's not the kind of snow that lasts.'

He lived in a large flat at the top of a Victorian house.

'An entire generation disappeared into places like this,' he had written to me just after the divorce, as if it was inevitable he would finish up in some bedsitter with a shared bath and lino on the stairs. 'What have they got now? A bookcase full of outdated sociology texts and some old records. They always wanted to go to Budapest, but somehow it couldn't be done.' As usual he had seen only what he wanted to see.

It was nearly dark as we made our way up the stairs. A curious thing happened at the top. While Lucas stood on the little landing outside his front door, fumbling with the keys in the cobwebby grey light, I heard a quiet, indistinct noise from inside the flat.

'Lucas! There's someone in there!'

Lucas seemed unnerved for a moment, then he laughed and explained, 'You get that every time they run the water next door. These walls might as well be made of plasterboard.' He opened the door. 'Let me go first. The light switches are difficult to find.'

The flat was two-bedroomed, with high moulded ceilings and

central heating. He had furnished its massive living room – which doubled as a study – with a kind of absent-minded energy, buying from junk shops one day and Habitat the next. As a result some gold brocade cushions hobnobbed with a black-and-chrome chair, while the tiny bulb of a very modern anglepoise lamp cast its light on a sofa covered with chintz. The fitted carpets were pale and neutral, the rugs old-fashioned and figured. The shelves bore a characteristic mix of books – Bruno Schultz next to Henry Miller; Cawte's *Ritual Animal Masks*; works of European history and modern literary criticism. The front windows had once looked out over gardens reminiscent of a London square, of which a few trees and some of the original railings remained. Lucas closed the curtains, switched on the gas fire, rubbed his hands.

'I'm sorry about the mess,' he apologised. 'I never get time to tidy up.'

Dark, peaty earth, studded with the remains of an earthenware plant pot, was scattered all over the floor. The plant itself, quite a large streptocarpus, lay in a corner where it had shed its thick white petals like a bag of prawn crackers. 'I knocked it off the mantelpiece last night,' Lucas said off-handedly. But I suspected that rage or misery had made him throw it across the room. Either way, the carpet was ruined. 'He was always so untidy!' I remembered Pam saying. This pretence – that Lucas was a child – had never entirely relieved her fear that he had some core of anger she could neither understand nor assuage. 'So untidy and so easily hurt.'

Lucas had been her life. Now she often forgot him altogether. Freed by her condition to be the centre of attention, she would talk for hours then fall asleep in the middle of a sentence; or refuse to talk at all, withholding herself almost as if she were blaming us for the illness. Riding an hourly see-saw of pain and morphine, she revised her memories, acted out her childhood in Cheshire and Silverdale, spoke in tongues: the coy whisper of the little girl, the boom of the father's laughter, the cooing of the mother. This eerie archaeological theatre was never fully performed. She needed help we couldn't give; asked questions we couldn't answer; wept distraughtly when we couldn't supply details she had forgotten.

She was three years old, escaping towards the sea with some other child's toy. It was an inflatable horse. It was blue. But what colour of blue was it? Lucas didn't remember. How could he?

'Go away then!' she told him. 'Go away.'

Her other relationships were equally confused.

'They've been so wonderful, whatever happens,' she would say suddenly of the doctors or nurses; only to beg a few minutes later, 'You've got to get me out of here! They won't tell me anything!'

We shared the visits. Since Lucas could rarely get away until four, I went to see her in the afternoons. Lucas took over when he had finished work. In the evenings I left them together as often as I could. I would go to the cinema, eat at McDonald's, call Katherine from a vandalised box on Oxford Road – 'Hello. I love you.' 'Hello?' – then go home and try to tidy up Lucas's flat. Afternoons were Pam's best time. On the cusp between one dose and the next, she sometimes salvaged half an hour of the Pam Stuyvesant I remembered. 'Aren't these gladioli beautiful?' she would insist: or, 'Have you seen the view from my window? I never get tired of it!' Looking out through the wavy Victorian glass you found the snow had melted to reveal a few trees and tilting board fences touched at that time of year with deep green lichen. Some sunlight, bright but dilute, slanted across the street, making you wish for frost, holly berries, one vigorous figure, one event which might give it the effect of a Christmas card. This didn't matter to Pam. 'It cheers me up, it really does.'

But the recapture of lucidity had dangers of its own. Two or three nights before Christmas Lucas came home early and complained: 'The whole time I was there, she just stared at the TV. *Celebrity Squares*. The whole fucking time! Can you understand that?'

Later, when he had calmed down, he added:

'She looked horrified. I don't suppose we'll ever know what she was actually seeing.'

I knew.

'How are you?'

Three thirty: Christie's. Two beds along from Pam on the other side of the ward, a fat woman stood up, retrieved her handbag, sat down again abruptly. She wore an angora wool skirt with a matching scarf; pinned to her head was a kind of trilby hat apparently made out of carpet material. She had been trying to leave for half an hour. 'Well, goodbye dear,' she said cheerfully each time she got up. 'I expect I'll see you this time tomorrow.' The air in Ward Three was brown and gloomy. Every so often, coloured light from the television flickered through it like sunshine through moving branches; discovered Pam's white face; and pulled the cheekbones this way and that in shifting relief. Her eyes were wide yet uninterested, her voice filled with a faint disgust.

'About the same.'

She seemed to be about to add something, but in the end only gestured tiredly at the screen. 'That about sums it up today.'

'What's the programme?'

'What do you think?' she said.

It was hard to say. Faces and limbs in some sort of crisis, filmed at odd angles by hand-held camera and lost in interference, had been intercut with pictures of sheep and goats running to and fro in an empty stone building. Gradually these images were allowed to leak into one another until there emerged something like a damp watercolour landscape – mud and rocks in umber colours: indistinct animals: another face staring anxiously out. This in its turn flared and darkened into soft ungeometric shapes which pulsed gently like the organs of the body. After a moment or two the colour faded entirely, as though the set had gone out of adjustment. Patches of whiteness began to merge and separate rhythmically against a uniform grey background. 'There!' said Pam. The picture had resolved again. I caught a single glimpse of white limbs intertwined, and looked away as quickly as I could. At the same time the soundtrack came up. 'In the afternoons.' I heard a faint dull voice say, 'it was too hot to sit still. She lay on her back on the sofa with her skirt pulled up and her hand between her legs. Her knickers were always damp. At night she would crouch down over him, push his cock into her, and move strongly up and down on it grunting and panting until she came.'

'Christ!'

'Ask everyone else what they're watching,' said Pam. 'It won't be this.'

'. . . this,' echoed the sound-track: 'His cock detumesced and fell out. Mixed sperm and juices ran out to cool and dry between his pubic hair and hers.'

Poor Pam! She was shaking. When I tried to put my arm round her shoulders, she moved away.

'No. No.'

'It's the morphine, Lucas.'

'I suppose so,' he conceded, 'I suppose it is.'

Morphine, heart's ease, hinge of truth. He had hauntings of his own, for which he had hardly begun to find comfort. It would only have distressed him further to know that she could see right through *Celebrity Squares* or *Take the High Road* to where the white couple hung just inside every TV set, smiling out at her while they clasped and pushed and panted and turned to and fro like a chrysalis in a hedge. To divert him I asked:

'What shall I do with this?'

We had decided we would clean the kitchen. A baking tray, earthenware casseroles of different sizes, the scorched oven glove shaped like a fish: Lucas had a way of handling each object as if he hoped to recognise something he had mislaid when he moved house years before. He took hours to cook anything and longer to wash up.

'I don't know.'

That evening it started snowing again. Wintery weather was

moving across the north-west on a broad front. Falls would be quite heavy, the television predicted; winds light. I went to bed early, and woke surprised not long after. Midnight. Laughter amplified by the cold air. Couples were still floundering past outside with linked arms, feet turned out, heads wrapped up dark and globular against the cold. People love snow. I lay there listening to them for a moment or two, wondering what had woken me. Then I heard a thud and a low cry from Lucas's room, followed immediately by an extraordinary outbreak of banging and crashing, as if someone was breaking up the front-room chairs and then throwing pieces of them about. 'Lucas!' I called. 'Are you all right?' Never a good sleeper, he was up and down all night, disturbed by his nightmares or making his way to the lavatory to pee noisily into the silence. Despite this, he would never switch on the lights. I assumed he had fallen over something at last. 'Lucas?' He said something indistinct but reassuring, then cried out suddenly in such an appalled voice I got straight out of bed and went to the door. Nothing sounds worse than a raised voice in someone else's house at night. Bad dreams, illness, self-pity in the small hours: you have no idea how to respond. Both bedrooms opened on to a short narrow passage painted white, an uncurtained window at one end of which admitted snow-light reflected up from the street. In this cold but buoyant illumination I could easily make out the pictures on the walls either side of Lucas's door, clip-framed photographs of a visit to some exotic country, Turkey perhaps, or Afghanistan, where very bright sunshine flooded through a deeply recessed window on to broad-striped orange and ochre rugs. I stood there in my underpants, shivering, and knocked. The noise redoubled. Something was flung heavily against the door itself, which flexed under the impact. I pushed. It resisted. Everything went quiet again.

'Lucas?'

Nothing.

'Lucas!'

I was about to turn away when the door jerked open and

Lucas stuck his head out so suddenly that I backed into the wall of the passage. It was hard to see what was wrong with him – the bedside lamp in the room behind him was flickering like a damaged fluorescent tube – but his face seemed both white and dirty, and there was blood running down one side of it from a cut above his eye.

'What do you want?' he said irritably, as if it was me who had called for help in the middle of the night.

'Lucas—'

'There's no need to come in,' he said. 'I had a bit of an accident. Go back to sleep now.' He closed the door until all I could see was his left eye and the cut above it, swollen, blue with bruised tissue. He was trembling. 'Go back to sleep,' he repeated. 'It's all right.'

'Lucas—'

The door closed suddenly.

'Lucas!'

Silence.

I went back to the spare room and stood at the window for some time with the duvet wrapped round my shoulders, staring down into the street. The snow directly beneath each sodium lamp was orange: a little further away it became a fragile tremulous pink, a colour on the edge of tenure, unassuming, shy, threatened. Though Pam was still alive, Lucas already felt bereaved. The bereft, we say, are less dismayed than in a rage; and I was afraid Lucas's rage would damage him. How can you protect someone from a grief which causes him to throw his furniture about in the middle of the night? This may have been the wrong question to ask. By now the street was empty. Parked for the night, the cars had grown strange and shapeless. In the morning, I knew, they would look as if they had been moulded from styrofoam – blind, blunt models in some early, uninteresting stage of design.

The next day Pam was moved into a small side-ward. Her bouts of pain and delirium had been upsetting other patients, the ward sister told us; it would be easier to manage her there.

'Easier to manage her death,' Lucas said bitterly.

Pam put a brave face on it. 'How nice to have a room of your own.' In the end though I think she would have preferred to stay where she was. 'They were real characters in Ward Three,' she said to me, as if I had been there to: 'Weren't they?'

She laughed.

'Oh, Lucas, aren't people funny?'

'I'm not Lucas,' I said.

She took my hand.

'I know that, really. Tell him I love him.'

That was one of the last lucid things she said to me.

When I got back to Lucas's flat late that afternoon, I found that he had been in at lunchtime and wrecked it. All the internal doors were propped open. The plates had been taken out of the kitchen and smashed in the bath; fragments of the bedside table from the spare room were scattered round the kitchen. Though he had chosen the hall outside his bedroom as the best place in which to wrench the house plants out of their pots, the earth they had been potted in now formed a thin careful layer over every carpet in the house. The bathroom wash-basin was cracked where it had been hit repeatedly with a ballpein hammer. Some of the kitchen cupboards had been emptied and their contents thrown around under the intense bleak light of the fluorescent strip – packets of dried soup, pasta, and tortilla chips, Marks & Spencer's coffee beans, bottles of vegetable oil and Hungarian red wine, in a congealing slick on the tiled floor. But the front room was the preferred site of destruction. The shades were off the lamps. The chairs were on their backs. Awed, I gazed round at Lucas's pictures, broken in half as if they had been snapped across someone's knee; the bookcases which lay on their faces in the centre of the room, volumes spilling out from under them like talus; the shattered plastic moulding and sheaf of coloured threadlike wires which was all that remained of the telephone. Lucas's grief had led him to tear up his own shirts. Finally, he had pulled all the papers out of the filing cabinet in his bedroom and thrown them in on top of the pile. It looked as if he had planned to make a bonfire in his lounge.

I stood there trying to take in the scale of it. The flat was so quiet you could almost hear him dragging the bulkier items from room to room, panting with effort, sobbing perhaps, repeating over and over again, 'Easier to manage her death. Easier to manage her death.'

'Lucas, for Christ's sake.'

An hour later I had righted the bookcases, vacuumed the carpets and cleaned the kitchen floor, thrown the pictures in the dustbin. Most of the books were undamaged, but it took another hour to pack them back on to the shelves. By eight o'clock I had gathered all his papers into a pile, made myself a cup of coffee, and come back to start sorting them out. I was pushing crumpled sheets of A4 into an old blue concertina file, when my eye caught the first sentence of the following paragraph:

'For two nights and a day the harbour had been in flames. In any case, there is no escape from inside the meaning of things. The Empress Gallica XII Hierodule, mounted and wearing polished plate armour but – in response some thought to a dream she had had as a child at the court of Charles VII of France – carrying no weapons, waited with her captains, Theodore Lascaris and the twenty-three-year-old English adventurer Michael Neville (later "Michael of Anjou"), for the last assault on the citadel. The outer walls were already weakened by three weeks of bombardment from landward. The labyrinthine powder magazines were exhausted. Smoke from the besieging cannon drifted here and there in the sunlight, sometimes like strips of rag, sometimes like a thick black fog.'

I looked for the title at the top of the page.

Beautiful Swimmers.

'What are you up to Lucas?'

I was fascinated. I put the sheets in order, made another cup of coffee, and began at the beginning—

Anima

'Concrete only yields more concrete. Since the war the cities of the Danube all look like Birmingham. When I was a boy you could still see how they had once been the dark core of Europe. If you travelled south and east, the new Austria went behind you – like a Secession cakestand full of the same old Austro-Hungarian cakes – and you were lost in the steep cobbled streets which smelt of charcoal smoke and paprika, fresh leather from the saddler's.'

The manuscript, though it amounted to sixty or seventy thousand words, was incomplete: the life of 'Michael Ashman' between 1947 and 1968 being sketched in with annotated cuttings from the *News Chronicle* and other newspapers of the time, a faded snapshot or two labelled 'Ashman in the Garden at Catesby' or 'Ashman's aunt', and a few thousand words of notes. Ashman's creative revision of history was documented at length, along with the conclusions he had drawn from it, in footnotes which referred to writers as far apart as Gilbert Murray (*Five Stages of Greek Religion*, 1933) and Norman Cohn (*The Pursuit of the Millennium*, 1957). One or two elements were preserved on the original postcards Lucas had sent to Pam in the early years of their marriage. Most of the text was typed, single-spaced and with very small margins, on the old Olivetti; much, though, had been handwritten at high speed in ball-point pen on the kind of ruled, punched paper students use. After the events at Burrington Combe, all pretence of an autobiography or memoir was abandoned. Instead, Ashman embarked on a dense, disconnected meditation around the theme of self-sacrifice (which he had originally described as 'the narcissism at the centre of Christianity'). He was trying to convince himself of something, though it was difficult to see what. 'Every sacrifice is a "sending on before", an attempt to prophesy or bring about the conditions of prophecy. All art, all religion, all "history", is only this pained clue dispatched to the future.'

Beautiful Swimmers took two hours to read, perhaps a little more. The final chapter began with such a barely coherent outpouring of delight I could hardly tell whether Ashman was describing 'the Coeur', or the world we already know—

'A rainbow like fire pouring down from heaven. Bare trees glimpsed through the violet end of the rainbow, transfigured, delicate, fragile and complex as a sea-creature in a bowl of water. Gold light on everything. Every object or event in this moment has idealised itself, every hawthorn hedge or gate in the twilight, every fold of a hill, every peach and silver line of cloud above an orange sun, every conifer in a suburban garden black against the house with its strings of fairy lights round each yellow window.'

Later, though, he passed into doubt and anger – 'We were all mad people, who heard voices and misinterpreted dreams' – to end with this strange and bitter cry:

'Willows bending over the roads, their leaves silver in the wind: comprehend the Heart, and you will never experience it.'

The flat was chilly, and I had eaten nothing since two o'clock that afternoon. Nevertheless, I sat for a long time with the manuscript on my knee, amused and thoughtful.

Remember, I knew nothing about this. In all those letters, miserable or elated, written to me over the years since their marriage, Pam and Lucas had been careful never to give anything away. I had never seen the word 'Coeur' written on paper, or heard it spoken down a telephone line. I was a publisher. It was easy for me to assume that Lucas – that dark horse! – had almost completed rather a clever novel. So I was quite unprepared for what happened next.

He got back from Manchester just after midnight and parked the Renault exhaustedly, sawing it up and down for several minutes in the snow. Then he came slowly up the stairs and stood in the centre of the room the way you stand in someone else's house waiting for them to make you feel comfortable. Last night's cut, inflamed and sore, embedded in its yellowing bruise, made his face look paler than it was. He had arrived at Christie's just after I left, he told me. He had been there ever since. 'That ward's bloody noisy in the evenings,' he said. 'You can't hear yourself think.' Then: 'She's not good today.' To make things worse, there was fresh snow on that side of town. 'I had a lousy drive back.' He blinked and rubbed the inside corners of his eyes with the tips of his fingers. I caught him staring in a vague way at the faded patches on the wall. Perhaps he was trying to remember where the pictures had gone.

'Lousy,' he repeated.

He took his coat off and sat down.

'Turn the fire on if you're cold,' I said, 'and I'll make you some coffee.'

I held out the manuscript of *Beautiful Swimmers*.

'What have you been hiding from me here?'

He took it, stared down at it in a shocked way, then up at me. Tears began to run down his face.

'Lucas! What's wrong?'

'I'm sorry.'

'What for? Lucas, it was a joke!'

'After Cambridge,' Lucas said, 'we couldn't believe that was the end.'

I stood over him. I touched his shoulder.

'Come on, Lucas. I only meant I didn't know you'd written a book.'

He didn't seem to hear.

'We'd done everything Yaxley suggested and nothing had come of it. Nothing could come of it. Pam was ill. Yaxley had vanished. You had lost interest in us.'

'All that was over years ago, Lucas.'

'Listen!' he said. He had to turn his head up at an odd angle to look at me. 'Just listen, for once!—

'The Pleroma isn't what the Gnostics thought it was. It's terrifying. Impossible to undertand. Without something like the Coeur to buffer it, Heaven is harder to bear than—' he made a helpless gesture '—all this. The world. Do you see? We had nowhere to turn. We had to believe something.'

I let him sob.

'What have you promised her, Lucas?'

'At least try to understand. It isn't just a book. She's the Heir. She's the Empress.'

'Jesus Christ.'

'She *is* the Coeur. She won't die. I've told her she won't die.'

13
Fatalité Intérieure

I hadn't slept properly all week. Tomorrow I would have to get up early, catch the train home, buy Christmas presents, put an ordinary face on it for Kit and Katherine. And now this again. I went over to the window. If I looked into the street I wouldn't have to look at Lucas. There was a clear moon through the trees. A few clouds high up redistributed its light, which had lent them the colour of a fish's skin. 'Lucas . . .' I began, but I couldn't think of anything I hadn't said a hundred times before, and I got no further. Lucas wasn't listening anyway. He had turned the gas fire up full and huddled close to it, his face lax and tear-streaked.

'You're always waking up at the exact moment your life goes away from you,' he said.

He added:

'That's what Pam thought.'

Hot and tired and a bit nauseated, I stood as close to the window as I could and gently touched my forehead to it. My breath bloomed on the glass, but I could still see moonlight glittering in the long thin discoloured icicles hanging from the sash windows on each side of the street, where condensation had run down the inside of the window panes to seep out yellow with tobacco smoke and cooking fumes.

'Life's aware of itself,' Lucas proceeded, 'even as you piss it down the drain. You're forever catching its last signal: the urge to laugh or fuck or give your money away which you've just ignored.'

'Lucas, we're free to change our minds.'

'Too late. As soon as you stop acting spontaneously, your life becomes a fiction.'

I could only laugh.

'That's a simple philosophy,' I pointed out, 'for a couple who invented their own Middle Europe.'

But he was already too confused to notice this.

'I won't live a lie—' he said.

An old Bengali woman came out of the house across the road and stood looking up and down the street. In the lighted passage behind her I could see a child's bicycle, a pair of stepladders. She wore cheap wellington boots, and over her traditional dress a council worker's coat. To her, snow was an alien, Sisyphean substance. Every day since the first fall she had been busy trying to clear her front steps, using a small red plastic dustpan. Morning, afternoon, quite late at night, you could see her shuffling to and fro across the pavement, the dustpan held stiffly out in front of her. It was too small for the job. Much of its contents remained compacted inside each time she emptied it. She had an air of inexpendable patience. As I watched, the wind got up and blew a cloud of spindrift round her. She bent down. I heard the distinct scrape of the dustpan.

Live a lie: it was one of Pam's phrases. You're living a lie. They're living a lie. I won't live a lie. Like all the others, it had signalled only a need for medication.

'—and Pam never would, either.'

'That was her trouble, Lucas,' I said bitterly.

The Bengali woman stopped work for a moment and went inside. When she reappeared, she had wound a coloured woollen scarf round her slack brown neck. Her breath puffed out white in the freezing air.

'Look, Lucas: the world's ours. We make it, minute to minute. Pam would never admit that. It frightened her to have responsibility for her own needs. She wanted the universe personalised. A father who would look out for her. Happy accidents. Gifts.

Things that came demonstrably from outside, so she felt special. That's the biggest lie of all.'

'Why are you talking as if she's already dead?' he shouted.

'Grow up, Lucas.'

I waited for a moment then added deliberately:

'Kicking this place apart every day isn't going to help you, either.'

There was a brief awful silence.

'You don't know anything!' he said. 'What do you fucking know?'

'Lucas. Don't. I'm sorry. I—'

He got up with such violence his chair fell over, and ran out of the room. 'Lucas!' I heard his footsteps all the way down the stairs and into the hall. The front door slammed. From the window I could see him floundering across the square, trying to run against the resistance offered by the snow. The Bengali woman watched him too. She remained there for a moment, her breath visible in the sharp air, then emptied her dustpan for the last time, drew her clothes tightly round her and went up the steps into her house.

'Lucas,' I said. My head felt like an empty cinema.

He was back some time in the small hours. He had forgotten his keys. He stood there on the doorstep, frail, tense, resigned, incapable of organising his own resources. It was his favourite act, and just for once I wanted to tell him so: all that came out was, 'You look utterly buggered.' Inside, he crouched down over the gas fire, coughing and rubbing his hands together.

'Look,' he said. 'You should go home tomorrow. Come back when you can. I really don't mind.'

He did: but he was losing ground against himself.

'You do mind, Lucas.'

He nodded. He narrowed his eyes. I could feel him measuring something. It turned out to be me. 'I do,' he admitted. 'And so do you. You know you do.'

'You're a bastard, Lucas.'

'You love her as much as I do.'

I made him have a bath while I got him something to eat. Then I went to bed and left him to it, and in the morning caught an InterCity 125 to Euston so I could spend Christmas at home with my family. If they found me miserable and withdrawn they didn't say so, for which I was grateful. 'How are things up there?' Katherine asked me on Boxing Day. 'Not good,' I answered. She put her arms round me. 'It will soon be over.' Kit had given me some marker pens and a new shirt. 'I wrapped them myself!' After some thought she had also given me her favourite postcard, featuring a Botticelli Venus with whom at that time she strongly identified. Lucas didn't telephone. I returned to Manchester, as I had promised, on the morning of the 27th. From the train, everything looked astonishingly beautiful: factory chimneys dissolving in a blaze of sunshine you couldn't bear to look at, smoke wreathing in the clear blue sky. Some children were playing with a tyre in a snowy field, enveloped in transparent, bitter air. The sun reflected pink and gold on the icy surface between them.

Lucas was at Piccadilly to meet me.

'I'm sorry,' we said to each other in unison.

As if she had been waiting for us to be reconciled, Pam hung on another day or so and then died.

'Make the most of your life,' she often repeated. 'It doesn't matter how,' She clutched Lucas's hands. 'Promise me you'll make the most of it.' In her brief moments of lucidity she could still be optimistic. She would look out of the window and say, 'Do you know, I don't regret a day that I was sent. Isn't that odd? Not a day!' Much of the time, though, she was in despair. You would have a job to recognise her in the games this caused her to play with us.

'Sit here. By me. I want to watch you commit suicide.'

She would open her eyes drowsily and smile.

A moment later, terror forced her back to the safety of

childhood, from which she recited nursery-rhymes, hymns, the nominies for skipping or ball-games, some of which had a deadly irony: 'Touch your head, touch your toes,' Manchester children recite when they see an ambulance, 'Never go in one of those.' Lucas was distressed. She eluded him increasingly in this surreal half-world of pain and morphine addiction. That is a bad way to put it, I know. It was Lucas and I who found it 'surreal', because of the contrast between the catheterised woman with the amputated breasts – nightdress riding up round her white body, emaciated, bed-sored and perpetually trembling – and the childish voice. God knows how she experienced it.

Somewhere down inside herself, you sensed, she was holding on with both hands when all she wanted to do was let go. She wouldn't relinquish the promises she and Lucas had made to each other. The Coeur, and through it the Pleroma, was all to be hers; and through her, his. She was the Heir. She could not die. She was determined to dispatch the 'pained clue' of herself into the future, accomplish on Lucas's behalf that extraordinary act of prophecy and sacrifice Michael Ashman had talked of in *Beautiful Swimmers*. Her glazed, taut expression was as much the result of determination as it was of fear, pain, the animal need to endure. Whatever Lucas had intended – and I'm sure it was comfort – he had ensured that her death would be as much of a struggle as her life. I couldn't forgive him that, despite what happened later.

'As children none of the women in that family would ever go to sleep,' he had once written to me.

'You see them in photographs at three years old, almost blind with tiredness, puffy-eyed, heavy-lidded as vamps from a silent film, white, thin, with expresisons as old and vulnerable as baby mice. They won't let go. They won't give in. In later life, rather than sleep, they smoke another cigarette, make another cup of instant coffee, read another page of *Lost Horizon*.'

At the very end, she wasn't anything at all. Whatever they had promised each other was a rag in the wind, the disease took it all away. Lucas stayed with her and held her hand, but I couldn't bear to look at her. I wanted to remember her ill but still human, saying something like, 'I never get tired of the view from this window.' Out in the corridor the afternoon she died, a little nurse with frizzy orange hair offered me a cup of tea and said,

'You can't imagine how we all admire her. We've never had a patient who sent her relatives away so happy.'

I stared numbly at the vases of flowers.

'I'm not a relative.'

Pam shrieked.

'The white couple! The white couple!'

Lucas wouldn't be comforted. His eyes vague with an undischargeable energy, he abandoned the Renault in Christie's car park and set out to walk through the snow into central Manchester. I followed him along Oxford Road trying to persuade him to take a taxi. 'Or at least get on a bus, Lucas!' I could hardly keep up with him. Every so often he turned back and said something unforgivable; but I could see that his hatred was for himself as much as me.

'Lucas.'

'Fuck off. You killed her.'

'Lucas!'

As the day began to fade, he made for the pedestrianised streets and softly lit malls where, preyed upon by greeds aroused but unassuaged by Christmas, shoppers clogged the replicated space, drifting slowly from window to window – past the ethnic knits and Barbourwear, the soft toys and 'collector' ceramics – looking for some way of relieving the emptiness between Boxing Day and New Year. Sensing this, wounded long ago in his own optimism, Lucas had no way of controlling his rage and misery.

'Look at these fucking bastards!' he said loudly. 'Haven't they got anything better to do?'

Women stared at him angrily.

He sneered.

'The middle classes are always on watch!'

I edged him along Market Street towards the monolithic tiled shed of the bus station. I still hoped to get him on a bus. Lucas gazed up into the dim ceiling structures, full of dust and diesel smoke from revving engines, then down at a Mars bar wrapper blowing along near his feet. Against the grey concrete it looked like a small dun bird. He nodded judiciously.

'See that?' he said.

Without waiting for me to answer he continued, 'It was very important to her to buy me a birthday present. Maltesers. I had to eat some of them in front of her.'

He said: 'I loved her, you know.'

A bus arrived, bouncing on its suspension with the weight of children inside. Lucas watched them nervily, but allowed me to buy him a ticket. We would be home in ten minutes: less. I felt able to relax. Two stops later he was on his feet. 'Let me off! I'm going to be sick!' This amused the children, who got down at the same stop to watch. I asked the driver if he could wait. It was snowing again, and I had no idea where we were. The illuminated signs of bed-and-breakfast hotels, electrical dealers and Chinese chippies receded along a wide street brown with slush, seamed and sagging with old repairs: halfway down I could see the trees at the corner of a park, traffic lights green and steady at an empty junction. Lucas leaned over a low brick wall and groaned his vomit out into the car park of the Floral Hotel. The bus driver grinned and shrugged as if to say 'Well that's that then,' and drove away before we could get back on. For a moment the children tried to push one another under his wheels then lost interest and dispersed without warning into the shops and narrow side streets. Five minutes later I could still hear them howling and shrieking motivelessly in the distance. They seemed to be speaking another language, African or Asian. Echoing away between the dark walls of the houses, their voices conveyed only excitement inflated out of all proportion, cries of fear and panic, urgent, insistent, penetrating.

'Christ,' said Lucas, wiping his mouth.

I knelt down facing him and held his head between the palms

of my hands. His cheeks were damp from the falling snow. I had the feeling that if I couldn't get him to listen, things would slip away from us for good.

'It was never your fault, Lucas.'

I made him look at me.

'None of it was your fault, Cambridge or any of it. All three of us chose to do it, whatever it was.'

He shook me off, stood up, and tried to turn away. 'What do you know?' he accused. Suddenly, the thin, intelligent lines of his face went flabby, his eyes wide and appalled.

'Lucas!'

He wasn't looking at me at all, but over my shoulder. He whispered something I couldn't catch, then: 'Not here. Please.' A small dark object came turning over and over out of the gloom behind me, landed on the snow at Lucas's feet with a soft wet thud, and burst, spraying his trousers with sticky, fizzing liquid. Someone had thrown an open soft-drink can at us. I stared up and down the road. It was still empty. 'Christ!' Lucas repeated. 'Not now!' He walked off quickly. Ten or fifteen yards on the left was the lighted doorway of a pub, the Golden Crown, and beyond that a dimly lit sign in yellow day-glo: IDEO CLUB. As Lucas passed beneath it, two motorcycles parked at the kerb fell down with a clatter. Lucas, who was nowhere near them, whimpered and brushed at his trouser legs. 'Go away!' he shouted, and ran off into the residential maze behind the pub. These old crescents of glazed red brick seemed deserted despite their renovated windows, figured glass doors, gardens full of clipped laurel and shiny-leaved holly. Snow whirled and eddied in the lamplight; snow lay thick in the open gateways.

Lucas hadn't got far when a small figure slipped out from between two parked cars and began to follow him closely along the pavement, imitating his typical walk, head thrust forward, hands in pockets. When he stopped to button his jacket, it stopped too, I thought at first it was a boy or girl about six or seven years old, in an adult coat which trailed around its feet. But when I called 'Lucas!' and started running to catch up, it paused under a street lamp to look back at me. In the sodium light I found myself looking at neither a child nor a dwarf but something of both, with the eyes, gait and pink face of a large monkey. Its gaze was quite blank, stupid and implacable: warning me off, but frightened of me too. Lucas became aware of it suddenly and jumped with surprise; he ran a few aimless steps, shouting, then dodged round a corner, but it only followed him hurriedly. I thought I heard him pleading, 'Why don't you leave me alone?' and in answer came a voice at once tinny and muffled, barely audible yet strained as if shouting. Then there was a terrific clatter and I saw some large object like an old zinc dustbin fly out and go rolling about in the middle of the road.

'Lucas!' I called.

When I rounded the corner I found that he was alone. He had fallen – or been knocked over – on his back in the slush at the side of the road, then turned half over and, like a dead insect contracting, curled up into the foetal position. His clothes were sodden. He was clutching his left wrist or forearm with his right hand. As I approached him, he tried to sit up.

'Christ,' he said thickly. 'Not again. Give me a chance. Oh, it's you.'

'What was that thing, Lucas?'

He laughed bitterly. 'That's my little gift from the Pleroma,' he said. 'That's what I got for wrecking my life all those years ago.' He winced, and sat down again in the half-melted snow. 'Once it starts, you never get free. I think the fucker's broken something this time.'

'Where does it hurt most, Lucas?'

After a moment he laughed wildly and pointed at his own head.

'Here,' he said. 'In here.'

He ignored the arm I was offering, struggled on to his knees, looked down at himself. 'It's hurt in here for forty fucking years,' he said. 'Ever since I was born.' He brushed disgustedly at the mess. 'What can you, a mere priest, do about that?'

'Lucas,' I warned him.

He shrugged and held out the heel of his hand.
'I scraped that when I fell.'
'You'll live.'
'I'm buggered if I will,' he said. 'Not this time.'
He staggered off into the sodium light.
'Lucas!'
Suddenly he stopped and turned back to face me.
'So much for the fucking Pleroma!' he shouted. 'Eh? So much for fucking magic! I got the dwarf. Pam got the white couple. What did you get? I'll tell you. You fell in the shit and came up smelling of flowers. No wonder you can afford to be so fucking patronising!'
'I'm going home, Lucas,' I said.
But I didn't. Sooner or later someone would have to spend time at Pam Stuyvesant's last cottage and there sort out her life – order it, if only in the sense of finding a home for the cats; ask, 'Is the father still alive?' and try to get in touch if he was; bring things to a close. It might as well be me, if only because it was always me. Lucas would never face up to it. I left him to his despair and his vile little familiar, walked back to the city centre, and then, after an hour's wait in the raw cold at Victoria Station, boarded a train to Huddersfield.

14
Burnt Rose

It was raining on the other side of the Pennines. Outside Huddersfield station I got into a taxi which smelt warm and sweaty, as if it had been used all day to transport dogs. The driver was wearing two or three unravelling cardigans; as I opened the door he reached out and turned the heater up. We went slowly through the town centre – it had a varnished appearance in the rain and orange light – while he carried on an interminable argument with his dispatcher. 'Well if you can't find it there,' he kept repeating, 'get Addie to try downstairs.' Once he said, 'Get her off her arse then.' Outside the town, he drove boredly, treating intersections and traffic signs with a kind of indolent irony as if he was too clever for whoever had put them there, occasionally looking sideways at the stone walls and farmhouses with no show of interest. 'Don't bother,' he told the radio eventually, his eyes focused somewhere off past the windscreen. 'I'm coming in. I'm getting nothing but rubbish tonight any way.'

'This will do.' I said, although I knew I would have to walk another four hundred yards to Pam's house: 'I'll get out here.'

He looked round at the empty village.

'Please yourself.'

He drove off slowly. I could see him staring at me over his shoulder, one arm stretched along the back of the passenger seat. I swapped my bag from my left hand to my right and wondered what he was saying to the dispatcher. The rain was still coming down. If I had wanted to look I could have seen my face in the gleaming pavement.

I found Pam's gate hanging open and a woman in a pale-coloured raincoat knocking at her front door. She seemed to have been waiting there in the shadows for some time.

'Can I help?' I called from the pavement, 'No one's here now.'

She stood away from the door with a sudden apologetic movement.

'Pam?' I said.

But it wasn't her. The face was that of a much younger woman, about my own height, with heavy dark hair which she pushed patiently out of her eyes, revealing them to be grey, rather large and childlike. They gave you the odd idea that at some time they had seen something she had not. I had no conception of what it might be, but later I was unable to stop thinking about it. Her smile had a kind of warmth and sensuousness. If her face lacked animation, the broad, full-lipped mouth warmed it; and the eyes, which knew something she didn't – or at least something I didn't – illumined it: together they rescued it from blankness and lack of affect and made it deeply attractive.

'I'm sorry,' I said. 'It's the light. I mistook you for someone else.'

'Are you the owner?'

'A friend of mine lives here,' I caught myself saying.

'I see.'

I wondered if she did. As far as I could understand, she was collecting for some charity, Oxfam or Christian Aid; or at least conducting on its behalf a preliminary survey.

'We don't reach as many people as we'd like to.'

'I'm not very religious,' I said.

She would have a Volvo parked further along the road; two children at a local school; she would live in a converted cottage on the road to Manchester, where her husband worked during the day in the personnel office of an insurance company. I could imagine her drying her hair with a white towel in front of the mirror when she got home, repeating, 'Not as many as we'd like,' to someone in another room. She had a very faint accent I couldn't identify.

Suddenly she said:

'Isn't this beautiful?'

Almost filling the little garden at the front of the house was a blackcurrant bush which Pam Stuyvesant had allowed to grow tall and woody because, she said, it obscured part of the lounge window and made net curtains unnecessary. Now the night was full of its pleasant musty odour.

'Isn't it?' I agreed.

The flowers, which I knew would be pink in the daylight, looked like yellow wax. I pulled some of them towards me – drops of water showered down – and broke them off. I was glad to have something to talk to her about.

'This smell always reminds me of my childhood—'

But when I turned back to offer her the flowers I found that she had walked off without a word. Her pale figure moved rapidly up the street into the rain, shoulders hunched as if she had lost interest.

'I can't think why, though,' I finished. 'Still, you often can't.'

Pam's house was exactly as I remembered it, a little colder, a little dustier from disuse. Her neighbours had been feeding the cats, which ran up purring, tails high, as soon as I switched the lights on inside, and began to weave about in front of me, rubbing their heads against the furniture. I went straight through to the kitchen and put the kettle on. Staring out at the passage where in another life Pam had been compelled to witness the mating of the white couple, I shuddered; I closed the blind. I gave the cats a tin of meat and liver dinner.

Then I remembered how late in the year it was.

'Christ!'

I rushed back out into the front garden, where the damp air was still haunted by the breath of flowers. I stood there in a kind of fury of understanding, staring first at the blackcurrant with its freight of delicate yellow candles, then along the empty street. I had been in the house for no more than a minute or two. I listened, and thought I could hear, a long way off, the tap of high heels.

'Hello?' I shouted. 'Come back!'

The door slammed behind me and I was filled with panic. I couldn't get my key into the lock. For a moment I thought I had the wrong one, but when I held it up to the stuporous orange light I saw that embossed on it was the logo 'Mr Minnit'. Soon after Pam became ill, Lucas had had two or three of these duplicates cut somewhere in Manchester, and they never seemed to fit as well as the original. Eventually it turned.

As I let myself back in the smell of the blackcurrant grew acrid and overpowering, and the sense I had of understanding something faded. I knew that if I looked back there would no longer be any blossom on the bush, only drops of water like tears on every stem.

By then, the conversation on the doorstep seemed distant and confused. At one point, I believed, I had heard her say, 'I wanted to die.' (Her eyes had closed, as if she were testing the idea briefly, then opened again.) I thought about this in Pam's front room while Pam's cats sat licking themselves companionably on the carpet. Rain blew against the window behind me; I turned up the gas fire and drank my tea. If she had been collecting for charity why had she talked of dying, and let so many silences fall between us?

I fell asleep in the chair and dreamed about her:

In the dream she came to me as Phoenissa, the muse who has 'whored with many'. This enabled me to understand clearly, though it would become meaningless to me once I woke up again, the paradox of the mouth that warmed, the eyes which knew. What I failed to understand then, though it would become plain within weeks and has stayed plainly with me ever since, was the origin – or simplicity – of the message she had brought when she asked me to fetch her some roses.

'Like those on the graves over there.'

I looked in the direction indicated and saw instead of graves, as if through the wrong end of a telescope, groups of sad, exhausted boys in a wood, digging wide pits amid the fallen trees and uprooted secondary growth. It was spring. The woodland rides were muddy and poached, filled with lines of emaciated women dragging the dead up from the burned and fallen City by the cartload, and the cold air smelled of rain, raw timber, excrement.

Phoenissa giggled and whispered,

'Did you see the way that boy smiled when he saw me? The one with the mark like a rust stain down his cheek? Another girl said to me, "He was brave in the fighting around the Basilica, but he has such a disfigurement, running down from the corner of one eye, exactly like the stain on the side of a building under a rusty bolt. As if he had been crying rust!" But did you see how he smiled at me?'

She touched my hand affectionately and then pushed me away with a laugh.

She drew me back. She said:

'Later he wrote me a note. Look!'

I woke up confused but still able to remember some of what the boy had written. 'Attar, the secret heart of the rose: one ounce of this colourless fluid may be extracted from the petals of two hundred and fifty pounds of Gallica roses by means of a suitable solvent.' It didn't occur to me to think of this as nonsense – dreams often speak, Yaxley had once been careful to teach me, in the very inappropriateness of their elements. It was two o'clock in the morning and so quiet I could hear a car change gear off towards Huddersfield. I yawned, stretched, switched off the fire and then the kitchen light. Pam Stuyvesant's cats purred; rain pattered in the garden outside the lavatory window. I went upstairs and opened the door of the bedroom and found Phoenissa waiting for me there.

She was sitting in the dark on the very edge of the bed, gazing fixedly into the reflector of a cheap electric fire, her hands clasped on her knees and her body curled forward over them. A deep orange light lay across her face, which was turned very slightly away from me, elucidating the line of the jaw, the long tendons of the neck but leaving her eyes in shadow. How long she had been there I couldn't guess. She hadn't taken her coat off, and while the air in the room was warm it smelled strongly of scorched dust, as if the single bar of the fire had only recently heated up. She had made some attempt to dry her hair on a towel which now lay like a small animal on the carpet near her feet. It seemed to take her a long time to see me. Eventually she murmured, almost to herself.

'Sometimes I think I'll never get warm again!'

I stood in the doorway, filled with an extraordinary excitement and tension. I could feel myself rocking a little with every heartbeat, as though I were being tapped politely but repeatedly between the shoulder-blades. The muscles of my arms and upper back were rigid. Phoenissa looked up from the fire, at the same time unclasping her hands so she could draw my attention to it.

'Isn't this lovely?' she said, like someone who had never seen one before.

'Pam and Lucas used to have dozens of them,' I heard myself answer. 'They could never get warm, either. Look,' I went on quickly, so as not to give myself time to think, 'I don't understand how you got in here.'

I switched the light on.

She jumped to her feet.

'I'm sorry,' she said. 'You were fast asleep. I just came up here, I suppose.'

'Did you have a key, then?'

'It was so wet. I had waited for a long time.'

'I thought you were collecting for charity,' I explained. I laughed. 'You should have said you knew Pam.'

At Pam's name a further wave of immobility – this is the only way I can describe an emptiness the warmth of her mouth simply could not redeem – crossed her face. She stared at me.

The unkind wash of electric light revealed her large eyes surrounded by smudges of make-up like bruises. She looked as awkward and impermanent as she had done when I first saw her, on the doorstep, in the rain. It was the raincoat, a brisk tailored design meant for a much older woman, which had made me think of Christian Aid. By now it had lost much of its crispness. Her hair hung damp and tangled over its sodden collar. Nevertheless in Pam Stuyvesant's bedroom under the unforgiving light it only increased her sexual attraction.

Quite suddenly I imagined her turning away from me, pulling it up over her behind to show underwear made of oyster satin, white skin a little reddened in the creases below the buttocks so that she seemed at once inviting and ordinary (or perhaps I mean real), and made vulnerable as some women are by their own sensuality. I entered her at once and with miraculous ease. She groaned, and I heard myself whisper, 'Christ, Christ.' The rain spattered against the window. 'I died in Birkenau,' she said. She did not know how she came to be here with me, even in a dream. The electric fire was burning my bare calf – I paid no attention.

To visualise this took only a moment. I had no control over it. At the same time I was asking her:

'Would you like another towel? For your hair?' and she was blinking as if a sheet of glass separated us and then saying with a quick smile like someone waking up,

'Yes.'

Outside on the landing I shivered convulsively.

By the time I came back from the bathroom carrying the towel across my arm, she had switched off the ceiling light and arranged the bedside lamp to face the wall. It was hardly brighter than the firelight. She had taken off the raincoat and hung it up. Under it she had been wearing only a shiny grey slip which bared her thin shoulders and clung to the sides of her body, accentuating every rib.

From the doorway I had a clear view of her.

She was kneeling over me where I lay naked on Pam Stuyvesant's bed, talking in a low, persuasive voice while she fanned out in front of my drawn, surprised face a handful of dusty picture postcards she had taken off a shelf at the head of the bed.

I didn't see how I could be in the open door with a towel in my hand, and at the same time on the bed, breathing heavily with my clenched fists at my sides and the blood pumping and aching in my sex: but there she was, astride me. The slip had ridden up round her waist. I could see the soles of my own feet, yellow like the soles of the feet in some painting by Munch or Schiele. An instant later I was inside myself there, looking only at her, past the offered cards, seeing only her mouth and eyes while I struggled to drag the satin slip up further, perhaps pull it over her head altogether, and she laughed and urged,

"Pick a card. First pick a card,"

so that in the end I had no option but to take one. While I was looking helplessly at it she reached down between her legs, adjusted herself slightly, then lowered herself deftly on to me. 'Oh!' I cried: and came, immediately and despairingly, as you often do in dreams. The rest of the cards showered down, spilled in an alluvial fan across the black and red motifs of Pam Stuyvesant's continental quilt and pattered on to the bare lino. Phoenissa's eyes were open but she could not see me; her lips were parted but she did not speak. I remember her smiling, moving on me for a few minutes in a slow, self-hypnotised parabola, raising herself in a long-drawn-out motion then sliding down with a quick limping flick, a rhythm with a strange lacuna at its heart, like a comet passing close to the sun. Then in complete silence her head seemed to transform itself into the head of a huge red rose, blind and perfect, and I shouted 'Phoenissa!' and fainted from pleasure or fear, to wake in the dawn with the bedroom empty and the fire unplugged, my semen drying stiffly on the sheets, and still clutching in one hand the postcard she had made me choose.

It was a colour print, mystified by the faint milky light coming through the window, of a Romanesque cloister or courtyard: perhaps the exact one from which Lucas Medlar had constructed, to pacify the young Pam Stuyvesant, the first myths and anecdotes of the Coeur – though when I sent it to him later he didn't seem to recognise it and, interested only in its curiosity value, described its architecture in a letter as 'less calm than dispassionate, less tranquil than detached'.

In the middle and foreground of the shot, neat flowerbeds, in which I could identify only the hyacinths – 'Lord, the hyacinths are blooming in the Roman garden' – surrounded a font built of pale rosy marble. Behind them was the low wall of the cloister, topped with serenely curved arches of the same stone as the font. In its dim recesses you could just make out a window, though whether it was glassed and modern was difficult to see. Growing across much of this part of the view were the blossom-laden branches of an old hawthorn tree. It was that type which flowers pink. You could imagine its heavy equivocal scent, half confection half corruption, filling the court; while a tiny jet of water sprang perpetually from the font, falling whitely back on itself in perfect order, so that you saw how passion and clarity need never be divorced again as long as they became aspects of some thing which is neither.

I got out of bed. I had a wash. I got myself something to eat. I was in love – as Lucas had often complained – with contradictions. The postcard I carried about with me from room to room the way you carry a paperback you are reading, propping it up by the soap dish, the kettle, and finally next to my plate. I stared into it, like someone staring into a shaving mirror, but found there neither myself nor the answer to the riddle which may be loosely stated:

'The house is empty but two damp towels lie on the bedroom floor.'

If I looked past the card and out of the window I could see the blackcurrant bush, its branches dark and wet, a few yellowed leaves still clinging to it out of terror at what their new lives might bring. In the north and the midlands, the weathermen were saying, more snow had fallen overnight. Though it was melting, the month would continue cold. Pam's cats ran in and out making sudden little noises of encouragement to one another: fights broke out between them, raced up and down the stairs like a burning fuse, then fizzled out. I thought I would go home that afternoon. At around eleven o'clock I had a telephone call from Lucas Medlar, who told me without preamble: 'Pam's come back.'

'You've seen her?'

Lucas said something that sounded like, 'No, of course not!' (although it might equally have been, 'The Course of the Heart!'), adding after a pause a sentence which made no sense whatsoever:

'None of us ever die,' and then 'Scars,' or perhaps it was 'Wounds.'

'Lucas?'

Unintelligibility was to mark this whole exchange.

The line was full of rushing noises which built up, saturated then discharged, in steady tidal patterns; distant voices were audible in them, like people calling to one another from boats; and sometimes voices not so distant, so that at times I wasn't even sure I was talking to Lucas. When I was, he was clearly distraught, often unable to finish one sentence before starting another, so that I was never sure if he was telling me about something which had actually happened, or about a dream of his own.

In an attempt to be sure I repeated again and again, as clearly as I could, the questions, 'You've seen her?' and 'Have you actually seen Pam Stuyvesant?'

'I can't hear you!'

'Did you see her last night?'

'Thank God for that.'

'Lucas? I said, did you see Pam last night?'

I tried to get him to put the phone down and try another line, but he ignored me.

'Like a lunatic!' he went on. 'Early this morning. Wandering about babbling and soaked to the skin on the moors—' I couldn't tell whether he meant Pam or himself, or someone else altogether. 'When I asked her why she said, "We talked about my heart." '

There was a silence, as if everything had flowed away out of the line, leaving it empty and transparent between us.

Lucas had time to say: '—taken up into the Coeur.'

Then the surf of interference rolled back in, and I had a sudden, clear, agonising memory of Pam describing her first epileptic fit, and the vision she had had along with it—

'It was very clear. A seashore, steep and with no sand. Men and women lying on the rocks in the sunshine like lizards, smiling at the surf as it exploded up in front of them – huge waves, that might have been on a cinema screen for all the notice anyone took of them! At the same time I could see tiny spiders making webs between the rocks, just a foot or two above the tideline. Though it trembled, and was sometimes filled with spray like dewdrops so that it glittered in the sun, every web remained unbroken. So close to all that violence! I can't describe the sense of anxiety with which this filled me. You wondered why they had so little common sense.'

'I saw her in a dream,' Lucas said reasonably. 'Taken up into the Coeur. We're to meet her tomorrow, perhaps for the last time.' A sound like frying drowned everything but the words 'clear instructions'. Then I heard the rhythmic clicking that signals a crossed line, and a woman's voice said:

'Is that you, Alex?'

'Can you hear me?' Lucas shouted suddenly. 'You must be mad if you think I'm saying any more on the phone!'

'Lucas?'

'Alex?'

The other voices on the line went on calling to one another, remote as voices at the small end of a telescope; but Lucas said nothing more, so I rang off, picked up the postcard again and turned it over in my hands.

15
Every Web Remained Unbroken

Carnforth is less a town than a kind of late efflorescence of the old A6 as it hinges away from Morecambe Bay, where you can sometimes hear the seabirds calling sadly in the morning. We met in a bookshop which claimed to have on its shelves a hundred thousand secondhand volumes. Lucas and Pam had visited it regularly over the years in search of texts which would enable them to develop their myth of the Coeur. By the time I got there, it was late on a raw morning, and Lucas – looking along row after row of books with his head on one side like someone who has noticed something missing, though he can't say what – was already puzzled and disappointed.

'Why did we come here?' he asked himself. 'We might as well have met at the railway station.'

'Because you're a romantic, Lucas.'

He shrugged.

'You'd know,' he said.

I laughed.

Lucas looked around him with a kind of amused helplessness. 'This isn't going to be one of my better days.' He offered me a copy of Bruno Bettelheim's *The Informed Heart*. 'Look at that,' he said in disgust. 'He's a saint.'

'Lucas?'

'He's a saint,' Lucas explained impatiently, 'and they want two pounds fifty for him, second hand.' He looked at his watch. 'We've got hours before the train,' he complained.

Over the years the bookshop had been knocked haphazardly

into dozens of finicky little rooms: section connected to section – however contiguous – by annex, passageway, steps up and down, often with bewildering changes of direction as each new builder strove to avoid knocking out structural members, so that you always seemed to end up back where you started. 'Two pounds fifty for that?' Lucas would say in a high pitying voice every time he saw the Bettelheim, and glance back over his shoulder, trying to decide what other turning we should have taken. 'It's absurd.'

Two women stood irresolutely on a top-floor landing.

'Oh Christine!' one of them was saying as we passed. 'And it was one of Daddy's favourite plays!'

'Don't touch my arm.'

Lucas glared at them. From somewhere below came a noise like a damp cardboard box full of books bursting as it fell down the stairs.

'Let's get out of here!' he said suddenly. He looked savage and ill. 'This old junk. I – Well, it isn't funny any more.' He wrinkled his nose. He could smell the stifled front rooms, vicarage studies, failed private schools all over the north-west, which had given up all these cramped, affectless, unread collections of *Men and Books*, *Books and Characters*, *Adjectives and Other Words*. Eventually we found the main door of the shop and were able to leave.

'If you spent too long in there your spirit would heave itself inside out!'

Lucas stood looking up and down the pavement.

'Let's meet Pam early!' he suggested. 'If we get a bus to Lancaster and then on, we could leave here now, without waiting for the train—'

'We were supposed to wait for this train.'

'Does that matter to you?' he appealed.

'You said it was part of the instructions.'

'Let's go now. Pam won't know!'

I thought about the dreams I had had the night before. I said tiredly, 'Of course she won't. Lucas, Pam's dead. She's dead.'

But he knew I would give him anything when he was in this mood, if only to prevent him damaging himself.

Even so, we didn't get away by bus. For some reason he could only explain by saying, 'I don't like to carry a lot of things around with me,' his briefcase and most of his money were locked in the left-luggage office at the railway station. When he discovered there would be no attendant to unlock it for him until the arrival of the next train down from Silverdale at two o'clock, he could only murmur softly and miserably, 'Fuck it, I always wondered what it would be like to be in Carnforth for more than an hour or two.'

'Now you know, Lucas.'

'There's a whole class of places like this. They wait for you as patiently as Medusa.'

'Come on, Lucas, don't be spoilt.'

Eventually we fetched up in the rain in front of the War Memorial. By that time it was only twenty minutes to wait for the train. Lucas was still tense but I could feel him relaxing. ' "Their name liveth for ever more",' he quoted contemptuously. 'I suppose we're lucky it isn't writen as one word.' Out of his jacket he pulled the two volumes he had stolen from the bookshop, *Moments of Reprieve* by Primo Levi, and the unexpurgated *Journals of Anaïs Nin 1931–1934*. He threw them down at the foot of the memorial in a wet flutter of pages. 'Forevermore,' he said. 'Forevermoreland.' With this gesture something was finally eased in him. He shivered, then laughed recklessly and pulled me away towards the station, his arm round my shoulder.

'I thought I could hear something on those stairs back there,' he admitted.

Suddenly he began to tell me how, after they were first married, he and Pam had found a wristwatch in the street. 'This will show you something about us, it really will,' he said. He gripped my shoulder and went on anxiously, as if he was afraid I might not be listening: 'We had this thing for six months. No one had claimed it. Neither of us had a watch of our own. But it was one of these modern things—' He moved his wrist to show me that he had one now, all these years later '—and we had no idea what to do with it. Every morning at ten o'clock the alarm went off, and we didn't know how to stop it. Every morning at ten o'clock it read eleven, because it was still on BST; and we had no idea how to adjust it. There it was, among all the other stuff—'

I could imagine it, on the sideboard next to the telephone, one of those items carefully picked up each morning so that Lucas Medlar's dwarf could fling them insanely about that night: the mystery novels, the coffee mugs with macaws painted on them, the artificial flowers and silvered pine cones.

'—recording some rhythm of its previous owner!'

'Lucas, you could probably have got an instruction booklet from the manufacturer.'

He shook his head impatiently.

'Listen,' he said. We were halfway across the road in front of the station; further up, some lights had released a thin stream of afternoon traffic. He stood in front of me and stopped and made me look at him.

'Listen, that isn't the point. It was just a tinny metonym of someone else's life. "Peep peep." We thought we'd penetrated the Heart, and we couldn't even work a watch!'

'Lucas, we'd better get out of the road.'

He made a bitter, impatient gesture.

'You, me, Pam Stuyvesant! Together we don't make up one whole intelligence.'

'What do you want me to say? "Perhaps that's the point"? I remember Yaxley telling me, "If you can comprehend the Pleroma you can never experience it." Lucas, please let's get out of the road!'

He looked at me with contempt. He knew that at this point I could never bear his pain.

'Believe that and you're worse than a romantic.'

'What did you expect to find in the bookshop, Lucas?' I asked him unfairly. 'The Library at Alexandria?'

He walked off without answering, and I let him go. The

station was deserted. I could see him wandering up and down at the far end of the platform in the streaming rain, looking first at his watch and then up the line. He coughed once or twice. He seemed all right, so I left him to it. At least he was out of the traffic. In case Pam had run out when we met, I got her a couple of packets of cigarettes from the machine on the down-platform. Then I remembered Pam was dead, and threw them one by one across the rails into the waste ground on the other side. Lucas watched this performance and then came up and said:

'I'm sorry.'

'Lucas, you always are.'

'I did expect the Library at Alexandria.'

'Lucas, you always do.'

We laughed.

'Fasten your jacket up.'

Shortly after that the pay train arrived from Silverdale. It was full of children with sore red faces who by the smell had been copiously sick just before we got on; and old men with veins like cables on the backs of their hands who walked up and down in a buckled manner carrying suitcases too heavy for them while their wives changed seats relentlessly. Lucas watched them as if they might be a message from the Pleroma, or from Pam, and then, deciding perhaps that it was impossible to decode, took a copy of *The Tartar Steppe* out of his briefcase and pretended to read it. A few hours later we were stumbling about on the steep windy slopes above Attermire Scar in Yorkshire, looking for a dead woman who had given Lucas the grid reference NGR 842642 but who never turned up there.

It was the last place I wanted Lucas to be. Up on the limestone you feel miles from anywhere, and he was already soaked and cold. It would be a nightmare to get him down again. He raced about in the dark in the big deteriorating amphitheatres and steep hollows above the Victoria Escarpment, putting his feet down rabbit holes and coughing helplessly. 'Pam, you bitch!' he shouted. 'My feet are getting wet!' But after an hour he fell asleep suddenly in the mouth of one of the bigger caves, whose cracked, water-polished walls went above him in the moonlight like something made. I put my coat over him and poked about at the foot of the Scar until I heard him call out in his sleep, 'Yaxley! Yaxley!'

By morning the whole of the Ribble Valley was under mist. Like the cloud you see from an airliner above the Atlantic, it was white, impeccable, solid-seeming. It shifted restlessly, though, against the sides of the hills.

Reluctant to go down into it, we sat on some clints above Settle in the bright horizontal sunshine. Every tussock of grass had a rich luminousness. Every shadow pointed into the mist – which, where it encountered the east wind blowing down the defile between Attermire and High Hill, advanced a little, retreated a little, boiled over a stile, lay there curling back on itself and pushing out faint wisps close to the ground, exactly like the mist in a sixties film. You had no idea whether it loved or hated the things it covered; you had no idea what they might be. Eventually it began to ebb, leaving a boulder which looked like a lamb, grassy slopes glowing like sun through a bottle. Across the valley the ridge leading up to Smearsett was revealed as a long, mysterious-looking island. Behind that Ingleborough, the ancient continent, inexpressibly bleak and far away.

Lucas who had got to his feet suddenly said in a savage voice:

'It was a real nightmare for her, you know. Fuck your common sense. Fuck it. You were in the Pleroma too, all those years ago!'

'Lucas—'

He stared intently out over the mist and said quickly so that I couldn't interrupt:

'Gallica, who called herself "the Slave of God" but who certainly loved Michael Neville, may not after all have died at the Carolingian Gate.' Soon he was shouting. 'Many of the wounded claim to have seen her after four o'clock, in the citadel itself, where she brought them great comfort. She was glimpsed several times during the three days of massacres which followed. Michael Neville, who though he lay all that time in the heap of dead and dying in front of the Eastern Basilica never saw her himself, recorded twenty years later: "Wherever she moved among them the smell of blood was transformed briefly to that of attar."'

He shivered and wiped his eyes.

'I made that up for Pam, years ago. It was a real dream. Fuck your common sense.'

'She never wanted to be the Empress, Lucas.'

Lucas looked round confusedly, exactly as he had done in the bookshop.

'She wanted to be the daughter,' I said. 'Let's go down.'

We took a wrong turn in the mist and were forced to walk for some time across rough grazing and moorland. Inside the mist it was silent, damp, cold. Lucas swayed and stumbled; he couldn't stop shivering. I pulled his jacket round him but it didn't seem to help. His shoes were coming to pieces.

'Where are we?' he kept saying. 'We should be down now.' And then:

'I hate it here.'

'I know you do, Lucas.'

Suddenly we were standing at the edge of a deep Gothic ravine in the limestone, at the dry bottom of which a well-defined path curved away between overgrown screes. Half a mile or less to the south white crags rose under the grey sky, their tiers of collapsing rock like teeth in a dead gum. Northwards, the path climbed abruptly into the recesses of the cleft and vanished. Light rain had begun to fall; I could hear it pattering quietly in the little bare larchwood at the lip of the ravine. We walked in silence along the cliff edge and stood in the rain to stare at the long featureless green sweeps of moorland stretching north.

'Christ!' said Lucas. But he seemed more cheerful.

The head of the ravine was a stony cleft hardly wide enough to admit two men. There the path came up to meet us, and we followed it down until we came to a village. Ducks honked from the shallows of the stream. A woman in a headscarf and gumboots stopped gardening to watch us pass, trowel in hand. Out on the main road, we waited half an hour for the Settle bus. When it came it was empty but for one bronchitic old man and his sly red-eyed collie.

Lucas was waxy and vague with hypothermia. I got him off the bus as soon as it stopped and took him into the first café I saw. That was a mistake. Warmth, laughter, and the smell of hot fat billowed into our faces as I opened the door: a New Year party was in progress, with a dozen people from one of the local agricultural businesses shouting, laughing and singing disconnectedly at a long table down one side of the room. They were wearing paper hats quartered in red, yellow and green. They all had red, polished, cheerful faces. The floor round their feet was littered with spent Christmas crackers, crumpled serviettes and strings of dried party-foam. Two or three middle-aged women in waitress outfits – old-fashioned belted black dresses with a severe little white collar – were beginning to clear the disordered remains of a second course of roast pork and apple sauce, in preparation for the pudding. Meanwhile a boy ten or eleven years old had the job of pouring out glasses of Tetley's for the men. A bit drunk himself, he ran about in his white shirt, little bow tie and neat black trousers asking hysterically, 'Would you like a beer? Would you like a beer?' The women in the party, who had decked themselves with tinsel and mistletoe, drank white wine. Lucas stood eyeing it all with horror, while the Muzak played first a xylophone rendering of 'Jingle Bells', then 'The Little Drummer Boy'. He didn't know what to do with himself. His shoulders were hunched under the sodden cashmere jacket, and he was shivering.

'I don't think I—'

'Lucas, at least have a cup of tea.'

I sat him down at a corner table where he turned helplessly away from the fun, his upper body stiff with rejection, while bits of talk floated round his head like strips of print on a clever advertisement—

'Pass us that mistletoe, Harry!'

'Ay, old Tommy Walker. Me brother used to work for him. He lost all his fingers and half his thumb, working potato machine.'

'Cost her twenty pound.'

'No, I think they saved some of his fingers – took them in with him and sewed them back.'

'White bread! Now that'll help your bowels come up.'

'Twenty pound? They're having you on.'

'He needed to. He needed to. Bring it up. He probably needed to bring it up.'

'Sorry, Harry!'

'Ay lad, yer will be.'

A large man in his early fifties who had at some time lost his left arm at the elbow, Harry wore a greenish tweed jacket over a maroon pullover not quite long enough to cover his shirt, which in its turn had popped open over a belly fat, smooth and hard-looking. In his youth his face must have been straight-planed yet heavy, quick to redden in the wind, and to develop broken veins. Now it had thickened under and around the jawline, and his lively blue eyes looked out from a lapping of fat. Harry was the most animated of them all. He liked the other men to listen to him. He liked the women, to whose attention he was always bringing his missing limb, to be a little shocked at the things he said. His idea of a joke was to drain a pint of Tetley's, exclaim loudly 'Ah'm not shuwer ah enjoyed that,' and finish: 'Now then! Ah'll joost av some of that *Perr*ier watter. Raght oop mah street.' I saw quite soon that something was going on between him and our waitress: they had some old score to settle, some business unfinished since early adulthood, perhaps even before. He would catch her eye and call challengingly across the room—

'Hey! You! Coom 'ere a minute! Ah've summat to tell you.'

'I bet you have, Harry. I bet you have!'

Then, to considerable laughter:

'I hope it's nowt to do with that arm of yours.' And, with a direct look: 'Because I haven't got it!' Harry enjoyed this a good deal, and so did his friends.

She was a well-built lively woman, thirty or thirty-five years old, dressed in what may have been a Monsoon frock, who in addition to waitressing took care of the till. Her eyes were direct and brown, her hair unruly, her forearms freckled. As she talked she held her body towards you, and her skin had a light, pleasant perfume.

'Somebody's having a good time,' I said.

She looked pleased.

'Ay, we're just this minute picking up the debris. They've only been in an hour and a quarter. To get them in and serve them four courses in one and a quarter hours isn't bad.'

'I think I'll have some tea,' I said, mainly to stop her from staring at Lucas.

She leaned her hip unselfconsciously against the back of my chair and stared at him anyway, with a kind of half-amused concern. 'You've been in the wars,' she advised him, 'and no mistake. What would you like?' Her friendliness seemed genuine, but she had never had to deal with anyone like Lucas Medlar. When he failed to respond she shrugged and told me, 'Well you'll have to order for him, won't you? Just two teas? Nothing to eat? Right.' When she came back with the teas a few minutes later she went on: 'It's been nonstop here all week. Turkey dinners! Every single table was packed.' She paused to shout in the direction of the kitchen, 'They're still waiting at table eight!' The sound of crockery answered her. 'People who didn't even know each other were sharing tables.' She drew my attention to Lucas, who was still staring over at the party. 'Are you sure your friend's all right?'

'Leave us alone,' said Lucas distinctly.

She laughed and returned to the till. There, she fussed with some receipts, changed the Muzak tape for a selection of popular choral classics, then, with a yawn, leaned her elbows on the counter and looked out across the café. Lucas and I drank our tea. One or two old ladies finished their lunch and, complaining about the weather, went out into the darkening air. The party, contemplating an afternoon at work with a bad head, had slid into an introspective mood. Even Harry was looking into his glass, sighing, and saying, 'Ay, well.' The woman behind the counter seemed amused by this. She folded her arms under her breasts and said into the silence, as if to herself but quite loudly:

'I'm sure I don't know what I've done to my neck, but it's ached since Wednesday.'

Instantly, the one-armed man was on his feet and making his way across to her.

'Ah know joost what you need!'

'Harry! No!'

Before she could avoid him, he had taken her wrist and pulled her out from behind the counter. He made her sit down on an empty table, stood behind her, and began to massage the side of her neck with his good hand. At first she laughed like a schoolgirl. Then, as his hand began to move down towards her shoulder, she let her body relax and began a pantomime of sexual arousal, looking up and back at him with large eyes, pushing her shoulder-blades back against his belly like a cat being stroked and whispering in a stage contralto—

'Oh, Harry.'

The blues and golds of her frock glowed like a stained glass window.

'By God!' shouted the one-armed man.

He slapped his hand to his forehead, slid agilely out of his jacket and pretended to undo his braces at the front. He panted loudly. His friends cheered and laughed at this demonstration of how his missing arm had somehow granted him more vigour than ordinary people. She, meanwhile, ducked away, darted round behind him suddenly and massaged his neck in turn. Harry rolled his eyes with appreciation; lolled his head; and let his tongue hang out comically. The waitress leaned forward; gave him a quick kiss near the mouth; then, before he could reciprocate, put the counter between them again. Further cheering broke out, and while Harry was bowing to the applause she slipped away into the kitchen.

What did this exchange mean? All you could say was that it was their party piece. Harry and the waitress knew one another of old, and they had done it before, and probably other things too. I was reminded of Ward Three at the cancer hospital, where among all the other wasted, wayward old dears (like a lot of moulting but cheerful parrots driven to testify at random from their smelly cage) there had been a woman called Doris. Against the odds of that place – indeed against all odds – Doris, seventy-eight years old, no hair and no teeth, pink flock dressing gown which shed all over the ward, radiotherapy implant and all, still enjoyed a rich and colourful fantasy life. 'I'll do most things,' she would carol out at the top of her voice in the middle of visiting hours, 'but I won't be buggered or bitten.' Or, 'Christ, that finger's been up two arses today. Look at it!' It was always unclear to me whether these were actually sexual memories of Doris's, or just some kind of loosening of the internal censors in the proximity of death. Much of the time, Pam told me, Doris irritated or upset the other women on the ward. 'It spoils their own memories.' But on occasion, especially in the middle of the night, when the building was full of their quiet, inturned, lunar despair, she actually seemed to give them an obscure comfort.

On balance, Pam had found her liveliness contagious. 'I think in the end the women did too, although they never joined in.'

I thought this might cheer Lucas up, but all he said was:

'Jesus Christ'

He finished his tea and walked out. I wanted to stay, but in the end followed him wearily.

Outside it was heavy snow. The air was flurried with it, and there was a thin, milky skim upon the setts. Whenever the wind catches falling snow, you seem for a moment to be rushing forward, as if your life has accelerated. Snow has been magical to me since as a child I stayed up late to gaze out of a downstairs back window and watch it fall through the night on to the dark lawn – soft, silent, huge as pennies. (It's easy to tell yourself: 'Memory is the great mythologiser. You were small. It was the first snow you had ever seen. Images like that become magnified out of proportion.' Now I wonder.) Pam Stuyvesant loved snow too. 'Yet if it falls for any length of time,' she used to say, 'I get the sense I'm watching something in slow motion which shouldn't be. It's very unnatural.'

Trying to find the bus stop, Lucas had become disoriented and was walking across the old Settle square – now a car park – towards some narrow lanes on the north side, where Castlebergh rises steeply, wooded like a Chinese rock, above the town. He seemed intent on something: NGR 842642 perhaps, and the image of Pam drawing him back. Halfway across the square, though, he stopped as if puzzled, a gloomy, stooped figure in the poor light. I could see him moving his head from side to side. He gazed up into the whirling snow. He put his hand out to gather some of it, suddenly dropped what he had caught as if it had scorched him. I stood in the shelter of the café doorway and called—

'Lucas!'

He didn't seem to hear me.

'Lucas!'

When I stepped out into the square, I found that it wasn't snowing at all. White rose petals were falling out of the sky. Their thick, Byzantine perfume filled the air.

We were folded into the heart of a rose. The heart of a rose! The whole square beat with it. Lucas Medlar stood distraught and lonely, lapped in attar. He shouted my name: and then, 'Someone's here!' Attar! We were in the heart of the rose, and it was already occupied. People say of someone, 'She filled the place with her personality,' without a clue of what they might mean. Perfume was like a sea around us. If we could not learn to swim in it we would drown. I was gripped by the panic of irreversible events. 'Hello?' I whispered. No one answered, but Lucas called again, more urgently, 'Someone's here! Someone's here!' Now she walked out of the great soft storm of rose petals, the goddess herself, the green – the grown – woman, the woman made of flowers. Her outline was perfectly sharp, it seemed to have no surfaces, and flowers came and went within it as she turned her head deliberately this way and that. She was like a window opened on to a mass of leafage after rain, branches of blackthorn, aglet and elder interwoven, plaits of grass and fern, all held together with rose briars, over and between which went a constant trickle of water. Her eyes were a pitiless chalky blue, without white or pupil. They were flowers, too. She knew we were there. She stretched her arms, standing with one leg bent and the other stiffened to take her weight.

'You are never simply yourselves,' she whispered.

This time she had brought for us a glimpse of her own place, the envelope of her eternal fall, which is perhaps of the Pleroma but not yet the Pleroma itself (thirtieth Aeon beloved of God, she cast herself out and fell into mirrors in Alexandria, Rome, Manchester, Birkenau): roses blooming in a garden. Between the lawns were broad formal beds of Old China Blush – 'China's in the heart, Jack. China's in the heart!' – with lilies planted between them. Burnet and guelder spilled faint pink and thick cream over old brick walls and paths velvety with bright green moss. White climbing centifolias weighed down the apple trees. Two or three willows streamed, like yellow hair in strong winter sunshine. Beyond this garden spread an intimately folded arrangement of orchards and lanes, of sandy eminences and broad heathland stretching off to hills. There, late afternoon light enamelled the leaves of the ilex, briars hung over the grassy banks, clematis put forth great suffocating masses of flowers. Everything was possible in that country beyond. A white leopard couched among the hawthorn; other animals paced cagily along its lanes – baboons, huge birds, a snake turning slowly on itself. I heard a voice not mine or Lucas's say: 'The Rose of Earth is the Lily of Heaven.' The scent of attar was as heavy as a velvet curtain: but through it, from the café behind me like flashes of light through a veil, came piercing human smells – hot fat, brandy sauce, perspiration, beer. I could feel the heat, see the yellow lights. For a moment it might have been possible to go back inside—

But the green woman!

She stared down at Lucas Medlar in his loneliness and offered him the whole garden.

To have it he must first accept her attendants. These creatures, denizens perhaps of the Fullness itself, have power over all transitional states, all re-drawing of borders, all human change. They are always with her:

Around her feet runs the dwarf which haunted Lucas for so long, poisoning the central experience of his life. In the air beside her, naked and joined, hover the white couple. I saw now that under the Manchester street lights I had been mistaken. The dwarf was only a child, a toddler full of delight and charm one moment, full of rage and frustration the next, trying to eat up the world but hampered by some old coat of Lucas Medlar's he forced it to wear. It was only Lucas's own unruly future, made futile by too much longing. As for the white couple: they are five million years old. Sustained by their tao on the perpetual edge between desire and release, they never sleep. Their faces are transitory, yet do not change. They are Harry's stump and the waitress's Monsoon frock; the unfastened buttons of the blind woman in the quarry, the sudden sweet smile on the face of her crippled boy. For a brief moment as I watched, they were Katherine and myself: 'Touch me here, then.' For an even briefer one, like a promise of some admission not yet ready to be made, they presented themselves as Lucas Medlar and Pam Stuyvesant. In such moments, perhaps, out of delight and disorder, the Coeur – if there was ever any such place – is finally brought forth.

As if in earnest of this, the green woman seemed to melt and shift and grow huge, until she towered above the town and Lucas Medlar found himself hardly a speck beneath her. Slowly, and with vast grace, she knelt before him and sat back upon her heels, the palms of her hands flat on her vast open thighs. Lucas fell down before the rosy door, then recovered, pulling himself slowly to his feet again. In response, wavering above him like water, the green woman became his Empress, Gallica XII Hierodule, her plate armour shining through the smoke at the gates of the Coeur: 'When the smoke cleared you could not bear to look directly at her. There is no escape from inside the meaning of things.' Immediately, she became the Empress's daughter Phoenissa, running through the cool rooms of morning to meet Theodore Lacaris by a fountain. 'Fuck me Theo oh fuck me now.' Now that the goddess is in the World, she is searching too. She sways on her heels above Lucas Medlar's silent figure. Is it here? No. Panicked, she becomes the Roman prostitute Eudoxia, wife of Mathaeus; then Godscall St Ives, then Godscall's sickly daughter Liselotte, then Alice Sturtevant, caught in a moment of yearning she can never express. 'Something burns within me,' Alice once imagined shouting as she stood looking in at her father who lay ill, 'but I am never consumed!' She felt a terrible emptiness, and ran to John Duck. Now the goddess has fallen into the world, where is it? Michael Ashman's gypsy prostitute offers Lucas the cards, brings herself off in the air above him with a quick limping flick of the pelvis. Is it here? (Floodwater was frozen in lakes, forty miles up and down the river.) For a terrified moment, the goddess finds herself as Lawson's twelve-year-old daughter, lying across Yaxley's table beneath Yaxley's pictures and her father's eyes. Then, with bewildering suddenness, she was Katherine; and Kit; and at last, leaping into stability and focus, Pam Stuyvesant as I had seen her that summer afternoon in her rooms at Cambridge, twenty years before, laughing up at me from the floor and whispering, 'This room reeks of sex.' Is it here? 'Don't let him in!' It is never anywhere. It is everywhere at once. The goddess is all those women and none of them, we seek her, she seeks us, less mater than matrix – the bitter world we know, the Pleroma we desire, the Coeur which intercedes. We are wrapped in the heart of the rose. Pam's face, now clear and specific, ages before us in the sky, after the divorce she is dyeing her hair, smoking fifty cigarettes a day, staring out into her garden. She has forgiven the world for not being ideal, and now bequeathes it to Lucas. The grown woman throws back her head in joy. A great open pink blossom fades like fireworks in the night.

I waited for a long time, just outside the café door. The winter air was dark. After a while the falling roses turned to snow again, the scent of attar faded, and Lucas Medlar was left standing in the middle of the car park with his head bowed.

'Lucas?'
'Someone was here.'
'Lucas?'
'I'll come back in.'

Pam's funeral took place a week later.

'A scent of roses,' I remember her saying once. 'How lucky you were!'

'It was a wonderful summer for roses anyway,' I answered. 'I never knew a year like it. All June the hedgerows were full of dog-roses, with that fragile elusive scent they have; I hadn't seen them since I was a boy. As for the gardens, they were bursting with Hybrid Teas and variegated Gallicas, great powerful blowsy things which gave off a drugged smell into the evening air. It was like a tart's boudoir. How can we ever say that Yaxley had anything to do with that, Pam? It would have been a good year for roses without his interference!'

But I sent some to her funeral anyway, though I didn't go myself.

EPILOGUE
Kenoma

What did we do, Pam, Lucas and I, in the fields of June, such a long time ago? I wish I could remember.

I don't think it was 'wrong' or 'evil'. Why should it have been? I think now it was one of those things that life offers you, from which you take the value you expect, or have been encouraged to expect, rather than some intrinsic goodness or badness. This is what Yaxley, in his corrupt way, might have been trying to tell us. If so, he forgot, and, though he sneered at Pam and Lucas for their lack of self-confidence, came away in the end with less than either of them.

'It is easy to misinterpret the Great Goddess,' writes de Vries in his *Dictionary of Symbols and Imagery*:

'If She represents the long slow panic in us which never quite surfaces, if She signifies our perception of the animal, the uncontrollable, She must also stand for that direct sensual perception of the world we have lost by ageing – perhaps even by becoming human in the first place.'

Lucas and I continued to correspond, although we never met each other again.

Shortly after Pam's death, he claimed he had remembered what it was we did to bring all this on ourselves. Indeed, it was Pam's death, he thought, which had somehow freed him to remember. He thought that in this sense her death was a redemption. The dwarf no longer haunted him. He had begun to write a book. He would not talk about what had happened to him in the snowy square in Settle. He did not remember a green woman, or a scent of roses. What he did remember, he believed, was his own affair. I agreed, although – from the hints he dropped, the obsessions he still had – I thought I could guess what it was. The search for the heart occupied him until his disappearance a year or two later. His letters are full of it. They glow like stained glass.

'The Coeur negotiates between the World and the Pleroma. It controls the dialectic between them. When it is in the Pleroma it cannot be in the World. When it is in the World it cannot be in the Pleroma. But it is never for long in one at the expense of the other. The fact that it has withdrawn from the World is the surest indication that it will return. Its presence in the World is the clear sign that it must Fall. It is less a country, or even a state of mind, than a counter which the World and the Pleroma must constantly exchange between them to maintain some balance we cannot understand.'

After he gave up teaching and went to Europe, I heard from him less regularly. He would spend a couple of weeks here, a couple of weeks there, moving erratically from Spain to Norway, then back down to the Adriatic. He stopped off at Arles to see the Romanesque cathedral there, perhaps because he remembered what Van Gogh had written. 'We must not judge God by this world. It's just a study that didn't come off.' Or perhaps simply because its cloister reminded him of the one at Cuxa, and the postcard which had begun it all. He wrote twice in a week from Amsterdam; after that not for a year. In the east, governments were going over like tired middleweights – saggy, puzzled, almost apologetic. At first he was unimpressed. Watching TV pictures of East Berliners pouring into West Berlin, he had the sudden impression – from their cheap, dated clothes, their pinched rather unhealthy faces, the way they tilted a bottle of wine greedily to their mouths – that it was in fact people from the back streets of Bolton or Tyne and Wear who were being given their liberty.

Then came the fireworks at the Brandenburg Gate. The fall of Ceauşescu brought lyrical footage of Moldavia: 'Ox-carts, bright peasant clothes and broken shoes, a near medieval society coming out from under the snow!' All this was accompanied by a terrible sense of risk, perhaps of guilt: 'At any moment it might go down like a card-house and take us all with it.' Aided more than hampered by a growing sense of his own inadequacy, he determined to re-enact the pre-war journey of his own invention, the travel writer 'Michael Ashman'; and after six months more in Western Europe crossed the border into Czechoslovakia, then Hungary. 'Things are quite different here now,' he wrote to me from a room overlooking Wenceslas Square. 'You can feel a real excitement, an extraordinary sense of something to be rediscovered.'

Budapest was less impressive. He had always wanted to see the tomb of Gul Baba, a Turk who was supposed to have introduced roses to Central Europe some time in the sixteenth century—

'I wandered about in the old Turkish Quarter. On Frankel Leo all that remained was a ruined mosque with a rusty dome, and, almost opposite, a flower shop. Eventually I found him, quite low down on the Hill of Roses, on a bleak hummock of earth and railed concrete. A few children were playing football on the worn-down grass round the shrine itself, which is a neat sunken garden laid out in squares, with a path of stones leading to the little domed turbe. The roses were tall and sad, covered in huge pale hips. The garden looked as if it would never flower again. But suddenly a thrush sang, the declining sun shed a gold light across the litter and broken-down houses on the hill above, and you could see how it might look in summer, if summer came again. Two or three other Western tourists were grouped about the railings. I heard one woman say clearly:

' "They don't seem to be any better at growing things than they were at socialism."

'It was an unfair comparison to make in February in Budapest. Nevertheless the only flowers I have seen are in the windows of shops, where they look as if they have been injected with wax.

' "Who would want to be Father of this?"

'At the Palace hotel the night before, a flautist had been practising in the room next door to mine, repeating each phrase of a quite complex piece slowly three or four times, then running them all together in an amazing fluid gesture, as if his failures and infelicities had never happened. You would never get that in a British hotel. Somehow I had expected to hear the same music on the Hill itself.'

A few days later he wrote, 'I'm having difficulty with the frontiers.' But he was determinedly pushing on down the Danube into East Croatia. Things were difficult there, he said. The West was still trying to broker a truce between factions. He would be in touch again as soon as things stabilised. I should take care of myself.

And then:

'Sometimes I think I understand it all so clearly!'

I never heard from him again.

As to my own search:

Shortly after Pam's funeral, I experienced a sudden, inexplicable resurgence of my sense of smell. Common smells became so distinct and detailed I felt like a child again, every new impression astonishing and clear, my conscious self not yet the sore lump encysted in my own skull – as clenched and useless as a fist, impossible to modify or evict – as it was later to become. This was not quite what you could call memory. All I recollected in the smell of orange peel or ground coffee or rowan blossom was that I had once been able to experience things so profoundly. It was as if, before I could recover one particular impression, I had to rediscover the language of all impressions.

But nothing further happened. I was left with an embarrassment, a ghost, a hyperaesthesia of middle age. It was cruel and undependable; it made me feel like a fool.

Katherine had learned to drive quite late in life, and like most people who discover a new skill in their forties, took to it with enthusiasm. Her first car was a little black Peugeot 205 GTi, with engaging plastic 'sports' trim and wheels so wide it looked exactly like a roller skate. By then we had moved out of London proper, and were living in Coulsdon, in a pleasant detached house on the northern edge of Sussex. She was soon whipping along the narrow Wealden lanes like a racing driver, redlining the rev-counter and tapping the clutch at just the right moment to slip from third to fourth gear without any loss of power. 'I love it!' she would say, laughing at herself. 'I love it!' Kit and I were less certain. Kit liked to sit in the back of my Volvo and look graciously out at the woods and flint-faced garden walls; she liked me to slow down for horses.

Sometimes the three of us would go down to Tunbridge in the Volvo after Sunday lunch, to walk on the downs; increasingly, though, Katherine preferred to drive herself, and meet us later. On a sunny Sunday, Coulsdon haemorrhages its BMWs and Jaguars into the surrounding tissues of Redhill, Reigate and Dorking, which flush and bruise suddenly under the strain. She hated to be in queues. One afternoon, following her at a leisurely pace down the M23 just south of Salfords, Kit and I found lines of stationary traffic winking in the sun. All three lanes were jammed solid. A police Land Rover, a small ambulance and a rescue vehicle raced down the hard shoulder. Every so often a kind of peristalsis shuddered through the lines of cars, a ten or twenty-yard gap which opened and closed to give each driver the illusion of movement. A quarter of an hour later we were still inching our way towards the accident. Up ahead we could see a tall black plume of smoke, its base somewhere near Outwood or Wasp Green; and once or twice we got a confused glimpse of flames through a hedge.

'There's a church near it!' cried Kit, craning her neck out of the open window. 'I can't see anything else!'

'Why would they be burning a church, Kit?'

'They're a funny lot in Wasp Green.'

But when we finally crawled past the base of the column, we found that a small black car had left the motorway and gone through the hedge into the churchyard, where it had shed its bonnet and one door then fireballed itself among the gravestones. A disgusting smell blew in through the windows and Kit threw up suddenly across the back seat. I stopped the car and shut her in it. She had begun to scream and kick. I walked back up the hard shoulder and said to the first policeman I saw, 'Does anyone know what make of car it is?' They weren't sure, but I was. The goddess gives, the goddess takes away.

A few weeks later, clearing up Katherine's papers, I came upon some letters, addressed to her from the Chelsea Arts Club, sympathising with her feelings of being 'stifled' by marriage and speaking of 'our long sexy afternoons together'. They were about ten years old. I didn't recognise the man's name. Kit and I drew apart in the following years. After she left home I couldn't seem to be bothered with the house, so I sold it. Bereavement numbed my hyperaesthesia. Then a year or two ago, for a few minutes one afternoon in May, it returned:

I had been sorting books all day. I still have a lot, some of which I have owned since Cambridge. They look their age now, browned by the tobacco smoke, gas fumes and evaporated cooking oil of the places I have lived in since things fell apart. By the shelf load they have a faint smell of dust. It is a cured odour, as if my way of life had been designed to preserve them by bringing about organic and chemical changes, in one-roomed flats like a chain of smoke-houses across London. I was thinking about that, and looking through an old paperback copy of *War in Heaven*, when up from it came a smell like cornflour, or even vanilla, so strong I thought a door had opened and someone I once knew had come in. It was the smell of the individual book – not dust, not decay, but cornflour and vanilla, some transformation of the glues and inks and paper: cornflour, vanilla, then hawthorn blossom like a drug!

I sat there on the floor and burst into tears:

It will soon be fifteen years since Katherine died. Kit has moved to New York, from where she sends me letters I don't understand, about politics and AIDS. Pam and Lucas walked away from me somehow, that scented, dew-soaked morning in Cambridge. I remember them all with such happiness.

SIGNS OF LIFE

Contents

1	Learning to Fly	231
2	Lost in Soho	243
3	Pictures from China	255
4	Burn Without Opening	269
5	Food for Thought	283
6	Nagy Secz	300
7	Trafik	314
8	What Could Happen	331
9	Fuck Everything and Run	345
10	Flying Blind	357
11	China's Syndrome	370
12	Icarus Flights	385
13	Makeover	400
14	Real Wings	414
15	Hi-pad London	430
16	The Signs of Life	444

EPILOGUE: In Jumble Wood   459

1
Learning to Fly

My name is Mick Rose, which is why a lot of people call me 'China'. Choe Ashton never did. That was one of the differences between him and Isobel Avens. Isobel was hooked from the word go. She would hold my face between her hands in the night and whisper dreamily over and over – 'Oh, China, China, China. China.' But it wasn't my name that attracted her to me in the first place.

The year we met, she lived in Stratford-upon-Avon. I walked into the café at the busy little toy aerodrome they have outside the town and there she was, serving meat pies and Kenco coffee. It was an old-fashioned café, full of mismatched wooden furniture, cracked melamine trim and the hot steamy air of an era before true fast food. Glass ran the full length of one side, so that you could watch the aircraft landing and taking off. Exhausted young mothers from Stratford favoured the window tables. There they could fill themselves with cigarette smoke while their children smeared jam on one another or stared out at the strip of grass and sky between the runway buildings opposite, hoping to see a helicopter.

'Mummy, can we have another cake?'

'No.'

Isobel was twenty-five years old then: slow, heavy-bodied, easily delighted by the world. Her hair was red. She wore a rusty-pink blouse, a black ankle-length skirt with lace at the hem. Her feet were like boats in great brown Dr Marten shoes. When she saw me looking down at them in amusement, she said: 'Oh, these aren't my real Docs, these are my cheap imitation ones.' She showed me how the left one was coming apart at the seams. 'Brilliant, eh?' She had a nice smile and she smelt of vanilla. She had a way of handing over a cup of coffee with both hands which made it seem a desperate gesture, precarious and fraught.

'I'd love to be able to fly,' she told me.

She laughed and hugged herself.

'You must feel so free.'

She thought I was the pilot of a little private Cessna she could see out of the window. In fact I had only come to deliver its cargo, an unacknowledged load for an unacknowledged destination, one leg of a journey that would end at some private medical research centre in Zurich, Budapest or the Near East.

I said, 'It isn't so hard to learn.'

'Flying?'

'It isn't so hard.'

She laughed again.

'I don't know,' she said.

She came back two or three minutes later and leant over me to wipe the table, rearrange the place setting.

'It won't be a minute now,' she said.

'No rush,' I said.

'I'm not used to waitressing.'

The deft movements of her hands, the sudden smell of perspiration beneath vanilla, the quick soft touch of her left breast on my shoulder, filled me first with excitement, then a strange, hypnotised calm.

'Is there much to do in Stratford?' I asked. 'Apart from the theatre?'

'Not a lot,' she said.

I watched her walk off between the tables to take another order. She called back over her shoulder:

'You'll never get into the theatre, anyway.'

'Listen to your heart . . .' Radio 1 was advising the mothers by the window. I wondered what they would hear if they did. Not

Radio 1; or two children arguing over half a Mars bar. '. . . It's gonna tell you what to do.' They knew what to do already. A milky opaqueness passed across their eyes and was gone. When Isobel came back with my egg and chips, she said:

'I'm going to a wedding reception tomorrow evening.'

Behind her the Cessna was taking off. I watched it go. Tomorrow was Saturday and I was due back in London.

She smiled.

'You could come to that.'

'I'd love to,' I said.

She looked down at my plate.

'Egg and chips,' she said. 'You've just reminded me how brilliant it is to have a fried egg for breakfast.'

I began to eat.

'Where will it be,' I asked, 'this reception?'

'I'll write it down for you,' she said.

Saturday, I woke early. It was a cold, damp winter morning. Over by the theatre the tourists were already telling one another: 'Look how swollen the river is.' I hadn't slept well, but I was excited and restless. I went out and bought the *Daily Express*. I went into the theatre foyer, where I picked up a lot of leaflets; then into the theatre restaurant to sit drinking hot chocolate with dark rum while I tried to read the paper. Yeltsin was visiting the West, in the wake of 'a new Star Wars offer'. The UN was pulling out of Yugoslavia, the UN was staying in. No, there, it was pulling out after all. Here at home, a 50 per cent rise in auto-crime. I couldn't settle to any of this. Every minute or two I found myself looking out across the Avon, which was a sullen brown colour and running quite fast between low muddy fields, its surface chopped and herring-boned by the east wind. Crows stumped about on the far bank. A kittiwake hovered above the water. The willows leant uneasily into the wind.

'Let's look at auto-crime,' a spokesman was quoted as saying. 'Let's take auto-crime. The public can do a lot more.'

Every figure in the distant gardens caught my eye: every oiled cotton jacket, every cyclist, every couple walking their Labrador dog over the bridge. Suddenly I realised why. I was hoping to see Isobel Avens among them.

I turned to the TV pages.

Auto-crime, I thought: crime against the self.

By half-past eleven I had found my way to a pub called the Green Dragon. The Green Dragon was part of some other Stratford, noisy, smelly, unreconstructed, full of boys in grey jeans or scuffed motorcycle leathers, with their student girlfriends, drinking bottled lagers while they listened to a curious mix of music from R.E.M. to the Bryan Adams hit 'Everything I Do'. I felt comfortable with them, perhaps because my attention span had become as short as theirs. I talked to the girl behind the bar. I found 'Raindogs' on the jukebox and played it twice.

All morning I was aware of the scrap of paper Isobel had given me at the aerodrome café. Once or twice I took it out and looked at it. 'Woodcotes Country Hotel,' she had written; adding a tiny aeroplane in blue felt-tip pen. 'Don't be late!' Her handwriting was careful, decorative, self-conscious.

'You shouldn't read that stuff,' said the girl behind the bar.

I stared at her.

'What?'

'The *Daily Express*,' she pointed out amiably.

'I never buy the *Daily Express*,' I said.

I never do. I folded it up carefully and put it on the bar.

'It'll rot your brain.'

'True.' I tapped the front page. 'We can always do a lot more auto-crime, though,' I told her. 'Is that a man's haircut?'

It was fifties-retro, dyed a harsh yellowy white above her ears.

'I like it,' I said.

'I'm flattered. Do you want another Holsten?'

'Yes, please.'

Later I drove the van about in the damp Warwickshire lanes for a bit, then parked it with the engine running, in a lay-by a little way down the road from the main gate of the aerodrome. Every four or five minutes I would remember something about

Isobel – the smell of vanilla, the way she pushed her hair away from her face – and find myself looking up with a shiver of anticipation. For the briefest moment there she was, walking towards me down the empty lane. I turned up the radio. R.E.M. again, 'Can't Get There From Here'.

It was two o'clock in the afternoon. I had no idea how I would fill up the rest of the day.

Woodcotes Country Hotel, just off the A40 about five miles out of Stratford. I don't know what I expected, but it turned out to be the ideal venue: a profoundly self-satisfied sixteenth-century house with heavily ornamented wooden beams. In the dining room you could see some famous wall-paintings, done in 1720 in 'vegetable dyes and blood'. They were kept covered now with little plum-coloured velvet curtains to stop them from fading. I arrived late and squeezed my van into the gravelled car-park between a sixteen-valve Golf ragtop and a steel-coloured V12 Jaguar. The dining room and the lounge adjoining it were packed and smoky. Everybody there had been successful at something in early middle age. They were still uneasy with it. They had finished eating – plovers' eggs, a sorbet and then saddle of lamb with rosemary, followed by a Belgian chocolate mousse – and they were ready to enjoy themselves. You could hear the younger single women, who lived in Putney and had come up for the day wearing a Harrods' hat, ask one another loudly:

'Have you ever had mussels cooked on a fire of pine needles?'

'Now that's an experience I've been waiting for all my life. You don't get that over here, do you? Where do you get that?'

And then, shouting and waving across the room:

'Debbie! Debbie!'

'It's Jane.'

'Jane. I'm good with faces but so bad with names. We're going to see you tomorrow evening, I hear. From John.'

'Are you? Are we? Oh.'

I was relieved to find Isobel Avens, sitting on her own

underneath the wall paintings. As soon as she saw me she got up and said:

'I thought you weren't coming.'

At exactly the same moment I asked, 'Did you get your egg?'

She stared at me.

'For breakfast?'

'Oh.' She laughed. 'Yes, I did.'

She led me back into the crowd.

'Come and meet Colin,' she said.

Before she left the house, her hair had been caught up for the evening in a big bow like a butterfly, black velvet to match her dress. But it had already escaped, and was falling in long untidy wisps round the freckled nape of her neck. Her shoes were patent leather, with very high heels which shortened her long, considered stride. In the black velvet dress, with its low square neckline and puffed shoulders, she looked older than she had in the aerodrome café. At the same time she looked vulnerable and young. I would have been content to follow her anywhere just to be surrounded by the smell of vanilla. All the tension had gone out of me as soon as I saw her.

'You'll like Colin,' she said.

Colin was the groom.

'Great,' he said vaguely, when we were introduced. 'Where have you come from?'

Tenerife, I told him. I had a business just back from the beachfront at Los Cristianos: African leather tourist goods. When he asked me how the journey had been, I replied, 'The flight was crowded, but they always are.' He was so nervous he said:

'Good, good.'

Colin bought print, but talked mainly about local cricket. He loved close fielding. By midnight he was kneeling on the floor of the hotel bar with his head up the front of his wife's skirt. A dozen guests egged them on. Earlier I had overheard her saying, 'I've just spoken to my ex on the phone and he managed to yawn twice in the first five minutes. I'm not used to being yawned at.'

Then, about a spray of orchids and stephanotis: 'They've gone up a bit. I must have paid ten pounds for each orchid in that.' Her name was Jennifer. She was toppling over into her forties, toppling over into Colin's close dependable hands. At the buffet in the corner her twelve-year-old son by the other marriage was learning how to pour beer. He stumbled about in his little bowtie and neat black trousers begging, 'Would you like a Grolsch? Would you like a Grolsch?'

Isobel watched me watching them.

'Why did you tell Colin you'd come from Tenerife?' she asked.

'I honestly don't know.'

'I mean I thought it was brilliant, but I know you haven't.'

She thought for a moment.

'You don't like this much, do you?'

I shrugged.

'I wish you'd worn your Doc Martens,' I said.

She looked down at the black velvet dress, then back up at me.

'With this?'

'With that. Look, let's—'

'What?'

And then before I could answer: 'They're staying here for the weekend, Colin and Jenny. They're working too hard to have a honeymoon. Do you want to see their room? It's full of the most marvellous flowers.'

I stared at her.

'Very much,' I said.

It was cool in there. The flowers, made up into careful arrangements like frozen fireworks, were still wrapped. A faint breath of florists' cellophane hung about them, later to become confused for me with vanilla essence and the smell of sex.

'I'll just put the table lamp on,' she said.

By now we were frantic. I started to say something like, 'What are we going to do about one another, then?' But as soon as I touched her she murmured, 'Oh,' in a surprised, musing voice and sat down on the edge of the bed. The black velvet bow fell out of her hair. She put her hand up to the side of her head. Suddenly she began to struggle with her dress.

'Here,' she said, when I tried to help.

She said: 'Here. The zip. No, the zip.'

In the end we couldn't do it, and she had to lie down and raise her bottom an inch or two off the counterpane so that I could take the dress by its hem and pull it up round her waist.

'Christ,' I said. I was shaking.

'Quick,' she said. 'Quick.'

She had her arms so tightly round my neck that I had to struggle away to get my trousers off. Entering her, I thought I would faint. Her legs went round me, her eyes snapped open, she opened her mouth silently and rolled her head from side to side on the pillow.

'Oh,' she said. Then:

'Fuck me.'

Fuck me, in a small panicky voice.

As if she meant, *Save me from falling*.

By the time we got back down to the party, it was over. One or two red helium balloons hung among the beams of the old hallway, but Woodcotes was quiet, empty, intent on itself. The hotel staff had tidied the dining room and were setting tables for breakfast, two or three middle-aged women talking in quiet local voices. Isobel waved at them as we went past; one of them laughed and waved back. In a hotel at night, things are comfortably in abeyance. All the odours are kind: carpet, floor polish, central heating. You feel warm, you feel tended. None of this, you think, takes place in the real world. Because of that, it can never end. Isobel smiled every time I looked at her. I walked with my arm round her waist, because I already loved to feel her hip roll and sway under my hand.

'I've got to find Colin and Jenny before we go,' she whispered.

I looked at my watch.

'We've been up there for three hours.'

We stopped and stared at one another in horrified delight.

'Oh no. Three hours . . .'

Colin and Jenny were in reception. Jenny had passed out on a chintz sofa with her mouth open. She had flung one arm up over the back of the sofa in the middle of some gesture. Her legs sprawled awkwardly: Colin had covered them with his jacket. There was no need to look closely to see the Yves Saint Laurent foundation caked into the laugh-lines round her mouth. Colin was staring down at her, pulling at his bottom lip in a puzzled way. At first I thought he was simply working out how he could get her upstairs. Then I saw that his eyes were full of wonder. There was some mystery for him in all this; how a print-buyer like himself, nothing much more than a useful pair of hands, had managed to capture someone so beautiful, so intelligent, so . . . Well, you saw that he could get no further, would always have difficulty getting further. As we went past, he looked up defensively. 'Ssh,' he said. The flesh under his eyes was grey; his cheeks were bright red, lacquered with the effort of remaining conscious. He had rolled up his sleeves and taken off his patent leather shoes. There were two great saddles of sweat underneath his arms. Isobel went up to him and kissed him on the chin. I saw her tuck something into the pocket of his dress shirt.

'Colin, it's half-past two,' she told him.

He looked down at his wife. I saw him *think*: My wife.

'Have a Glen Morangie,' he invited us.

He said: 'We're having one.'

'Bye bye Colin.'

Outside, the air was cold and sharp. The car-park had emptied itself of Audis and BMWs an hour before. Only a faint smell of money remained – unleaded fuel and sophisticated catalysers, German iron. 'Look up there,' Isobel said. 'How brilliant. All those stars.' Then after I had unlocked the passenger door for her and we were sitting waiting for the heater to clear the windscreen: 'Colin and Jenny deserve to have the best time they can.' I shrugged. I switched the headlights on. Beyond the car-park, through a dark fringe of hedge, I could see an empty field. 'You mustn't feel superior to them,'

Instead of replying, I asked her:
'What was that you gave Colin?'
She blushed.
'The room key,' she said.
'They all knew?'
She said: 'None of them knew.' Then: 'Jenny knew.'
I peered out into the car-park, put the van into first gear.
I admitted: 'I'm not a pilot.'
Isobel smiled.
'I guessed that,' she said.
'Don't you care?'
'No.'
I knocked the van out of gear again and leant over.
'Kiss me then.'
'China.'

Before six months were out we were inventing one another hand over fist. I went back to see her every weekend. Spring came early. It was an extraordinary summer. You have to imagine this:
 Saturday afternoon. Stratford Waterside. The river has a lively look despite the breathless air and heated sky above it. Waterside is full of jugglers and fire-eaters entertaining thick crowds of Americans and Japanese. There is hardly room to move. On a patch of grass by the water, two lovers, trapped in the great circular argument, are making that futile attempt all lovers make to get inside one another and stay there for good. He can't stop touching her because she wants him so. She wants him so because he can't stop touching her. A feeding swan surfaces, caught up with some strands of very pale green weed. Rippling in the sudden warm breeze which blows across the river from the direction of the theatre, these seem for a moment like ribbons tied with a delicate knot – the gentle, deliberate artifice of a conscious world.
 'Oh look. Look,' she says.
 He says: 'Would you like to be a swan?'
 'I'd have to leave the aerodrome.'

He says: 'Come and live with me and be a swan.'

Neither of us had the slightest idea what we were talking about. But by the end of July I had persuaded Isobel to leave Stratford and come down to London with me. On the morning of her last day at the aerodrome, she woke up early and shook me until I was awake too.

'China,' she said.

'What?'

'China.'

I said: 'What?'

'I flew!'

It was a dream of praxis. It was a hint of what she might have. It was her first step on the escalator up to Brian Alexander's clinic.

'I was in a huge computer room. Everyone's work was displayed on one screen like a wall. I couldn't find my C-prompt.' People laughed at her, but nicely. 'It was all good fun, and they were very helpful.' Suddenly she had learned what she had to know, and she was floating up and flying into the screen, and through it, 'Out of the room, into the air above the world.' The sky was crowded with other people, she said. 'But I just went swooping past and around and between them.' She let herself fall just for the fun of it: she soared, her whole body taut and trembling like the fabric of a kite. Her breath went out with a great laugh. Whenever she was tired she could perch like a bird. 'I loved it,' she told me. 'Oh, I loved it.'

How can you be so jealous of a dream?

I said: 'It sounds as if you won't need me soon.'

She clutched at me.

'You help me to fly,' she said. 'Don't dare go away, China. Don't dare.'

She pulled my face close to hers and gave me little dabbing kisses on the mouth and eyes. I looked at my watch. Half-past six. The bed was already damp and hot: I could see that we were going to make it worse. She pulled me on top of her, and at the height of things, sweating and inturned and breathless and on the edge, she whispered, 'Oh lovely, lovely, lovely,' as if she had seen something I couldn't. 'So lovely, so beautiful.' Her eyes moved as if she was watching something pass. I could only watch her, moving under me, marvellous and wet, solid and real, everything I ever wanted.

2
Lost in Soho

Choe and Isobel disliked one another the moment they met. It would be easy to say that she felt threatened by him; that he felt displaced by her. But things between them were more complex than that. They were more alike than they seemed. I loved them both, but you could hardly say which of them was the more dangerous.

To begin with, you would have thought it was Choe. I had known him for about two years. Between us, we were running a courier service we called Rose Medical Plc. Our fleet comprised a single Vauxhall Astravan into which Choe (you pronounce it as in 'Joey' or 'Chloe') had dropped the engine of a two-litre SRi insurance write-off. We specialised. If it was small, we guaranteed to move it anywhere in Britain within twelve hours; occasionally, if the price was right, to selected points in Europe. Choe kept the fleet operating. I touted for business. We shared the driving. We would move anything – transplant organs in ice, small runs of a new drug, diagnostic technology designed to bolt on to existing computers. But we preferred the really profitable loads. Recombinant DNA; viruses at controlled temperatures, sometimes in live hosts; cell cultures in heavily armoured flasks. What the stuff was used for we had no idea. I didn't want an idea until later; and that turned out to be much too late.

The day I met Isobel Avens, it was Choe's turn to drive. I had phoned him repeatedly the night before: no answer. I did the job myself, then rang him again. Nothing. He was away for three or four days. I began to worry. Finally he picked the phone up.

'Where have you been, Choe?'
'What can I say? I went to France.'
'What?'
'I met someone I knew in a bar, Mick. We went to France.'
'Choe, you unreliable fucker.'
'I know. It was real, though.' He laughed. 'What's happening?'
'Weird stuff, Choe. I'm still in Stratford—'
'It's a girl,' he said. 'Isn't it?'
'Choe, you don't know that.'
'Ho, ho. Oh yes, I do. Brilliant. Is she a tart, Mick? Is she a *real fucking tart*?'

This was Choe's highest form of praise.

'I bet she is,' he said. 'I bet she's a real fucking tart.'
'Stop trying to talk me round, Choe. It was wrong of you to go to France.'
'I know. I *know* it was wrong. But I can't seem to *care*.'
'Choe—'
'Do you forgive me? I bet you do. I bet you forgive me . . .'

I had been forgiving him one thing or another since December 1989, the weekend Bush talked to Gorbachev on the *Maxim Gorki* in half a gale in Valetta harbour. In those days I still worked for other people.

Ten past ten on a Saturday night. The upper rooms of a media drinking club in central London. In the East, governments were going over like tired boxers – saggy, puzzled, almost apologetic. Here, we were celebrating the birthday of an agency boss called Andy Dawes – 'Ada' to his friends. I knew him vaguely, the rest of the people in the room hardly at all. The women were in PR: the last of the power dressers. The men were in advertising, balding to a ponytail. Men or women, they all had a Range Rover in the car-park at Poland Street. They were already thinking of exchanging it for one of the new Mazdas. Soon they would be giving Dawes a cake in the shape of his nickname, on which had been iced the words 'Just Do It'. Meanwhile they were eating pasta.

'Now that's *two* thousand calories.'

'So far I've had cheese but not much else, which is interesting . . .'

'Are we going to get that fettucini we've paid for?'

'How much more do you want?'

I moved away and went to stare out of the window. Over towards Trafalgar Square the sky looked like a thundery summer afternoon. The buildings stood out against it, and against one another, like buildings cut from cardboard. I followed an obscure line of neon. A string of fairy lights slanting away along the edge of a roof. Then cars going to and fro down at the junction by St-Martin-in-the-Fields, appearing very much smaller than they were. I had been there about a minute when someone came up behind me and said:

'Guess what? I was just in the bog.'

'That's interesting.'

'No, come on. I switched the hand-drier on and it talked to me.'

I stared at him as flatly as I could.

'I expect it did,' I said.

He was delighted.

'Why do you say that? Has it happened to you, too?'

He was in his forties, short and wiry, full of energy, with the flat-top haircut and gold ear-ring of a much younger man. His 501s were ripped at the knees. With them he wore a softly tailored French Connection blouson, which made his face, reddened as if by some kind of outdoor work, look incongruous and hard one moment, shy the next.

' "Choe, I really like drying your hands." I'm not kidding you, you know. It talked to me.'

I shrugged.

'You don't believe me, do you?'

'No.'

'OK. Give us a fag then, if you don't believe me. Eh?'

'I don't smoke,' I said.

'Come on,' he wheedled. 'Every fucker smokes. Dawsie only knows people who smoke. Give us a fag.'

I laughed.

'I honestly can't help you.'

'All right then,' he said. 'Let's fuck off to Lisle Street and have a Chinese. Eh?' He gave me his sly, beautiful smile, just an ageing boy in a French Connection jacket. 'Come on, you know you want to.'

I did. I was bored.

As we were leaving, they brought the birthday cake in. Ada made several efforts to blow the candles out, to diminishing applause. He ended up pouring wine over them until, fizzing and bubbling grossly, dripping thick coloured wax down the sides of the cake, they blackened and cooled. There was a loud cheer as he cut inaccurately into the first A of Ada. Then an odd thing happened. The candles, which had seemed to be completely extinguished, began to burn again. Blinking happily around, Dawes took this as a powerful metaphor for his own vitality. He poured more wine on them.

'Did you see that?' I asked Choe Ashton.

But he was halfway out of the door.

At first we walked rapidly, not talking. Head down, hands rammed into the pockets of his coat, Ashton paused only to glance at the enormous neon currency symbols above the Bureau de Change on Charing Cross Road. 'Ah, money.' But as soon as he recognised Ed's Easy Diner, he seemed content to slow down and take his time. It was a warm night for December. Soho was full of the most carefully dressed people. Ashton pulled me towards a group standing outside the Groucho, so that he could admire their louche haircuts and beautifully crumpled chinos. 'Can't you feel the light coming off them?' he asked me in a voice loud enough for them to hear. 'I just want to bask in it.' For a moment after he had said this, there did seem to be a light round them – like the soft light in a seventies movie, or the kind of watery nimbus you sometimes see when you are peering through a window in the rain. I pulled him away, but he kept yearning back along the pavement towards them, laughing. 'I love you,' he called to them despairingly. 'I love you.' They moved uncomfortably under his approval, like cattle the other side of a fence.

'The middle classes are always on watch,' he complained.

We dodged briefly into a pick-up bar and tried to talk. The only free table was on a kind of mezzanine floor on the way to the Ladies. Up there you were on a level with the sound system. Drunken girls pushed past, or fell heavily into the table.

'I love them all!' shouted Ashton.

'Pardon?'

'I love them.'

'What, these too?'

'Everything they do is wonderful.'

Actually they just sat under the ads for Jello-shots, Schlitz and Molson's Canadian and drank Lowenbrau: boys in soft three-button shirts and Timberland boots, girls with tailored jackets over white silk trousers. I couldn't see how they had arrived there from Manor House or Finsbury Park, all those dull, broken, littered places on the Piccadilly line; or why. Eventually we got sick of bawling at one another over the music and let it drive us back out into Cambridge Circus.

'I was here this afternoon,' he said. 'I thought I heard my name called out.'

'Someone you knew.'

'I couldn't see anyone.'

We ended up in one of those Lisle Street restaurants which specialise in degree-zero decor, cheap crockery and grudging service. There were seven tables crammed into an area smaller than a newsagent's shop. The lavatory – with its broken door handle and empty paper roll – was downstairs in the kitchens. Outside it, on a hard chair, sat a waitress, who stared angrily at you as you went past. They had a payphone: but if you wanted to use it, or even collect your coat from the coat rack, you had to lean over someone else's dinner. Choe Ashton, delighted, went straight to the crêpe-paper shrine mounted in the alcove to show me a vase of plastic flowers, a red and gold tin censer, from which the stubs of old incense sticks protruded like burnt-out fireworks, two boxes of safety matches.

'See this? Make a wish.'

With considerable gentleness he put fresh incense in the censer and struck a match.

'I love these places . . .' he said.

He sat down and rubbed his hands.

'. . . but I'm bored with Hot and Sour.'

He stared away from the menu and up at the industrial ceiling, which had been lowered with yellow-painted slats. Through them you could still see wires, bitumen, ventilator boxes. A few faded strings ejected from some exhausted Christmas party-popper still hung up there, as if someone had flung noodles about in a claustrophobic fit or paddy.

'Let's have some Bitter and Unfulfilled here,' he called to the waitress. 'No. Wait a minute. I want Imitation Pine Board Soup, with a Loon Fung calendar. But it has to have copulating pandas on it.'

After that we began to drink Tsing Tao beer. Its packaging, he said, the pale grey ground and green, red and gold label, reminded him of something. He arranged several empty cans across the table between us and stared at them thoughtfully for some time, but nothing came of it. I don't remember eating, though we ordered a lot of food. Later he transferred his obsession from the Tsing Tao label to the reflections of the street neon in the mirror behind the bar. SOHO. PEEP SHOW. They were red, greenish-yellow, a cold blue. A strobe flickered inside the door of the peep show. Six people had been in there in two minutes. Two of them had come out again almost immediately. 'Fucking hell, sex, eh? Why do we bother?' said Choe. He looked at me. 'I fucking hate it,' he said. Suddenly he stood up and addressed the people at the nearer tables. 'Anyone who hates sex, stand up,' he tried to persuade them. 'Fucking sex.' He laughed. 'Fucking, fucking,' he said. 'Get it?' The waitresses began to move towards us.

But they had only come to bring the bill and offer him another beer. He smiled at them, moved his hands apart, palms forward, fingers spread.

'No thanks,' he said shyly.

'The bill's in Chinese!' he shouted. He brandished it delightedly at the rest of the diners. 'Hey!'

I agreed to drive him home. For the first few minutes he showed some interest in my car. At that time I owned an Escort RS Turbo. But I didn't drive it fast enough for him, and he was silent again until we were passing the Flying Dutchman in Camberwell. There he asked in an irritable voice: 'Another thing. Why is this pub always in the same place?' He lived on the other side of Camberwell, where it nudges up against Denmark Hill. It took him some time to find the right street. 'I've only just moved in.' I got him upstairs, then consulted my watch. 'I think I'd better sleep on your floor,' I said. But he had passed out. It seemed like a nice flat, although he hadn't bought much furniture.

I woke late the next morning. Ten o'clock. Sleet was falling. A minicab driver had parked his Renault under the front window, switched its engine off, and turned up Capital Radio so that I could hear clearly a preview of a new track by the Psychedelic Furs. Every thirty seconds he sounded his horn. At that, the woman who had called him leant out of a fourth-floor window in one of the point blocks on the other side of the road and shrieked:

'Cammin dahn!'

Beep.

'Cammin dahn!'

Beep.

'Cammin dahn!'

Beep. Beep. Beep.

'Cammin dahn! Cammin dahn!'

The back of the flat overlooked a row of gardens. They were long and narrow and generally untended between walls of sagging, sugary old brick; so choked, some of them, with bramble, elder and buddleia stalks, that they reminded you of overgrown lanes. In the bleaker ones, you knew, a dog would trot restlessly all day between piles of household or builders' rubbish, under a complex array of washing lines. Choe Ashton's garden had once been kept in better order. There was a strip of lawn and a patio of black and white flagstones like a chess board, a few roses pruned savagely back to bare earth, a little pond full of leaves. Suddenly I saw a fox sniffing round the board fence at the bottom of the garden.

At first I thought it was some breed of cat I had never seen before: long-backed, reddish, brindling towards its hindquarters and long tail. It was moving a bit like a cat, sinuously and close to the ground. After a minute or two it found the pond and drank at length, looking up every so often, but too wet and tired, perhaps too ill, to be wary or nervous.

I watched with my heart in my mouth, afraid to move, even behind the window, in case it saw me and ran off. Choe Ashton came into the room.

'Fucking hell,' he said. 'Are you still here?'

'Sssh. There's a fox in your garden.'

He stood beside me. As he watched, the fox wandered into the middle of the overgrown lawn, pawing and sniffing at the earth. It yawned. I couldn't see anything there it might eat. I wondered if it had smelt another fox. It sat down suddenly and stared vaguely into the sleet.

'I can't see anything.'

I stared at him.

'Choe, you must be blind—'

He gripped my arm very hard, just above the elbow.

'That hurts,' I said.

'I can't fucking *see* any fucking fox,' he said quietly.

We stood like that for thirty or forty seconds. In that time the fox went all round the lawn, not moving very fast, then crossed the low brick wall into the next garden, where it vanished among some elders, leafless laburnum bushes and apple trees.

'OK Choe.'

People like Choe are like moths in a restaurant on a summer evening just as it gets dark. They bang from lamp to lamp, then streak across the room in long flat wounded trajectories. We make a lot of their confusion but less of their rage. They dash themselves to pieces out of sheer need to be more than they are. It would have been better to leave him alone to do it, but I was already fascinated. I spent the rest of the day phoning everyone who might have something to tell me. No one knew the whole story. But they all agreed that Choe was older than he appeared and, as Andy Dawes put it, 'Career-wise at least, a bit of a wimp.'

He was from the north of England. He had taken one of the first really good media degrees – from Sussex – but never followed it up. He did occasional design jobs for the smaller agencies that operate out of top rooms above Wardour Street. In addition, he had some film work, some advertising work. But who didn't? The interesting thing was how he had filled his time until he appeared in Soho. After Sussex he had moved back north and taken a job as a scaffolder; then joined a Manchester steeplejacking firm. He had worked in the massive stone quarries around Buxton, and out in the North Sea on the rigs. Returning to London, obsessed with motorcycles, he had opened one of the first courier operations of the Thatcher boom. He never kept any job for long. Boredom came too easily to him. Anything hard and dangerous attracted him, and the stories I heard about him, true or not, would have filled a book. He told me some of them himself, later:

Stripping old render near the top of a thirty-storey council high-rise in Glasgow, he found himself working from scaffolding fifty feet above a brick-net. These devices – essentially a few square feet of strong plastic netting stretched on a metal frame – are designed to catch dropped tools or bits of falling masonry. With a brick-net, you don't need safety bunting or a spotter on the ground to protect unwary pedestrians. Ashton quickly became interested. He thought about the brick-net in his digs at night. (Everyone else was watching *Prisoner, Cell Block H.*) During the day everything that fell seemed to go down into it in slow motion. Things were slow in his life too. One cold windy Monday, ten minutes before lunch, he took a sly look sideways at the other jacks working on the scaffolding. Then he screamed and jumped off, turning over twice in the air and landing flat on his back. The breath went out of him – boof! Everything in the net flew up into the air and fell down again on top of him – old mastic tubes, bits of window frame, half bricks.

'I'd forgotten that stuff,' he said with a grin.

'Were you injured?'

'I walked a bit stiff that week.'

'Was it worth it?'

'It was a fucking trip.'

Later, induced by money to take a long-running steelworks job, he decided to commute to Rotherham from London on a Kawasaki 750. Each working week began in the early hours of Monday morning, when, still wobbly from the excesses of the weekend, he pushed this overpowered bright-green monster up the motorway at a hundred and fifty miles an hour in the dark. He was never caught, but quite soon he grew bored. So he taught himself to lie along the Kawa with his feet on the back pegs, wedge the throttle open with a broken matchstick so that he could take both hands off the handlebars, and roll a joint in the tiny pocket of still air behind the fairing. At the right speed, he claimed, Kawasaki engineering was good enough to hold the machine on track.

'The idea,' he said, 'is not to slow down.'

I wasn't sure boredom was entirely the issue. Some form of exploration was taking place, as if Choe Ashton wanted to know the real limits of the world, not in the abstract but by experience. I grew used to identifying the common ground of these stories – the point at which they intersected – because there, I believed, I had found Choe's myth of himself, and it was this myth that energised him. I was quite wrong. He was not going to let himself be seen so easily. But that didn't become plain until later. Meanwhile, when I heard him say, 'We're sitting on the roof one dinner time, and suddenly I've poured lighter fuel on my overalls and set myself on fire,' I would nod sagely and think of Aleister Crowley's friend, Russell, discharged from the US Navy after he had shot up forty grains of medical-grade cocaine and tried to set fire to a piece of glass by willpower alone.

'I just did it to see what people would do,' Choe said. 'They had to beat me out with their hands.'

In a broad fake-northern accent he added:

'I'm scared of nowt, me.' Then, in a more normal voice: 'Do you believe that?'

'I think I do,' I said, watching with some interest the moth on its flat, savage, wounded trajectory.

He gave me a look of contempt.

But that didn't stop him from flirting with me all winter. I don't know why. Perhaps he had sensed something changing as the eighties slipped inexorably into the nineties. If I remember being dissatisfied with what the decade had shown me, how much more might Choe feel it, who was always looking for something new? I pursued him, and he slipped away – although never too far – between the sets of a comically complex personality. He was always waiting for me to catch up, or catch my breath. 'You can't make me out, can you?' he boasted. He was like a conjuror or a tart, always revealing something hidden – a taste for expensive food or difficult books – always keeping something back. He was a member of the ICA, the British Film Institute. He would telephone me late at night to recommend a photographic exhibition, invite me to some performance event in Princelet Street or sneer at the *Late Show* coverage of 'virtual' art. 'I'm not kidding,' he once insisted, arriving at the ENO dressed in an immaculate designer two-piece with baggy trousers and immense shoulder pads: 'I'm into Philip Glass, me.' And then announced:

'I've got the Kawa parked round the corner.'

'I'm sure you have, Choe.'

'You don't believe I came on it, do you?' And again, appealing to a foyer full of people who had arrived in 8-series BMWs:

'This fucker doesn't believe I came on me bike.'

To see how far he would go, I took him to a dance version of *Beauty and the Beast* at the Royal Opera House. He sat there quietly, entranced by the colour and movement, quite unconcerned by the awful costumes and Persil-white sentimentality, until the interval. Then he said loudly: 'It's like the fucking fish tank at the dentist's in here. Look at them!' He meant the audience, who, gorgeously dressed and vaguely smiling, had begun to come and go in the depopulated front stalls like moonlight gourami or neon tetras nosing among the silver bubbles of the oxygenator. Quiet, aimless, decorative, they had come, just like the dancers, to be seen.

'They're a bit more self-conscious than fish, Choe.'

'Are they?'

He stood up.

'Let's go and get some fucking beer. I'm bored with this.'

3
Pictures from China

Isobel and I bought a tiny, one-bedroomed flat in Peckham. Though it was quite empty when we viewed it, it took three months to buy. We loved its two skylights, its proximity to the park. We were less certain about the plump, ear-shaped growths at the junctions of the bathroom walls. 'It must be the cheapest flat in London this summer,' our solicitor said uncertainly. 'Is it really that cheap?' He remained calm when the freeholder tried to charge us for the right of way over the pavement outside. We bought a copy of Muriel Spark's *The Ballad of Peckham Rye* to read while we waited for the land searches to come through.

'My God,' Isobel said, the day we moved in. 'Why have we done this?'

Round the kitchen, at the height of a young child or a biggish dog, ran a gluey black dado impregnated with hair. Above it three layers of wallpaper were peeling stiffly off the plaster. The gas cooker alone had taken all afternoon to clean. In its grill pan I found three-quarters of an inch of solid fat with a whole fish in it – a complete fossilised fish, with the silver skin and black, intelligent eyes of a fish in some old Russian story.

'We'll soon have it finished,' I said. I hugged her. 'This is nothing.'

But she was already staring away from me, down into the street, where a firm of contractors had been working since nine that morning to make an irregular hole about a foot deep, now filling rapidly with brown rainwater. A British Gas engineer bent over it as we watched. He began baling with a two-litre plastic container, while a lime-green JCB went busily back and forth behind him, bouncing on its suspension like a toy.

'They'll never put the gas back on,' said Isobel. 'I know that.'

I loved her sudden despairs because they were so rare and – unlike my own – so easy to divert. At that time I loved everything about her. She was a resource, densely stratified, embedded with objects whose significance I might never understand. 'Oh, I've had *that* for years,' she would say dismissively of a record, an old menu, a faded pink satin camisole. But as soon as she had left the house to go windowshopping at Compagnie Internationale Express, I would play the record; let the underwear run through my fingers like cold water; glance over the menu, trying to imagine how Isobel had looked as she ordered from it before I met her. 'Did you *really* like Marillion?' There would always be something new to find out. Isobel, delighted at first, soon became impatient.

'Why are you courting my mother so hard?' I remember her saying suspiciously, after we had been together for some months.

'Because she knew you before I did.'

'You don't even like one another much.'

'True.'

Margaret Avens was a broad, muscular woman of about sixty, who had retired, on the death of her husband, to a cottage conversion in Gloucestershire with extensive views of Cleeve Hill. This she shared with three noisy, affectionate Burmese cats. She took the *Daily Telegraph*, claimed to find Nigel Lawson sexually attractive, and brought home her weekly shopping from Cheltenham in an F-registered maroon Daimler.

'Everyone calls me Maggie,' she had encouraged me the afternoon we met. I could never bring myself to do that. But if we had nothing else in common we had Isobel, and I soon persuaded Margaret to lend me a shoebox of crumpled Instamatic snaps, the earliest of which – summer 1968 or 1969 – showed a curved beach, an ebbing tide, a small, naked, sturdy toddler, her features washed out by the light.

Isobel stared emptily at this version or abandoned prototype of herself.

'Give me that,' she said. 'I'm warning you.'

I moved it out of reach. 'Tell me what you were up to, then,' I bargained.

She thought for a moment.

'I'm going to kill my mother for this,' she said. She said: 'I was three before I would walk. They tried everything, but I just sat there and looked at them. I wasn't a "late walker"; I knew quite well what to do. I just didn't need it for anything.'

'What made you change your mind?'

'Give me the photo back now. You promised you would.'

'Tell me,' I said. I was intrigued.

'I had to be able to walk to steal toys from the beach.'

'What?'

'The beach was mine. I was there the whole year round: the other children were just visitors. If I liked what I saw, I took it. See that rubber swan? It's a swimming ring. I hit the girl to get it.'

She laughed.

'They went mad about that.'

Her first memories were of a café owned by her parents at Sennen Cove. 'We had an ice-cream cabinet, and about five tables inside. My father cleaned and set them every morning.' He had decorated the walls with local paintings of fishermen in yellow oilskins. 'They were as stiff as Woodentops. Do you remember the Woodentops, China?' What Isobel remembered best was looking out of the window at the grey Atlantic waves smashing against the base of Aire Point. 'There was always a man walking two dogs on the beach.' Whenever the wind changed, she said, or the air pressure fell, the window pane gave out a soft, distant booming sound. 'At the end of the day the clouds parted for a moment. They sent down great sheaves of light to the west over the water.' Caught suddenly in that light, so that they looked like seabirds in a water-colour, the young herring gulls picked about on the tideline until dark; or, bracing themselves against the sky, turned impassively out to sea and let the cold air slip by them. Most of her childhood had been spent like that. Beaches had seemed to stretch away from her forever. 'We always lived in Cornwall.'

'What did you like best about it?' I asked her.

'I hated it all.'

'Isobel! No one really hates anything at that age.'

'Don't you believe it.'

'I do believe it.'

She shrugged.

'More fool you,' she said. Then: 'At least the gulls could get away.'

Her father, already in late middle age, surprised perhaps to find himself a father at all, had moved his family steadily north along the Penwith coast, urged on by vague commercial dissatisfactions. 'He liked anything new,' Isobel recalled. 'He liked everything to be new.' The way she put this made me imagine the two of them, staring out of the café window in Sennen. While the young Isobel willed herself away – 'I didn't know where, just anywhere.' – her father willed the future towards him, bearing its extraordinary freight of possibility. It was a future not just of tourists, but of surfers, divers, sailboarders, hang-gliders. All those fluorescent plastics to sell. Black Lycra from America, violet neoprene from Australia, hotfoiled with names like Gul and Quicksilver. Open-topped Japanese offroaders, bouncing on their huge polished alloy wheels down the narrow lanes to the bay. Whole new ways of being by the sea. His own father had been a butcher in Cheshire, hidebound and smug. Determined to live differently, he stared out of the café window, and took a flying lesson every Wednesday afternoon at the St Just aerodrome, and Isobel was perhaps the last thing in his mind.

'So after that,' I said, 'you moved to Newquay.'

'After Sennen we moved to St Ives. *Then* eight years in Newquay.'

'Tell me something else.'

'When I was young I kept hamsters.'

'Something else.'

'I lost most of them behind furniture and up chimneys. I lost a rabbit.'

'How careless. Something else.'

'I read a lot.'

'Something else.'

'China!'

'Something else.'

'I believed that books had feelings. I was afraid to say I didn't like a book in case I hurt its feelings. Now that's enough.'

'One more thing.'

Isobel sighed.

'One more thing and you can give me the photographs back. Promise me, China.'

'I promise.'

'After we left Cornwall we moved to Wales. My parents bought a huge, run-down old guest house above the A5 in Gwynedd. They built it up from nothing into a good business. I had a room in the roof, with a Velux window. Every night I would stick my head out and watch the mist creep down the valley towards Betwys. I felt magical and exalted. After about three years my father died. He was sixty-eight years old, I was eighteen. We sold the house the following autumn.'

She was silent for some time.

'Hello?' I said.

'There was an overgrown orchard on the sloping ground at the side of the house. The day we moved out, my mother decided to pick all the apples. When I asked her why, she said, "It's a shame to let them go to waste."'

For an hour or more the two women had scrambled about in the damp leaf mould and the growing darkness. Their faces alight and excited, they had shaken the upper branches of the trees with a long pole, pounced on windfalls, run backwards and forwards to the house for cardboard boxes. Leaves had floated down. Apples had thudded on the soft floor. Then quite suddenly the night had enveloped them, and they were puzzled to find themselves there, tired out, staring at the old house which hung emptily above them, one big window yellow with light. Eight years later, Isobel was still puzzled.

'We'd never bothered with the apples before,' she told me. She laughed. 'Two grown women as impulsive as children.' Then she said:

'It was a harvest.'

I had seen photographs of the house, pebbledashed and foursquare on its damp Welsh hillside. I could imagine the road from England rumbling endlessly past in the bottom of the valley.

I said: 'I don't understand.'

'Neither of us would be going back there. Picking the apples was the last thing of that kind we could have together. My parents had worked hard for so many years, and my father was dead, and soon enough my mother would be too. It was the harvest of their whole lives together.'

She shook her head.

'That isn't it, either,' she said.

She said: 'It was panic. Have you got any idea what I mean?'

'No.'

'The whole thing was on and off like a tap. Don't you see? Twenty minutes later the boxes were packed in the boot of the car and we'd forgotten them. The next day we drove off and never saw the place again. She was a widow and I was going away to university: we picked the apples out of pure panic. Give me the photographs now, China.'

Isobel had a love of anything odd or old or cheap; anything that seemed exotic. This led her to furnish the Peckham flat with reclaimed pine bought under the railway arches at Camden Market, ancient velvet-covered sofas from Austin's on Rye Lane, lace curtains and kitchen chairs she had found one Friday afternoon in Camberwell. She liked chenille, in deep reds and purples, burnt orange. She was drawn to the colours of unfinished wicker, tarnished brass and Afghan carpets. She painted the front-room walls a pale terracotta and covered them the same afternoon with art posters, favouring anything warm, anything Klimt, anything Pre-Raphaelite. She bought little African tables, draped coloured shawls over them, scattered the shawls with jackdaw things, shells and pebbles, a dried starfish, ceramic roses, broken ear-rings, bits of leather and hessian, cheap brass bowls, Moroccan pottery, Chinese fans, painted plaster suns and moons, fake icons, and mirrors the size of postage stamps in heavy moulded frames. She uncovered the bedroom fireplace (which turned out to be Victorian), enamelled it gold and filled it with dried flowers. From the bedroom ceiling, by invisible nylon thread, she strung her collection of birds: strangely articulated wooden parrots in sombre colours from Indonesia, an ancient paper mobile of hummingbirds that looked like a shoal of small fish, owls and hawks and seagulls assembled from thin card, whose wings curled and curved in realistic shadows on the walls. Red and blue balsa-wood macaws perched on the windowsill. The eastern light fell through a peacock's tail of stained glass which scattered the headboard of the bed with oblique lozenges of cobalt, cadmium yellow and green.

It was like living with Kate Bush.

'Wouldn't you like a real bird?' I suggested.

'China, they *smell*.'

She lived in the moment. She woke to find you beside her and that was enough, whoever you had been before she met you. We were quite different in that respect. I was glad, because I hadn't kept much of anything to show her. 'At fifty,' I told her, 'you've left all your snapshots with your ex-wife.' Luckily, Choe Ashton was the only part of my past that made Isobel in the least curious. By then I'd known him for two years, perhaps a little longer. While I was always willing to talk about him, I didn't always know how to begin.

'When I first met him,' I would say tentatively, 'he was talking to a hand-drier.' Or: 'Choe's the sort of person who will set fire to himself if he gets bored.'

Isobel wasn't sure how to take this kind of thing.

'Is that supposed to be clever?'

'Well . . . funny, anyway.'

'Boys will be boys.'

'Look, do you want to hear about him or not?'

'I'm sorry, China.'

I thought for a moment. 'What can I tell you?' I asked, more of myself than Isobel. And then: 'I know. We once went to the Mumbles for a weekend, with a friend of Choe's called Stevie—'

'The *Mumbles*? You're making this up.'

'No I'm not. Listen . . .'

The universe, I remember reading, simply knitted itself together one day, out of numbers. One moment there was nothing. The next, this. What we have. All of it. Just numbers, knitting themselves together because their rules left them no option. A compact, elegant idea. If you want to know why it's wrong, go to the Mumbles for a weekend. The Mumbles, stamping ground of Dylan Thomas and other Welsh drunks, lines the western curve of Swansea Bay like hair in an armpit. Rain swings in over the grey arc of water, and through the rain you glimpse the cooling towers of Port Talbot across the bay. You note seven churches in half a mile. If the Mumbles was knitted out of anything, it was the strangled howls of Perry Como in a breakfastroom full of pensioners, something that calls itself 'SAS Coffee' and two Welsh salesmen talking in the Foreshore café.

'Fresh mackerel,' one of them says. And: 'Get some fresh mackerel off it.'

Off what? You won't ever know.

Choe and I arrived late one Friday afternoon. Though the weather was good, endless motorway roadworks had given Choe a pinched, resentful look. The first thing he saw on the Mumbles seafront was an old woman in a white mac, dragging her reluctant Cairn terrier along the pavement parallel to the slow-moving traffic. After a moment, she encouraged the dog to squat down and, staring straight at Choe, waited for it to extrude one small perfect chalk-white turd. Then she slipped a plastic bag over her hand to pick the turd up, wiped the dog's bottom with a bit of Kleenex, and tottered off.

'Christ!' said Choe.

He said: 'I wish we hadn't come here.'

'It was your idea, Choe.'

'Did you see that?' he said.

He said: 'She wiped the fucker's arse!'

He stopped my car so suddenly it stalled.

'This is the pub here,' he said.

'Bloody hell, Choe.'

It was whitewashed. It was half-timbered. Inside, it smelt of dust, mice and microwaved pie-filling. It was crowded. Choe bought two beers and sat down at a table already occupied by a woman of about thirty wearing a Mickey Mouse sweatshirt, black trousers with plaid turn-ups and black shoes on which had been appliquéd, just in front of the arch of the foot, a design of small red, green and yellow flowers. Pale lipstick gathered in the corners of her mouth, and a liquid redness at the rims of her eyes. In front of her on the table stood four empty glasses and one still half-full. All five had some kind of sediment crusted on to the rim. Choe stared at her for a moment, gave her a brief, empty grin and then said loudly to me:

'All over Europe women go into the sea with bare tits. Here they don't feel right without a swimsuit. And even then they have to pull a Snoopy T-shirt on over it before they can bring themselves to walk across the fucking beach.'

'Choe,' I warned him.

'Yet they'll shriek and run out into the fast traffic at the slightest excuse. You know? Especially at night when crossing an unlit road from one pub to another.'

He grinned at the woman.

She smiled uncertainly back.

'Had a nice time today?' he asked.

'Oh, lovely, thanks,' she said.

'Lev-ly,' mimicked Choe. 'Buy anything nice?'

'Choe,' I said.

'I bought some lovespoons,' the woman said. 'At the Lovespoon Shop.'

Choe stared me down.

'I reely lev levspoons,' he said.

'Would you like another drink?' the woman asked us. She got up unsteadily. 'I'm having margaritas,' she explained.

'No shit,' said Choe. 'Beck's.'

On the way to the bar she changed her mind suddenly and veered towards the Ladies.

Stevie turned up wearing patched 501s and a dirty white T-shirt. He was a slim, depressed-looking man, just out of his twenties, with big feet and bedraggled shoulder-length hair the brown side of blond. He had spent most of his life in Chorley or somewhere like that, and he had the indescribable snuffling Lancashire accent which goes with those places. He and Choe had done steeplejacking together up there, before Choe moved to Soho in search of other kinds of work. They had once been around a lot together. He came over to our table and began kicking morosely at me legs of Choe's chair. The little finger of his left hand was splinted and wrapped in a wad of bandage.

'This is Stevie,' Choe told me, not looking at him.

'Fuck off, Choe,' Stevie said, not looking at me.

He scratched his armpit and stared vaguely into the air above Choe's head. He said:

'I want the money first.'

Neither of them could think of anything to add to this, and after a pause Stevie wandered off to the bar.

'He's always like that,' Choe said. 'You don't want to pay any attention.' All week he had been promising me, 'You'll get on well with Stevie, though. You'll like him. He's a mad bastard.'

'You say that about all the girls.'

'Oh, Stevie should be in a strait-jacket.'

Stevie came back from the bar with a pint of Guinness. He sat down facing away from Choe and spoke only to me. If you said anything that impressed him, Stevie replied: 'That's through the other side.' What he meant by it I have no idea. He had been up the coast all that week, he said, at Pembroke Dock. He was working on one of the cracking-plants there.

'There's always a lot of that kind of work down here,' he said. 'Oil work. Chemical work.' He asked me, 'You getting plenty of work?'

I said I was.

'What kind of thing?'

'TV advertising,' I told him. 'That kind of thing.'

'What?' he said. 'You—'

'I write the adverts,' I said.

'Yeah? Through the other side.'

'I don't know about that.'

Choe said: 'For fuck's sake, Stevie.'

He took four or five notes out of his pocket and offered them across the table.

Stevie grinned suddenly.

'I've got some E back at the bed and breakfast.'

Choe laughed.

'It had better be *fucking* good stuff.'

I stared up at the clock above the bar. Not yet seven. I could see what sort of weekend we were in for. We would eat at the Quo Vadis, just along the front, a restaurant so uncertain of its own identity that it displayed next to its tariff board, as an idealisation or dream of itself, two or three colour photographs of the Acropolis. Choe and Stevie, having dropped the E at Stevie's bed and breakfast – some warren with asbestos fire doors, locks that didn't work and heavy-duty plastic covers on the mattresses – would annoy the other diners by telling them how beautiful they were, and how much they ought to love one another. Full of the benign language of the drug, as energetic as toddlers out of a playpen, seeing the world as if for the first time in every broken seashell, they would run about on the beach all night, calling to one another, 'I love you Choe.' 'I love you too, Stevie. Have you ever honestly *looked* at your own hands?' and eventually be trapped by the tide at Caswell Bay.

But this time Choe had other ideas.

'Down the coast,' he said, 'there are some fucking fantastic limestone caves that *look just like cunts*. You think I'm joking, don't you? But they do. They look just like cunts a hundred feet high.' He said, 'We get in the van and drive over there in the dark – fucking brilliant empty lanes – and drop the E in a giant cunt.' He laughed delightedly. He said: 'Get it— ? Drop it in a giant cunt.' He said: 'That's the plan.' He said: ' "Love is the plan. The plan is death." ' Stevie began to laugh too. 'Fucking hell, Choe. Right through the other side.'

'I'm not sure I can be bothered with this,' I told them.

'Don't be a wanker, Mick,' Choe said.

'No, come on Mick,' said Stevie. 'Don't be a wanker.'

The woman in the Mickey Mouse sweatshirt came back from the toilet. She had been to the bar and was carrying a tray with two Beck's and a pint of Guinness on it.

'There,' she said.

'Ask her to say "pub",' Choe advised me.

'Go on,' he urged. 'What do you bet me it comes out "peb"?'

'That's right through the other side, Choe,' I said.

'Don't be a wanker, eh Mick?'

He laughed.

'Not all your life.'

It was late before we got away. By midnight the seafront was alive with psychotic middle-class teenagers from Swansea: two hundred would-be estate agents and aerobics teachers – the boys and girls of summer – all trying to manoeuvre their mid-range GTIs and white Suzuki four-tracks out of the car-parks at the same time, in a fog of alcohol, bad blood, missed gears and lead-free exhaust. Choe's brilliant empty lanes weren't much better. Chains of high-intensity fog lamps glittered across the black emptiness of the peninsula, as if to anchor Mumbles Head to Rhossili. It was one-way traffic, windsurf traffic, jet-ski traffic, Caravan Club traffic, coming in bad-tempered and wiped-out after a hard drive down the M5 from the suburbs of Manchester and Birmingham. Stevie's vehicle, an ex-post office delivery van bought at auction and with only one functioning brake light, bobbed and weaved among them, lurching on its fucked-up shock absorbers and smooth tyres, brushing the vegetation on the wrong side of the road every time he tried to pass. He was successful twice in every five attempts. Through the rear windows of the van I could see three silhouettes against the bald glare of oncoming headlights – Stevie hunched over the wheel, his elbows sawing up and down energetically like the wings of some badly planned bird; Choe turned in profile, mouth opening and closing; and the Mickey Mouse woman, staring rigidly ahead. I wondered what she was thinking.

Failing to take off, Stevie changed his mind and plunged into the narrow back roads around Penrice and Hangman's Cross, hoping to find a way through to the B4247. I kept up with him for about five minutes. Then he turned right so suddenly that ten inches of air appeared under his offside rear wheel and I couldn't brake fast enough to get round after him. I wasn't going to rack my Cosworth up just to stay with a drunk in a dented post office van. I let them go. By then it was half-past one at night, and I didn't have much idea where I was. Gusty onshore winds had brought the rank smell of the sea to the whole peninsula. The lanes were like dark tunnels. I drove up and down the coast road from Rhossili to Scurlage, to see if they had already parked the van somewhere. Nothing. I went back into the lanes and drove around slowly in case I met them coming the other way. Nothing.

'Fuck it,' I said.

I was lost. I was ready to give up. I came round a blind corner to a T-junction about a mile east of Llanrhidian, and there they were. Stevie had driven straight across the junction into a steep grassy bank planted with rhododendrons. In his anxiety to avoid the local telephone box he had knocked down a road sign. The impact had crushed the bonnet of the van and popped all its doors. It looked deformed but at the same time opened up, like a rare species of moth in the moonlight. Stevie, who looked nothing like a rare moth, had banged his face on the windscreen and was leaning against the back doors, sniffing and wiping his nose with the back of his hand. Whatever he did, blood continued to pour out. The woman in the Mickey Mouse sweatshirt was vomiting freely into a drain she had found by crawling carefully along the interface between the road and the bank. I got out of the Cosworth to look at her. There were some cuts around her mouth and neck. Between each spasm she shivered and whispered to herself, 'Oh dear. Oh dear me.' When she felt my hand on her upper arm, she said, 'I'm sorry,' as though she had failed me in some way.

'You're OK,' I said. 'You're OK.'

Choe eyed me from the front passenger seat of the van, where he was fiddling with the radio as if nothing had happened.

'I can't get this fucker to work,' he called.

'Don't be a wanker all your life, Choe,' I advised him.

I decided to telephone 999. Nothing. A brief warm squall of rain blew in from the south, buffeting the rhododendrons. I held the receiver tightly to my ear and stared at the stone wall behind the telephone box. In the yellow wash of light I could see several brown spiders, some of them quite large. Despite the rain they were running in and out of the crevices between the stones. They had orange marks on their legs. I decided to drive the Mickey Mouse woman to Swansea hospital.

Behind me, Stevie began laughing.

'Look.'

I put the handset down and watched him walk uncertainly round to the nearside door of the van, using the edge of the roof as a handrail. He urged Choe out into the road.

'Look,' he said. 'Fucking look at this.'

'What?' said Choe.

'The sign! The fucking road sign!'

The road sign said: 'De Gwyr.'

'More like de pits,' said Stevie.

Suddenly they were both almost helpless with laughter.

Stevie said: 'De fucking pits. Get it?'

4
Burn without Opening

That was only the first of many attempts. Choe and Isobel had no common ground. There was no language that would describe them to each other. Despite that, they swam around in my head like bits of the same unfinished fish. Every time I told her some anecdote, Isobel asked in a bemused way: 'Why are you laughing—? You're talking as if you think it's clever to act like that.' Then, getting out of her chair and walking away across the room: 'It just seems like bad behaviour to me. It just seems childish.'

'I suppose you had to be there.'

One day she said: 'I'm sorry, China.' She said: 'I just don't want to think you're the same kind of person.' She said: 'I know you're not.'

When I didn't answer, she said:

'Tell me some more.'

'About what?'

'Tell me about Rose Services.'

'There wouldn't be a Rose Services without Choe. It was his idea.'

She sat on the sofa, leant forward and put her arms round me. 'Don't be defensive,' she said. And, eyeing me closely: 'Sometimes I don't quite know what to make of you, China.' I pulled her legs across mine and began to stroke them.

'I love that,' she said.

She curled round me like a shell.

'When I met Choe he still had all the connections he'd built up as a motorcycle courier.'

'Yes, do that,' said Isobel. 'Oh.'

'He knew someone who wanted some waste moved. It wasn't difficult. None of that stuff is particularly bulky or heavy. I hired the van. It didn't cost much. Choe drove it to some brand-new trading estate in Bermondsey, just off Rotherhithe New Road.'

'I love you to touch me.'

'We loaded the stuff and took it to a dump.'

There was a silence.

'I can hear you breathing,' I said. 'Inside.'

'That's how you started?'

'That's all there was to it.'

I didn't tell her where we had dumped the waste, or what it had turned out to be. I didn't tell her I'd been in two minds about the whole thing from the start.

'It was a cold night in November,' I said.

'Touch me like that again. Yes. That's . . . Yes.'

'Choe came without a coat.'

We got there early in the evening. Fog and dog shit lay in the hollows of the bleak strip of parkland south of Millwall football ground. We could hear a floodlit game in progress – meaningless roars, a loudspeaker playing current hits at half-time. We could smell hamburger, puddles full of leaves, industrial disinfectants leaking out on to the local roads from the legal tip under the railway arches off Bolina Road. Choe huddled between a stack of pallets and a Biffa waste tub, shivering patiently in his old cap-sleeved T-shirt and grey Italian army trousers. Under the halogen lamps, his upper arms looked varnished with the cold. He kept consulting his watch. Every so often a train would rattle past on the embankment above us, while we waited, on its way to London Bridge from the quiet, ordered life of East Sussex.

'For God's sake, Choe.'

'It won't be long.'

He was right. A dark blue diesel Transit pulled into the parking area and rolled to a stop about ten yards away. It was a site vehicle from some small construction firm – bald tyres, a mass of dents in every panel, rust breaking out round the inexpertly welded sills, engine rattling as unevenly as dice in a cup. Choe walked over and spoke quietly to its driver – their voices were thick, hesitant; there was a sudden laugh. Then he went round to the back. The doors creaked open.

'Good enough,' I heard him say to himself.

He jumped in and began moving things about.

'Come on Mick,' he called.

The load was packed in a dozen high-impact cardboard boxes, unmarked, ordinary-looking, a bit battered as if they had been used before: very light to carry. Someone had sealed them carefully with yellow biohazard tape. In five minutes we had moved everything across to our own van, stripped off the blue rubber gloves Choe insisted we wear and taken our money in cash. An hour later we were ploughing up the M1 like a barge on a freezing canal.

'I think I'll have game casserole with a spicy dumpling,' Choe told the barmaid, who had dressed for the evening in jeans and a promotional T-shirt for some old horror novel, Chinese red on black and yellow. When she spoke it sounded as if she was eating what she said, dipped in glutinous sauce from a Morecambe chippie. Choe rolled his eyes at her. 'Fucking hell! Savoury dumpling, eh?' He stared at the menu again. 'No. No I won't. I'll have steak, Guinness and Stilton vol-au-vents.'

He warned me: 'I'm paying.'

'With a smile like that,' the barmaid said, 'you can have it for free.'

We had ended up in the lounge bar of a 'country' pub tucked up among leafless oaks and little brown valleys under an arm of the Pennines south-east of Preston. The Boar's Head: maroon carpet, tan velvet seat covers, ceiling beams; the usual collection of fake firearms, horse brasses and cheap copper jugs. In addition, the walls were hung with landscapes, all by the same artist. He had painted something wrong and sentimental into the light – something unsuitable and at the same time lucid, as though the moors and fells, the little Lake District crags and tarns, were embedded in a clear, gel-like substance. Despite that, or perhaps because of it, you wanted to run away into them and hide.

Outside it was heavy rain, low cloud. While we were waiting for our food, three local men arrived, pink-faced with cold and shaking out the Barbour jackets they had worn over suits and ties to cross the car-park. You couldn't tell whether they were upper-class farmers from the Trough of Bowland or middle-class accountants fresh from the trough in Bolton. Between them they ushered in a frail-looking woman, perhaps seventy years old, wearing a red silk shirt tucked into her white wool skirt. She had thrown an expensive American raincoat loosely over her shoulders. Her face was heavily lined, especially round the mouth, where tiny vertical creases intersected her upper lip so that it looked like a badly stitched seam. Articulate and attentive, they settled her down at the bar. Did she want a stool? Or would she prefer to sit down by the fire? (Here they looked vaguely in our direction in case we might want to help, perhaps by giving up our seats.) They bought her a large G&T and a foil bag of dry-roasted peanuts.

'Oh,' she said. 'What a lovely idea.'

She pronounced it 'aydeah'.

When he heard that, Choe raised his head and said distinctly:

'Ay up! Fox and chips!'

'Actually I was trying to find you some cashew nuts,' apologised one of the men. The foil bag being just too clever, she smiled helplessly at him until he opened it for her. 'I know how fond you are of cashew nuts,' he reminded her.

'Still, it's a lovely idea.'

Aydeah.

'Fox and fucking chips!' repeated Choe, raising his voice in case they hadn't heard.

'Eat your vol-au-vents, Choe.'

He stared emptily past me.

'When I woke up this morning,' he said, 'I could 'ave sworn there were a maggot on me face. I were that depressed.'

He emptied his glass.

'Aren't they delicious, these nuts?' said the woman in the silk blouse.

Her voice carried. Choe's voice carried too.

'Fuck me, a maggot on me face, I thought I'd had it. But it were only a dream.'

'I've often thought they'd do well with cashews in these places.'

'Fact were, I just needed a piss.'

'Aren't they delicious?'

'*I just needed to piss.*'

In an attempt to divert him, I asked Choe:

'What's in the boxes?'

He had the grace to look amused. 'We don't want to know,' he said. He consulted his watch. 'Soon be time to drop them.' He pushed his chair back. He looked directly at the woman in the silk blouse and called over in his idea of a cut-glass Cambridge accent:

'Actually, I *am* off for a piss, this awfully moment.'

If it's glib to claim 'By the time you're fifty you've left all your snapshots behind with your ex-wife,' what should I have told Isobel? That when I was tired it still seemed inconceivable I could escape the frustration, the depression, the cloudy rage I had dragged around with me until I met her? That by simplifying my life to a place, a glance and a voice whispering, 'Fuck me, fuck me,' in the night, she had returned to me the optimism eroded by what seemed a long and ordinary life?

I don't know.

I could have explained: 'You took me away from someone else and I can't pretend I never loved her.' I could have told her: 'Some people marry young to hide.' I could have said: 'My whole generation had an obsession with authenticity we found it impossible to shake, and so we were always old but never grew up.'

I could have admitted:

'I let Choe Ashton persuade me to illegally dump fifteen cardboard boxes of low-level biological waste because it was a way of breaking with everything I had ever been.'

Would that have been any less glib?

In a cabinet in a corner of the Boar's Head lounge, someone had assembled a collection of real and yet meaningless bits of brass machinery – parts of old engines, beautifully turned valves and cylinders – whose origin and purpose was now completely lost. If I stared at it I became so puzzled I had to focus my attention somewhere else. I was tired out. When I closed my eyes I could still feel the M6 winding past me as if the van was stationary and the landscape moving, bridge after bridge, at seventy or eighty miles an hour. I could still see Choe's sharp, unreadable face next to me in the feeble dashboard illumination, and hear the roar and rattle of the Luton van. I tried to let the warmth of the Boar's Head seep into me. I tried, without turning round, to separate a single voice out of the babble at the bar—

'So that's the connection, then. Frederick North was her father.'

'Ah, the Shuttleworth connection. Yes.'

'Marianne North. She's the daughter of Frederick North. His second wife was a famous Shuttleworth. Her work—'

'Yes, please. Some more of that and another drink.'

'Her work . . . all of it in Kew Gardens, and some of it . . . the book explains . . .'

'Food, that is.'

'Oh yes?'

'. . . the book explains . . .'

'My father inherited two tied cottages on the estate. He was so softhearted he could never put up the rent. Two families at three pounds a week, and we're paying that in rates. More than that. They must think my father is a complete idiot.'

'. . . never seen by the public!'

'Excuse me. Excuse me. Could I have one of those? What is that? Oh good, I'll have one of those.'

'Sometimes I wake up in the night, thinking of all that money.'

All that money. Choe had returned from the lavatory. He was shaking my arm. I stared up at him dry-mouthed, barely able to remember who he was, while he looked down into my face with an amused, almost tender expression.

'Ay up Mick, tha's bin asleep.'

'What's in the boxes, Choe?'

'You'll love this,' he said. 'There's a sign in the lavatory, "CONTINENTAL EXCITER CONDOMS – USE FOR FUN ONLY".'

'Choe, what's in the boxes?'

He shook his head.

'Rubber johnnies, I suppose. I didn't *buy* any.'

He said: 'It's time we got on.'

'Where are we going?'

'You drive. I'll tell you when to stop.'

Outside, he seemed to wince for a moment in the wind and rain. Then he hunched his shoulders; walked over to a bottle-green Daimler V12, the only other vehicle in the car-park; and, in one long, sensuous motion, dragged his keys down the side of it to leave a deep scratch curved like a wave. 'There,' he said simply, ignoring the *wah-wah-wah* of the Daimler's alarm – which sounded, as he put it, just as piss-pointless as the fuckers in the bar – 'They'll love that, won't they?' His eyes were quite blank.

'For God's sake, Choe.'

'Go left out of here. Left.'

After a mile or so, he made me take the narrow gated road of the local North-West Water catchment area. There, a bulky Victorian architecture of revetments, ramps and spillways petered out among broken vernacular walls, eroded gritstone earth, unsurfaced tracks: as if, anxious to warn his audience about the natural world and its encroachments, the architect had designed a steady, homiletic movement from order to chaos.

Soon we were bumping along two ruts, hardcored with brick and crushed tarmac, which wound up steeply beneath black rock outcrops. I couldn't see much. Rain flew into the headlamp beams like insects. Wind tore through the sedges and rocked the van on its suspension as it wallowed and strained against the gradient. 'Fucking hell,' complained Choe. 'I fucking hate the outside.' His face was pressed up against the windscreen. He seemed uncertain, nervy. 'Right! No, go right!' The rain stopped, leaving a few clouds to redistribute the moonlight, which had given them the colour of a fish's skin.

'*Yes*,' said Choe suddenly. 'Not bad for someone who's only been here twice.'

He made me stop the van. He got out. 'Wait,' he ordered. He slammed the door, then called: 'You can turn the engine off.'

To the left I could see as far as the faint, ghostly sweep of Morecambe Bay. To the right, beyond a stone wall in poor repair, the ground fell away steeply to open space and very distant street lights flickering on the eastern slope of the watershed – Blackburn, Burnley, perhaps Colne. All I could hear was the wind rumbling across some large obstacle; the ticking of the engine as it cooled. Choe was gone for some time. The rain started again, harder than before, rattling and booming on the back panels of the van. I turned up the collar of my leather coat and watched the big clouds rush across the moon. The moor smelt like cinders. The wall seemed to go on for miles in both directions, punctuated by empty gateways opening on to nothing but rough pasture and bog-cotton. Suddenly Choe was hammering on the offside window. When I opened it, he shouted:

'We'll not get the van near enough to tip the stuff over the top.'

I could hardly hear him. The rain had plastered his T-shirt to his bony chest. His cheeks looked as if they had been peeled for some cheap cosmetic enhancement. His nose was running, he was shivering uncontrollably and his eyes were full of excitement.

'We'll have to carry it down.'

'What?'

'I said we'll have to carry it down.'

'I can't hear you.'

'Weather won't be so bad down there.'

He vanished. The back doors of the van burst open on a gust of freezing wind. He started to drag the boxes out.

'Come on Mick,' he said angrily. 'Don't fuck about.'

Then he was gone again.

I took a couple of boxes and scrambled awkwardly over the wall. Two feet the other side of it everything fell away without warning into a deep quarry choked with rhododendrons and young oak trees. It was a hundred and fifty foot drop into darkness. There was no wire, no sign. The edge was marked only by some crumbling red blocks of stone and two or three stunted birches. For a minute or two all I could do was teeter there in the wind, soaked to the skin, so close to falling I couldn't even speak. 'Choe!' I managed to call eventually. 'Choe, why don't we just throw them off the top?' But he had already started down, so I was forced to slither after him, clutching at the tangled rhododendron stems. Damp, friable brown soil soon caked my hands and feet. I dropped one of the boxes and had to feel about for it in the dark. Later, the whole episode would seem hallucinatory to me, a descent in more ways than one.

'Choe!'

At the bottom, worn aimless paths curved between heaps of spoil in the bluish, rain-dirty moonlight. Up under the steep sodden rock walls the earth was packed and hardened by years of use. Into it had been trodden a kind of light urban silt – layer after layer of smashed safety glass, broken battery cases, blue fertilizer bags, bedsprings rusted down to a powdery deposit, railway sleepers rotted and fibrous. Three or four burnt-out cars lay sprawled on their collapsed shock absorbers and rusty brake drums, as if they had maintained a perfectly straight and level stance during their fall from the ridge above, bounced once and come to rest. Burst laundry bags lay everywhere, children's clothes spilling out of them across the standing puddles and flooded ruts.

'Choe!'

I remember thinking, Who would want to do this? Who would want to do this? But the worst was still to come.

'Choe? Choe!'

A great frail wing of rock, like an eighty-foot razor blade, had caught itself years ago in the act of toppling from the main face and now, balanced precariously on a foundation of loose blocks, divided the quarry floor into two. When I walked cautiously round it, there was the real tip – one huge collapsing mound of plastic drums, bent strips of metal oxidised to white, cardboard boxes split and pulped by the rain, heavyweight plastic bags slashed open by the broken laboratory glassware inside, all resting in an expansive pool of water five or six feet deep and iridescent with escaped chemicals. There was a dead sheep in the shallows, bloated and grey. Around it floated literally hundreds of used latex gloves, their whitish transparent fingers ghostly as live squid in the dim light; swatches of asbestos waste like clumps of wool; detached biohazard labels the colour of willow leaves on a village pond. A thick, rotten smell came up, palpable as a touch, corrupt and chemical at one and the same time. But if I closed my eyes and listened to the rain, pattering straight down on half-submerged polyurethane and cardboard, it sounded as comforting and steady as rain on the roof of a garden shed.

'Choe?'

I couldn't see him.

'Choe?'

'What?' he said softly.

There he was – still as a lizard on a rock – impossible to separate from his setting until I had understood the shape and size of it. He had got as close to the water as he could. His eyes were narrowed and one leg was tensed to bear his weight. The cardboard boxes rested negligently on his hip. I don't know if I can describe the way he looked to me at that moment. He looked as if he was watching something, some animal that might be frightened away if we spoke loudly. At the same time he had the musing expression of a professional sailor wondering how he would navigate some small, newly discovered sea.

'Choe?'

'What?'

And then, as if he had really said *Don't bother me now*:

'Be careful.'

Then he was turning towards me in swimmy slow motion from the edge, his mouth opening, his eyes widening in amazement and wild surmise.

'Choe?'

'Fucking hell, Mick! *Look* at it!'

He stopped, coughed, choked, clamped his hand over his mouth. With a violent, despairing overarm gesture he hurled the cardboard boxes into the water – they turned over and over in the air, yellow tape flickering – and stumbled towards me. He clutched wildly at my upper arms.

'Mick!'

I pushed him away.

'It wasn't like this before,' he said. 'It was nothing like this.'

I said: 'I'm not coming down here again.'

He grinned.

'Oh yes you are, Mick,' he said. 'Go on. You know you are. Eh?'

'I'm not.'

'You know you want to.'

'I don't.'

'I can't do it on my own,' he wheedled.

'Bollocks, Choe.'

I knew exactly what he was trying to do. But in the end I would never be able to defend myself against him – Soho, 1989; ageing boy; French Connection jacket; sly, beautiful smile. 'Let's fuck off to Lisle Street and have a Chinese. Eh? Come on, you know you want to.' Somehow that would always pull me back, steady me down. Choe could always steady me down. He could always get on the right side of me. We made six trips between us, cutting a furrow in that soft, steep, unpleasant earth between the rhododendron roots: and an hour later we stood on the edge of the pool to toss the final box on to the great stinking tangled raft of stuff in the centre. We were filthy and exhausted. It was like standing on the shore of a completely unknown future.

'This water's *warm*,' Choe whispered wonderingly.

A faint, milky steam lay above it.

'Here we go,' I said.

'Wait,' he ordered. 'Look at this.'

Peeling a length of yellow biohazard tape off the box, he offered it to me. It was two inches wide and printed with bold black capitals.

'BURN WITHOUT OPENING.'

'Jesus, Choe.'

I hurled the box away from me as far as I could and blundered off across the quarry, straight up a short steep slope of half-stabilised spoil and into the stripped frame of a 1979 Vauxhall Chevette, which had once been pale blue. I hung on to it helplessly, panting and groaning and peeling off flakes of rusty paint like dry skin, repeating, 'Why would anyone want to do this? Why would anyone want to do this?' until I felt calmer. When I was able to look back, I saw Choe on his knees, his back curved like a foetus', throwing up into the pool.

'Choe!'

'*Fuck off back to the van.* I'll catch you up.'

I had the engine going by the time he reappeared. He stood swaying and retching into his hand as I turned the van round to face downhill. He opened the passenger door and then stood there gazing in at me like a drunk, unable to summon up enough strength to get into his seat. 'I'll need directions,' I said. And when he didn't answer: 'Choe, I'm just going to find the motorway, OK?' The van lurched forward, Choe's door swung open. He didn't say anything or do anything. He just sat looking tiredly ahead. He sat that way for thirty miles, then suddenly straightened up and looked around.

'Christ,' he said. 'Where's this?'

'It's the M6, no thanks to you. How do you feel?'

'Fucking desperate.'
'You should have stayed out of that water.'
'It wasn't the water.'
'What was it then?'
'Stop at the next services. I've got to drink something.'
'If it wasn't the water, Choe, what was it?'
He stared out of the side window.
'I had a look in one of them boxes.'
'Christ, you moron.'

It was raining again. From Chorley on south, both inner lanes had been jammed with vast ARC carriers hauling high-grade road materials from the great northern limestone quarries down to bypass projects in Sale or Oldham, daubed to their cab windows with white mud, shifting in and out of view in a groaning aerosol of water and red light. I moved into the outside lane to overtake; moved back. Lights flashed behind me out of chaos; flashed again.

Choe ducked his head and grinned suddenly.

'Aren't you going to ask me what was in it?'

'No, Choe, I'm not.'

He frowned at something: perhaps his own reflection in the windscreen.

'Well, I'll tell you anyway,' he said. 'It was full of dirty bandages. What do you think of that, Mick? Fucking dirty bandages.'

I looked sideways at him.

'We could have burnt them in your back garden and saved the petrol money,' I said. Then it occurred to me to ask: 'You didn't touch anything, did you?'

With Choe around, it was always a wrong move to display anxiety.

'I fucking *licked* one,' he claimed.

I crossed all three lanes as quickly as I could, and pulled to a halt on the hard shoulder. Trucks rushed past, shaking the van on its suspension, spraying it with their sour emulsion of mud and oil and butyl rubber. I leant across Choe and opened the passenger door.

'If you as much as touched that crap,' I told him, 'you can fucking walk home.'

I was shaking.

Two weeks later I bought the Astravan from an advert in the north London edition of *Auto Trader* magazine. When he saw it, Choe laughed.

'What's this?'

I was hurt.

'What does it look like?' I said.

'It looks like a shed.'

'It was cheap,' I explained. 'And I've got the offer of the engine from a newer model.'

'Take the brakes too,' was Choe's advice.

'Fuck off, Choe.'

He kicked one of the wheels.

'I'll see what I can do with it,' he said.

He uprated the suspension to handle serious loads, fitted big discs front and rear to stop them. He shook his head at the diesel engine I showed him and went off to find a two-litre petrol unit of his own. 'Fell out of an SRi,' he boasted. 'It'll go like shit off a shovel.' It did. Within a week we had used it to move our first live consignment, a thousand transgenic moths for release into a timber plantation in Argyll. Six months after that we were carrying anything we could lay our hands on, from cellular raw materials to apparatus and computers (including a secondhand DNA sequencer, which we wrapped in an old mattress of Choe's in case it broke); from 'passive immunity' vaccines to artificial antibodies and speciality bloods designed in the US. We moved plant specimens shipped quietly in by air from the Third World so their seeds could be patented by self-financing university research departments in the Midlands. We had our foot in the door of the genetic supply industry. We were on our way.

5
Food for Thought

In the end Isobel never asked me why anyone would pay two thousand pounds to have some cardboard boxes taken to Lancashire. All she said was, 'It's a big boys' game to you two.'

I shrugged.

'I quite like it, really,' she said.

I knew I was giving her too simple a picture of Choe, but I couldn't seem to stop mythologising him. He put an end to this himself, a week or two after I told her the Lancashire story. From then on, he was in charge of his own myth.

It was a cold November night, but he came on a motorcycle wearing one of his extraordinary Paul Smith suits, winding his way east from Chalk Farm, where he now lived with his girlfriend, into Mile End so he could take the Rotherhithe tunnel – where he tried to reach a hundred and twenty miles an hour along the deep interior straight with its 20 m.p.h. speed limit and Toytown carriageways – and into Peckham from the Jamaica Road. His right wrist was in a lightweight cast. 'This fucker got broken a couple of weeks ago,' he explained, as if the wrist itself were at fault. 'Throttle hand, too.'

We were standing in the sodium light on the pavement outside the house. 'You've just *got* to come out and see this bike,' he had told us when we answered the door. 'You'll kill yourself if you miss it.'

Isobel shivered.

'I've never broken anything,' she said.

She said: 'Did it hurt?'

'I felt nowt,' he reassured her.

He grinned.

'I won't tell you how I did it,' he said. 'But I'll tell you what I did after. Shall I?' And then: 'Shall I tell you?' as if he was really asking both 'Ought I to tell you?' And 'Do you want me to tell you?'

Isobel folded her arms under her breasts.

'I'm cold out here,' she said.

'Ask me this,' he said quickly. 'Did I get back on the bike and ride it to the nearest hospital?' He gave her a cocky grin and added parenthetically: 'I could have done, you know. Do you believe me?'

Isobel opened her mouth to speak.

'No,' he said. 'I did not.'

What he had done instead was to catch the bus to his local Sainsbury's. There, he had gone straight to the poultry produce aisle, extracted from its box a nice brown middle-sized *free-range* egg, and unobserved, dropped it on the floor. 'It broke,' he told us wide-eyed, as if this fact – the fragility of the egg, of eggs in general – surprised him even now. 'After that I thought I'd buy a few things.' He smiled reminiscently. 'So I got a basket and went round. The way you do.' He had picked up a nice cake, rum and butter; some Fetherlite condoms; and a packet of Ariel Ultra. ('I used to use Ecover but it costs more and it just doesn't fuck the environment up the same way.') Walking absent-mindedly down the poultry produce aisle again, he had slipped on the broken egg and fallen awkwardly into the shelves. 'I'm suing the fuckers,' he told us brightly. He held up his arm in its cast. 'Lucky it wasn't worse.' He shook his head. 'I was gobsmacked,' he said. 'They're supposed to take care of you in a place like that.'

He grinned at Isobel's expression.

'Fourteen hundred quid,' he said. 'That's what I'll get for a broken wrist. Brilliant. Eh? Don't you think?'

Isobel didn't know what to think.

'Anyway, come and look at this,' he said. He took her by the hand and pulled her across the pavement towards the motorcycle. It was that year's Honda CBR Fireblade, essentially a 900cc racing machine barely detuned for the road, with canted twin headlights the shape of a Japanese warrior's eyes, and the bright orange flames of some psychokinetic conflagration raging across its plastic skin. It was manga. It was *Akira*. It was ludicrous. Nobody knew that better than Choe. 'Isn't that fucking *over the top*?' he demanded.

Isobel, who could barely tell a motorcycle from a roller skate, made a disconcerted gesture with her whole body. She looked at me.

Help, said her eyes.

'I don't know what it is,' she said.

'You do,' Choe told her.

'I don't.'

'This,' he said, 'is the most phenomenal motorcycle ever made.'

He laughed up at her.

'*And now you're going to have a ride on it.*'

'China, no,' she appealed.

She tried to push Choe away from her.

'I'm not,' she said.

'You are.'

She started to laugh, stopped.

She said: 'No.'

She said: 'Can I have my hand back, please?'

Choe shrugged and let her go.

'I like it,' she said. 'But I won't go on it.' Suddenly she pointed to the Honda's exhaust. 'The back's hot,' she said. 'Is that bit supposed to be so hot?' She laughed. 'I don't even know what this is,' she said. 'It's a motorbike, isn't it?'

Choe stood back and appraised her performance. Then he looked over at me.

'I was right,' he said with satisfaction. 'Mick, she's a real—'

'Choe!' I warned him.

'Let's go in,' said Isobel, pulling herself away and running up the steps to the house.

'Let's eat.'

I had never seen her so confused.

'Fucking hell,' said Choe, towards the end of the meal. 'Marks and Sparks custard sauce.' He looked at Isobel, as if seeing her in a new light. 'My fucking favourite,' he said: ' "Delicious hot or cold." '

'He's reciting that from memory,' I said.

'I don't doubt it,' Isobel said.

'From the *heart*,' Choe insisted. 'I'm reciting it from the heart.' He stared at Isobel. 'I'm not reading the fucking packet, you know.'

Despite herself, she had begun to smile.

'I know everything about custard,' he claimed: 'Me.'

She looked down at her plate.

'Eat it then, Choe,' she said carelessly.

She looked back up again.

'Eat the custard.'

Coming back from the kitchen with the coffee a few minutes later, we found him sprawled on the sofa. He had selected a CD remastering of some Champion Jack Dupree tracks from the 1940s, and was playing 'New Low Down Dog' quite loudly. The CD remote control dangled from his damaged right hand, while with his left he was holding to his eye – the way you would a lens – a bracelet of Isobel's. Celtic nouveau in cheap silver plate, the bracelet was thick and heavy, coppery at points of wear and a little weak at the clasp from over-use. Isobel had taken it off that morning and left it on the coffee table among half-read novels, scattered copies of *Scientific American* and *New Scientist*, and a slippery fan of catalogues from the genetic, medical and biological supply industry – glassware and electronics manufacturers, packing agencies, software firms.

'Here's your coffee, Choe,' Isobel said.

He didn't answer. He was reading – or pretending to read –

through the bracelet. She put the mocha down on the table in front of him.

'Do you want this?' she said.

Choe looked up at her, the bracelet still to his eye.

'Through this ring I see the future.'

Isobel started to say something, but he had turned away and was staring up at the light fixture. 'The future,' he said in a resonant voice, 'is in Hanford-style sites. Trenches, cribs *in situ* vitrification.'

'Not in Britain,' I said.

We had had this argument before.

'What's Hanford?' asked Isobel.

'You don't want to know,' Choe said.

Isobel stared at him angrily.

'What's Hanford, China?'

'It's an open chemical toilet in Washington State,' I explained. 'Mainly radiotoxics. They lost control, overfilled the site, panicked. In the end the only way to stop it all draining into the Columbia River was to pump so much electricity into the ground everything turned to glass.'

Hanford Reserve: great feathery subsurface plumes of carbon tetrachloride, radioisotopes in solution, completely arbitrary combinations of wastes, even the organics like rubber and oil cooked into new substances. No records had been kept. Heat – radio heat, chemical heat – kept the cribs simmering. They cooked and cracked and leaked. Then everything turned to glass, like a fairy tale. The river was saved when everything turned to glass.

'They call it "uncertain chemistry",' I said. 'No one knows what's in there anymore.'

'China, how horrible.'

'China's real name is Mick,' said Choe, very quietly to himself. He reached down slowly and, still staring into the light, tapped the front of the current *New Scientist*. ('Can We Grow Younger?' asked its cover, across a picture of a nervous woman in a raincoat waiting for a train.) 'It will come,' he told me. 'It will be legalised and controlled, and people will make less money as a result.' He grinned to himself, as if that was all right with him; as if it was a challenge he badly needed. 'I see the future of anything,' he went on, 'but only when I look at it. Everything around it is a kind of rushing grey fog.' He turned away and hung over the arm of the sofa, making vomiting noises. 'It's nauseating, the unstructured future rushing past us like the wind.'

'Does he always behave like this?' asked Isobel.

I grinned.

'I've done something wrong, haven't I?' Choe appealed. 'The music's too loud, isn't it? Is that it? Oh God, I'm sorry, Mick.'

He spun Isobel's bracelet round his index finger until it became a silvery blur.

He shrugged.

He said to me: 'Maybe you're right.'

He listened for a moment to Champion Jack Dupree, then added:

'I can't understand why the educated classes make such a fucking fuss about Robert Johnson. You'd think he was the only fucker who ever played the blues.'

'He's the only fucker most of them have ever heard, Choe,' I said.

'Shall I leave you two boys to smoke your cigars?' Isobel asked.

She drank her coffee.

'Can I have my bracelet back?'

Choe looked at his watch and jumped to his feet.

'Fuck,' he said. 'I forgot.'

It was ten o'clock. He had to leave. He had promised to spend the evening with Christiana, his girlfriend. 'I'd better get back,' he said, standing up reluctantly. 'She's not feeling too well.' It wasn't so much he regretted leaving us, I thought, as that he regretted leaving any gathering, any occasion. 'Show me out,' he ordered. 'Or I'll never go.' At the door, he kissed Isobel, pressed the bracelet into her hand like a gift – closing her fingers round it gently with his own – and grinned fleetingly at me.

'Fucking hell mate,' he said.

Isobel snapped the bracelet closed on her wrist.

We stood in the hall together for a long time afterwards, listening to the Honda weave its way away through the night. Every time you thought it had gone out of earshot at last, you would hear its engine shriek up to the red line again – faint, distant, undeniable, eerie as an event on another planet – as Choe pulled out from under some dark railway arch in Bermondsey, wound it up tight, and went for the next roundabout with the front wheel off the ground and the fuel tank in his armpit at a hundred and ten miles an hour. Eventually, silence.

'Well, that was a bit tiring,' said Isobel.

'I thought he was on good form.'

'That's good form, is it?' she said. We were back upstairs, and she was walking vaguely round the dinner table, picking up the used dishes and putting them down again. 'What was all that business about the girlfriend?' she said. And then, before I could devise an answer: 'Do you think he really was supposed to be spending the evening with her?'

I thought it was very likely. I said:

'Who can tell?'

'For God's sake,' Isobel said suddenly. 'Come and help me here.' Then: 'What's she like?'

I heard myself sigh.

'She's the sort of woman who always thinks she's seen the waiter somewhere else.'

'China—'

'It's true.'

A girl on a bus, a boy at the zoo; they always remind Christiana Spede of someone you both used to know. 'Just have a look,' she urges you. 'It's X when she was younger.' You look but you can never see the resemblance. It hinges on some tiny factor around which all the others have realigned themselves in Christiana's mind – a turn of the head, a way of holding a knife, the first syllable of a laugh – seen or heard fifteen years ago.

'He's just a type,' you say of the waiter, and she looks brutally disappointed.

One of the first things I remember hearing her say was:

'I thought I saw a dead dog in the lavatory, but it was only an old coat.'

That was at the ICA, some time in the early eighties; some time, anyway, when we were both a bit younger – though Christiana was always a lot younger than me. She had intense blue eyes; a face like Claire Bloom, twenty years old, which she framed between a kind of orange post-punk haircut and a short black leather motorcycle jacket; and all the cultivated wrongness of that time. She shaved one eyebrow. She wrong-footed you with everything she said. Her body language was wrenched and odd. She was a performance which offended everyone she met until one day she smiled across some café table and they were seduced. She used the word 'transgressive' a lot.

She was never more than a friend of mine, though at that time I hardly liked anyone better.

I had walked down to the Mall from Piccadilly station one dark night in February to see an exhibition with her, knowing she would be late. It was one of those central London winter evenings with high winds, pissing-down rain, cold puddles. Commuters try to walk through you as if you aren't there, taxis will kill you on zebra crossings, the homeless are crushed up into the doorways to get their legs out the way. But on Regent Street, just before it met Pall Mall, among the Volvos and bottle-green Saabs like padded cells on wheels, someone had parked a little red Greenlight-modified M3: boxy lines, left-hand drive, yellow four-spoke alloy wheels and all, it was an amazing note of hope in a dull place. I stood near it for a moment, feeling a kind of psychic warmth come off the cold bonnet. I wanted to touch it but I was afraid of its alarm, and all too soon – a member for a day – I found myself in the ICA bar, grinning around like a feral dog at the hot pink décor and Rentokil condom machine or whatever it is they have there on the wall.

Christiana Spede wasn't in much better shape. She sat down next to me, wrenched at her red tartan micro-skirt until it covered the gusset of her tights and, after the comment about the lavatory, said:

'Every face I saw on Oxford Street I'd seen before.'

She offered me a drink from a bottle of Beck's, which I accepted.

'Cold out tonight,' she said.

She said: *'Institute of Cultural Anxiety*. I look round this place and I want to scream "Bollocks!" and walk out backwards, like a gunfighter in a film.'

She cocked her index finger and threatened some posters with it. I looked at her feet.

Steel-toecapped workboots.

I wasn't in advertising then; I wasn't in Soho. Neither of us had any money then. We could have made money, but not by doing the things we wanted to do. I learned about that, but Christiana never did. Some of those late seventies, early eighties people are easy with life. Others aren't. They manage to stay one step ahead of themselves on the high wire. They're always catching themselves just before they fall. It's a tiring performance. But I suppose it's better than the long drop.

'Tell me about it, Christiana,' I said. 'You could kick them to death,' I suggested.

Two years later we fell out over a Ken McMullen film, which, though it was interesting, just didn't make any really serious attempt to transgress gender boundaries, and I lost sight of her until she turned up with Choe at the other end of the decade.

During that time she had been a singer, a dyke, a dyke singer and a radical feminist dyke, before settling down as a wholesale wine salesperson travelling for Roederer champagne. By now her blue eyes seemed a little pale and watery. As she talked they would rest briefly and vaguely on other things: the cruet, a picture on the wall, the street outside whatever café you were in with her, sometimes on people coming and going in the room. It was unnerving to be the object of this attention, however briefly, because you felt you were drawing it away from its proper recipient. And it was always shocking to see her with Choe because although they were of an age he looked so much younger than her. Until she laughed – and she laughed less often than before – that peerless Claire Bloom face was lined and crumpled and sleepless-looking, wrinkled deeply at the corners of the eyes.

I couldn't decide why. Some private tension had worn her out. Or perhaps the decade itself had done for her, the way it did for so many: perhaps, I thought, she had simply never recovered from the attempt all her generation had made to politicise their inner lives, growing – without ever suspecting it – more and more exhausted by the attempt to resolve the appalling inconsistencies of their position in an age when even the Left had picked up Thatcherite rhetorics of self-reliance and economic necessity. I was close. If I had just said to myself that 'something inside' had aged Christiana, I would have been closer. But in the end I decided to believe that she had worn her face out by living in it, that the lines about her mouth and eyes were lifelines, the record of too much laughter and tears, eating, drinking, fucking.

About that I was completely wrong.

'I want to meet her,' Isobel said, and about a month after Choe had ridden his CBR out of Peckham and into the dark, she arranged for all four of us to have dinner. She chose the restaurant without asking anyone. It turned out to be at the wrong end of Frith Street, some staid survivor of the old Soho – brown walls, brown menus, dark brown food – a long way away from the new one. 'When in doubt,' I advised her, 'at least pick L'Escargot.' Christiana and Choe arrived half an hour late. Choe was already drunk. Christiana was wearing a fur coat. 'I'm feeling better than I did a couple of hours ago,' she said, as if one of us had asked. She stared vaguely into the middle distance. 'I'm trying to remember when that was.'

'I thought you might choose us some wine,' Isobel suggested.

'Oh God, I'll drink any old muck.'

'She'll drink any old muck,' Choe said. He glanced uninterestedly at the menu. ' "Sausage and mash with onion gravy." I've had that in hospital.'

'Shall I eat calamari?' Isobel asked herself.

Christiana shuddered.

'I don't like octopus. Well, they remind you of genitalia.' She thought for a moment. 'It's that great big bag of bits, isn't it?'

'She got that from Jean Genet,' Choe told us.

'Mind you,' he was forced to admit, 'she *has* seen them. On the fish counter at Tesco's.'

'Don't worry, love,' Christiana reassured Isobel. 'It's not me he hates, it's my alcoholism.'

Isobel picked up the wine list.

'Why don't we try this Mâcon Village?'

'Not at twenty quid a bottle.'

'Not at twenty quid a bottle,' mimicked Choe. 'Nothing good is good enough for her,' he informed me. 'Ever met people like that?'

'I just meant it was a bit expensive,' said Christiana.

She touched his hand and he moved it away.

'It's just a bit expensive for what it is, that's all.'

I could see it was a private game of theirs. He would pick a fight. When she tried to placate him, he would retreat into himself. The outcome would be much later and not in the restaurant at all. It wasn't a game for beginners: once or twice I caught him looking at her with real distaste, as if he was watching the behaviour of a stranger at some other table. In the end, Christiana seemed to give up. She started talking to Isobel instead. They drank house white. They put their heads together and laughed. I heard Christiana say, 'Mind you, what did that matter to me? I'd seen my first corpse at age fifteen, anyway.' And then a little later: 'I tried to be a beatnik when I was a kid but I got a rash from my pullover.' Choe curled his lip. He had won the game and lost his opponent. He sensed this.

'Let's go and have a piss,' he invited me, after the main course. To get there, we had to pass the sweet trolley.

'Fucking hell,' said Choe. 'Look at that lot.'

In the loo he asked me suddenly: 'Have you ever wanted to piss on a wasp in the bath—? I'm serious. I mean, seen a wasp settled on the bottom of the bath and wanted to piss on it there and then?'

He stared expectantly up at me over the partition between the urinals.

'I have,' he confided, when it became clear I wasn't going to say anything. 'More than once.'

After a moment he said mournfully:

'I don't think your tart likes me.'

I had spent all day feeling as if my eyes were focusing at different lengths. Every so often, things – especially print – swam in a way which suggested that for one eye the ideal distance was eighteen inches, while the other felt happier at twelve. Choe was the perfect object for this augmented kind of vision, swimming naturally in and out of view, one part of his personality clear and sharp, the rest vague and impressionistic. Any attempt to bring the whole of him into focus produced a constant sense of strain, as your brain fought to equalise the different focal lengths.

'Choe, her name's Isobel. She isn't my tart.'

'She fucking is, mate. Best I've seen.'

'Come on, Choe. Stop showing off.'

I got him to zip up and go back into the restaurant. On the way past the sweet trolley, he said, 'Want some strawberries with your tart?' When I didn't answer, he reached out and took a couple. 'Choe, you're an arsehole,' I said. He grinned. 'I won't be any more trouble, Mick,' he said. 'You'll let me stay, won't you?' At about half-past ten he looked around suddenly and said in a bright voice as if he was opening a conversation rather than interrupting one:

'So. Where are we, then?'
Isobel stared at him. After a moment, Christiana explained:
'We came in a cab. I don't think he looked out of the window once.'
'If I can find Oxford Street, I'll be all right,' Choe said. 'I can get home from there.'
'"We", darling,' Christiana reminded him. 'We can get home from there.'
She put her hand on his arm.
'Who's "we"?' said Choe, gently removing it.
Suddenly he said to her:
'Close your eyes and open your mouth.'
'Why?'
He winked at me.
'Just close them,' he said.
'I'm not very good at this sort of thing.'
'Go on,' he insisted.
While her eyes were closed, he produced one of the strawberries he had stolen on his way back from the lavatory.
'Open your mouth.'
'Is it something awful?'
'How will you know until you open your mouth?'
She tried, but her eyes popped open instead. Deftly, he hid the strawberry again.
'I can't do it,' she said.
Every time she lost her nerve, he hid the strawberry. She could close her eyes or open her mouth, but not both at the same time. A physical force seemed to drag her eyelids apart; a physical force closed her lips. Eventually she made herself do it. He popped the strawberry on to her tongue as deftly as he had stolen it. Several expressions passed over her face: horror, puzzlement, then delight.
'You sod,' she said, when she had swallowed it. 'It tasted like rubber when it first went in.'
'You say that to all the boys.'

*

When we got home, Isobel said:

'He's just cruel, China.'

'Oh, come on, it was funny.'

'It was cruel.'

'Christiana loved it.'

'She loved the attention,' said Isobel.

'There's nothing wrong with that.'

'Yes, there is,' she insisted.

'Look,' she said: 'Even in low heels Christiana is an inch or two taller than him.'

'I can't say I noticed.'

'Exactly. He makes you feel . . .' A pause: 'I can't say it, I can't find a way to say it. It's sexual, I suppose; there's that extraordinary sexual attraction he has . . .' She laughed. 'No. That's not it, either. I don't know. He's demanding, but it's not you he wants. He's—'

'What?'

'He's constantly trying to make you feel awkward with yourself,' she tried to explain. 'The way you were at fifteen. If you're a woman, I mean.'

'It's very clever, what he does.'

And finally, with a helpless shrug: 'You want him to do it.'

'What?' I said. 'Do what?'

'For God's sake, China. Confuse you. Mystify the world, so he's your only safe place in it. You get on the back of the motorbike once: you have to trust him forever.'

She saw that I didn't understand.

'Forget it,' she said suddenly.

She looked round the bedroom.

'I love this house, China,' she said. 'Don't you love our house?'

By then, it seemed odd to be living in two or three rooms in Peckham.

'When you get tired of it, we can easily afford somewhere in west London,' I said.

Isobel shivered.

'I'll never get tired of it,' she said.

Certainly she never seemed to tire of the work it meant. 'Don't you hate fitted carpets?' she asked me the next morning. I wasn't really listening. It was still dark and I was still half asleep. I was late for a pick-up I had promised to make in Reading.

'I suppose I do,' I said.

That evening when I got home the whole house smelt of sawdust and varnish. She had hired a sander from Travis Perkins and stripped the floorboards to bare wood. She was delighted with herself.

'Take a photograph,' she said.

Isobel always wanted a photograph. I had photographed her in expensive restaurants and at other people's weddings. I had photographed her on the back of a camel during a two-week winter break in the Canaries; on mule-back in Yosemite National Park. At Refugio Beach, off Highway 101, I had photographed her sitting on the bonnet of a fat white rental Toyota; in Stratford, feeding a swan. We had albums of before and after shots of the Peckham flat, every step forward out of chaos, every room. 'Look. You won't believe the things they left behind,' Isobel would tell our friends. 'That's a postcard of Andrew and Fergie's wedding on the shelf. And look at the colour of the *radiator*.' Every time I bought a new suit or a new car, Isobel had to have a photograph. Isobel would photograph the dinner table if she thought she had made a special job of it.

'Go on,' she said.

And so I did; and in that shot, if you could find it, you would still be able to see her as I saw her then, standing in the middle of the living-room floor wearing industrial safety glasses, an Ecuadorean cardigan over her best flowerprint frock and Doc Marten boots. Every crease and fold of her clothes was caked with fine sawdust. An Indian silk scarf was tied round her lower face to keep the worst of it out of her mouth. In her arms she cradled a Bosch Professional CPT.

'What do you think?' she demanded.

'I think you look like Arnold Schwarzenegger. No, you look like Buddy Holly.'

'Thank you, China.'

I hugged her.

I said: 'Don't you ever get tired?'

'I love it,' she said. 'I love it all.'

She pushed her hair out of her eyes with the back of her hand. 'China, I want it to be *brilliant*.'

If Isobel's delight was invested in the flat, then mine was invested in Isobel. At the same time, in some way I find it hard to explain, Isobel *was* the flat. How can I put it? Like this:

Our back door opened on to a bitumen roof, about twelve feet square, sheltered from the wind by a low wall. Isobel called it 'the roof terrace'. One Saturday afternoon she painted the wall white and bought some terracotta pots into which she planted geraniums, morning-glory and miniature roses. 'Come here and look at your garden, China.' As early as the first weekend in March, I found, I could sit there and turn my face gratefully up to the sun, which cleared the upper storey of the house at one or two in the afternoon. The wall's shadow filled the rooftop like a pool, leaving a strip of sunlit about three feet wide which rapidly became too hot to sit in. My exposed skin tingled. I felt as if it was being gently stripped away, to reveal a fresher layer beneath.

'It probably is,' Isobel told me.

She had come to the door and was standing there in the well of shadows looking out at me with a smile possessive and ironic.

'What would you like to eat for lunch?'

By summer the heat was so strong that passing insects toppled out of the air paralysed; struggled for a moment on the soft bitumen of the roof where I lay reading Scott Fitzgerald; then blundered on.

Even in the winter, I used to stand out there in the rain and stare at the City of London in the distance and imagine the roof as the prow of a ship, pushing forward into time. The ship was my life, and the excitement of being on board it was so powerful as to be physically astonishing.

The last time anything strange or intense happened to me out there was one very hot August night. I got up for a piss at three o'clock, then staggered outside half asleep and half naked. Heat-lightning filled the sky. I stared up at it – pulse after pulse of weird silent green light reaching from the horizon to horizon – feeling drunk, elated, puzzled, lonely, all at once. I felt irradiated, but God knows what by. Something compelled me to dance about in my underpants, under the peculiar light, waving my arms in the warm air until I felt breathless and foolish. Then I went back to the bedroom and stared down at Isobel with an intensity of love I have never felt for anything since.

She, on the other hand, dreamed of some long, soaring, heartbreaking flight.

6
Nagy Secz

Business began to take up most of my time. Out of an instinctive caution, I dropped the word 'medical' from the company description and called myself simply Rose Services. I had someone design me a logo. We looked at several images, but the one which made most sense featured a rose and a reaching hand. Over the next eighteen months Rose Services became twenty quick vans, some low-cost, heavily fenced storage space off Ilderton Road in Bermondsey and a licence to carry the products of the nascent genetics industry to Eastern Europe. During that time I decided that, if I was to take advantage of the expanding markets there, I would need an office on the spot.

'Let's go to Budapest,' I suggested.

Isobel hugged my arm.

'Will there be ice on the Danube?' she said.

'There will.'

'Oh, China.'

When I put it to him, Choe liked the idea too.

'Fucking ace,' he said.

'Does that mean yes?'

'Ace to fucking base.'

'Bring Christiana,' I suggested.

'Do I have to?'

'Yes,' said Christiana. 'You bloody do.' She said: 'Thank you for inviting me, China.'

Choe looked at her, then out of the window at the passing traffic. We were in a café-bar called Gill Wing's just down from

Highbury Corner, and Christiana had ordered us a bottle of Gamay de Touraine. 'I've never been to Budapest,' Choe said. 'That's in Hungary, isn't it? Is that in Hungary?' He turned away from the window, leant towards Christiana and ran his finger quickly down the back of her hand. 'Now tell me: Hungary. Is that left of Austria, or right?'

'Piss off, Choe.'

'I mean, as you look north?'

He tried the Gamay.

'Some days,' he concluded, 'you just can't get the taste of toothpaste out of your mouth from the word go.' Then he said to me: 'There's someone you ought to meet before we leave.'

'Arrange it then, Choe,' said Isobel.

Choe ignored her.

'His name's Ed,' he said.

'That's very informative,' Isobel said. She tipped back her chair so that her shoulders touched the wall. A long brown wool skirt from Comme des Garçons at Harvey Nichols fell into an attractive fold between her slightly parted legs. We had been at Gill Wing's for half an hour and it was the first time she had spoken. 'What does Ed do, do you think?' she asked me, as if Choe and Christiana weren't there: 'Insurance fraud?' She glanced down at her starter. 'We all look forward to meeting Ed,' she said, and then: '*Is* this fried Gruyère?'

Choe gazed levelly at me.

'Well, Mick, is it?'

'Choe,' said Christiana, 'are you going to drink that wine or am I?'

'Is it fried Gruyère, Mick? Don't be shy to tell us. Because to me, you know, it doesn't look like that at all. It looks just like—'

'Choe!' Christiana warned him.

'Drink that wine,' he mimicked.

He looked from Christiana to Isobel and back again. Then he grinned at me.

'Don't bloody whine,' he said. 'Eh, Mick?'

*

Ed, it turned out, was an American of Central European extraction. His surname was Cesniak: or so he said. 'Pronounce that with a "Ch".' During the late eighties he had made money out of the border between Poland and Belorussia and now he was looking for somewhere to invest it.

'Bring him to supper,' I suggested.

Choe seemed nervous.

'What can we lose?' I said.

I said: 'Set it up.'

At seven o'clock one cold night in January, an hour before they were due to arrive, Choe phoned to apologise: they would be late. 'OK,' I said. Fifteen minutes after that he rang again. Ed couldn't make it at all – the meet was off. 'Fair enough,' I said. Almost immediately it was back on again. But Ed only drank Valentines: could I go out and buy some? 'Of course,' I said – although I wasn't even sure I knew what Valentines was – and put on my coat. Predictably, this irritated Isobel.

'Couldn't you have taken him out somewhere?' she said, 'and all been boys together?'

When I got back from the off-licence in Camberwell it was eight o'clock. No one had arrived. Isbobel stared at me and then at the boeuf en croûte with chicken-liver pâte and fennel.

'How's it looking?'

'I might save it,' she said.

At nine a car pulled up outside. The phone rang. 'We're downstairs,' said Choe, when Isobel picked it up.

'He's calling from the *car*,' she told me in a voice of disbelief. She offered me the handset across the room. I shrugged and shook my head, no. 'Are you new to mobile phones?' she asked Choe loudly, and hung up. 'He's like a fucking seven-year-old.'

They were waiting for me when I got down, Choe grinning and turning over the junk mail on the hall table; the American swaying slightly, rubbing his hands together in the cold and wiping his feet compulsively on the thinning sisal doormat. Ed Cesniak was perhaps forty years old, an inch or so taller than Choe, and his front teeth had been comprehensively caried by amphetamine abuse. He was wearing a purple silk suit, five hundred dollar Rocket Buster cowboy boots in calf and kidskin, and a broad buff-coloured tie with port-wine skulls woven into it. A slender, mobile face, white from lack of sleep, made him look impermanent but determined. Ed would hang on, you sensed: he would endure. He would be there long after everyone else had left, or slept, or died. He had a Sony Sports Walkman in one hand – its headphones making a tinny noise like distant anger – and a cigarette in the other. He was shaking.

'Hi,' he said to me, putting two or three syllables into it. When he talked to you, he stared vaguely off over your left shoulder, as if he had seen something hallucinatory on the wall there. He gestured to his head. 'Robert Johnson,' he explained. '".38 Special". I have to hear it every day.'

'Well you do, don't you?' said Choe.

'Every day.'

'Ah,' I said, wondering what Isobel would make of that. 'Come up.'

In the end, she seemed rather charmed by him, perhaps because Ed was continually overcome by her cooking, groaning and murmuring in appreciation, then looking round to see if anyone had left anything he could finish. He switched the Walkman off but smoked Marlboros throughout the meal – holding them up close to his face, between the thumb and first two fingers, the remaining fingers loosely curled – and drank his Valentines in doubles, on the rocks. 'A while ago I thought I might be getting diabetes,' he confided, as he shovelled down the food.

'I'm surprised,' said Isobel.

'My grandpa developed it late. He was eighty.'

He looked uncertainly across the room.

'Is that a TV?' he asked. 'Do you all get CNN over here?'

'I think we only get the CIA,' said Choe.

Ed blinked.

'That's good, Choe,' he said.

He said: 'That's very good.'

We found him the Ceefax foreign news, an item of which immediately amused him; or seemed to.

RUSSIAN POLICE: SEVEN BODIES IN CAR

Russian police found seven bodies in a Mercedes that was being towed through St Petersburg last night. All seven had been shot and wrapped in a tarpaulin. According to reports, the car towing the Mercedes was being driven by an unemployed man from Dushanbe in Tajikistan, who was armed with a pistol. The owner of the Mercedes, described as a company director, was later found dead at his home.

Ed grinned around.

'I heard this was on,' he told us with a chuckle. ' "Company director." Isn't that fine?'

Isobel stared at him.

'I forgot,' he said. 'You guys didn't know Ive Kerensky, did you?'

Choe laughed.

'We'll never meet him now,' he said.

Ed stared at Choe, his smile fading. He took his cigarette out of his mouth.

'Some day you will,' he pointed out.

Choe looked away.

Isobel always worked hard to make her supper tables attractive. This one featured a centrepiece of stiff creamy-white lilies in a blue glass bowl which had originally belonged to her grandmother. From the start of the meal, Ed had been fascinated by the lilies, regarding them, as he became drunker and drunker, with expressions ranging from delight to puzzlement – as if he enjoyed seeing them there but couldn't work out what they were for. Now, suddenly, he reached out and with a movement almost too quick to follow, broke off one of the flowers and offered it to Choe.

'Hey, Choe,' he said: 'Want one of these?'

'No thanks, Ed,' said Choe. 'I've already had one.'

A complicated expression passed across Ed's features. Then

Signs of Life

he got up, switched off the TV and sat down on our Heal's sofa with the Valentines bottle and a fresh pack of cigarettes.

'So you guys move waste,' he said. 'Interesting trade.'

He stripped the cellophane off the Marlboros. 'Could you empty this ashtray, honey?' he called to Isobel. 'So where's the future for waste guys like you? Cribs? Trench dumping?'

'Not over here,' I said quickly.

I tried to explain: 'People won't accept that over here.'

'Well' – he pronounced it *warl* – 'no,' he said. 'Not right here in Great Britain. I was thinking of further east.'

He winked at Choe.

'I think the future lies further east for all of us, really,' said Choe.

'Here's your ashtray,' said Isobel. 'Do you want some ice cream?'

Ed saluted her.

'I was thinking of a long way further east,' he said, and lit another Marlboro from the stub of the last.

'Do you want some ice cream?'

Later he stopped shaking, but by then speech had become so difficult for him he had begun to lose his temper with it. He had finished a dish of Ben and Jerry's Chunky Monkey, stubbed out several Marlboros in the remains, then forgotten and tried to eat them with a spoon. Choe and I got him downstairs. It was two in the morning and, from Ed's ear-phones, Robert Johnson was still singing that he had a .32-20 and he guessed he'd burn in hell. Choe, who wasn't in much better condition than Ed, intended to drive him back to his hotel. 'I hope to God they get there,' I said.

'I hope to God they stay there,' Isobel said.

She came up and put her arms round my neck.

'Let's not do the washing-up,' she said.

She affected a corrupt drawl, wavering somewhere between Kentucky and the Upper West Side: '"Could you empty this *ash*tray, honey?"' She smiled. 'I really rather liked him.'

I smiled too, but I couldn't sleep.

'I'm not sure about Ed,' I admitted.

All evening his face – its powder whiteness, its curious dead-and-alive mobility, its air of being somehow both impish and ruined – had reminded me of someone. I couldn't think then who it was; although I was to remember quite soon.

Fourteen days later, Isobel and I descended into Hungary in a warm red light, the late sun blessing houses, woods and fields, the mist at the edge of the world. The approach was full of excitement; a great sudden swoop, then lots of manoeuvring. Servos whined, the control surfaces shifted, bronze light flickered suddenly along the wing. Banked hard over, the aircraft showed us long brown lanes, great tracts of birch and alder, roofs, smoke, a cemetery.

'I don't like it!' screamed a panicky toddler. 'I don't like it!'

'I love it,' whispered Isobel. 'I love it.'

She had never been out of Britain. Except in her dreams, she had never flown. She was as fascinated by the cramped seats and narrow aisle of the Tupolev as by the glimpse she got of its cockpit, finished a dull green and studded with obsolete little round dials; as delighted by the air-conditioning system and its bank of dirty plastic nipples as by the view out of her scratched and condensation-blurred plastic window. The interior design amazed her. She thought it was all part of flying. She craned her neck to stare at the other passengers – men with the soft brown eyes, dark moustaches and apologetic gazes of drunks, women whose heavy bodies and tired sensuous smiles would soon be shopping down by the Danube, wrapped in honey-coloured fur hats and coats.

'China, somebody has wallpapered the inside of this aeroplane.'

And then, in a fierce whisper:

'Are those *Hungarians*?'

'No,' I said.

I was enjoying it less than Isobel. Malev coffee had turned out to be instant, served with old-fashioned powdered milk which dissolved slowly and partially. I had flown before, in aircraft which did not have such obvious rivets.

I said: 'They're people who've just failed job interviews in Bolton.'

The toddler screamed. The Tupolev turned and swooped. Ferihegy airport rushed up to fill the windows. We filed down the boarding tunnel.

'Thank you and goodbye,' said the stewardess.

I had booked us into a hotel called the Palace, at the top end of Rakoczi Street on the Pest side of the river. That was a mistake. Like Budapest itself, the Palace had once been something: now it was a dump. Patches of render had fallen off its façade. Bare wires hung out of the light switches on the fourth-floor corridors. The wallpaper had charred in elegant spirals above the corners of each radiator. If the air was too hot, everything else – coffee, food, water from the cold tap – was lukewarm. But there we were at last, in the heart of Europe, where the hotel keys came attached not to a plastic tag but a strange hard black rubber ball, and clusters of opalescent lamps hung in the dining room like mystic grapes. There was a chambermaid, we discovered – a wispy, transparent old woman, who knocked very quietly at the door whenever we were in the room and made an incoherent attempt to speak German to us. And our room had french windows opening on to a balcony with wrought-iron railings, from which, bundled up against the freezing cold, Isobel could gaze at the other balconies, across a sort of high courtyard with one or two flakes of snow falling into it, each with its lovers, its yellow-lit window, its bottle of white wine left out to chill. That first evening, she loved it. She loved it all.

'China, isn't this romantic? Isn't it?'

'It is.'

'Well, put your arm round me then.'

'I wonder if Choe's here yet?'

'China!'

By the time we got downstairs it was late. Choe and Christiana had arrived, on a British Airways flight. We met them in the empty dining room, where the staff in their shabby striped waistcoats stood about quietly, adjusting a tablecloth or holding a knife up to the light. Next morning the same waiters would serve us eggs broken on to a layer of thin ham in the bottom of an oval glass dish, lukewarm and barely cooked. Christiana, asking for orange juice, would, after a twenty-minute wait, receive a glass of tepid orange squash. For now she stared around her, less startled by the frozen *Jugenstil* exuberance of the interior than by the way her cutlery had been presented, wrapped in half a carefully torn paper napkin. The first thing Choe said was:

'Mick, there's a fucking espresso machine over there with *three tits*.'

Then he said: 'Ed's in Szentendre.'

Isobel sighed.

'Look at this,' Christiana urged her. 'Have you ever seen anything like this?'

'He says he can't wait long,' Choe said.

'Good,' said Isobel.

Choe eyed her quietly for a moment.

He said: 'We should talk to him, Mick.'

Christiana put her hand on Choe's arm. She tried to show him the knife and fork. 'I can't believe this,' she said. 'Honestly, have you seen this?'

Without looking away from Isobel, he murmured:

'Will you just for now fucking shut up about the fucking cutlery?'

'Choe!'

Choe laughed.

'I mean, have a drink or something,' he said.

Budapest is a prime site for dreams: the East's exuberant vision of the West, the West's uneasy hallucination of the East. It is a dreamed-up city; a city almost completely faked; a city invented out of other cities, out of Paris by way of Vienna – the imitation, as Claudio Magris has it, of an imitation. Nineteen seventy-seven: representatives of fifteen countries gathered beside the

Danube to ratify the Budapest Treaty, a dream of a document which, coming into force three years later, would govern the patenting of genetically engineered micro-organisms. Patentability means profit: commercial biotechnology dreamed its own dream here, and was brought forth in a welter of kitsch and whipped cream, one dream dropping – as slippery as a sac of amino acids – from another.

The dream I woke from on our first night at the Palace Hotel was one of rooms; opening out in front and closing behind. (They were layered and imbricated, like a handful of photographs. They were strange and familiar, large and small. I entered them and left them. They were rooms.) I had dreamed it once before, in Peckham, after Ed Cesniak came to supper. Now, as then, he featured largely: a curious, 1950s comic-book figure, icon of menace or fun according to which room he occupied, wearing a black and green chequered revolving bowtie. Tarot cards showered from the cuffs of his plum-coloured jacket. A point of bright light winked from the edge of his undependable, caried smile. Towards the end of the dream he bent over our bed. Isobel was enchanted. With a drowsy laugh she invited him, 'See if you can fuck me without waking me up.' And that certainly woke me, sweating and dry-mouthed beneath the peculiar fake-fur bedclothes they give you at the Palace. It was 3 a.m. The bathroom was even hotter than the bedroom. It smelt faintly of very old piss. When I turned the cold tap on to splash my face, nothing came out of it. I stood there swaying in the dark.

In Peckham the dream had left me unable to sleep. Instead I had gone into the kitchen and washed up the supper things, and then spent the rest of the night staring down at the cars parked along the street. At nine the next morning Choe Ashton phoned to ask:

'Well, what do you think of him?'

'I don't know what to think. He reminds me of the Joker. You know? Batman and the Joker?'

'Sometimes I wonder about you, Mick.'

In Budapest there was no washing-up to do, so I went back into the bedroom and touched Isobel's shoulder.

'Isobel?'

She was fast asleep. Her dreams, I assumed, were the same as always. We can't know other people's dreams. Her face was pressed into the pillow, her mouth a little open; she looked hot and irritated in her sleep, like a toddler with an infection. 'I don't like Ed,' I whispered, perhaps in the hope that she would hear me and sympathise. Lukewarm water gushed suddenly from the tap I had left turned on in the empty bathroom.

Next morning it was bright sunshine.

In Budapest in winter you can always find your way to the Danube. The temperature drops as you approach, the cold is like a force pushing you away; at the same time, the light seems to increase, the streets become livelier and more modern, the arcades fill with western goods. We left the hotel at nine and walked down Dohany Street past the 'Moorish-Byzantine' synagogue with its patterned brick and pale onion domes; then via St Stephen's and the Vaci utca pedestrian precinct to Belgrad Quay. As we went, Isobel raced out in front of us like an excited dog.

'China! The river!'

There it was, immense, placid, rafted with ice, full of reflections. Light lay on the pink-gold water, on the bridges and on the churches of the Buda shore, as shimmering, nacreous and delicate as a thirteenth-century blessing. The air itself seemed like light; substanceless, vibrant. For a minute we blinked across at the mirrored spires, unable to think of anything to say; then crossed by William and Adam Clark's bridge and made our way up on to Castle Hill. There the air seemed denser but still clear, the wintry trees and yellow walls of houses distinct and photogenic, the infamous *faux*-Romanesque battlements of Fisher Bastion a perfect Disney-white. (Reflected imperfectly in the windows of the Hilton Hotel, these arches and little mushroom-capped towers already seemed drunken, melting, pixillated as a *Snow White* dwarf, as if the whole thing were made of sugar and cream collapsing over a base of sponge: the architecture of torte.)

'Shit hot,' Choe said.

'All those bridges,' whispered Christiana. 'Look at them in the sun.' She had bought a new camera for the trip, quite an expensive Pentax with a motor-wind and zoom. 'I want you all in this one. Stand over there, Choe. No, *there*, you idiot.'

Before he left the Palace that morning, Choe had carefully pushed back the sleeves of his unstructured Paul Smith jacket. Underneath it he was wearing a black cotton T-shirt. The whole time we were in Budapest, I never saw him dress for the weather. Now he shivered, turned up his collar and whistled through his teeth. 'Shit hot,' he repeated, but I could see he was beginning to be bored. 'I'm just going to make a phone call.' Five minutes later he emerged grinning from the Hilton lobby.

'Tomorrow,' he told me. 'Lunch.'

'I suppose we ought to do some business,' I admitted. 'Now we're here.'

At this, snow began to fall, in flakes the size of five-forint pieces.

'China,' cried Isobel. 'See?'

She took my right hand in both of hers and tugged. 'Come here,' she said fiercely. 'This is the most wonderful river in Europe, and now you are going to look at it.' She made me stand with her on the fan cobbles at the edge of the Bastion, where the snow eddied around us and down on to the bare trees and the broad elegant white stairs in the gardens below. Too close a look and you saw that the trees were full of plastic bags, the gardens trodden into bare frozen mud. Yet the tranquillity of the stone forced itself on this landscape of defeats; and on the other shore, Pest – a boom-town twice in one century – seemed to stretch away indefinitely into the east. 'China, I can see Dohany Street.' She hugged my arm. After a minute or two the snow thinned out, then stopped.

'Oh, damn. Oh, China, damn.'

*

Over the next three days Ed rang to cancel lunch at the Hilton, breakfast at the Hungaria coffee house and tea at the Gellert Hotel. Feeling more relief than agitation, I shopped for office space instead. Isobel came with me, and in the afternoons we toured the city. We photographed one another beneath the huge winged woman at the top of the Gellert Hill. We stared into hardware shop windows full of ordinary artefacts made bizarre by distance – tea-strainers, tins of shoe polish, Magyar Brillo pads as outlandish as a political slogan. We translated the titles of the newsstand paperbacks.

'What does this mean, "*Nagy Secz*"?'

'You know very well what it means, Isobel.'

I looked at my watch.

I said: 'It's time to eat.'

'Oh no. Must we?'

Isobel hated Hungarian food.

'China,' she would complain, 'why has *everything* got *cream* on it?'

But she was enchanted by the street signs, 'TOTO LOTTO', 'TRAFIK' 'HIRLAP'. She loved the underground with its bookstalls, display cases and echoing, brightly lit expanses of tiled floor, slicked and patterned like lace with muddy water brought in on boots. The city's drunks delighted her, the way they swayed through the traffic like marine life, eyes focused on something inside themselves, a soft, childlike expression of interest on their faces. She was entranced by hats – 'China, don't you love the *hats*!' – honey-coloured fur hats, caps with earflaps, watch caps, ski caps, woollen caps with a bobble on a string, flat round leather caps with a peak, pork-pie or Tyrolean hats, chubby with fake fur. She loved the red and grey buses. She loved the children, racing down the broad grand steps of the Nemzeti Museum.

On Thursday morning she got out of bed and pulled up the blind.

'China,' she cried.

'What?'

'China.'

Half an inch of snow had fallen on the balcony. We stood there naked and looked out. Snow. Snow out of Russia, snow which had swung stealthily across Central Europe towards us in the night, to lodge as icing on the cake façades and ornate ledges, fill the bent elbows of plaster caryatids beside the grandiose doors of every hotel on Dohany, plug the holes in the bonnet of each abandoned Trabant, gather in the forks of trees and, at last, muffle the sound of the taxis, slowing them down for just an instant to the speed of traffic in a normal city.

'China. Snow.'

Now Isobel could embrace Budapest at last – take the whole of it deep inside her without further thought and let it advantage her there – a city, white, clean, redeemed, dreamy, finally picturesque.

7
Trafik

In the Café Hungaria, where we had taken to breakfasting, we found Choe and Christiana. 'That waiter's actually rather nice,' Christiana was saying. She was already a bit drunk; or perhaps still drunk from the evening before. 'Well, he would be if they dressed him properly. He's got an unused look.' She kissed me hello and indicated her espresso. 'Why do you always get a glass of Andrews Liver Salts with this?'

'I've no idea, I'm afraid.'

'Oh, you're from *England*,' she said delightedly, as if we had never met before. 'For some reason I thought you were a local. It must be the haircut.'

I looked at Choe. He shrugged.

'Don't ask,' he said.

'It's snowing again,' Isobel announced. 'And I'm going to have two eggs.'

Although its Venetian chandeliers have long gone, the Hungaria, haunt of obsessive card-players and circus artists before the First World War, is still blowzy with arches, velvet curtains, little barley-sugar columns, mirrors and gilt ceilings, which every evening spray the light about above the heads of the diners in a kind of empty splendour. In the heyday of the Hungaria it was known as the 'New York', and the Danubian intelligentsia packed themselves in as tight as late arrivals on Ellis Island. They wrote polemic and edited journals. It was all laughter, politics and spilled ink. The playwright Ferenc Molnar threw the keys in the river, so that the waiters could never lock up.

Their caricatures remain, along with the marble floors and tabletops: but that morning the café was empty except for a few locals smelling of damp wool, clustered round a litter of espresso cups on a table near the door; and a tall middle-aged couple from Germany, who had come dressed as money. He wore fawn slacks and a cream cable-knit sweater. A black Filofax the size of the Old Testament was placed squarely on the table in front of him. Her delicate bony frame supported a string of pearls and a blouse with high padded shoulders. A sleepy heat prevailed.

Isobel sat down next to Choe.

'Look, Choe: Germans. Tell us what they're saying.'

But before Choe could open his mouth, Christiana proposed: 'He's saying, "My friend, an Albanian, has recently taken up kendo, but finds it difficult to buy a sword."'

Choe gave her a withering glance.

'No he isn't,' he said.

'Then he's saying: "Our neighbour's hedge has been eaten by a cow."'

'He's not.'

Christiana's smile faded.

'What is he saying, then, Choe?'

'He's saying fuck off,' Choe told her. 'He's saying invent your own game.'

He winked cheerfully at Isobel and turned his attention back to the 'international' edition of the *Guardian*. '"Very cold air from Russia,"' he quoted. 'But that was yesterday. Hardly worth one hundred and fifty forints. What the fuck is a forint?'

Christiana had started to cry quietly.

'Choe, you're such a fucking bastard,' Isobel said.

He thought for a moment and then grinned.

'I such a fucking am,' he said. 'Aren't I?'

'I've been looking at the map,' I intervened. 'Why don't we go to the zoo this afternoon?' I gave Choe what I hoped was a warning look. 'After we've seen Ed,' I said. Choe didn't seem to be interested. He stared into the sediment at the bottom of his espresso cup.

'I can tell fortunes,' he revealed.

I said: 'You mean, "You will go to a place with many fissures . . . ?"'

'". . . And meet a man whose right ear is upside down." Yes.'

Christiana brightened up.

'I want to see,' she said.

'No.'

'Let me see.'

Between them they upset the cup.

'Look at that.' Choe pushed his seat back and stood up. 'The future's ruined, you stupid bitch,' he said.

'Choe!'

'You stupid drunken bitch.'

'For God's sake, Choe,' Isobel said.

He beamed at her suddenly.

'Only joking.'

He sat down again and stared away at the junction of Dohany and Lenin.

'There's no fucking future here anyway.'

By now, the dirt which always blows about Budapest – dirt from the Hungarian Plain, fall-out from the chemical plants up and down the Duna, domestic dust from courtyards – had turned the melting snow into a kind of fawn syrup, which was being pushed aimlessly about by teams of street sweepers with old-fashioned brooms, while pedestrians quickly churned to espresso anything that remained. Over the road a little knot of people, perhaps the staff, were trying to get into the Horizont cinema, which had the look of all empty cinemas at ten in the morning. It was showing *Cocoon*. After a bit they separated, shrugging, and went away in different directions. An old man slithered into view through the traffic on Lenin. He had a hat with fake-fur earflaps, and he was pushing a long two-wheeled handcart piled with flattened cardboard boxes, trotting patiently up into his load like a horse.

'Look at that,' Choe appealed. 'Handcarts are still big business here.' He laughed. 'I bet he got that hat at Asda. Don't you?' In an attempt to mollify her, he touched Christiana's arm. 'Don't you bet he got that hat at Asda?'

Christiana wiped her eyes and looked away from him.

If the cafés make you drowsy with comfort, the cold streets of Pest soon wake you up again. Choe and I left the Hungaria shortly before eleven and walked north-east along Dohany towards Varosliget. Choe kept his hands in his pockets and his coat collar turned up. Around us the city became progressively less international. The snow was thicker. Currency touting was less a way of life. Every block was hollow, the way people once imagined the earth to be, containing secrets – a garden, washing lines, sometimes a shabby arcade of shops, where you couldn't buy a Kodak film, a cream cake, or a single postcard of the Chain Bridge at night.

After about ten minutes we came to a courtyard off Damjanich, behind the China Museum. Access was by tiled archway, high and dark. The arch framed a well of grey light into which snow fell as slowly as the snow in a Tarkovsky film, every flake intensely visible, making the courtyard seem at once depthless and too deep, a lighted space the revelatory nature of which could only be experienced from outside.

'This is it,' Choe said.

Five floors of apartments surrounded the yard. At first they seemed abandoned. Dry render was flaking off the walls. The balconies, strung with winter-browned ivy and dead vines like rotten electrical cable, were falling to pieces. But after a moment a door slammed a long distance away and I heard children rushing about on what I thought was the second floor. Eventually a woman came out of her flat to the dustbins. A strong smell of vegetable peelings filled the courtyard. She looked down at us and called out cheerfully in Hungarian.

'What's she saying, Choe?'

Choe looked at me and shrugged.

'She's telling us to invent our own game.'

The stairs were cold, though the people who lived there had

layered them with carpets – red, gold and black. Ed Cesniak was waiting for us on the fourth floor.

One room and a kitchen, that's how I remember it. Probably there were other rooms I didn't see. It was papered throughout in a water-streaked, pearlescent grey which had faded over twenty or thirty years from another colour. Most of the furniture had been pushed up against the walls, as if for some dull but desperately energetic dance, to reveal a black and white chequered floor-covering – less lino than a kind of compressed cardboard – buckled and worn into holes with sandy edges. The soft furnishings were burst or threadbare. From the kitchen issued a pervasive smell of wet gnocchi and paprika, steam from ancient boiled fish; beneath that the recent memory of a stopped-up toilet.

Ed's associates were lounging about in there like minicab drivers waiting for the pubs to close. To help pass the time they had set up three TVs, the largest of which, manufactured in East Germany, resembled a tank. They had it tuned to the local station, NAP – where someone who looked as if he used to run Butlins was interviewing someone who looked as if he used to run Bulgaria. The other two were Aiwas with flat screens, one downloading some sort of financial teletext from Tokyo via satellite link, while the other played a VTR tape loop – highlights from an old *Ren and Stimpy Show*, of which the cab drivers were clearly big fans. One of them grinned out at Choe as we came in. 'Play nice,' he warned, shaking his index finger.

Ed, who was sitting at a dining table in the main room, laughed loudly.

'Great guys,' he said. 'Great sense of fun.'

The table was covered in cigarette burns and overlapping ring-shaped stains. Veneers thin as a layer of varnish bubbled up at its edges to give a *mille-feuille* effect. In front of him on this corroded surface Ed had arranged a half-empty bottle of Absolut vodka, bought that morning on Vaci utca; a carton of two hundred Marlboros, as yet unwrapped; and his Sports Walkman, the batteries of which he was trying to replace. There was also a white ceramic bowl decorated with traditional designs like spidery drawings in dark blue ink. Ed would select a Duracell AA from the thirty or forty in the bowl: then, when it proved to be dud, throw it back in with the rest. The Sony headset was disconnected, but he was still wearing it. Every so often an exasperated expression would cross his features and he would work the earphones deeper into his ears, as if he wondered why he couldn't hear anything. His face was startlingly pale, filmed with moisture, the spots of high colour under the cheekbones exactly like those on the face of a ventriloquist's dummy.

'Could you get them to turn the noise down?' I asked him. I had to shout.

He shrugged. He could, though he seemed hurt to be asked. 'You should meet these guys,' he said. 'These guys used to steal cars with me.' He waved over at the men in the kitchen and they waved back. 'In the old days,' he said, 'we were moving a thousand units a week across the Polish border alone. We got them from all over – Mercs from Munich, Alfas from Amsterdam, BMWs from Birmingham.' He pronounced it *Birming Ham*. 'I once hid an 830 Csi under a ton of potatoes.' He chuckled. 'Adaptive gearbox and all. A ton of fucking potatoes!' He tried another battery. Nothing. 'Mind you, we never went much further than Minsk,' he said. 'Our part, we acquired the car, fitted it with papers and a driver, and took care of him maybe as far as the Beresina river.' He thought for a moment. 'Yeah. In some cases we would go that far. The Russians would take over from there. That was their part.' He lit another Marlboro, tried another battery. 'They were jealous about that,' he admitted. He blew smoke across the table. 'Still, everyone did business.'

'That's what counts, Ed,' Choe said.

'That's what counts, Choe,' Ed agreed pleasantly. 'I made money out of cars,' he told me. 'What I'm hoping to do now is move it over the hump.' He added: 'Crime to capitalism, tell me about it.'

'Hamlet Goes Business,' Choe said softly.

'Shut up, Choe,' I said.

Ed scooped a handful of batteries out of the Hungarian bowl and hurled them into the nearest corner, where they landed with a single compact thud, making a visible dent in the plaster.

'Fucking fuckers,' he said.

His associates chuckled amiably; you could see they had been waiting all morning for him to do something like that. On the TV, Ren and Stimpy began to break up. The story was that they had gone to another planet, lost their coherence and become no more than an ear, some wildly tapping fingers, a vapid ecstatic smile. 'Fucking fuckers,' Ed repeated, more quietly. He spread his hands out and examined them. He showed them to us. 'Still shakin' like a leaf,' he said. 'I want to move Russian know-how out. I want to move that other stuff in. The stuff we talked about.'

'Where's the profit?'

'Everywhere.'

Ed looked around him as if he was in a cartoon too, and I was in it with him, and the walls of the room were transparent. 'There's profit everywhere.' Then he laughed. 'OK. To you? Now? You corner the work from Brits who can't dump at home. You're cheaper than your competitors. More importantly, *you can handle stuff they can't.*'

He nodded vaguely eastwards.

'You can dump anything over there. Those people have been shitting in their own kitchen for sixty years.'

'What else?'

'You move product in the other direction,' he said. 'Secure containers, software.' He stubbed his cigarette out half-smoked on the table. 'That kind of thing.' Suddenly I noticed that his hands had stopped shaking. 'Nothing you don't already do.' He gave me a direct look and added: 'Except maybe live hosts.'

He said: 'Maybe the odd live host.'

'Animals?'

'Animals. People too. People need the work.'

I felt suddenly depressed and hopeless; I didn't know why.

Perhaps it was the smell from the kitchen. The painted white chairs and torn lino looked like a set from *Stalker*. They looked like furniture from a bed and breakfast in Barnsley in 1948. I got up and went to the door.

'I won't do that,' I said.

'For Christ's sake, Mick,' said Choe. He seemed genuinely worried, and I was glad. He pushed back his chair, which made a shrieking sound loud enough to hear above the TVs in the other room. One of the men in there wandered over and leant against the kitchen doorway. Unlike the others – who wore longish black leather jackets belted at the waist, or acrylic pullovers with simple black and white designs – he had on a suit. He was short, five foot three or four, with curly hair, a dirty blond colour, surrounding his hard triangular little face. The suit was a kind of forest-green corduroy. Its jacket was cut too tight across his shoulders and too loose at the waist. Its crumpled trousers gathered above his shoes. The effect of this should have been laughable: instead it seemed deliberate, a costume chosen to be raw and to offend.

He studied me, then grinned. 'Hey, Steempy,' he said. 'What's it all about?' He made a ring with the thumb and index finger of his right hand and moved it up and down rapidly in front of him.

'Get this fucker off me,' I said to Ed.

'He's advising you not to be a wanker all your life,' Choe said.

'Fuck you, Choe.'

'It's a universal sign, Mick.'

'Get him out of my way,' I said.

Choe made a tired, rejecting gesture of his own, then turned his back on me.

'For Christ's sake, Ed,' he apologised.

Ed Cesniak shrugged.

'If he won't deal, Choe,' he said, 'he won't deal.' He looked at me. 'Maybe another time,' he said. He coughed. Then he selected two batteries from the bowl and slipped them deftly into the

Sony. He plugged the headset in and switched on 'All the doctors in Wisconsin', Robert Johnson boasted tinnily out of the headset, 'sure couldn't help her none.' To leave we had to push out past the man in the suit. His bright blue eyes were full of broken veins, the taut skin over his cheekbones reddened and pitted. 'Steenky,' he said to me. 'Eh? Steeeenky.' He burst out laughing. He watched us go down the stairs and out into the snow.

Outside, Choe said:

'I'm just fucking puzzled, that's all, Mick. I'm just fucking puzzled as to why you aren't interested in making some fucking money.'

'Live hosts, Choe? Women with patents *in utero*?'

'Oh come on, Mick. You've done worse, only you just don't know it.'

I stopped and pushed him against the wall.

'I'd better not have, Choe,' I warned him. 'I'd better not have.' I felt very tired. 'He had a gun under his coat,' I said. 'I felt it there. The little bastard had a gun.'

In the parks, where it had been allowed to lie, the snow was two or three inches thick. The four of us walked across the northeastern tip of the Town Park, Varosliget, from Heroes' Square. It was our last day in Budapest. Bored soldiers hung about on the steps of the Museum of Fine Arts in fatigue trousers and earflap hats. In the distance strings of children skated to music on the ornamental lake. Attracted by the hot-food kiosks, then the shabby frontage of the circus featuring a giant poster of performing bears, we zigzagged towards the zoo: to find that the weather had rendered it miraculous, a little piece of some endless, entangled imaginary Middle European wood. The city sounds were absorbed by the snow before they penetrated to these softened trees, padded hummocks and blurred little pathways. Few animals were about. Isobel found a pair of white owls staring interestedly from their hutch at the weather; but even they had ceded their ambition to the crows. The crows pecked about half-heartedly, sometimes working themselves up into a ludicrous, floundering run.

It got dark. From the zoo we took a taxi across town to have tea. By now the snow was falling thickly again, huge flakes slanting through the street lights and on to the expensive German cars parked in front of the Gellert Hotel. Visibility was down to four or five hundred yards. A tram crept past in the direction of Lagymanyos. The river had vanished. We sat in the steamy heat and bright light, the smells of the coffee house – marzipan, ground hazelnuts, hot milk – and drank mocha-and-chocolate.

'It's like Christmas,' said Christiana.

She sniffed at the sleeve of her coat, then wiped at it ineffectually for the fourth or fifth time with a handful of paper napkins. She had already tried washing it at the sink in the women's room.

'Oh dear,' she said. 'I still smell.'

The big cats of Budapest zoo are kept in an Art Nouveau building which conceals a line of old-fashioned cages each fifteen feet by ten. The air in there is dark with ammonia and pheromones and the great coughing grunts of the trapped cats. Edging down the narrow viewing aisle that afternoon, we had come upon the biggest leopard I have ever seen, working itself into an extraordinary temper – pacing to and fro, turning suddenly on its haunches, slamming into the bars. Quick as lightning (as Christiana put it), the animal had presented her with its arse; quick as lightning, she had shrieked and jumped back. Too late.

Now she said:

'Animals are always doing that to me. A sea lion soaked me when I was eight.'

I was impressed.

'You've been pissed on by a sea lion?'

'No. It jumped into the water near me, and I was soaked. Later a pelican ate my best doll.'

She dabbed at her sleeve again.

'I never forgave it for that.'

'Not many people can say they've been pissed on by a leopard,' I pointed out.

Isobel said: 'It's probably lucky.'

'It fucking isn't,' said Choe. 'Nobody with any brains gets pissed on.'

By five o'clock the pavement outside the Gellert was white, the road a dark, chocolaty brown, the central reservation fawn, the far pavement white again. 'Oh no,' said Isobel. 'Layer cake. I'm going home.' For some reason we decided to walk back to the Palace. It was the rush hour. Ladas and Dacias huddled together on the bridges, slow and hesitant in the growing dark and flying snow. Electricity flared from the tram wires overhead in showers of blue-green sparks. The Margaret Bridge was packed with commuters spilling out of Pest, hunched and huddled in fur hats and coats, clutching their briefcases, shuffling through the slush. Isobel led the way. She still tended to walk ahead of us wherever we went; but now her hands were deep in the pockets of her dark blue rever jacket, and her stride had become the determined trudge of a child who has taken on too much but won't admit it. Halfway across the Danube she dropped back until she could put her arm through mine. She looked up at me; I smiled down in surprise. 'Pull me along, China. I'm cold and I'm tired.' For a moment we walked together like that. Then she murmured:

'China, will you do me a favour?'

'You know I will.'

'Will you talk to Choe about Christiana?'

I looked back. Choe and Christiana were dawdling some yards behind. I didn't know whether they had made it up yet, but they too were arm in arm. A foreign city will do that for you.

'Choe's not talking to me just now,' I said ruefully.

That evening Isobel and I ate alone at the Senora, a Korean restaurant which advertised, 'Grill yourself at the table without any smell'; then, planning to go to bed early, we went back to our room at the Palace. There we found that the chambermaid, tipped a few forints, had left us a new roll of lavatory paper – pink, but still with the texture of the stuff they give you to wipe your hands with at a motorway petrol pump – and a very small cake of scented soap (roses). Isobel was pleased.

'Oh good. Now I can have a wash.'

While we were undressing, I said: 'I've no idea what's got into Choe.'

'Oh, come on. It's so fucking obvious.'

'I'm sorry?'

'You're such a child. He's finally found someone he can be impressed by.' As if he was in the room with us, she congratulated him. 'Good choice, Choe: a fucking gangster.'

She looked at me in the mirror and smiled.

'The fact is, Choe's in love. Isn't that sweet?'

Budapest is rarely quiet, even late at night. The traffic, death oriented and wild like the ride of the Erl King, never stops. Ambulances and police cars warble musically past on their way to the carnage. Drunks scream suddenly or make noises like animals. From the start, these noises had worked themselves into our sleep: but all I dreamed of that night was the steward of the outgoing flight, Malev MAO116, with his sad eyes and soft black moustache. All night he pushed a trolley up and down the aeroplane aisle of my dreams, pronouncing the word 'dollars' as 'dollas' or even 'do las' . . .

'You like to buy something, please? Scarf for the lady? Tie for you? You like to buy something? It is very nice, this Chanel Number Five. You like to buy this tie?'

'WELCOME,' said the advert on the side of the trolley, 'TO THE CHEAPEST DUTY FREE IN CENTRAL EUROPE.' Discovering that the tie cost forty do las and realising with terror that I was going to make him an offer, I woke up to find a little grey light leaking through the metal shutters of the room. The heat was like magma in the central-heating pipes. The radiators were vibrating against the wall. I worked my tongue against the roof of my mouth. I sat up, swung my legs out of the bed and went over to look through the shutters. Isobel groaned and pulled the blanket over her.

She said reasonably:

'It's a system fault.'

After a moment she said, 'Oh no. Oh no,' in such a quiet and sad voice that I went back to the bed and touched her gently.

'Isobel. Wake up.'

She began to whimper and throw herself about.

'The system's down,' she tried to explain to someone.

'Isobel. Isobel.'

'The system.'

'Isobel.'

She woke up and clutched at me. She pushed her face blindly into my chest. She trembled.

'China.'

It was midnight, February, perhaps two years after we had met. I didn't know it, but things were already going wrong for her. Her dreams had begun to waste her from the inside.

She said indistinctly: 'I want to go back home.'

'Isobel, it was only a dream.'

'I couldn't fly,' she said.

She stared up at me in astonishment.

'China, I couldn't *fly*.'

She was inconsolable. In the end I made her get up and dress.

'Come on,' I said. 'It's not so late.'

'China, why?'

'We're going to find you a bridge.'

On the way we drank bitter espresso in an Italian restaurant at the corner of Regi Posta and Apaczai Csere Janos. The waiters were sleepy, but amused. They offered us torte and whipped cream, and a bottle of Chianti in a raffia basket. Behind the till was a notice which said in English: 'NOBODY IS UGLY . . . AFTER 2 A.M.' Isobel looked at the waiters and then pointedly at her watch. The waiters laughed. Outside in the street again, she hugged my arm. Her breath surrounded us, warm and comforting in the bitter night.

Signs of Life

'Trust us to find the worst restaurant in Budapest,' she said.

'I don't think I've seen Chianti bottles in raffia baskets since nineteen sixty-three. And that was in Coventry.'

'I wasn't born in nineteen sixty-three.'

'I know you weren't.'

She pulled me towards the river, a vast black sweep outlined in light, draped in light, to the Erzebet Bridge.

'I love it, anyway,' she said. 'China, I just love being here.' She said:

'Look. China, it's fucking huge. Isn't it fucking huge?'

I said: 'Look at the speed of it.'

We stood in the exact centre of the bridge, gazing north. Szentendre and Danube Bend were out there somewhere, locked in a Middle European night stretching all the way to Czechoslovakia. Ice floes like huge lily pads raced towards us in the dark. You could hear them turning and dipping under one another, piling up briefly round the huge piers, jostling across the whole vast breadth of the river as they rushed south. No river is ugly after 2 a.m. But the Danube doesn't care for anyone: without warning the medieval cold came up off the water and reached on to the bridge for us. It was as if we had seen something move. We stepped back, straight into the traffic which grinds all night across the bridge from Buda into Pest.

'China.'

'Be careful.'

You have to imagine this:

Two naive and happy middle-class people embracing on a bridge. Caught between the river and the road, they grin and shiver at one another, unable to distinguish between identity and geography, love and the need to keep warm.

'Look at the *speed* of it.'

'Oh China, the Danube.'

Suddenly she turned away.

She said: 'I'm cold now.'

She thought for a moment.

'I don't want to go on the aeroplane,' she said. 'They're not the real thing after all.'

I took her hands between mine.

'It will be OK when you get home,' I promised.

Everywhere in Budapest that night, mysterious and crude road repairs were being done. At one junction we found a shallow floodlit crater. A line of men holding strange, long-handled spades blinked benignly into the glare, while three engineers stared at the great mass of thin fibrous wires that had escaped from a broken telephone trunk line. Their hands were full of wire. Clearly they would never understand it. Just before dawn they would scratch their heads, stuff it all back into the conduit and go home, leaving the patient men with spades to fill in the hole.

One of the last things we saw, as the taxi conveyed us like parcels to the airport the next morning, was the graveyard of a little Serbian church, all its gravestones wrapped in sacking to insulate them against the frost, and its walls decorated low down with neat, careful reproductions of Western brand names – Adidas, Nike, Levi. They were less graffiti than cave-paintings, pictures of the prey. After that it was foggy leafless woods and lines of colour-washed houses – ochre, green, dark pink, pale blue – then motorways, diagrammatic beyond sense, slabs of cement raised on lines of tubular greyish-brown piers, all the way to Ferihegy.

The cab stopped suddenly.

'What is it?' I asked the cab driver.

He turned down the radio and said something in Hungarian.

'Can you make any sense of that, Choe?'

'I can't make any sense of anything mate. Not since yesterday morning.'

'Thanks a lot, Choe.'

'What's going on?' asked Isobel, who had been dozing on my shoulder.

As she spoke, someone opened the door nearest me and raw

wet air filled the cab. A boy of about twenty extended his big pale hand in front of us. There was a machine gun slung over his shoulder on a black leather strap. The sleeve of his combat jacket had a damp, somehow reassuring smell, like the clothes displayed outside the Army and Navy store on Camberwell Road. An empty landscape opened up behind him: a few trees; a wire fence; some fields, flat and snowy; and in the middle ground, three or four other men in uniform going through the boot of the car in front of us. You couldn't see the airport. You couldn't see the city. For a moment, in a place like that, nothing has any personal identity. The snow comes down. Water vapour billows up to meet it from the car exhausts. You sit and wait in your good-quality clothes, feeling like people trying to step carefully from one window ledge to the next, three floors above an empty street.

'Choe, have you and Ed done something?'

'*Done* something?' he said. 'It's passports, Mick. It's a passport check.'

'Passport and tickets,' agreed the boy with the gun. His eyes searched mine, flickered with a brief interest, only to retreat immediately into an apathy not so much personal as national. He had a cursory glance at our Malev boarding vouchers, then with an abrupt laugh motioned us on.

Choe grinned out of the window. 'Done something,' he mouthed silently.

'Fuck off,' I said.

'Don't be a wanker all your life, Mick.'

They were still searching the car in front of us. As the taxi moved slowly forward and around it, I thought I saw a civilian, a short blond-haired man wearing only a badly tailored corduroy suit and slip-on shoes despite the weather, pulling suitcases out of its boot. The soldiers had dropped back to let him get on with his work. He was opening the suitcases and dumping people's things in the snow in front of them, making no effort to hide his pleasure in the act. I was sure that if he saw us we would be stopped again. He would have us out of the car and into the snow; push his raw triangular face up close to Isobel's as he searched her; then empty her jeans and clean underwear on to the road. Finally, opening his coat to give her a glimpse of the 9mm pistol in its thick brown leather holster underneath, he would mimic the last thing he had heard me say, in the courtyard off Damjanich Street;

' "The bastar'. The little bastar' have a gun." '

8
What Could Happen

'It will be all right when we get home,' I had promised Isobel on the Erzebet bridge. But London didn't seem to help. For weeks I woke in the night to find she was awake too, staring emptily up at the ceiling in the darkness. Unable to comprehend her despair, I would consult my watch and ask her, 'Do you want anything?' She would shake her head and advise patiently, 'Go to sleep now, love,' as if she was being kept awake by a bad period. In the day it was different. Suddenly, the flat she had so loved seemed small, unsuitable, full of naive objects. As her dream of flight failed her she began to do pointless, increasingly spoiled things to herself. She caught the tube to Camden Lock and had her hair cut into the shape of a pigeon's wing. She had her ankles tattooed with feathers. She starved herself, as if her own body were holding her down. She was going to revenge herself on it. She lost twenty pounds in a month. Out went everything she owned, to be replaced by size nine jeans; little black Lycra skirts; expensively tailored jackets, which hung from their own ludicrous shoulder pads like washing.

'You don't look like you any more,' I said.

'Good. I always hated myself anyway.'

'I loved your bottom the way it was,' I said.

She laughed.

'You'll look haggard if you lose any more,' I said.

'Piss off, China. I won't be a cow just so you can fuck a fat bottom.'

I was hurt by that, so I said:

'You'll look old. Anyway, I didn't think we fucked. I thought we made love.' Something caused me to add, 'I'm losing you.' And then, even less reasonably: 'Or you're losing me.'

'China, don't be such a baby.'

We weren't always at one another's throats. I bought the house in Stepney at about that time. It was in a prettily renovated terrace with reproduction Victorian street lamps. There were wrought-iron security grids over every other front door, and someone had planted the extensive shared gardens at the back with ilex, ornamental rowan, even a fig. Isobel loved it. She decorated the rooms herself, then filled them with the sound of her favourite music: The Blue Aeroplanes, 'Your Own World'; Tom Petty, 'Learning to Fly'. For our bedroom she bought two big blanket chests and polished them to a deep buttery colour. 'Come and look, China. Aren't they beautiful?' Inside, they smelt of new wood. The whole house smelt of new wood for days after we moved in: beeswax, new wood, dried roses.

I said: 'I want it to be yours.'

It had to be in her name anyway, I admitted: for accounting purposes.

'But also in case anything happens.'

She laughed.

'China, what could happen?'

What happened was that Choe threw a tantrum.

Budapest had left him depressed and lethargic, a condition characterised in Choe by the short periods of ferocious, undirected enthusiasm which interrupted it. He went to the cinema every afternoon, but seemed confused when you asked him what he had seen. Later you found out he had been watching, over and over again, the opening twenty minutes of a film called *Stargate*. Such preoccupations caused him to lose interest in Rose Services. He was often late with deliveries; sometimes he failed to turn up at all. If he visited the office it was only to spend an hour reading out loud from the trade catalogues, an incongruous and over-produced literature that pitched its wares in the language of restriction enzyme and biocompatible liquid chromatograph:

'At last!' GenEx Plc International of Coventry were pleased to announce. 'We can offer Fractimaster, an attractively priced yet competitively specified low system for Gradient Elution Applications!' And they followed with the stark but chatty: 'Work Safe with Radiochemicals!'

'Listen to this, then, Mick.'

'Choe, I'm trying to work.'

'No, honestly, you'll kill yourself if you miss this one. Listen.'

'Choe.'

'But just listen to this.'

'What?'

' "Samples from the Dissolution Bath." '

'It's good,' I had to admit. 'But not as good as "Large volumes of mobile phase".'

There were no limits to biosupply, an industry so new and expansive it couldn't keep up with its own jargon, or indeed invent new jargons fast enough: there was no end to the money that could be made. We were taking on a lot of contract work the medium-sized companies like Abney no longer had time to handle. But there were bigger and more interesting fish floating around down there in the standing pool. It would have been useful to have help netting them. When he put himself out, Choe could be impressive. The biologists – overweight boys who, barely out of university, had already taken up golf and a once-a-week facial sauna – were charmed despite themselves by his stories of solo rock-climbing and fast motorcycles. He got them tickets for ENO, and they loved that too. But now, when I asked him to be at a meeting, he would only shrug and say vaguely, 'Nothing real is ever worthwhile.' And then: 'Nothing worthwhile is ever real.' Or he would arrive at the offices of HDC Biotech, D'Courtney Cabe or FUGA-OrthoGen and refuse to come in. We would have an argument in the lobby or a corridor, which he would terminate by shouting:

'Why should I take any notice of a bunch of fucking twenty-five-year-old wankers in *chinos*?'

'Because they're our bread and butter.'

'Off to fucking conferences in fucking Marks and Spencer shirts—'

'Choe, they can hear you.'

Who gives a shit? You know what, China? You know what?'

'What?'

He lowered his voice.

'Every one of them is already infected.'

'What?'

'*E. coli*, mate. Mutated *E. coli*. Class five organism. Dormant now, but in ten years' time—'

'Oh, for God's sake, Choe.'

'Know what it'll do then, Choe? Eh? Go on: ask me. Ask me what it'll do in ten years' time.' And then, on an ascending triumphant note when I refused to join in: 'Melt the fucking fat off their bones. Melt it off like wax off a fucking scented candle.' He grinned. 'They'll *shit* it off, Mick. To the accompaniment – no, listen, *to the accompaniment, mate*, of sensations so pleasant as to amount to ecstasy.'

The business bored him. It was too successful. It was too ordinary. He wanted a share of Ed Cesniak's world. He wanted to be a gangster. He drew into himself and became elusive in a way no one – not me, and certainly not Christiana Spede, it turned out – could engage.

Two or three weeks after we came back, he sent me an expensive old edition of Turgenev's *Sketches from a Hunter's Notebook*, on the front endpapers of which he had written in his careful designer hand:

> Turgenev records how women posted flowers – often pressed
> marguerites and immortelles – to the child-murderer
> Tropmann in the days before his execution. It was as if
> Tropmann were going to be 'sent on before'. Each small
> bouquet or floret was a confused memory of the pre-Christian

plea 'Intercede for us', which accompanied the sacrifice of the king or his substitute. But more, it was a special plea: 'Intercede for me'. These notes, with their careful, complex folds, arrived from the suicide provinces – bare, empty coastal towns, agricultural plains, the suburbs of industrial cities. They had been loaded carefully into their envelopes by white hands whose patience was running out between their own fingers like water.

I phoned him up.
'Choe, what a weird quote. Where did you come across it?'
'I'm not stupid, you know,' he said, and put the phone down. He had written it himself. For two weeks he refused to speak to me, and in the end I won him round only by promising him I would go to the Tate and spend a whole afternoon with the Turners. He shivered his way down to the Embankment from Pimlico tube station to meet me. The sleeves of his jacket were pushed up to his elbows, to show off slim, but powerful forearms tattooed with brilliantly coloured peacock feathers which fanned down the muscle to gently clasp his thin wrists.
'Like them? They're new.'
'Like what, Choe?'
He laughed. I was learning. Inside the gallery, the Turners deliquesced into light: *Procession of Boats With Distant Smoke*, circa 1845; *The Sun of Venice Going Down to Sea*, 1843. He stood reverentially in front of them for a moment or two. Then the tattooed arms flashed, and he dragged me over to *Pilate Washing His Hands*.
'This fucker though. It can't have been painted by the same man.'
He looked at me almost plaintively.
'Can it?'
Formless, decaying faces. Light somehow dripping itself apart to reveal its own opposite.
'It looks like an Ensor.'
'It looks like a fucking Emil Nolde. Let's go to the zoo.'

'What?'

He consulted his watch. 'There's still plenty of daylight left,' he said. 'Let's go to the zoo.' On the way out he pulled me over to John Singer Sargent's *Carnation, Lily, Lily, Rose*. 'Isn't that fucking brilliant?' And, as I turned my head up to the painting, 'No not that, you fucking dickhead, the *title*. Isn't that the most brilliant title in the world? I always come here to read it.'

Regent's Park. A cold April. Trees like fan coral. Squirrel monkeys with fur a distinct shade of green, scatter and run for their houses, squeaking with one high-pitched voice. A strange, far-off, ululating call – lyrical but animalistic – goes out from the zoo as if something is signalling. Choe took me straight to its source: lar gibbons. 'My favourite fucking animal.' These sad, creamy-coloured little things, with their dark eyes and curved arthritic hands, live in a tall cage shaped like a sailing vessel. Inside, concrete blocks and hutches give the effect of deck and bridge fittings. The tallest of these is at the prow, where you can often see one gibbon on its own, crouched staring into the distance past the rhino house.

'Just look at them,' Choe said.

He showed me how they fold up when not in use, the curve of their hands and arms fitting exactly into the curve of their thigh. Knees under their chins, they sit hunched in the last bit of afternoon sun picking over a pile of lettuce leaves; or swing through the rigging of their vessel with a kind of absent-minded agility. They send out their call, aching and musical. It is raw speech, the speech of desires that can never be fulfilled, only suffered.

'Aren't they perfect?'

We watched them companionably for a few minutes.

'See the way they move?' Choe said suddenly. Then: 'When someone loves you, you feel this whole marvellous confidence in yourself. In your body, I mean.'

I said nothing. I couldn't think how the two ideas were linked. He had turned his back on the cage and was staring angrily away into the park where, in the distance, some children were running and shouting happily. He was inviting me to laugh at him. When I didn't, he relaxed.

'You feel good in it,' he said. 'For once it isn't just some bag of shit that carries you around. I—'

'Is that why you're trying to kill yourself?'

He stared at me.

'For fuck's sake,' he said wearily.

Behind us the lar gibbons steered their long strange ship into the wind with an enormous effort of will. A small plaque mounted on the wire netting of the cage explained: 'The very loud call is used to tell other gibbons the limit of its territory, especially in the mornings.'

I thought that was a pity.

'This is a bit different from the last zoo we were in,' I said; but Choe didn't answer.

'China, what could happen?'

What happened was that a couple of months later, in early June, I had a phone call from Christiana.

'Is Choe with you?' she said hesitantly.

She hadn't seen him for a week.

'Neither have I,' I said. 'I shouldn't worry, Christiana.'

'You're as bad as he is.'

She rang off.

The next day she came into my Bermondsey office with Isobel. Outside in Ilderton Road they had a black cab with its meter still running, and they were struggling with two or three large pieces of Louis Vuitton luggage. Christiana kept her head turned away and wouldn't look at me. She was crying openly, sniffing and wiping her nose with the back of her hand. She had smeared lipstick across her cheeks, and her eye make-up had run down to join it. She looked tired and defeated. But Isobel was furious enough for both of them.

'What's going on?' I said.

Isobel gazed at me as if she wasn't sure what species I belonged to.

'Your friend walked out on her,' she said. 'I don't suppose you know where he is?' It was less a query than a sneer; and she wouldn't say anything more until she had got Christiana back into the cab, which pulled away north towards Rotherhithe and the tunnel. Isobel watched it go, then came and sat down wearily on the end of my desk. 'Sometimes I wish I smoked,' she said. When I tried to hug her, she moved away. She indicated the luggage.

'Christiana wanted to do this by herself. I told her his stuff was too heavy.'

'What's happened?'

At first she wouldn't answer. Then she said:

'I never liked that little bugger.'

'I know, Isobel—'

'When you do see him, give him these' – she kicked one of the suitcases – 'and ask him what he said to her to finish it.'

'Isobel—'

'Just ask him.'

I shrugged. I knew she would tell me when she calmed down. 'Whatever you think,' I said, 'I honestly don't know anything about this.'

'You'd better not, China.'

It was a few days before Choe phoned me.

'Ay up, Mick.'

'That's not going to get you anywhere, Choe.'

'I know, Mick. I know it isn't.'

There was a pause. Then he laughed.

'I suppose I just can't stop doing it,' he said, as if he was talking about someone else – someone whose Martian levels of dissociation and unreliability impressed even him.

'I suppose she hates me,' he said: 'Christiana.'

'For God's sake, Choe.'

He said: 'I could do with a beer.'

We met that afternoon. It was London summer: dogs barking; air baked yet humid; the continual unresolved murmur of conversations in the street. We sat on the Victoria Embankment, on a bench in the shade of a plane tree, and, surrounded by the continual groan and thud of the traffic, had a look across the river. The tide was down as far as the first pier of Waterloo Bridge, beneath which roiled water the colour of milk chocolate. Seagulls busied themselves on the shingle, planing out of the Embankment shadow and into the sunlight, then back again. The receding water had sorted the stones into neat lines and strands. Pleasure boats patrolled up and down, stubby and peeling. That afternoon the whole of the Strand – street after street spread out in the strong sunlight – had smelt of roasting coffee.

'Did you have to tell her she was old?' I asked him.

Instead of answering directly, he said:

'For weeks I thought I could hear a dog howling two or three houses down the street. But when I went out there was nothing there. No noise, no dog. Then, as soon as I was back inside again . . .'

He looked suddenly restless, got up, said, 'Let's have a look at Cleopatra's Needle,' and as we walked went on: 'It was a delusion, Mick. There was no dog. Have you ever had anything like that?'

I didn't know how to answer.

He stopped and stood in front of me so that I had to stop too.

'I'm really serious, Mick. Some buried part of me had cracked. It was giving out this signal.' He began to laugh. 'Mick, that howl was a sign of *deep inner mourning*.'

'Oh, grow up, Choe.'

'I got you, though, didn't I? You believed me.'

'Just grow up.'

When we arrived at the Needle it was surrounded by tourists: Germans amused by the Victorian lamp standards with their bizarre design of intertwined fish; Japanese photographing barges in midstream – THAMES & GENERAL LIGHTERAGE COMPANY. A woman on her own stared at us, then thoughtfully down the waterstair.

'We never fucked, anyway,' said Choe. 'Christiana and me.'

Then he said:

'It was making *me* feel old.'

A light breeze brought us the smell of the Thames mud, causing the tourists to laugh uneasily and move away.

'You're a bastard, Choe.'

'I know, I know.'

He grinned.

'It's better than being a wanker though. Don't you find that?'

'China, what could happen?'

What happened was that I asked Isobel to make a delivery for me. The way it happened was this: Choe had been filling in. Without him, I had to reshuffle to cover my national commitments. As a result I was temporarily down on local help.

I told Isobel: 'It's not far. Just across to Hammersmith. Some clinic.'

I passed her the details.

'A Dr Alexander. You could make it in an hour, there and back.'

She stared at me.

'*You* could make it in an hour,' she said.

She read the job sheet.

'What do they do there?' she asked.

I said irritably: 'How would I know? Cosmetic medicine. Fantasy factory stuff. Does it matter?'

She put her arms round me.

'China, I was only trying to be interested.'

'Never ask them what they use the stuff for,' I warned her. 'Will you do it?'

She said: 'If you kiss me properly.'

'How was it?' I asked, when she got back.

She laughed.

'At first they thought I was a client.'

Running upstairs to change, she called down:

'I quite like West London.'

*

'China, what could happen?'

What happened was that, in the end, nothing helped.

When I think about that time now, I see us like this:

We are in the nice new kitchen area in Stepney, with its Whirlpool hob and pale oak floor. We are pursuing a dull argument about ourselves, or about Choe Ashton. Isobel, who has a summer cold, is trying to ease her sinuses according to some prescription of Margaret Avens' involving an infra-red lamp which she has arranged on the stainless-steel work-top. The lamp surrounds her head with a violent corona, throws pale green shadows on the white walls. She leans forward and stares intently into it with closed eyes. Sitting the other side of the beechwood table on a rattan chair from Heal's, I hold the *Daily Telegraph* up to the side of my face to keep from being dazzled.

I see this as a photograph, oblique and odd, without any aids to interpretation. Who are these two people, in their little open-plan house which runs the kitchen seamlessly into a quasi-minimalist living room relieved by one or two framed Leendert Blok autochromes of tulips? How do they relate to one another? The photographer is not telling us. We see the books on the shelves, the litter on the table, the infra-red reflected like a tiny star from the flat black screen of the television. A telephone with answer-, fax- and call-splitting facilities. On a side table, two pieces of chalk like lumps of eroded bone. These things are not in any sense aids to navigation. We are left with a feeling that everything in the room is alienated from everything else. A photograph you might put down with a shiver, a film from which you might walk out because it is too modern to understand.

In late June or early July we had a short holiday in Tenerife. Neither of us wanted it. 'I suppose I can just lie on the beach for a week,' Isobel said. In the event she rarely got that far, but sprawled face-down on a recliner on the tiled surround of the San Marino Apartments pool, while I drove a rental SEAT to Las Cañadas and the El Teide parador; or toiled upwards in the heat under the blistered walls of the Barranco del Infierno. Caught in the slanting light of early morning, the distant pantile roofs and campaniles of the partly finished Los Cristianos hotels and bars took on a translucent quality, as if they were made of porcelain. But in the afternoons the sunlight was like a fierce violet transparency laid across the burnt beachfronts, rubbish, stray cats and dogs, old people who stared into space, the English girl in the wheelchair pushed by the fat boy with the butterfly tattoo. (They had hoped for so much, they told me, before she contracted muscular dystrophy. They were going to have this holiday anyway, 'Whatever happens.') And there! Lizards! A flicker of bitter light off a broken terracotta tile. Balconies replicated giddily in the sun; and the squared-off helices of the exterior staircases, with their hanging mats of pink and purple flowers, ascended diagrammatically towards the air where all buildings finish and can never go.

I thought: It's the perfect place for people like us.

Isobel, photographed sunbathing at Médano:

She lies on her stomach, the upper part of her body raised on her elbows, her skin shiny with Clarins sun lotion. She has a drink, a towel, an unopened book. I hardly recognise her. Heavy-framed Raybans make her seem oracular, equivocal: half skin-diver, half sphinx. Half pilot. Is it her – can three halves be anything at all? – or quite some other woman? The beach curves away in the background to something that might be rocks or, equally, a laurel forest.

'China, what could happen?'

What happened was this:

One afternoon, a week after we got back, she came downstairs to the living room, where I was trying to read a book called *The Language of the Genes*. We hadn't been speaking. Since Tenerife she had spent her mornings on the phone, then taken herself off to shop in a preoccupied way at Waitrose, where she bought oranges, olives, anything that reminded her of the sun. She came

Signs of Life

and stood by the arm of the sofa. I took my reading glasses off and looked up at her.

'Hi.'

'Hi.'

She looked at me uncertainly.

'China, I want to talk to you.'

I knew exactly what she was going to say.

'China, I . . .'

There was a kind of soft thud inside me. It was something broken. It was something not there any more. I felt it. It was a door closing, and I wanted to be safely on the other side of it before she spoke.

'What?' I said.

'It's . . .'

'What?'

'China, I haven't been happy. Not for some time. You must have realised. I've got a chance at an affair with someone and I want to take it.'

I stared at her.

'Christ,' I said. 'Who?'

'Just someone I know.'

'Who?' I said. And then, bitterly: 'Who do you know, Isobel?' I meant: Who do you know that isn't me?

'It's only an affair,' she said. And:

'You must have realised I wasn't happy.'

I said dully: 'Who is this fucker?'

'It's Brian Alexander.'

'*Who*?'

'Brian Alexander.'

I had no idea who she was talking about. Then I remembered. 'Christ,' I said. 'He's just some fucking *customer*.'

She went out. I heard the bedroom door slam. I stared at the books on the bookshelves, the pictures on the walls, the bar of dusty gold afternoon light. I couldn't understand why it was all still there. I couldn't understand anything. Twenty minutes later, when Isobel came back in again carrying a soft leather overnight bag, I was standing in the same place, in the middle of the floor. She said:

'Do you know what your trouble is, China?'

'What?' I said.

'People are always just some fucking this or that to you.'

'Don't go.'

Two days later, when it was clear she wouldn't come back, I left the house and moved in with Choe Ashton, who had bought the upper maisonette of two in a large, shabby Edwardian house just off Green Lanes, midway between Turnpike Lane and Manor House. Like much he owned it was expensive but disused-looking, as if he had loved it once and then walked away. There were French film posters on the walls and piles of fading adventure-sport magazines subsiding day by day into dusty moraines on the living-room carpet. I found its shabbiness intensely comforting. Not that I had much comfort at that time.

9
Fuck Everything and Run

Afternoons were the worst.
So were evenings.
Nights were the worst.
I kept imagining her at orgasm. It made me masturbate helplessly. I had her mixed up with the Sophia of Valentinus. I had her mixed up with my own anima. I had her mixed up with Kate Bush, singing 'Hounds of Love'. You can't get much more mixed up than that. Staring up at the ceiling of my room, hearing the restless creak of the cheap wicker rocking chair downstairs in Choe Ashton's lounge as Choe watched *Nigel Mansell's Indycars* late into the night, I would begin to miss her for no reason, only to realise after a moment what the noise reminded me of: the slow, delighted rhythm of sex in some hotel- or boarding-house bed when we were still new to one another.
Mornings were the worst.

Listen. I'm not here now. I'm free now. Nothing has ever happened between me and Isobel Avens. All I'm doing now is driving slowly through the wet city streets in my favourite car. Make? I've had them all. Model? You choose. The interior has that unmistakable smell, acrid and comforting at the same time, of new plastic trim. The sound system – let's say it's a 120-watt Alpine RDS CD tuner with a six-disc changer in the boot – is playing Patti Scialfa, 'Rumble Doll' from the album of the same name, so quietly I can almost hear it, while the lights of approaching vehicles star out in the droplets of water on the unswept part of the windscreen. Brake lights flare ahead. Traffic lights change from orange to red. Intersections appear slowly and slowly move away, to the right or the left and always to the rear. Brightly lit shop windows drift by, full of comforting goods. I'm not driving quickly. Do you understand? I am making only the required decisions. While I drive with care and keep the music low, nothing that can happen to me here is significant. I may reach absently into the glove compartment, looking for something I have forgotten even as my hand touches it. A paper tube of sweets. A book of matches (Ruby in the Dust, Camden Town, her favourite restaurant for a week). A packet which contains one cigarette. I may even light the cigarette, although I have not smoked for twenty years. But I will never leave the city however far I drive. Johnny Rocket's Original Hamburger will precede Hip Bagels. Each pizza house will be succeeded by a Thai palace recommended – as Thai palaces inevitably are – by *Time Out*. Patti Scialfa will pass on to 'Spanish Dancer', just loud enough to hear, but never loud enough to centre herself in my awareness.

I can do that because I'm free now.

To start with, I was unwilling to drive. Everything was raw. Everything stuck out at the wrong angle. Everything was amputated, or needed amputating. Do you know what I mean? Everything smelt too strong in the mornings. All I had was panic and the sudden sickening calm that follows it, as if you have been given a painkilling drug you don't want. I felt like an invalid. If I drove my car, I told myself, I would only make some appalling error of judgement. Lose interest suddenly and run over a pedestrian. Coast to a halt on the South Circular somewhere near Catford, having forgotten who or what I was, while the early-morning traffic piled up behind me, at first confused and then enraged.

I couldn't drive so I walked. I walked the first week away. I got up early every day and, in Caterpillar boots and a leather coat, walked to Turnpike Lane tube station. Then I walked back. It was always raining, and I took care at kerbs. I knew I wasn't fit to be allowed out. But what else was I to do? As long as I was moving I could eat, even at seven a.m., when eating is hardest for the recently bereaved, the recently divorced, those who have lost their children or their houses or their jobs or all of those things. The recently dead, as Choe Ashton was later to put it. First I could eat a hot bacon sandwich. Then I could remember which café to order it from. Then I could begin to wonder why every morning as early as half-past seven there was an old woman reading Lawrence Durrell in the Green Lanes all-night launderette. It's true. She had grey, thinning hair, spectacles with violet frames, a pink crocheted top over pale blue cotton trousers, Dr Scholl sandals. Her skin was stretched and full of broken veins, her ear-lobes swollen, her upper chest reddened, grainy and mottled, as if she had recently spent time in the sun. She wore an old-fashioned man's watch with an expanding metal bracelet. By her feet was a green cloth shopping basket. She would read a paragraph of *Mountolive*, look up with a vague, digestive expression. There was her washing, going round in the machine.

Then one morning I put an old pair of Adidas squash shoes on and went out to look at my car. It was still parked half up on the disintegrating pavement a few yards down from Choe's house, where I had left it with the driver door hanging open the evening I arrived. Choe had locked it up, but he hadn't taken care of it. Scraps of waste paper were plastered to its windscreen. There were streaks of road mastic running down from the old wiper marks at the rear. In the dirt, someone had written with a finger: 'LORA IS A SPOLT BITCH.' It looked abandoned already. But when I disarmed the security system, and got in, and turned the key in the ignition, it started immediately. Welcome home, I thought. I released the handbrake. I selected first gear, let the clutch come up, and faces appeared at windows all along the street. One and a half hours later I was drinking pale grey coffee from a styrofoam cup in a petrol station on the outskirts of Stratford-upon-Avon. I rang Choe.

'Jesus, Choe,' I said. 'Where am I?'

Choe said: 'Fucked-up Street.' He laughed. 'How would I know, dickhead? Can you see any road signs from there?'

'I can't see any fucking thing.'

We both laughed. I could hear music in the background. If I turned up the gain on the Vodafone and listened carefully I could hear Lou Reed singing 'What's Good' from *Magic and Loss*. *Magic and Loss* was Choe's favourite album that month, just as *Rumble Doll* was mine; and 'What's Good' was his favourite track.

'I bet you can't get back here before half-past eleven,' he said.

I looked at my watch.

'What's good, Choe?' I asked him.

He said: 'Not much at all. I bet you can't do it.'

He was right. But I got a hundred and thirty up on the clock somewhere south of Oxford, in broad daylight, with all my lights on.

'I'm back, Choe.'

'That's what you think today, sucker.'

After that, from being my worst, mornings became my best time. I drove to Dunwich in Suffolk and walked along the beach; I drove to Cambridge, I drove to Reading.

I often went back to Stratford, where I sat in the cool early-morning air on Waterside, watching the river go past and whispering, 'You fucking bitch, Isobel. You fucking spolt bitch.' And once I drove to the car-park of the Woodcotes Country Hotel, and tried there to remember our first night together. All that came back was our first fuck. All that came back was saddle of lamb with rosemary, the fat Colin with his safe pair of hands and Isobel saying, 'Colin and Jenny deserve to have the best time they can. You mustn't feel superior to them.' I couldn't for the life of me now see why. It was lunchtime, but nobody was in the place. Beyond the deserted car-park, through a dark fringe of hedge, I could see a field. There was a single magpie hopping about in it. One for sorrow, I thought, and then rejecting that instantly: fuck off. Wherever I went after that, it was *one for sorrow, fuck off.* Wherever I went I rang Choe from the Vodafone and asked him where I was.

Choe hated it. 'You moron, I was asleep.' By the time I got home he had managed to make himself a cup of tea and, in a black singlet and a pair of those very loose, pleated black trousers Asian boys wear, was sprawled in the rocking chair watching television. The dusty, buff-coloured curtains were still drawn. His tattoos seemed to fluoresce in the stale light. Whenever he was at home he watched TV all day. He liked cartoons. He liked *Biker Mice From Mars, Talespin, Rude Dog and the Dweebs.* (Rude Dog, the cool California bull terrier, had an outline so radical it made him look like a diagram of a dog, a fashion sketch of a dog done with one economic line.) But much of the time he sprawled on the sofa and watched with the sound turned down.

'I'll fucking kill you if you do that,' he said, the first time I walked into the front room and tried to turn it up.

'Choe, it's the news.'

'Who gives a fuck? This is *prophecy*.' He grinned. 'Prophecy's more important.'

I stared at him wearily.

'Choe—'

'Look, I'll show you how to do it.'

He made me sit down. He gave me the TV control.

'Change the channels,' he said.

He said: 'Watch.'

He said: 'What do you see?'

On all four channels people were opening doors. The news they got was good, bad, good, good.

'See?' said Choe. 'A good chance of success in any project you might be pursuing.'

'Choe—'

'That's a very pure example, of course. It makes the method easy to understand: good news outweighs bad.'

He took the control from me.

'But what if you turn on the set to find one man looking out of a caravan window, while another one seems to be straining his head in through the same opening to look out of the set and talk to you?' Surfing absently into cable – I saw Hitler, I saw Stalin, I saw a snowboarder wipe out on some almost vertical slope, I saw a fraction of a scene from *Basic Instinct*, fat Michael Douglas, every woman's dream – he said: 'What if they both look dead? I suppose you can switch to another channel for confirmation: any direct mailing ad, especially one for stain-remover – stay at home that day; *Gardeners' Question Time* – perhaps not so bad, but avoid dogs.'

Suddenly, he switched the set on to standby and swivelled round on the sofa to stare as closely into my face as Isobel had ever done.

'Whatever you do,' he said, 'when using this method, *never turn up the sound.*'

He got up and stretched.

'What's for lunch?' he said.

I hated to eat with him.

'Know what my favourite food is?' he had said one day. 'I bet you can't guess. Go on. Try.'

'I don't know, Choe.'

'Told you. Well, it's this: get fish and chips from down the Green Lanes chippie, melt half a pound of St Agur cheese over it in the fucking microwave.'

He licked his lips.

'Brilliant,' he said. Then:

'You don't think I mean it, do you?'

How could anyone tell what Choe meant? He was working on the rigs again, two weeks on, two weeks off. He had more money than ever. He was more restless than ever. He was more unassuaged. Enthusiasms passed through him in a week, left him shaking but complacent. His life was full of objects but drained of anything else. He seemed to relish that. He would not talk about Christiana. He gave up kick boxing and took up cave diving. 'The most dangerous fucking sport in the world.' He bought two or three compact discs a day. His tastes were fluid:

Lou Reed, Joe Satriani, a brilliant Brazilian jazz guitarist called José Neto he had heard one night at Ronnie Scott's. 'Listen to this. It's fucking amazing,' he would insist, play it the once, and stop listening halfway through, his expression sliding into vagueness. He took up mountain biking, and bought a machine the composite *frame* of which cost fifteen hundred pounds. 'Just look at that,' he would whisper in awe. 'Isn't that fucking obscene?' It hung on the wall of the lounge, its exotic alloys glowing with interference patterns, like a huge insect: within a week it was gathering dust. A week after that he had given up his job.

'I'm going to take the CBR round Europe,' he said in explanation. 'You need the dosh to pay the speeding tickets.'

He thought for a moment. 'I like Europe.'

And then, as if trying to sum up an entire continent:

'I once jumped over a dog in Switzerland. It was just lying in the middle of the road asleep. I was doing a hundred and ten. Bloke behind me saw it too late and ran it over.'

'Have a good time, Choe.'

He was away for two weeks. The day he came back it was the last good weather of summer.

'Ay up, kid,' he said.

He was wearing Levi 620s, brand new sixteen-hole DMs, a black sleeveless T-shirt, which had faded to a perfect fusty green, and a single gold ear-ring. We had a drink, then drove over to Camden and walked up between the market stalls to Camden Lock, where we sat in the sunshine blinking at the old curved bridge which lifts the towpath over the canal. Choe's arms had been baked brown in Provence and Chamonix, but the peacock feathers still rioted down them, purple, green and electric blue, a surf of eyes; and on his upper left arm one tiny perfect rose had appeared, flushed and pink.

'How was Europe?' I asked him.

'Fucking brilliant,' he said absently. He seemed nervous. 'It was great.'

'Get many tickets?'

'Too fucking right.'

'I like the new tattoo.'
'It's good.'
We were silent for a bit. Then he said:
'I want to show you something.'
'What?'
'It would mean driving up north.'
I said: 'I've got nothing else to do.'
'Are you sure you want to know this?'
I wasn't sure. But I said yes anyway.

He wheedled me into letting him drive. A blip in the weather brought strong south-west winds which butted and banged at the Ford as he stroked it up the motorway at a steady hundred and twenty. Plumes of spray drifted across the carriageways, so that even the heaviest vehicle, glimpsed briefly through a streaming windscreen, seemed to be moving sideways as well as forwards, caught in some long dreamlike fatal skid. Beyond Nottingham, though, where the road petered out into roadworks, blocked exits and confusing temporary signboards, the cloud thinned suddenly.

'Blue sky,' said Choe, braking heavily to avoid the back of a fleet Cavalier, then dipping briefly into the middle lane to overtake it. Hunched forward over the steering wheel until his face was pressed against the windscreen, he squinted upwards.

'I can see sunshine.'
'Will you watch where you're fucking going?'

He abandoned the motorway and urged the car into the curving back roads of the White Peak, redlining the rev counter between gear changes, braking only when the bend filled the windscreen with black and white chevrons, pirouetting out along some undrawn line between will and physics.

'Bloody hell, Choe.'
'Don't talk.'

After about twenty minutes he stopped the car and switched the engine off.

'This is near enough for now.'

We were in a long bleak lay-by somewhere on the A6. The

road fell away from us in a gentle curve until it reached the flatter country west and north. Down there I could see a town – houses for quarry workers, a junction with traffic lights, a tall steel chimney designed to pump hot gases up through the chronic inversion layers of spring and autumn.

'When I was a kid,' Choe said, 'I lived a few miles outside that place.' He undid his seatbelt and turned to face me. 'What you've got to understand is that it's a fucking dump. It's got that fucking big chimney, and a Sainsbury's and a Woolworth's, and a fucking bus station.' He adjusted the driving mirror so that he could see his own face in it. 'I hated that fucking bus station. You know why? Because it was the only way in and out. I went in and out on one of those fucking buses every day for ten years, to take exams, look for jobs, go round the record shop on a wet Saturday afternoon.' He pushed the mirror back into its proper place. 'Ever spend any time in bus stations?'

'Never.'

'I didn't think you had. Let me tell you, they're death on a stick. Only people who are recently dead use a bus station.'

Everything warm, he said, went on at a distance from people like that. Their lives were at an ebb. At a loss. They had to watch the clean, the happy, the successfully employed, stepping out of new cars and into the lobbies of warm hotels. If the dead had ever been able to do that, they would never be able to do it again. They would never be able to dress out of choice or eat what they would like. Nothing they had been or wanted to be would ever come to anything.

'They're old, or they're bankrupt, or they've just come out of a long-stay mental ward. They're fucked.'

All over the north of England they stood around at ten in the evening waiting for the last bus to places called Chinley Cross, or Farfield, or Penistone. By day it was worse.

'Because you can see every fucking back-end village you're going through. The bus is fucked, and it never gets up any speed.' He appealed to me: 'It stinks of diesel and old woollen coats. *And the fuckers who get on are carrying sandwich boxes.*'

I laughed.

'There's nothing intrinsically wrong with a sandwich box,' I said.

'Do you want to hear this or not?'

'Sorry Choe.'

'I hated those fucking buses except for one thing:'

He was seventeen or eighteen years old. It was his last summer in the town. By September he would be at Sussex, doing his degree. He would be free. This only seemed to make him more impatient. Women were everywhere, walking ahead of him on every pavement, packed into the vegetarian coffee shop at lunchtime, laughing all afternoon on the benches in the new shopping plaza. Plump brown arms, the napes of necks: he could feel their limbs moving beneath the white summer dresses. He didn't want them. At night he fell out with his parents and then went upstairs to masturbate savagely over images of red-haired Pre-Raphaelite women he had cut from a book of prints. He hardly understood himself. One afternoon a girl of his own age got on the bus at Stand 18. She was perfectly plain – a bit short and fat, wearing a cardigan of a colour he described as 'a sort of Huddersfield pink' – until she turned round and he saw that she had the most extraordinary green eyes. 'Every different green was in them.' They were the green of grass, of laurel leaves, the pale green of a bird's egg. They were the deep blue-green of every sea-cliché he had ever read. 'And all at the same time. Not in different lights or on different days. All at the same time.' Eyes intelligent, reflective of the light, not human: the eyes of a bird or an animal. They seemed independent of her, as if they saw things on behalf of someone else: as if whatever intelligence inhabited them was quite different to her own. They examined him briefly. In that glance, he believed, 'She'd seen everything about me. There was nothing left to know.' He was transfixed. If you had ridden that bus as an adult, he said, and seen those eyes, you might have thought that angels travel route X39 to Sheffield in disguise.

'But they don't. They fucking don't.'

After that first afternoon she often travelled from Stand 18. He was so astonished by her that when she got off the bus one day at a place called Jumble Wood, he got off too and followed her. A nice middle-class road wound up between bungalows in the sunshine. Above them, on the lip of a short steep gritstone scarp, hung the trees: green and tangled, rather impenetrable. She walked past the houses and he lost sight of her: so he went up to the wood itself. Inside it was smaller than he had expected, full of a kind of hot stillness. He sat down for a minute or two, tranquillised by the greenish-gold light filtering down into the gloom between the oaks; then walked on, to find himself suddenly on the edge of a dry limestone valley. There was a white cliff, fringed with yew and whitebeam. There were grassy banks scattered with ferns and sycamore saplings. At his feet purple vetches twined their tendrils like nylon monofilament round the stems of the moon daisies. He was astonished by the wood avens, pure art nouveau with their complaisantly bowed yellow-brown flowerheads and strange spiky seed cases. He had never seen them before: or the heath-spotted orchids, tiny delicate patterns like intaglio on each pale violet petal.

When he looked up again, sunshine was pouring into the narrow valley from its south-western end, spilling through the translucent leaves of young ash trees, transfiguring the stones and illuminating the grassy slopes *as if from inside* – as if the whole landscape might suddenly split open and pour its own mysterious devouring light back into the world.

'So what did happen, Choe?'

Instead of answering he stared away from me through the windscreen, started the car up and let it roll gently down the hill until, on the right I saw the turning and the sign:

'JUMBLE WOOD.'

'You decide,' he said. 'We'll walk up.'

I don't know what he wanted me to see, except what he had seen all those years ago. I found what he had already described –

the wood, smaller than you might expect, full of dust motes suspended in sunshine – and beyond that, on the knife-edge of the geological interface, the curious little limestone valley with its presiding crag like a white church.

'You're going to have to give me a bit more help,' I said.

He knelt down.

'See this? Wood avens. I had to look it up in a book.'

He picked one and offered it to me.

'It's pretty. Choe, what happened here?'

'Would you believe me if I told you the world really did split open?'

He gazed miserably away from me.

'What?' I said.

'Somehow the light peeled itself open and showed me what was inside. It was here. She walked out of it, with those eyes every green in the world.' He laughed. 'Would you believe me if I said she was naked, and she stank of sex, and she let me push her down there and then and fuck her in the sunshine? And then somehow she went back into the world and it sealed itself up behind her and I never saw her again?'

'Choe—'

'I was eighteen years old,' he said. 'It was my first fuck.'

He turned away suddenly.

'It was my only fuck,' he said. 'I've never done it since. Whatever lives here loves us. I know it does. But it only loves us once.'

He drove back to London in silence, parked the Ford on Green Lanes and walked off towards Manor House tube station.

'Choe,' I called.

No answer.

10
Flying Blind

Never any answer.

After he had gone I kept to the flat, playing *Rude Dog* reruns in the gloom until half-past seven or eight in the evening, when I could switch over to *EastEnders* with its obscurely comforting theme music. Dust continued to gather on the piles of books and magazines. Choe was gone three weeks, then four. The phone didn't ring. Waste paper rustled and scraped along the pavement outside, children howled and shrieked motivelessly along the road, their voices echoing away between the houses; I barely heard any of it. I was trying to reconstruct my life with Isobel.

She was easy to see, even at that distance. I remembered her asleep on an Intercity express to King's Cross, just after we had met, curled up so tight she hardly took up the space of one seat. I saw her perched not much later on a bar stool at the Criterion brasserie, drinking Kronenburg from a bottle. I saw her in grey jeans and black DMs. I watched her frowning amusedly at herself over a new frock in a long mirror at Monsoon in Covent Garden. I saw her in a camisole top the colour of ivory and nothing else at all. It was easy to remember the pattern of frost on a south London window, the confused song of a bird in the middle of the night, a photograph of a pair of her shoes nesting in a spill of satin things she had just taken off. It was easy to see Isobel. What was hard was to make anything of her. With each new item of clothing, each new image of herself, she had changed completely and yet somehow become more completely the person I already knew. Almost as soon as we met, she had been warning me:

'Don't be a baby, China. Nothing stands still.'

Isobel had always been easy to see and impossible to see past. Somehow she had taken cover behind her own image, long before she forgot how to fly, or met Brian Alexander. Washed up on Green Lanes among Choe Ashton's abandoned toys, I understood suddenly how I had begun to mourn her *before* she left, hardly daring to revisit my memories of Stratford or our first few months in Peckham, because by then the colour of sunlight in the morning, the angle of a shadow across the bedroom carpet, was never quite enough to bring it all back.

I wrote these things down every night, in letters which I did not post to her. The word I used most often was 'remember'. 'Do you remember this?' I asked her: 'Don't you remember that?'

Remember how couples in restaurants in Chelsea and Bloomsbury and Covent Garden came over to our table to tell us how special we looked together, as if that might give them good luck in their own faltering and fucked-up affairs? Remember how the traffic hushed, slowed, held back, *parted* for us on Shaftesbury Avenue at eight o'clock on a summer evening? How we were Oberon and Titania, and not just to each other, but also to the waitresses at Peppermint Park, whose hair was peroxided a violent white-blond to go with their spotless white aprons and little black bowties, a uniformity which made them look more rather than less human?

'Remember,' I wrote, 'how all of that happened, and isn't just the false memory of hallucination of someone who used to be in love?

'Look, don't you even remember St Helier?'

Two weeks in a fifth-floor suite directly under the sign at the Hotel de France. We lay awake every night listening to the neon tubes creak as the wind streamed through them. 'Or I did, anyway. Now I begin to wonder if you didn't just go to sleep.' The wind in the neon. You could see that sign from all over the town. We had always known where our room was – there, a little left of centre, under the 'el' of 'Hotel'.

'Don't you remember?'

If Isobel remembered, she was saying nothing. She had begun to abandon me again, every morning at about five o'clock, in dreams. She was openly and aggressively unfaithful, yet we lived on in the same house. I couldn't make her help me, I couldn't make her leave: I couldn't make myself leave. I was financially dependent, afraid of heights and stairs, of falling. I cried easily in the afternoon. Each dream was different; they were all the same. I was in a mess. I woke up shocked and cold, or full of a pure, convulsive aggression. I woke up with my mouth thick and dry and a throat full of something which felt like hot cotton wool.

But the worst dream seemed to have nothing to do with us at all. In it, I was someone else. I was someone else, dreaming every night of trying to find out what had happened to the woman I loved. Isobel was someone else too – a pianist and a writer with her blond hair in a complex braid. We had met in New York when she played a concert of American and British music. She had reminded me how I was once able to dance. Now, some time later, she had come to Britain to find me. But she could no longer speak, only weep. How had she travelled here? Where did she live? What was she trying to say? It was a dream heavy with sadness and urgency. All avenues of inquiry were blocked. There were people who might know about her, but always some reason why they could not be asked, or would not tell. I walked up and down the streets, examining the goods on the market stalls, my only clue the reissue date of a once-banned medicine. She was close. She was *that far* from me, I knew I wouldn't find her.

I woke up shaking. I wrote:

'I know you hate me for needing you, I know you hate me for only having one argument – *Don't leave me, I love you.*'

Of all the letters, I sent that one.

Isobel replied by return of post on expensive paper, thick,

lavender-coloured, heavily recycled to have the writing surface of raw chipboard. She was happy, she said, though she missed me. Things were hard for her too. 'I don't hate you, China,' she wrote. 'Why should I hate you?' She asked me if I would like to meet her one day: perhaps for early-evening drinks.

I crumpled up the letter and threw it across Choe's front room.

'For Christ's sake, Isobel,' I told her quietly. *'Early-evening drinks*? Where do you get this stuff from?'

Two days later I was waiting for her in a pub near the south end of Hammersmith Bridge, already wondering where she would go on to, and who with; and why the wound was still so raw.

The bar of the New Buccaneer was a bleak and windswept runway dedicated to someone's scrubby, vanished myth of flight. Perhaps that was why Isobel had chosen it. A wooden propeller hung on one wall, and, above the spirit optics, two whitening colour photographs of old-fashioned naval jets climbing steeply away from an aircraft carrier on a storm-tossed but somehow gelid sea. Scattered here and there were equally faded prints of Canadian Pacific short-haulers of the 1940s, fitted for desperate landings above the Arctic Circle.

Six o'clock. The weather was bad, and nothing much was flying in or out. Four middle-aged women had stalled on the runway. As a group they were bright, noisy, attentive to one another; left alone for a moment, they slumped and studied the bar furniture with an interest bordering on anxiety.

'Well, anyway, psoriasis,' one of them said suddenly.

'I'll have a Beck's,' I told the barman.

'Will you want a glass with that, sir?'

'No, I won't.'

'Is that all then, sir?'

'No it isn't.'

I stared past him at the optics.

'I'll have a Captain Morgan, too.'

'That will be five pounds altogether, sir.'

Signs of Life

'Christ.'

I sat down in a corner. Every time the street door opened I looked up, though I had promised myself I wouldn't. The wash of neon in the open doorway was the exact colour of early daylight as if the women, the barman and I had already drunk ourselves into the next morning. I got up again and wandered around. I looked at the pictures. I looked into the deserted restaurant section, where girls were laying tables for dinner. They reminded me of Isobel as I'd first met her. What would happen when I saw her now? I would be able to smile: I was sure of that. But she would be smiling too. She would come in with that swinging, sexy walk, stooping slightly as if she was a taller woman. She would be smiling, but it wouldn't be the smile I remembered – unarmed, candid, whole. She would be smiling as if I was an appointment. She would be someone who said 'early-evening drinks', and 'six for six-thirty'; someone who said 'K' when they meant 'thousand'. Someone who had gone so far away I would never be able to interpret her smile again.

By six-fifteen, when I next looked round, one or two regulars had come in to erratic crosswind touchdowns, oil-pressure at zero and instruments undependable. An old man with an artificial hand sat trembling at the table underneath the 'Toilets' sign. Just down the bar from him, a Jack Russell terrier dashed repeatedly at its owner's foot, barking, while he laughed and fended it off with mock growls. (If he looked round for applause, it was all for the dog.) A tall wasted boy in ripped jeans and leather jacket dragged himself from table to table as if he could forget the pain of his last crash-landing only so long as he was on the move. Leaning tiredly over the juke box, he twice selected the old Roxy Music hit 'Virginia Plain'. Finally he sat down between the man with the dog and the man under the 'Toilets' sign and, without giving any indication that they knew one another, all three began to talk at once. It had been an early Jack Higgins' novel for them – a long haul through thick air and electrical storms – and I thought I heard one of them say:

'She can't bear to touch the chickens.'

This sentence brought me a clear vision of my future without Isobel. I would live in a two-star hotel in the Mumbles. I would buy an Austin Allegro. Every night I would drive it to some pub like the New Buccaneer and – after a period of aimless walking up and down – join the other cripples at the bar. 'Supports *cats*, does she?' I would hear myself say. 'Bloody waste of money, that.' One night there would be a smell hanging on the stairs next to the men's lavatory; it would be the exact smell of a fat-rendering factory in Preston. I would try not to smell it – too late – and it would lodge inside me, recurring unpredictably, always at one crucial juncture, souring my joy, undermining my confidence, marring my life forever.

I sat down again. Let Isobel come to China, by the Hammersmith Bridge. I would see her in the mirror behind the optics, underneath the picture of the climbing Buccaneers, long before she saw me.

Six-thirty. Nothing.

I thought: The traffic will have made her late. She will be parking her car. Why did she suggest this? Why did I agree? I heard one of the cripples say to the other two:

'If you killed yourself I'd never speak to you again. I just wouldn't respect you.'

At this, the Jack Russell yapped, the barman smiled as if he understood some joke no one else had caught, the women looked up briefly then went back to their drinks. One of them said:

'Now you *are* in on Monday aren't you, dear?'

'Yes, yes I am.'

'And—' turning to someone else '—you are too, dear, because I've just arranged a whole new pricing structure.'

The door opened. Isobel Avens was caught in the wash of neon, thin, hesitant, angular, oddly posed with one hand still raised to the door as if she was leaning against a wall in some alley. For a moment she looked confused and terrified. She looked ill. I had a clear memory of her saying: 'China, I couldn't *fly*.' Behind her I glimpsed an endless stream of cars going to and fro across the Thames, and Budapest went across me like a pain in the heart, a crack across the mirror, and we were on the Erzebet Bridge at midnight watching the ice floes race towards us through the Middle European night, and Isobel was in my arms and whispering:

'I thought I'd never hear from you again.'

Everything inside me suddenly went very still.

'I—'
'Would you—?'
'No, let me—'
'I—'
'Let me.'
'You look nice.'

We stepped back as suddenly as we had embraced. Isobel took out her purse.

'You look so nice.'
'I'll get these.'
'Is it raining?'
'I got a taxi.'
'Are you . . . ?'
'I came over from Putney.'

She had dressed for dinner, in a long, clinging black frock.

'It's a John Rocha. Do you like it?'
'Turn,' I said.
'I love it,' I said.

She laughed and turned again.

'John Rocha,' I said.

I said: '*Very* upmarket.'

She had been shopping all afternoon. She had visited some friends. 'I wasn't even sure you would be here,' she said. She had come in a taxi, straight to me from Putney, wearing a John Rocha frock. Only Isobel could have chosen something so inappropriate.

'Let's have a drink, then go on somewhere else to eat,' she said.

She thought for a moment.

'Let's go to dell 'Ugo's.'

Instead of 'dell 'Ugo's? In a John Rocha frock?' I said: 'Brilliant.'

I would have gone anywhere for another hour with her. I would have gone anywhere for another ten minutes.

'Brilliant,' I said.

'Oh China, I have missed you.'

She looked around the bar, smiling vaguely. The barman smiled back; while the women, ashamed for her without entirely knowing why, avoided her eyes.

'I'll fetch the car,' I said, a little later. 'It's a couple of streets away.'

'Don't be silly, China. I'll walk.'

'If you're sure.'

It had stopped raining, and a feeble quarter of moon was hauling itself up over Arundel Terrace. A Claude Montana raincoat slung across her shoulders, arms folded beneath her breasts for comfort, Isobel walked with her upper arm brushing mine. Unsure, perhaps, how close she should get to me, how far into her new self she could safely admit me, she spoke only to admire the red-brick apartment houses or complain about the cold wind from the river. 'You don't have to be so careful,' I wanted to reassure her. I wanted to say: You were never so wary before. But how could I know that? Some people, I thought, always withhold themselves: some people give themselves to you without ever giving you anything at all – an accusation which hung there between us on the edge of being spoken, where it only added to Isobel's uncertainty.

I had parked my Greenlight Cosworth at the end of the road, next to the weed-infested concrete expanse of the Harrods' Repository yard. She stood expectantly by the passenger door.

She said: 'The old Sierra.' She said: 'China, I'm so glad you kept it.'

When I failed to respond, except to disarm the Cosworth's

security system and advise her, 'It's open,' she got in, gave a shrug so minimal I almost noticed it, and added suddenly:

'Brian's got an XJS.'

I wanted to say: Shit car, that. Instead I adjusted the driving mirror.

Isobel smiled as if to say, Yes. That's how you always adjusted your driving mirror, China. I remember.

Neither of us knew how to act. In the confined space of the car everything became meaningful; everything meaningful was dangerous; and I couldn't think of anything to talk about at all. Isobel fastened her seatbelt – staring at the mechanism for a moment as if she didn't quite understand it – then sat facing straight ahead with her raincoat folded in her lap. Occasionally she would turn her head to study a brightly lit window display. At traffic lights she peered into the dim interiors of the more expensive cars we stopped beside, as if she expected to recognise some celebrity or politician, or perhaps just some new friend she had made in Brian Alexander's company. Once I heard her say softly, 'Oh look, China.' But I missed whatever she was trying to draw my attention to, and it didn't seem to need acknowledgement anyway.

In the end I stopped trying to talk and instead of listening to the things Isobel said, concentrated on the sound of her voice. Her smell was soon mixed up with the smell of the warm car. Street lights picked out the curve of her shoulder, the long line of her arm, her fingers where they rested on the dash. I wanted to be able to remember all those things when she was gone again. In an hour, two hours, the memory would be more important than the event itself – or indeed Isobel herself. She seemed to sense that. She asked once if I would turn the heater up.

'Whose is the field mushrooms?'

'Happy birthday, Charlotte. Have a lovely evening.'

'I've got to go and buy something to make myself pretty with tomorrow: wedding.'

'Oh God.'

'What's a wedding anyway—?'

'Field mushrooms? Who's having the pan-fried field mushrooms!'

'Earth, Air, Fire, Water, Hype. Hype, the Fifth Element!'

'—just a lot of failed princesses in powder-blue lace.'

'I do agree.'

'They give you a ring with a stone on it the size and colour of a boiled sweet—'

'Field mushrooms on tapenade toast?'

'I think that's mine. Oh no. It isn't. Did I order that? I'm sure I didn't.'

'We're going to see you tomorrow evening.'

'Are you? Are we? Oh!'

'—Gavin Bryars. Sort of an anorexic Donald Pleasence, but he's actually fairly awake.'

'Alice is down in Oxford tonight.'

'Oxford?'

'She's a trustee of the Lewis Carroll Society. They're trying to raise some money. What they're trying to do is set up a centre—'

'—a sort of Lewis Carroll theme park?'

Laughter.

'It was mooted. It's been mooted.'

'Who's having the pan-fried mushrooms on tapenade toast.'

'What's a wedding anyway?'

'Charlotte, did you order this?'

dell 'Ugo's was hot, crowded and full of the smells of food and coffee. Isobel stared around unashamedly, drank a lot of Côtes de Rouffach, and ordered thyme muffins with glazed crab, oysters and crispy bacon. All evening the John Rocha frock added to her air of shyness and vulnerability. Against its confident lines she seemed unformed, girlish, labile. Perhaps that was the idea.

'I love it here,' she insisted, holding out her glass. 'Let's stay until they close.'

'What's that?' she said, poking at my plate.

'Chargrilled bananas, I think.'

She whispered loudly, 'China. China. That's *Muriel Gray*. No, over there.'

Suddenly she asked me: 'Do you think they'll ever get the lid back on Yugoslavia?'

I stared at her, astonished.

She stared back.

'What "lid"?' I said brutally. I said: 'Why would you care?'

'Because of all the children,' she said.

She looked down at her plate, as if this admission had disconcerted her as much as me.

I said: 'I'm sorry.'

By then it was nine or ten o'clock.

I said: 'I didn't – Look, I'm a bit jumpy . . . I . . .'

She took my hand gently.

'I know, China.'

'It's difficult,' I lied. 'Here.'

But the real trouble wasn't even dell 'Ugo's, with its freight of self-conscious TV comedians, journos and publishers. The real trouble was this: behind Isobel's voice – behind early-evening drinks and chicken hash-cake with wilted spinach – behind the whole lot of it – I had suddenly heard the received wisdom of Brian Alexander. He might have been standing behind her chair. I was filled with contempt. At the same time it came home to me with bleak clarity how being with him had 'grown her up'. That was a meaningless thing to think. But its corollary was obvious, and as the evening went on I kept getting glimpses of the pair of them together – down at Margaret Avens' cottage in Gloucestershire; visiting the Tate; and finally, of course, in the bedroom at Stepney, where the box of tissues by the bed, the scented candles burning on the mantelpiece, the satin underwear scattered on the pink carpet, would be as perfectly familiar to me as the things she murmured to herself while he fucked her.

Against the odds, dell 'Ugo's had eased Isobel's nerves; and perhaps that made me angry, too. I said:

'You aren't telling me much.'

'About what?'
'Your life,' I said.
I meant: Your life with him.
Isobel said: 'I never know how much you want to know.'
'Only that you're happy,' I said.
She reached over quickly and took my hand.
'Oh, China, I am,' she said. She said: 'I love him.' She said: 'But it isn't just that. He's going to help me to fly.'
I pulled my hand out of hers.
'You always said I helped you to fly.'
She looked away.
'It's not your fault it stopped working,' she said. 'It's me.'
'Christ, you selfish bitch.'
'He wants to help me to fly,' she repeated dully.
And then:
'China, I *am* selfish.'
She tried to touch my hand again, but I moved it away.
'I can't fucking believe this,' I said. 'You want me to forgive you just because you can admit it?'
'I don't want to lose you, China.'
'Christ.'
Towards the end of the evening, she said:
'I never trusted you. That was the problem.'
I remembered how we had been at the beginning.
'If you could hear yourself,' I said. 'If you could just fucking hear yourself, Isobel.'
She left a long silence after that.
Suddenly she said:
'Can't we be friends? Neither of us knows what we might want in the future.'
'You're confused, Isobel. He's your friend now.'
'Grow up, China.'
'You grow up, Isobel. People come whole. You can't just take the bits you want and throw the rest away.'
She looked across the restaurant. She blinked once or twice.
'Take it or leave it,' I said.

'If that's what you want,' she said.

I shrugged. We sat not looking at one another.

'You can't expect friendship from someone you've hurt,' I said.

'I didn't hurt you.'

'What?'

'For God's sake, China, this kind of thing happens to everybody all the time. Why do you have to make it such a tragedy?'

'I can't believe I'm hearing this.'

She pushed her chair back savagely and got up.

'It's the nineteen nineties, China.'

I didn't see her after that. I did have one letter from her. It was sad without being conciliatory, and ended: 'You were the most amazing person I ever knew, China, and the fastest driver.'

I tore it up.

' "Were"!' I said. 'Fucking *were*!'

11
China's Syndrome

By that time she had moved in with him, somewhere along the Network South-East line from Waterloo: Kew, East Sheen, one of those old-fashioned suburbs on a bladder of land inflated into the picturesque curve of the river, with genteel, deteriorating houseboats, an arts centre and a wine bar on every corner. West London is full of places like that – 'shabby', 'comfortable', until you smell the money. Come to think of it, almost everywhere you go is full of places like that.

   Isobel kept the Stepney house. I visited it once or twice in September, ostensibly to collect my things, ended up crying in the lounge, and after an hour took away with me a compact disc I had bought her, an American fleece shirt she had bought me. Every object in that place frightened me with its potential for memory and pain. It was necessary to be careful where I looked, even among my own belongings; among hers there was no relief. On the second visit I came across the photographs Isobel's mother had given me the first year we were together. They had been kept all that time in the same old shoebox, which, faded to beige and fastened with perished elastic bands, still smelt very faintly of salt air, seaside towns. It was an object from another age. The prints too seemed older than they were, small, oddly proportioned slips of pasteboard, made to last. In them, eyes were cast down, faces turned aside, less through shyness or embarrassment – though clearly there was some of both – than in a vain attempt to look away from the sun. A strange, blanched seaside horizon transected each image. The shadow of the photographer lay oblique and truncated in every foreground, among inexplicable objects and piles of light-coloured clothing.

Out of the box they tumbled, to spill across the polished floor, dusty and a little warped as if something heavy had been thrown carelessly in on top of them a long time ago.

'Look at her,' Margaret Avens had exclaimed when she first showed them to me. 'She was a *horrible* toddler.'

That was at Cleeve Hill, the first year we were together. I still remember Margaret in Country Casuals skirt and jumper, sitting on a wingback chair with the shoebox in her lap. Late afternoon, winter. The air outside was raw and damp. Mist crept down the hill towards Cheltenham, or, trapped by the inversions, layered itself in the growing dusk along the sides of the valley. Inside, a log fire burned up bright, slowly filling the grate with pure white ash.

Isobel was in the kitchen making scones. All afternoon I had been keenly aware of her there, moving in a kind of dreamy dance between the Aga and the work surfaces. Margaret's Burmese cats stared into the fire, or, with rapt reflective eyes, sat on the windowsill to study the wintry garden: everywhere they went, they went together. Is it possible to 'shiver with comfort'? I suppose not. But if I thought about it for a second, comfort and excitement were equally mixed in what I felt that afternoon. Comfort and excitement. Can you understand that?

'Still, she grew out of it,' Margaret said. 'They always do.' She glanced at me over the rims of her gold reading glasses. 'In fact, she really did turn into quite a nice little girl. Look.'

She offered me another print.

'Don't you think?'

I had already dismissed the dull brown bunches of hair and self-tutored smile of the ten-year-old. It was the face, I had decided, of a growing anxiety to please – a face always turned towards the nearest adult.

'Mm,' I said noncommittally.

I thought: Who wouldn't prefer the toddler?

'I love them all,' I said.

'I'm sure I'm right,' said Margaret.

This exchange has somehow entangled itself with my memory of finding the shoebox again after Isobel left. I remember kneeling on the floor. I remember sorting the snapshots into chronological order. I remember arranging them face-down, then turning them over again, one by one. There she sat, an Isobel puppy-fatted and unassuaged, scowling out from her cluttered little territories in the sand. 'I had to be able to walk,' she had admitted to me, 'to steal toys from the beach. If I liked what I saw, I took it.' How could I ever have romanticised this monster, with its uncontrollable rages and misplaced pets? More importantly, how could I have failed to detect it, installed in the grown woman, every preoccupation intact?

I stayed all afternoon. Weak sunshine had thrown a bar of light across the varnished wooden floor. I remember how it moved across the scattered pictures, and then slowly round the room until it fell on a few dried flowers in one of Isobel's tall brass vases, isolating them from their background so that they looked like the demonstration of some well-known illusion. The visual structure of that part of the room – a corner, the table with the vase on it, some bookshelves – was subtly altered, as if it were possible to have lenses or eddies of greater depth in different parts of the same space.

By then Stepney was as bitter a memory, as irretrievable a paradise, as Cleeve Hill. I looked down at the photographs. Had Margaret Avens been warning me against her own daughter? I thought: I don't suppose I'll ever know.

I didn't go back again, I couldn't face the bedroom, with its wooden chests and paper birds. It always seemed to have filled up further with dust. Despite that I could never quite tell if anything had changed. *Had* they been in there, the two of them? Was that Isobel I could hear, whispering, 'Do you want to *fuck* me? Do you want to *fuck* my *cunt*?' Was that his answering groan? 'Say, then. *Say* you want to.' I stayed in the doorway so as not to be certain, and then – when the possibility got too close to ignore – drove back as fast as I could to Tottenham. There, sick of *Rude Dog and the Dweebs* at last, I was drinking a lot of Michelob beer, going listlessly through Choe's collection of unknown female rock singers on CD and watching Channel Four movies while I encouraged Rose Services to go down the drain.

Some films I liked better than others. I liked the beginning of *Alice in the Cities* a lot. It was such an intense replication of space and sensations: but nothing at all like standing between two mirrors. More as if these things just went on and on as you moved towards them, into them, through them. As if America really was infinite once you got past the boundaries of New York, a country in which people communicate by leaving notes for one another. They look out of windows and someone is always walking away. Someone is always asleep in the next room. They switch endlessly from TV station to TV station; and unassuagable from the very outset, unwrap sandwiches from a plastic pack. I cried all the way through *Alice in the Cities*. I wasn't sure why. But I knew why I was cheering Anthony Hopkins as *The Good Father*.

'What fucking crap,' Choe Ashton said, when I tried in a confused way to explain all this.

He had returned the day before from some New York of his own, one he wasn't prepared to relinquish to Wim Wenders or anyone else. America always put Choe in a dangerously good mood. You often found it hard to get out of him why he did the things he did. But once he started, he couldn't stop telling you about them:

'I went to Union Square, I went to Madison Avenue. Listen, I went into a *blind pig*. Fucking Tom Waits country – are you listening? People had cut so many initials in the tables they looked *carved*. It was red neon, but completely dark at two o'clock in the afternoon. But do you know what the best graffiti in the bog was?'

'No, Choe. I don't.'

'DAVE WAS HERE FROM EASTBOURNE.'

He grinned.

'You don't believe that, do you? But it's true. Fucking Eastbourne!'

He had been all over the Village, from Jane Street – which for some reason he remembered from William Burroughs, 'A dirty, furnished room in a red-brick house on Jane Street,' home of Marvin the waiter, a junkie allergic to junk – to the Cowgirl Hall of Fame, where he had eaten Frito pie and catfish fingers. He had ridden the subway to the Bronx and beyond; and convinced a taxi driver to go back and forth across the Brooklyn Bridge seven times.

'I had these fucking *sweet potato chips* somewhere else . . .' He had to stop for a minute to think '. . . I forget where. But they were fucking ace. Fucking brilliant. The best thing of all, though . . .' A broad smile passed across his face. '. . . the best thing of all was Sioux City Cream Soda. I drank five glasses of it.'

He had drunk them down, one after the other, at the Cowgirl Hall of Fame.

'I threw up after that.'

'Don't boast, Choe. Anyway, only a dickhead goes to New York to get sick on pop.'

He laughed. 'I know. What's happening?'

'I'm going bankrupt,' I told him. 'This afternoon.' I explained: 'I'm not entirely sure why.' I asked him if he'd like to sit in on the meeting, as an ex-Rose Services' shareholder. He looked at me as if I had gone mad.

'Fuck off, Mick,' he said.

'Go on, Choe, you know you want to.'

Suddenly he clapped his hand to his forehead and fumbled about in one of his jacket pockets. 'I forgot,' he said. 'I got something for you.' And he offered me a cutting, folded and furry, from some cheap DTP magazine. 'This is an East Village thing called *New Biology*: some kind of political sheet at the consumer end. More a print-out from their Web site than a magazine.'

I took the cutting and opened it. It was a brief CV.

*

Brian Alexander worked for some years developing patentable human cell lines for a California company called FUGA-OrthoGen; and later on transgenic farm animals under the auspices of a privatised university department known since 1989 as Agritrans Cambridge Plc whose literature boasted that it was 'one of the first companies to offer a transgenic service'. The Alexander group of clinics, in Florida, Chicago and Milan, are a partly owned subsidiary of FUGA-OrthoGen (now a transglobal with offices in Geneva and Budapest).

Dr Alexander's publications include 'New Work with Plasmids' *British Journal of Molecular Biology*, 1982: 'Firing the Genetic Bullet' OMNI, November 1994; and 'Grow Your Way to Freedom' Alexander Publications, Chicago.

I turned the cutting over. Nothing else.

'Who gave you this?'

'Is it him?' Choe said. 'It's him, isn't it?'

'Why give me this?' I said.

He shrugged.

'Let the ferret see the rabbit,' he said. 'After all, the fucker stole your tart.'

'Grow up Choe.'

It was his turn to shrug.

In the end he did turn up at the bankruptcy meeting, although his main contribution was to sit on a chair in the corner and stare appraisingly at the liquidator, who turned out to be a pleasant young man from Hither Green called Tony. So many bankruptcies were available at the moment, Tony told us. They occupied 50 per cent of his time, where once it had been 15. But he did do other kinds of work. Tony wore a Marks and Spencer suit and had trained himself to say 'I see' with a variety of different intonations, some less encouraging than others.

'I see,' he would say. 'Things are pretty bad then.'

And he would move smoothly on to the next point. As the shortfall between the estimated and the book value of the business grew plainer, so Tony became more and more impersonal, reserved his judgement more and more. 'I see. Well, I think that's it as far as the form-filling's concerned. If I could trouble you to get those accounts again?'

'Trouble you to get those accounts?' mimicked Choe softly. 'Here,' he said. 'Let's do some blow.' He began to go through his pockets. 'Well, that's fucking odd. I'm sure I had some somewhere here—'

'Choe,' I warned him. Too late. He had made eye-contact with Tony.

'I see that we're missing my favourite nature programme, Tony, did you know that? Do you watch a lot of daytime TV? Well, this afternoon it's *The Flight of the Condom*. Have you watched that one, Tony, at all? There's some very interesting camel-fucking in that one. Ever watched two camels fucking, Tony?'

Tony shook his head slowly.

'I see,' said Choe.

'I wonder . . .' Tony began. Had he ever met anyone like Choe before? 'I wonder if—'

'Well you do,' said Choe. 'Don't you?'

'Choe!'

'You do wonder,' Choe said.

He laughed quietly to himself. '*The Flight of the Condom*,' he said.

Tony cleared his throat.

'I wonder if I could see the records of these medical waste transactions?' he asked me. 'They seem to have been the mainstay of the business—'

'We didn't actually keep records of those.'

'I see.'

I said: 'I must admit the details are a bit vague in my own mind.'

'They're a bit vague in his mind,' Choe said.

Tony thought for a moment.

'Well,' he decided, 'if the directors aren't aware of it I can often argue back to the company that it's invalid.'

'You often can, can you?' said Choe.

He laughed.

Tony looked at him. He rubbed his face. Then he asked us: 'Is there anyone who would want to pick up these assets?'

Who knew? By then, the only asset Rose Services actually had left was a 1985 BMW M3. I had bought it to race, but it was just too old to be competitive, though it had done well as a BTCC privateer for two seasons in the late eighties, coming in ninth or tenth most meetings against the team Toyotas and Vauxhalls: once even seventh. I had paid someone in Brixton to legalise the electrical and exhaust systems, put in proper seats, bulkhead insulation and a CD player, and paint out the promotional decals for RipSpeed and Demon Tweeks. But the roll cage and six-speed powertrain were still in place, the car remained quite noisy inside and it sat down into tight bends in a distinctive, predatory fashion. It was practically uninsurable.

Choe loved it.

'Coke dealer's choice,' he had complimented me the day I bought it. 'Fucking ace car.'

After Tony had gone, he looked at his watch.

'Let's get ripped and see if we can drive to Shrewsbury before the pubs close.'

'Why Shrewsbury, Choe?'

He looked at me as if I was a moron. *'Because I've never fucking bin there,'* he explained patiently.

'Fair enough.'

'I've got a better idea than that, even.'

'What?'

'Let's go and beat up that fucker who stole your tart.'

'Jesus, Choe.'

'Go on, you know you want to.'

'Perhaps you're right,' I admitted. But what I wanted least was for Choe to be involved. So one evening at about seven I left him watching *Channel Four News* with the sound turned down; drove across town; and parked the BMW at the kerb outside Brian Alexander's clinic, which was in a postmodern block at the

Hammersmith end of Queensborough Road, not far from the Broadway. Some light rain was falling. I sat with the engine running and watched the front entrance. The security staff looked back at me from behind their wraparound desk. After about twenty minutes a receptionist came out, put her umbrella up, and walked quickly off towards Hammersmith tube station. A bit later Alexander himself appeared at the top of the steps, a tall thin man, middle-aged, grey-haired, dressed in a light wool suit. He seemed worried. He looked along the street towards Parsons Green, then down at his watch. I wondered if he was waiting for Isobel; I didn't know that by then Isobel wasn't even in Britain. I was disappointed by him. 'It makes me sad to lose you, China,' she had written. 'You were the most amazing person I ever knew.'

Why did you pick this prick, then? I thought.

I wound down the nearside passenger window.

I called: 'Brian Alexander?'

I called: 'Need a lift?'

He bent down and looked into the M3.

'Do I know you?' he asked.

I thought: Say the wrong thing, you fucker.

I said: 'Not exactly.'

'Then—'

'Forget it.'

He stood back from the car suddenly, and I drove off.

'What a waste,' said Choe, when I got back. 'You should have twatted him.'

He was still slumped in front of the TV. He had the remote control in one hand and a bottle of Dos Equis beer in the other. He added, 'I would have,' and turned the sound up. He seemed to have recorded part of the news.

I said: 'Could we have less of this fucking stupid Yorkshire act?'

'You want to watch this,' Choe advised.

'Listen,' I said, 'I just went to see what he was like. OK, Choe? Is that OK with you?'

'. . . illegally dumped uranium,' said the TV.

I switched it off.

I said: 'Could you listen to me, Choe? Could you do that for me?'

I said: 'Is that OK with you?'

He stared up mildly from the sofa.

'Please don't hurt me, Mick. It's my first time.'

'Fuck off.'

I went into the kitchen to get a beer. While I was gone, Choe switched the TV on again.

'Watch this,' he said, and rewound the tape.

'Experts,' the TV said, 'have begun the delicate task of moving a quantity of illegally dumped radioactive waste from a Lancashire quarry.'

I stared at the screen – where police vehicles were moving about in confusion in the rain and mud – then at Choe.

'Choe, that's where we . . .'

He shrugged.

'Don't look at me,' he said. 'I didn't do it.'

'Removal of the drums of uranium 238, used as ballast and for balancing aircraft wingtips, was delayed this morning when AEA inspectors realised they were in a heavily corroded condition.

'A spokesman said the material could have been lying unnoticed since last year. The alarm was raised when a local scrap-metal dealer sold three drums of the waste to a Leeds processing company.'

The picture changed to security fences, falling sleet, articulated lorries reversing carefully through the late-afternoon gloom.

'When the drums were driven through *these gates* an automatic alarm sounded.'

'Jesus, Choe,' I said.

'It wasn't him, either.'

I said, 'But nuclear waste . . .'

He shook his head wearily.

'Where did you think this kind of stuff went?'

'But for God's sake, Choe. Fucking *uranium* – we never dumped anything like that.'

'I think you live on another planet,' he said.

After a moment his expression softened.

'Oh come on,' he encouraged me. 'Eh?'

He said: 'Don't be a prick all your life. Let's do some of this blow.'

'You know what upsets me most?' I asked him later.

'What?'

'You wouldn't remember him in the street,' I said bitterly. 'You just wouldn't remember that fucker's face in the fucking street.'

'Who?'

Two or three days later, I had a card from Isobel. It had been posted in Florida. The picture was an old sepia-tint of the Wright Brothers' first flight. I stared at it. Where you expected brown paper and string, a technology fumbling on the edge of Dada, you saw only hope and energy.

'Wish me luck!' Isobel had written.

As a reprisal, perhaps, I telephoned Christiana Spede.

We met in Upper Street, Islington, outside a jazz café called the Blue Saloon. 'You'll find it easily,' Christiana had assured me. But on that windy autumn night Islington was an empty, Hopper-like vault. Distracted by a handful of people round a table in the brightly lit Pizza Express, I went in the wrong direction. The Blue Saloon turned out to be on the other side of the road, directly across from Angel station. I found Christiana standing underneath its neon sign, her hands cupped round her eyes and her nose pressed to the window. She was wearing a short imitation leopardskin coat and a bright red cloche hat she had made herself. I wondered how long she had been there, peering into the deserted, unlit space.

'Hello,' I said.

'Well, there it is, then,' she said, as if we'd been together all day and this was just part of some discussion we were having. Inside the Blue Saloon, strange, futuristic metal chairs were stacked on the tables. The wind threw a handful of rain against the glass. 'Closed on Mondays', said the sign on the door; and, 'VISA'.

'Do you know,' Christiana said. 'I could have sworn it would be open?'

She looked tired and disappointed. Before leaving the house, she had applied very red lipstick with such a precision edge that by contrast every wrinkle, every slack curve of her face was accentuated. Her eyes were enwebbed, panicky. They were too direct: the eyes of a much younger woman. It was like a cruel lighting effect. Since the break-up with Choe, I realised, none of us had been in touch with her. Quite suddenly, as if the two things were connected, I had a lucid memory of her ten years before, in the Jai Krishna vegetarian restaurant on Stroud Green Road, saying of David Hare (or was it Ian McEwan?), 'He couldn't sell bananas to a monkey.' Until now I hadn't realised how fragile these kinds of pronouncements – less provocative than nervous, issued out of some passing irritability and retracted almost at once – had always made her seem.

I hugged her. Her hair smelt faintly of Neutralia shampoo.

'Come on. Let's go to Gill Wing's instead.'

'That would be nice,' she said.

Gill Wing's: flimsy petrol-blue menus, deco lights and marble-topped tables. It was a slow night. Towards the back of the room sat a couple enjoying a quiet, lethal argument over the remains of foie de veau aux anchois. 'It's not a matter of that, David,' the woman said. 'It's a matter of you fucking her on my sofa.' David, a frail, boyish-looking man of about thirty-five wearing a denim shirt under his new Gap jacket, looked bemused. 'The thing is, you never fucked *me* on that sofa, David. How do you think that makes me feel?' David shook his head. He didn't know what to think, he said. The rest of the clientele were pretending not to listen, reading that morning's *Independent*, accumulating empty cups and glasses, staring out of the window at the Hen and

Chickens Theatre Bar across the road. If Upper Street had been quiet, Highbury Corner was like a grave. I would have preferred the Pizza Express, with its cheerful garlicky steam.

Christiana sat down at one of the tables near the bar. She undid the fake leopardskin coat, but kept it on. Under it she was wearing a black polo-neck top. 'Every time someone opens the door here you freeze,' she complained. She sighed, 'I don't think I'll eat anything. I don't feel hungry, do you?' She lit a cigarette.

'So,' I said. 'What have you been up to?'

She stared at me.

'What,' she said. 'Since nineteen eighty-four, you mean?'

I began to feel like David.

'I'm sorry,' she said. She reached across the table and took one of my hands between both of hers. 'China, I honestly didn't mean it to sound like that.'

I said: 'Tell me anyway.'

'Where would I start?' She blew smoke over the wine list, narrowed her eyes at something there, laughed suddenly. 'You must have been surprised when I turned up with Choe after all those years.' I couldn't think of anything to say. She shrugged. 'Or maybe you weren't.' She stubbed her cigarette out half smoked. 'Christ, China, you're hard work.' And then when, unnerved by her impatience, I still didn't reply: 'Perhaps I will eat something.'

After sausage and lentils and two or three glasses of Château Laurens, she cheered up briefly.

'I bet you didn't know I had a child.'

'Never.'

She laughed.

'Well, I did. She's eight, and her name is Vita.'

'I don't believe you.'

'She's all right, Vita is. She'll be OK.'

Vita had been born on a beach in Portugal, at six o'clock in the morning. 'She came a month early. I was performing out there. Sleeping on the beach.' I tried to imagine Christiana, alone in pale slanting light, simply giving birth there and then on the white Atlantic sand. Of course, she wouldn't have been alone. It was a seductive image all the same, full of the sound of the waves, the power and otherness of Christiana's ideas. I tried to imagine what kind of character a child born like that might have.

'Weren't you frightened?'

'No.' She lit another cigarette. 'Pour me some wine.'

'It must have been hard for you later.'

'Why?'

'To look after a child—'

' "—and have a career?" Is that what you were going to say?' She laughed. 'Jesus, China, that's what people like you always say.' She stared across the bar as if everyone in it was part of a conspiracy.

'It was easy,' she said.

I waited a moment and then, because it seemed a safe enough thing to ask, tried:

'What's she like?'

I meant: How tall is she? I meant: What colour is her hair? I meant: Are her eyes like yours?

I meant, I suppose: Does she look like you?

'Oh, Vita's OK,' said Christiana. 'She lives with her grandmother. She does well at school. She already reads a lot. She's very independent.' She paused. She sounded almost puzzled. 'Vita's OK,' she repeated. 'We went all over Europe together when she was a baby. Prague. Munich. Amsterdam. She was a member of the band. Her father was a man called Gram, who thought he looked like David Bowie. He did look a bit like David Bowie when he was twenty. I still see him occasionally. He never supported her.'

Suddenly she turned her face away from me, and I saw her wipe her eyes.

'Why are you crying?'

'I'm sorry,' she said. 'I miss him.'

'Gram?'

'Oh, for God's sake, China! Are you stupid? Choe. I miss *Choe*.' She pushed back her chair and got to her feet. She pulled her coat together at the front, sniffed, wiped her eyes again. 'Look, China, I think I'll go now.'

'Christiana—'

'I'll buy you a beer, China,' she promised. 'Soon.' She tried to smile. 'Let's find somewhere quiet and really talk. Would you like that? To really talk?' She glanced at me appraisingly. 'You look as if you need to talk,' she said.

I watched her walk away.

I thought: You'd know.

12
Icarus Flights

Christiana ransacked north London for Turkish and Lebanese restaurants. She also dragged me to the Daquise, near South Kensington tube. 'I can't believe you've never *been* here. I can't believe you've never eaten Polish food.' Though she liked Soho she hated almost every restaurant I knew there. 'I'll drink any old muck,' she had once told Isobel over the dinner table. In fact she wouldn't. Without Choe to keep them in check her snobberies were revealed to be florid, interwoven, less inverted than reversible. She would have coffee at Pâtisserie Valerie, but not Maison Bertaux. She would go anywhere that served café latte, but edge away from me if I ordered hot chocolate and Captain Morgan rum. She really hated L'Escargot. One evening, after I had suggested Kentucky Fried Chicken as a compromise between Brick Lane and the Soho Brasserie, she said, 'We could go home and *cook*. Wouldn't you like that, China?' And then, as if making a remarkable new discovery: 'After all, it's probably cheaper than eating out.'

She lived on a curious side street in Chalk Farm. One side of it was very middle class, with flowering cherry trees, newly painted iron railings, resident parking. The other backed on to railway yards, and every other basement was boarded up. During the fifties Christiana's house had been split into two self-contained maisonettes which she had bought at auction at the height of the Thatcher boom, intending to knock them back into a single dwelling. 'Somehow it never got done. I never had the money. Mind you, I've got two of everything.' She had –

although she only ever used one of each. Kitchens, lavatories, showers: all in an engaging state of disrepair. She would eye them morosely and say, 'Oh well, at least the mortgage is almost paid off.'

'Then why don't you borrow the conversion money against your equity?' I suggested.

'Oh God, don't talk about it. Put some music on instead.'

Christiana liked a lot of torch singers I had never heard of. She liked Gavin Bryars. At first I thought we had Tom Waits in common, but she only really liked *Frank's Wild Years*. If I played an old Iggy Pop track, she would always ask, 'Can you remember where you were and what you were doing when you first heard this?' She liked Laurie Anderson. Sometimes, especially on Saturday evenings, I found myself staring out at the railway yards wishing I could listen to Bryan Adams.

After we had eaten, we talked. I talked about Isobel. Christiana talked about anything that came into her head. In practice this meant that we talked about sex.

'Isobel and me . . .' I might begin, and then be unable to continue. 'I don't know how to say it.'

'For God's sake, China.'

'Things were so physical between us.'

'Of course they were. At the beginning you can't stop fucking one another, can you? It's just fuck, fuck, fuck.'

She looked thoughtful, then laughed.

'Vita's father and I found things in the bed.'

'Pardon?'

'Well, strictly, it wasn't a bed the first time, it was the toilet on an InterCity 125. Afterwards I found a perfect little wood anemone on the seat. The first time we actually slept together, a piece of straw turned up in the bed. It hadn't been there before.' She described Gram doing 'this really brilliant awed whisper', his eyes wide and naive: ' "Did we *make* that?" ' (Mimicking him, her own eyes widened, sly, innocent and self-conscious, and she looked about five years old.) Two days later it was half a tomato. 'He ate it,' she said, 'without a thought.' She stared into space, smiling all over again at Gram and herself, kneeling naked on the bed in some fleapit hotel in Amsterdam or Cracow, laughing over the things they had fucked into existence: a beer-bottle top, two strands of coloured wool, a small apple with woody, very sweet flesh. All her male lovers had had short names, like the names people give sheepdogs: Al, Bill, Ed. From their photographs they looked like big, dependable men, but none of them had been, much. 'Oh, Gram was a bastard. But something always caught fire when we were together. Life was never dull with Gram—'

'I know what you mean,' I began to say.

'—and then suddenly one day we went to Brighton, and nothing happened. I spent the entire afternoon remembering other times we'd been there.'

Looking east towards the town from Palace Pier, she had remembered how it floated between grey sea and sky a deep stratospheric blue, between each side of the century, real gold, buildings biscuit and cream, suspended there in the horizontal sunlight which also illuminated the seaward side of the waves before they fell and broke on the beach. She had remembered Gram for some reason shouting gleefully, 'No, it goes up your leg. Sea air is well known for going up your trouser leg.' But this time nothing like that had happened. They had walked about all afternoon. They had visited every antique shop in the Lanes. They had played an electronic motorcycle game on the pier, then hung over the railings, discovering in the low muddy swell by the stanchions two frozen-looking surfers in wetsuits. 'We caught the six o'clock train home. It was such a shock to me. Wherever we'd gone previously, something had happened to us. It was as if the very fact of us had been enough to generate a good time. Do you know what I mean? I was really quite shocked when I realised we were bored.'

'Mm,' I said.

'I've always blamed Brighton.'

'You can't tar a place with what happened there,' I thought of saying; and then, remembering how much I hated west London, went on instead, 'I didn't mean just the beginnings of things. It never went away for Isobel and me.'

'I don't think I loved him anyway,' said Christiana. 'And he certainly—'

She stopped and looked hard at me.

'It goes away for everyone, China,' she said. 'The only good luck you can have is that it goes away for both of you at the same time.' She contemplated that: shuddered. 'Relationships are so strategic. They come down to what you can offer one another.'

I looked at her.

'You don't believe that for a moment.'

'I do.'

'What about Choe?' I said.

She blinked and looked away.

'Perhaps you're right,' I said.

'No,' she said.

But perhaps she was.

Inevitably we tried to become lovers. It wasn't very successful at first. We were all arms and legs. The angles were wrong. I felt as if I might hurt her, and sometimes I had no idea what she wanted.

She said: 'Sex is very *phallocentric* for you, isn't it?'

She said: 'Is this what Isobel liked?'

She said in an amazed voice: 'You don't know my body. You don't know my body.'

'Christiana, how could I?'

But I loved her little bedroom, with its off-white walls, pale blue cupboards and single shelf of books above the narrow single bed. I loved that it had no curtains, just a raffia blind she never drew, so that all night the strange metallic halogen light from the railway yards hardened her thin, strong swimmer's body until it looked like enamel. And in the end we did get it to work, and she whispered, 'China, what are you *doing* to me?' and, 'Oh yes, oh, China, oh yes, very good, very good.' And then – to herself, but almost as if to some third party in our dark, warm transaction – 'I want to come, oh, I want so much to come.'

Except each other, we never found anything in the bed afterwards. Instead I lay tracing with the tips of my fingers the curious, raised web of scars beneath her tiny breasts, where, she told me eventually, her ribs had been laid open again and again for heart surgery.

'I was born with valve stenosis.'

At ten years old she had been admitted to hospital and offered a choice. They could replace the bad valve with an artificial one, in which case she would have to take anti-coagulants for the rest of her life. Or she could have the appropriate valve from a pig's heart. Her parents had helped her choose the latter, advising, 'It does seem more natural, dear,' only to discover that a pig's heart lasts exactly the lifetime of a pig. 'Every eight years the new valve dies and has to be replaced.' From that moment she had felt betrayed: by her mother and father, by the doctors, by her own body. Thirty years later, her sense of continuity was deeply undercut. She could be as pragmatic about this as about everything else that had happened to her, shrug and repeat, 'No expectations, no regrets.' But her heart had aged her – the anxiety, the drugs, each bout of surgery wearing her away – and sometimes she would stare at the railway lines and admit, 'It tires me out, China. It's tired me out.'

I wasn't sure what to do for her at moments like that. She didn't want comfort. I tried silence, but she didn't want that, either. In the end I stroked her scars very lightly one night and said:

'Wasn't that a bit politically difficult for you? A pig's heart?'

'China, you fool.'

She took my hand in her own and moved it down.

'I love the way you touch me,' she said. 'But there's no need to be so gentle.'

The sun shone through Christiana's kitchen window for about an hour every morning. Then it moved behind a point block until noon, when a few pale, oblique rays fell across the desk in the corner of the front room, illuminating a glass jar full of pens. That was usually the last of it until the next day. But sometimes the sunset would be reflected into the room for a minute or two by a window across the road. A ray of light fell across the empty living room on to the rosewood piano she never played – or, in the bedroom, across a pile of plain white underwear – and I shivered with the strangeness of her, the austerity of her life, her house, her furniture, both actual and emotional. In that light, even her books seemed strange. I would browse the shelves and wonder how she could reconcile Julia Kristeva with Alan Garner, or who had given her *The Earth Wire* by Joel Lane. She would be saying:

'The whole of the fifties looked like a caravan site in the rain. It looked like a bungalow on the Welsh coast.'

Or: 'Cross-Channel ferries. Don't tell me. I get sick on a flannel.'

She had the untidiness of some small animal trying and failing to make a nest. A litter of unpaid credit-card bills and music cassettes (some with the tape spilling out of them) had to be cleared off the table in the evening before we could eat. An eczema of dried soapsuds had to be wiped off the tiles behind the bathroom sink before I could wash. She was always trying to mend a broken cup with Pritt paper glue. Her kitchen smelt. A draught was enough to clear it. But as soon as the breeze dropped, there it was again, pervasive, intricate and hard to forget. Perhaps it had always been there. Costa Rica coffee grounds, the water in which pasta had been cooked, clarified butter: the primordial smell of human habitation in the London Basin.

One afternoon, in the middle of some argument I forget, she looked out of the window and said:

'The dead never answer you back.'

Christiana drove around in a down-at-heel old Citroën BX

Safari. It was silver. The hydraulics leaked, and she had hacked off one of its wing mirrors and part of a plastic bumper during some disagreement with a delivery van double-parked outside a deli in Camden. I always knew when she had been out to buy groceries. The BX would be parked outside the house, one wheel up on the pavement and its lights on at two in the afternoon. She would take the shopping out of the car and then leave it in the hall, and move it item by item across the next day or so into the kitchen. A pile of vegetables would diminish by two aubergines and some sweet potatoes: the rest would remain for several hours before she went back to worry at it again. 'Don't go near that stuff, China,' she would warn me. She had forbidden me to cook the day she caught me measuring ingredients. Also, I had admitted that I shopped at Sainsbury's and had no idea how to add the water to an authentic paella.

One Friday evening, with the last of the rush-hour traffic growling up the wet hill outside towards Hampstead, and a thin cold rain in the air, I arrived to find her sitting on the hall carpet, crying silently. She was surrounded by half a dozen grocery bags and there was a brown envelope in her lap.

'Christiana!'

I took the envelope from her. She had pulled it raggedly open with her hands and then lost whatever was inside. I put my arms round her and tried to get her to her feet but she resisted.

'Christiana. What's the matter?'

She gave me a dull look.

'Tests,' she said. 'I have to go in for tests.' She pushed me away and struggled upright. 'Sorry,' she said. 'Nothing's broken.' She sat down again and moved the grocery bags about. 'I don't think I broke anything.'

'Oh, Christiana.'

'It was due a month ago, but I put it off.'

She wiped her eyes and offered me a bottle.

'Australian chardonnay,' she said. 'They describe it as "broad-shouldered". Can you believe that? Broad-shouldered? That means it tastes like corned beef.'

'At least you won't need any dinner.'

I took the bottle off her and opened it in the kitchen and filled the two biggest glasses I could find. Then I went back into the hall and sat down next to her. The light thinned, the traffic quietened. Up and down the road people were turning on their televisions to get the news; they were making supper. Soon I could smell London Basin cuisine: frozen lasagne, microwaved chilli, the odd chicken casserole. 'I'm starving,' Christiana admitted, but she made no move to get up. We drank. We talked. 'Ever had Pineau des Charentes?' she asked. 'Unfermented grape juice with brandy, about seventeen per cent proof.' She stared into her glass. 'Actually, this stuff isn't bad.' Every time she fell silent, I asked her something else about herself. One of the things I asked her was, 'What did you do all those years we weren't speaking?'

'Oh, this and that,' she said.

She said: 'You know most of it already.' She gave me a little wry grin. 'I once spent a year fucking anyone who answered an advert in the back of *Time Out*. I was quite bi by then.'

'Bye bye then,' I said.

'Have you ever done anything like that?'

'What?' I said. 'Been bi?'

'No, you fool: put an ad in the back of *Time Out*.'

'I don't think I have.'

'Don't bother. You get this phone call, you go all the way to bloody Waterman's Arts Centre, and your date's a bloke wearing a lovat safari waistcoat with a copy of *Viz* sticking out of one pocket. He asks you if you want the couscous or the vegetarian goulash. Everyone with any youth or energy left is in the bar getting pissed, and they look at you as if you're dead, if they look at you at all, and the play is something by Eugene O'Neill.'

'I thought you liked couscous.'

'They drink a lot of Pineau des Charentes in East Sheen, China,' she said. 'I'm afraid you're grown up enough to know that now.'

'*Miaow*.'

Later, she said:
'For a while I thought Vita would be enough.'
'And isn't she?'
'Of course she is.'
'Well then, why—'
She made a little impatient gesture of the head, pursed her lips. 'Vita's going to be OK. It's not that,' she said. 'It's just . . . Well, look, she's got the most beautiful voice, but she won't sing. She's got a fantastic eye and a natural hand, but she won't draw. I've tried everything.'
  'She's only eight,' I pointed out. 'It's a bit early for St Martin's.'
  'I know,' said Christiana.
  'What does she want to do?'
  'At the moment she wants to be a psychologist.'
  '*What?*'
Soon we had finished the chardonnay, and I had been to the kitchen to open another bottle, and it was eleven o'clock and quite dark in the hall. After a long silence Christiana said:
  'I loved the band most of all. I loved every show we ever did. We had a sixteen-wheel truck just for the lights and things. We went all over Europe and America. Vita came with us and jumped about in the audience every night. China,' she said, 'I once drove a sixteen-wheel truck into Prague at five o'clock in the morning. Look at me now.'
  'You're an extraordinary person,' I said.
  She sniffed and wiped her eyes.
  'I know,' she said. 'I *know*. But what does that matter, when you can't have what you want?'
  'Christiana, Christiana.'
  'I've hardly been out of the house since he left,' she said suddenly. 'I loved him, even when he wasn't kind to me. Is that awful?' She began to cry in earnest. 'Isn't that awful? I've hardly been out. China,' she said: 'What if I'm agoraphobic?'
  I held her hand and looked down at the scattered shopping. I thought of all the Turkish restaurants she had taken me to in Stoke Newington.

'I don't think you're agoraphobic, love,' I said. 'Honestly.'
She shivered.
She said: 'I was ten years old when they landed me with this. *Ten years old.*' She said: 'China, I'm cold sitting on the floor here.'
'Well let's get up then.'
'China, will you come with me to the hospital tomorrow?'
I don't believe she had ever asked anyone that before.
'Of course I will,' I said.

Understaffed and underfinanced, obscured by scaffolding, King's College Hospital expands just too slowly to detect with the naked eye along the upper slope of Denmark Hill, SE5. What funds there are have been assigned at random, so that while the School of Medicine and Dentistry is quite new, outpatients of the Maudsley drug dependency unit find themselves ringing the bell of a tired Edwardian house. None of the more modern buildings match, (Few of them even give the feel of structures finished and purposive.) The older ones seem simply unwelcoming and dull. A place with no firm boundaries, always petering out into its surroundings or into rows of Portakabins, King's has less an architecture than an oncology. The bulk of this tumour issued from the silver trowel of Edward VII some time before the First World War. It is fibrous and deepseated. Corridors a stale cream colour darken to tobacco as you move inwards. There are cobwebs soft with dirt in the ceiling corners. The cracked lavatory tiles smell like the urinals of some blackened northern town four decades ago. Nothing is clean. You can't find your way. The signs at stairways and junctions use a different descriptive system to the one on your appointment form. Ask directions: heavy-duty masonry drills fill the corridors with a continual resonant grinding noise which prevents you from hearing the answer. In the end, the department you want turns out to be a cul-de-sac in which three old people wait uncertainly on tubular chairs: a cubicle behind a curtain where a few shelves curve under the weight of concertina files: a tired-looking woman who says patiently, 'Take off your jean jacket, please,' and weighs you on the digital electronic scale. At night, an occasional bus grinds past. Drunks and madmen stagger up the long incline from Camberwell Green, hoping to have A & E stitch up wounds like lips. 'I was pushed,' they claim, and laugh softly. Later they will get lost and fall down again among the builders' yellow waste chutes and stacks of Hi-Seven breeze blocks. From its vantage point on Champion Park, the barracks of the Salvation Army Officers' Training School – its own walls homogenous and four-square, thick with charity, thick with good, honest funding – looks down sardonically. From up there the street seems lunar and empty, the hospital abandoned forever. But by nine next morning the local traffic is nose-to-tail again, and you can't park a car within half a mile of the Bessemer Road entrance.

' "The Changing Shape of Hospital Care." ' quoted Christiana. 'Jesus.'

We were in and out of King's for a fortnight. They lost her notes between visits. At reception they stared at her as if they had never dealt with her before. They could find nothing. Records could find nothing. The cardiac clinic was in chaos anyway – a new system, all three specialists on leave, no direction home. It was a ship without a rudder. No one could find anything this morning. 'I was here the day before yesterday,' Christiana reminded them. 'No one could find anything then, either.' She was able to point out her name on a sheet of computer output in plain view on the reception desk.

'Oh yes,' said the receptionist dismissively, 'you're on the com*pew*ter.'

'I'm going to sit here all morning,' Christiana warned her. 'If I have to.'

'You can go to radiology straight away.'

By that time it was half-past eleven. The clock in the radiology waiting room said twenty to eight. 'Ah yes, Miss Spede,' the radiology co-ordinator welcomed us. She was a cheerful woman with curly grey hair and spectacles. 'They've just rung up about you.'

'The appointment was made a week ago,' Christiana said, and turned away as rudely as she could. Later, in the waiting area, she told me: 'Last week this room was ECG reception.'

She looked around bleakly. 'It still is, for all I know.'

'Miss Spede? Miss Spede?'

'What?'

Sometimes Christiana told me:

'I don't want you with me today.'

'Will you be all right?'

'Yes.'

But she would be trembling when she returned at four in the afternoon. She wanted to be held, although she didn't know how to ask for that and could only stand awkwardly in the hall a little too far in front of me, still in her soaking wet coat, waiting until I saw what was needed.

While I sat on a tubular chair in cardiac, they put her into a copious white smock stencilled with the warning 'CAMBERWELL HEALTH AUTHORITY HOSPITAL PROPERTY'. It was designed to hang open at the back. Wearing it made her feel vulnerable and silly at the same time, the way she had often felt as a child. It was easy to imagine her wandering from corridor to corridor in this garment, tired and misdirected; returning every so often to the waiting area full of a vague anger she no longer knew what to do with. In fact she bore everything with a kind of blunt passiveness she didn't expect to share. She had been through it so many times before: and anyway was caught up, distant, filled with anxiety. If I spoke, she frowned and looked at me for a moment as if I were some hospital stranger: just someone else she didn't know.

'Pardon?'

'I said: Does it hurt?'

She shook her head.

'I just feel odd,' she said vaguely. 'You know? It's just this odd feeling.'

Suddenly her eyes focused and she looked round. In the row of chairs facing us, a baby was asleep on its back across its mother's knees, hands held in little lax fists each side of its head. On the wall above were pinned some curled leaflets and a sign saying, 'NHS prescriptions: some people get them free. Can you? If not, you could still save money with a season ticket.'

'A season ticket to hospital,' I said.

Christiana whispered. 'I hate this so, I really do.'

Outside in Bessemer Road it was raining heavily.

I looked at my watch.

'Christiana?'

'China, I—'

'Come and sit down.'

'I'm all right. What did you do today?'

'Not much.'

'China, wouldn't it be good if we could have a proper coal fire in here?'

'Wouldn't you like that?'

'A proper coal fire, and sleep in front of it together?'

One day she came back and said:

'Those fucking bastards in haematology. I'm not going again.'

She sniffed and wiped her nose with her hand.

'Really, China, I'm not going back this time. You know?'

I sat her down and gave her a cup of tea.

'It's Earl Grey,' I said. 'Look we could have this done privately. I've still got BUPA, PPA, a whole bunch of stuff like that. I know it's bad politics, but . . .'

She stared at me.

'Just listen to yourself, China,' she said bitterly. 'Just fucking listen to yourself. How would that help anyone? How would that help the poor old fucker I saw this morning?'

'I don't know,' I said. 'Because I wasn't there.' I said: 'Drink your tea.'

She smiled suddenly.

'And he was such a nice old man. *Very* middle class, in a proper tweed jacket and polished brown shoes. They were old shoes, but you could see your face in them.' (Oh yes, I caught myself thinking: just the sort of old man you love, Christiana.) 'He was reading *Aspects of Antiquity* in this faded old Pelican edition.'

She burst into tears again.

'I'd rather die, China. I would.'

'What is it, Christiana?'

'He didn't hear his *name*.'

And that was all I could get out of her. The more I tried to understand what had happened in the open-plan haematology department – where two women take your sample in the waiting area itself, with all the other patients watching – the more she repeated: 'He just didn't hear his name, that's all. They said his name as if it was part of a conversation they were having. Oh, China, that poor old man.' Her anxieties had overwhelmed her at last. Whatever humiliation the old man had suffered was her own humiliation; her own sense of worthlessness in the face of King's.

'I'm not sure what you're trying to tell me,' I said. 'Won't you think about BUPA?'

'I'm not trying to fucking tell you anything!' she shouted. Then she took my hand and laid her cheek against it. 'Thank you for offering, anyway,' she said. 'You will come in with me, won't you?'

I didn't spend all my time at Chalk Farm. I wasn't comfortable there. If I found Christiana too easily irritated, I knew I was often too dull for her. Anyway, she hated to have the M3 parked outside her house. To avoid conflict, I would return to Choe's place in Haringey every two or three days, and wait until she phoned me.

'Why haven't you been to see me?'

'Because you said my car looked like a cheap stereo set.'

Choe was rarely at home. In his absence everything covered itself further with dust: the posters featuring Adjani and Huppert, Béatrice Dalle and Nathalie Baye, in films five or ten years dead – *L'Été Meurtrier, Les Soeurs Brontë, 37C Le Matin*; the CDs of Lori Carson and the Golden Palominos stacked on the old-fashioned sideboard after being played once – 'Fucking brilliant,' Choe would say, but he soon lost interest; the piles of specialist magazines, *Photo, Vox, Motorcycle News*, subsiding day by day into yellowing fans on the carpet. Dust made rolls and mats beneath the sofa. In the kitchen there was dust thick enough to unpeel from the half-empty yoghurt cartons and unanswered correspondence.

The third of November I spent the evening watching TV. Some story of love and transfiguration, cropped into the wrong proportions for the small screen. Christiana's operation was due at the end of the week. Outside, Haringey stretched away, an endless sprawl of minicab firms, deserted bakeries, social clubs. Turn the TV off and you could hear the young Turkish Cypriots prowling Green Lanes in their Hartge BMWs and Cosworth-engined Mercedes 190s. Turn it back on and the film unrolled, passages of guilt with lost edges, photographed in white and blue light. At about half-past eleven the phone rang.

I picked it up. 'Hello?'

It was Isobel Avens.

13
Makeover

'Oh China,' she said.

I knew what had happened.

I said: 'Can you drive?'

'No,' she said.

I looked at my watch. 'I'll come and fetch you.'

'You can't,' she said. 'I'm here. You can't come here.'

I said: 'Be outside, love. Just try and get yourself downstairs. Be outside and I'll pick you up on the pavement there.'

There was silence.

'Can you do that?'

'Yes,' she said.

Oh China. The first two days she wouldn't get much further than that.

'Don't try to talk,' I advised.

London was as quiet as a nursing-home corridor. I turned up the car stereo. Tom Waits, 'Downtown Train'. Music stuffed with sentiments you recognise but daren't admit to yourself. I let the M3 slip down Green Lanes, through Camden into the centre; then west. I was pushing the odd traffic light at orange, clipping the apex off a safe bend here and there. I told myself I wasn't going to get killed for her. What I meant was that if I did she would have no one left. Traffic on the Embankment is light at that time of night. I went through it in sixth gear at eight thousand revs, nosing down fairly heavily on the brakes at Chelsea Wharf to get round into Gunter Grove. People were careful to let me through. By half-past twelve I was on Queensborough Road, where I found her standing very straight in the mercury light outside Alexander's building, the jacket of a Karl Lagerfeld suit thrown across her shoulders and one piece of expensive leather luggage at her feet. She bent into the car. Her face was white and exhausted and her breath stank. The way Alexander had dumped her was as cruel as everything else he did. She had flown back steerage from the Miami clinic, reeling from jet lag, expecting to fall into his arms and be loved and comforted. He had told her, 'As a doctor I don't think I can do any more for you.' The ground hadn't just shifted on her: it was out from under her feet. Suddenly she was only his patient again. In the metallic glare of the street lamps, I noticed a discoloration around her lips and gums. I switched on the M3's interior light and saw it was blood, sores.

'It's just a virus,' she said. 'Just a side-effect.'

She put her arms around me and sobbed.

'Oh, China, China.'

It isn't that she wanted me; only that she had no one else. Yet every time I smelt her body in the closed car my heart lurched. Alexander had made everything fucked up and eerie and it would be that way forever.

I said: 'I'll take you home.'

'Will you stay?'

'What else?'

The next morning I phoned Choe Ashton.

'Choe, it's Mick.'

'Yes.'

'I won't be at the flat for a bit.'

'Good.'

'Choe, she's back. Isobel's back.'

There was a silence.

'Choe, she's really fucked over. She needs help.'

'It's your life.'

'Choe?'

'Take care of yourself, Mick. What can I say?'

'Nothing. I'll fetch my stuff.'
'OK. See you.'

The worst thing you can do at the beginning of something fragile is to say what it is. The night I drove her back from Queensborough Road to the little house in the gentrified East End, things were very simple. For forty-eight hours all she would do was wail and sob and throw up on me. She refused to eat, she couldn't bear to sleep. If she dropped off for ten minutes, she would wake silent for the instant it took her to remember what had happened. Then this appalling dull asthmatic noise would come out of her – 'zhhh, zhhh, zhhh', somewhere between retching and whining – as she tried to suppress the memory, and wake me up, and sob, all at the same time.

I was always awake anyway.

'Hush now, it wears off. I know.'

I knew because I had been there too.

'China, I'm so sorry.'

'Hush. Don't be sorry. Get better.'

'I'm so sorry if I ever made you feel like this.'

I wiped her nose.

'Hush.'

How much had Alexander promised her? How much had she expected from the Miami treatments? All I knew was that she had flown out obsessed and returned half dead. Whatever they had tried to do to her, it hadn't worked. I had seen her last as Isobel – a bit thinner than the Isobel I loved, but Isobel none the less. Two months later, here she was: anorexic, covered in sores and open to every infection in London. I unpacked her luggage: it rustled with drugs in foil, state-of-the-art antibiotics, bizarre steroids with incomprehensible names. In the days that followed she tired easily and moved like someone in a dream. She didn't bother to dress. She walked bent forward a little from the waist, clasping her hands across her upper abdomen. She was cautious with herself, but she couldn't rest. Instead she shuffled endlessly between the bed to the window (out of which, confused, she sometimes called the name of Brian Alexander's pet cat) and the wardrobe, where she went perplexedly through the clothes she had loved before she left. I would find her stalled out on the stairs, too exhausted to go up or down. I would wake in the night to find her staring into the tall bathroom mirror like a teenage girl, half afraid, half asleep, half expectant. Can three halves make anything? Her eyes were huge with need and wonder. When she saw me looking at her over her own shoulder, her skinny hands flew together to cover the pubic mound of her image in the glass.

She didn't offer to tell me what Alexander had promised her, and I never asked. I was too shy, too angry, too jealous. Anyway, to ask would have meant using his name, and I wouldn't willingly have done that then. All I could do was look after her and hope she got well. That part was easy. I could dress her ulcerated lips and watch for whatever else might happen. I could hold her in my arms all night and tell lies and believe I was only there for her. But after a day or two she asked me, 'Will you live here again, China?'

'You know it's all I want,' I said.

She warned: 'I'm not promising anything.'

'I don't want you to,' I said.

I said: 'I just want you to need me for something.'

'Choe?'

'Yes.'

'Choe, it's Mick.'

'I didn't think it was the Queen of Sheba.'

'What?'

'My old dear used to say that: "I didn't think it was the Queen of Sheba".'

'Choe, she wants me to move back in with her.'

'Who? My old dear?'

'For fuck's sake, Choe. Isobel.'

'Ah, the Queen of Sheba. Ask yourself what she wants, Mick.'

'I don't think she knows what she wants.'

'I know what she's got.'
'Whatever it is, I just want her to need me for something.'
'She's got you by the cock.'
'I can't seem to care, Choe.'
'She always has had.'
'Choe, I just want to look after her.'
'Wrong.'

I was sick of Choe. America had worn off, and he was bored. I knew the signs. A general failure of his obsessions to satisfy him. Provocative behaviour in pubs. Loud music, bottled lagers, a Silver Palm Leaf pipe like a credit card designed by NASA. He grew sentimental and was attracted impulsively to animals and children encountered in the street, favouring bull terriers, foreign pedigree cats, and – especially – any bright three- or four-year-old girl turned out in pastiched adult clothes. 'Christ, I'm fucking broody at the moment. Look at that little sod. Don't you think she's perfect?' New toys appeared in the Haringey maisonette: a Power Mac 8100; B&W MATRIX 801 speakers, with Kevlar cones; two silvertip burmilla kittens, whose perpetually amazed green eyes seemed the size of saucers. On the concrete hard-standing outside, the Honda CBR had been replaced by a Lotus Super 7. To start with it was, 'See this, Mick? Eighty mile an hour: not fast. But look at things this way: *it'll get there from a standing start in four seconds*. It's a fucking slingshot.' Two weeks later he was passing it in the morning without a backwards glance. Sticking his head out of my car as he thugged it through midday traffic, he would call, 'Shit bike, mate!' to anyone who cycled past on less than a Klein.

As soon as he got back from New York he had been at pains to tell me:

'All that Jumble Wood stuff: I made it up. I bet you believed me, though, didn't you?'

By then, of course, I hardly cared.

'Perhaps I did, Choe,' I said.

For no reason at all I had a sudden memory of Isobel saying in a tired voice over the dinner table, 'Eat it then, Choe. Eat the custard.' Then a flash of Jumble Wood – the secluded little valley itself, with its sun-warmed oak and mountain ash – along with which came a strong sense of the outside world as an intimate place closed like a hand around human affairs in some way none of us could understand.

'Perhaps I did,' I repeated.

But Choe wasn't listening.

'I bet you did, whatever you say. Well, I only told you that to get you going, you know.'

I thought of the wood avens, flowering in the sun. I thought: what if the world is enchanted by us, and not the other way round?

'Choe?'

'It's Mick, right?'

'Choe, I'm sick of you.'

That whole November we both needed taking care of, Isobel and me. We were as awkward as children. We didn't quite know what to say. We didn't quite know what to do with one another. We could see it would take time and patience. We shared the bed rather shyly, and showed one another quite ordinary things as gifts.

'Look.'

Sunshine fell across the breakfast table, on to lilies and pink napery. (I am not making this up.)

'Look.'

A grey cat nosed out of a doorway in London, E3.

'Did you have a nice weekend?'

'It was a lovely weekend. Lovely.'

'Look.'

Canary Wharf, shining in the oblique evening light.

In our earliest days together, while she was still working at the aerodrome, I had watched her move about a room with almost uncontainable delight. I had stayed awake while she slept, so that I could prop myself up on one elbow and look at her and shiver with happiness. Now when I watched, it was with fear. For her. For both of us. She was so thin; and hot as a child with fever. When I fucked her she was like a bundle of hot wires. I was like a boy. I trembled and caught my breath when I felt with my fingertips the damp feathery lips of her cunt, but I was too aware of the dangers to be carried away. I didn't dare let her see how much this meant to me. Neither of us knew what to want of the other any more. We had forgotten one another's rhythms. In addition she was remembering someone else's: it was Alexander who had constructed for me this bundle of hot, thin, hollow bones, wrapped round *me* in the night by desires and demands I didn't yet know how to fulfil. Before the Miami débâcle she had loved me to watch her as she became aroused. Now she needed to hide, at least for a while. She would pull at my arms and shoulders, shy and desperate at the same time; then, as soon as I understood that she wanted to be fucked, push her face into the side of mine so I couldn't look at her. After a while she would turn on to her side; encourage me to enter from behind; stare away into some distance implied by us, our failures, the dark room. I told myself I didn't care if she was thinking of him. Just so long as she had got this far, which was far enough to begin to be cured in her sex, where he had wounded her as badly as anywhere else. I told myself I couldn't heal her there, only allow her to use me to heal herself.

At the start of something so fragile the worst mistake you can make is to say what you hope. But inside your heart you can't help speaking, and by that speech you have already blown it.

Her dreams were uneasy. To begin with she could hardly recall them. We would wake at three in the morning to the bedclothes flung about, and find both water and medication knocked off the little African table at her side of the bed. A quiet voice had asked her: *Why do we plant the crocuses deeper than the daffodils*? She had woken up swearing.

'China.'

'What?'

'China, I had a dream. You and I were in a room with bare floorboards . . .'

'Then what?'

'I don't remember.'

'Go back to sleep, Isobel.'

'No. China . . .'

'What?'

'China, you and I were in a room, and Brian was in there with us.'

'Fuck off, Isobel.'

'No! China!'

She took my head in her hands and made me face her. She put kisses on my mouth, on my eyes.

'China, listen, please listen. The three of us were in a room . . .'

The three of us were in a room: the two of us were fucking her.

'I was wetter than I'd ever been.'

'Isobel, I can't deal with this.'

'No, China, please. I lay down on you and put you in me. I looked you in the eyes. I was so wet. Then Brian knelt over us both and fucked me from behind. China, he was so careful. We loved each other, all of us. We were fucking in a room, and Brian was pulling something out of my back. Whatever it was got longer and longer. It wasn't at all painful, but I could feel it coming out through my skin, exactly the way it feels when you pull a hair out of your mouth. China, it was wings. When I saw them, I just came and came.

'China, fuck me now.'

'No, Isobel.'

'China China China.'

'Isobel, no.'

And then, to listen to her, she was a child again, and it was Christmas; and instead of her father – who was to have travelled from St Ives by train – she found a man in a wheelchair waiting for her outside the sugary-pink 'Beauty Heaven' display at

Hamley's in Regent Street, where pre-pubescent manikins attended to one another's hair in a salon with walls apparently of Bacofoil. His expression was dull and puzzled as he searched the lunchtime crowds for her face. His ankles were crossed, knees apart – a posture hieratic or apathetic. An artificial hand rested on his right thigh.

'China, he was like a gate-keeper.'

Why do we plant the crocuses deeper than the daffodils?
So they won't come up and trouble our dreams.

After about a week, emerging from somewhere too deep inside her to guess at, illness took a more determined hold. To the sore throats, stomach cramps and short-lived rashes we already knew were added bouts of vomiting and diarrhoea. She could keep nothing down but mineral water. Viruses ripped through her like supernatural weather – subtropical weather, Miami weather – three distinct, low-key infections in one day, cyclical highs and lows presenting symptoms from inflamed nasal membranes through arthritically swollen joints to a case of vaginal thrush that was gone in an hour. Across one rainy Thursday afternoon, her temperature reached 102, lowed-out at 93 and normalised again before five o'clock. She began to suffer constant dysmenorrhoea. Her dreams were filled with images of self-scarification, body-horror: and, above all, failed flight. Night after night Isobel soared up from her internal runways. Night after night she smoked across the sky like an Icarus dully unsurprised by failure, to wake intact but sobbing. These flights began, like the dreams of our Stratford days, with a computer screen:

'Isobel, wake up.'
  'What?'
  'Isobel, you're OK. You're OK.'
  'China, we were in a room.'
  'Let me get you some water.'

'We were in a *room*, China.'

'Isobel—'

'China, I don't *want* any water. We were in a room, and everyone's work was displayed on this huge screen. China, I could see *myself* up there, I could steer myself about . . .'

Suddenly she had learned what she had to know, and she was floating up and flying into the screen to join herself 'up in the air above the world'. At first the sky was crowded with other people, she said. 'But I went swooping past and around and between them.' She let herself tumble, just for the fun of it: she rose and levelled off, her whole body taut and trembling like the fabric of a kite. Her breath went out with a great laugh.

'China, I loved it.'

But at the top of the dream her collarbones cracked suddenly with the weight of the wings. They made exactly the sound a dry stick makes when, kneeling in front of the empty grate in the morning, you break it for kindling. ('Shall I make a fire?' 'Let's have coffee first.') She never felt the pain. There was only that appalling dry domestic crack somewhere not far away from her ear: then she fell, and as she fell a paper fire burst out of her head, a fire of newspaper and sticks to melt the wings – although they continued to move cruelly and rhythmically, levering her clavicle and upper ribs out through the skin. She knew she would never make it back to the ground, which by now looked like a city – or anyway the motherboard of some vast computer – its every parallel avenue shining with silver solder. The ground, the sky and for a moment some place which was neither: it all swung in a delirious arc round her, as if her failure was necessary so that everything else could fly. Eventually, the wings began to lever out her internal organs, which bagged and fluttered in the airstream like dark-coloured washing, like tangled parachutes, making a sad, wet flapping sound. She watched them for a moment and came to the conclusion: The only way to fly is change. 'I need to lose *these* wings.' There was barely a teacup of blood.

*

Anima

During the fevers even her smell changed.

I would wake in the dark with my hackles raised, like a dog which has detected an intruder, to find that I couldn't recognise her. Her smell was different, her body heat was different, everything about her seemed strange. She shook perpetually, and reeked of cinnamon, yeast, water pouring over a weir. For a day I smelt her sex all over the house. Her eyes were huge, and with her face close to mine, and her hands placed on either side of my face so I couldn't look away, she breathed her newness upon me.

'China, I'm going to be sick.'

'Choe.'

'Yes.'

'It's me. Choe, she's no better.'

'Let her go to the doctor.'

'Come on, Choe.'

'Worry about yourself, Mick.'

'If you're the only person who can help someone, they become your responsibility, whether you want it or not.'

'Bollocks.'

'I believe that.'

'You fucking don't. Anyway, listen to this: HOT CARS 24-HOUR MINICAB & COURIER SERVICE. A SAFE AND CARING COMPANY. What do you think?'

'It's nice, Choe.'

'It's shite.'

'Why ask, then?'

'I'm not worried about you. You lost your touch years ago.'

'Thanks, Choe.'

'It's me I'm worried about. HOT CARS? Fucking shite. Shall I tell you why?'

'You might as well.'

'*Because old ladies take taxis too.* HOT CARS. Fucking shite. Still. I've got the office.'

*

Signs of Life

The office turned out to be a narrow storefront on the corner of St Ann's Road and Green Lanes. There was a net curtain up at one window; pelargoniums and spider plants were dying in plastic pots on the windowsill of the other. 'Drivers Wanted.' Some previous tenant had painted the brickwork pink. Above it, an impressive yellow and orange sign announced: 'Domani Children's Wear'.

'They got the apostrophe in the right place,' I said. 'I'm surprised.'

On a desk pushed up against the left-hand window stood two old Akai receivers, the dispatcher's radio and an expensive plastic model of a Ferrari Berlinetta, opened up to show a tiny pristine silver engine. The bulk of the room was occupied by a half-size pool table without cues or balls, and several greasy office chairs had been arranged round the walls. The fax machine whistled, peeped and bustled to itself in a corner under a shelf made of two cheap angle-brackets and a piece of veneered softboard. In summer, air-conditioning would be provided by an electric fan, the wire guard of which was held together with brittle nicotine-coloured twists of Sellotape.

'Look,' urged Choe. 'TV and microwave.' For a moment I found it hard to tell one from the other. 'The microwave's for the drivers,' he explained. While I was trying to think of a suitable reply to that, he said: 'Fucking hell, Mick, you might be a bit more enthusiastic.'

'It's the smell, I think.'

'Awful, isn't it? Let's go out and get a beer.'

A thousand pigeons circled in the big air above the decaying Coliseum at the junction with St Ann's. We turned on to Green Lanes and bought some pastries at Barnaby's. 'I love this street,' said Choe. 'It's the only place in London where the bakeries *smell of pepper*.' He tugged my sleeve. 'Can you account for that, Mick? I'd say you can't. I'd say you can't account for that.' On the whole, enterprise had made him a little more cheerful. 'I love these fucking Turkish women with the hooked noses, too. Don't you? Thin and nervous and full of themselves. I could eat those fuckers all night.' I wondered if he did.

Later we sat at the dispatch desk. Business was slack. Drivers came in to watch the TV and stayed. They were fattish Greek Cypriot men wearing sweaty short-sleeved white shirts; lean and vicious-looking Ethiopians in tight trousers too short for them, who drove slagged-out Volvos which smelt of cleaning fluid. The TV was black and white and kept skipping channels – as Choe said – off its own bat.

'See that?' he said. 'Christ.'

We were watching ads.

'From Bodyform towels to prawn curry in less than a tenth of a second.'

He appealed to the drivers.

'Can you believe that?'

They stared back at him emptily.

'Sure, Choe,' said one of them at last, pronouncing it as in 'Joe'.

We watched part of *EastEnders*. We watched part of a *Horizon* programme about schizophrenic perception, which led to us having an argument about what Choe called 'community of experience'.

'All that's fucked,' he asserted. 'That's all over now.' He seemed half puzzled, half aggressive. 'There isn't anything like that any more.'

He examined his own hand.

'We all go to a different wedding,' he said.

He laughed.

'You ask me, "Wasn't the bride a piece? Wasn't she a real *piece*?" No point in me answering. I don't even remember who those people are.'

'Choe, I don't know what you're talking about.'

He looked impatient.

'Every fuck you ever had with that tart of yours was separate and perfect. They don't *make* anything, those experiences. And they weren't *shared*. What do you know about what she knows? Fucking nothing.'

He looked up.
'What do you *want* to know? The same.'
Then he said:
'Do you want a job? I've got one if you do.'
He looked across at the drivers.
'None of these fuckers is any good.'

When I got back to Stepney it was late. The house was quiet. Isobel lay face-down, one long leg drawn up, in a bar of moonlight on the thick rose-coloured carpet outside the bedroom. She was naked, very white, weeping tiredly; the skin around her eyes looked bruised and dark. Waking to an empty house, she had thrown up on herself before she could get to the toilet. 'China. Where were you? I'm sorry.' The vomit was clear and almost odourless; but tonight Isobel herself had a faint, tarry, bizarre smell of bitumen and musk, which reminded me of something in childhood. I carried her to the bathroom, ran a lot of warm water into the bath and helped her in. She kept her arms round my neck as she made the awkward step over the side. Her feet slipped. I felt her draw breath nervously. 'Come on now, let go and be washed. Let's make you nice again. It's just one of your bad days. Tomorrow you'll be fine.' I looked down at her in the clear water and heard Choe say, 'That tart of yours,' and suddenly felt unreasonably angry. Her pubis, waxed to an exotic, feathery stripe, looked only vulnerable. There was no more flesh on her for illness to burn off. She seemed too long for the bath, her legs folded awkwardly to one side, her shoulders presented front-on, thin as fishbones, her head turned in profile. Every day she was easier to carry, hotter to the touch. It was as if her fevers were permanent. She was so precious to me. She was so precious.

14
Real Wings

'Mick!'

'That's Choe Ashton, isn't it?'

'Fuck off Mick and listen to this. I've got it. SHOGUN CARS. *Shogun* cars! Ace, eh?'

'That's right through the other side, Choe.'

'Don't be a wanker all your life. I'm getting the sign changed.'

Isobel made progress. The nightmares eased. Her internal weather stabilised. On a good day, the state of her body frightened her less. She examined herself minutely in the mirror each morning when she woke. 'Tell me what I look like, China. No, tell me.' She greeted each new group of sores with a kind of puzzled hope – though she often seemed bemused too, as if she had expected something else. I still couldn't bring myself to ask about Miami: Isobel offered no information. When she talked, she would talk only about the flight home. 'I could see a sunrise over the wing of the airliner, red and gold. I was trying to read a book, but I couldn't stop looking out at this cold wintry sunrise above the clouds. It seemed to last for hours.' She stared at me as if she had just thought of something. 'How could I see a sunrise, China? It was dark when we landed.' Her dreams had always drawn her away from ordinary things. All that November she was trying to get back.

'Do you like me again?' she would ask shyly.

It was hard for her to say what she meant. Being thin was only part of what she had wanted. Standing in front of the mirror in the morning, in the soft, grey slanting light from the bedroom window, dazed and sidetracked by her own narcissism, she could only repeat:

'Do you like me this way?'

Or at night in bed: 'Is it good this way? Is it good? What does it feel like?'

'Isobel . . .'

In the end it was always easier to let her evade the issue.

'I never stopped liking you.' I would lie, and she would reply absently, as if I hadn't spoken:

'Because I want us to like each other again.'

And then add, presenting her back to the mirror and looking at herself over one shoulder:

'I wish I'd had more done. My legs are still too fat.'

If part of her was still trying to fly back from Miami and all Miami entailed, much of the rest was in Hammersmith with Brian Alexander. As November died into the first few cold days of December, I found that increasingly hard to bear. She cried in the night, but no longer woke me up for comfort. Her gaze would come unfocused in the afternoons. Unable to be near her while she pretended to leaf through *Vogue* and *Harper's*, I walked out into the rainy unredeemed streets. Suddenly it was an hour later and I was watching the lights come on in a hardware shop window on Roman Road.

Sometimes it seemed to be going well. I couldn't contain my delight. I got up in the night and thrashed the M3 to Sheffield and back; parked outside the house and slept an hour in the rear seat; crossed the river in the morning to queue for croissants at Ayre's Bakery in Peckham, playing 'Empire Burlesque' so loud that if I touched the windscreen gently I could feel it tremble, much as she used to do, beneath my fingertips.

I was trying to get back, too.

'I'll take you to the theatre,' I said: '*Waiting for Godot*. Do you want to see the fireworks?'

I said: 'I brought you a present . . .'

A Romeo Gigli dress from Browns. Two small stone birds for

the garden. Anemones, and a cheap Boots' nail-brush shaped like a pig.

'Don't try to get so close, China,' she said. 'Please.'

I said: 'I just want to be something to you.'

She touched my arm. She said:

'China, it's too soon. We're here together, after all: isn't that enough for now?'

She said:

'And anyway, how could you ever be anything else?'

She said: 'I love you.'

'But you're not in love with me.'

'I told you I couldn't promise you that.'

We were working on the house again. Isobel wanted new floors; she wanted space and light; she wanted *height*, she said – she wanted the loft opened so she could perch up there and look out across Stepney Green towards Limehouse Basin and the Thames. She wanted a Linn proactive stereo system so she could listen to the recent Counting Crows album. One afternoon I was fitting the speaker brackets for that when the Bosch struck rotten brick, its motor racing and throwing out sparks. I looked down and saw damp orange sand pouring out of the drill-holes. Little conical piles of it were building up on the white skirting board.

'Isobel, look.'

'They lived in a sandcastle,' she announced wryly.

'The sea never quite came in . . .'

'. . . But neither did their ship.'

'Oh, it's coming in all right,' I told her. 'Don't you worry about that.'

'It's my turn with the drill now.'

'But you've had it all week.'

'China, give me the drill.'

The way I went to work for Choe was this:

'Incidentally,' he said one Monday morning, wiping condensation off the office window so that he could stare out at my car parked against the kerb in the teeming rain, 'I'm glad you kept the Bavarian iron.' He was sitting on the dispatcher's desk drinking instant coffee from a styrofoam cup. 'It's nice.'

'I'm not using it as a taxi,' I warned him.

'Has anybody asked you to? Be fair. Have I *asked* you to use it as a taxi?'

He swung round and grinned at me.

I have not,' he said.

'Choe, I can hear you thinking a mile off.'

He put down the cup and got off the desk. 'No, Mick,' he assured me quietly. 'You only think you can.' And he offered me a yellow Post-it slip, on which he had written in his careful designer hand, 'FUGA-OrthoGen', followed by an address in SW1. I turned it over, then back again.

'So?' I said.

'So make a pick-up.'

He stared at me.

'She's a hundred-thousand a year girl since she went to the doctor, Mick.'

'Choe, leave her alone.'

He tapped the piece of paper in my hand.

'They'll tell you where to take it,' he said.

'Whatever it is.'

'Whatever it is,' he agreed.

So all through November and December I worked for Choe, which was almost like working for myself. Every trip required speed and discretion. To Eastern Europe I ferried data archived by optical drive; to Manchester, ceramic sample cases with complex electronic locks. I visited Cambridge in the middle of the night carrying an unbranded sub-notebook computer and a single transgenic mouse in its own sealed environment. My instructions were to hand both of them over at a private house. I had been given forty-five minutes to complete the trip. I settled the mouse on the front passenger seat where I could keep an eye on it, then got Choe on the cellphone. 'Have a word with this mouse,' I told him, and offered the mouse the phone. 'Ay up,

Mickey,' I heard Choe say: 'No shitting on the floor.' I rang off. The mouse ran about in its transparent plastic box, and I chatted to it. It was still alive when we arrived, though less active.

After that job I often talked to the mouse. Being away from Isobel made me feel raw and lonely; it made me angry with her again. By day I counted magpies – *one for sorrow, fuck off; one for sorrow, fuck off*. At night I listened to Lori Carson tracks and talked to the mouse.

'How's it going, Mickey?'

It was going like this: straight down a tunnel of shaking halogen light. Noise, speed, music like a second engine; something valuable on the back seat. I was often tired. Sometimes I didn't change gear for a hundred miles. Motorway signs came up a kind of living crystalline blue in the night. Above eight thousand revs, BMW engines produce a distracted whine, as if they are trying to tell you, 'Don't bother me now'; behind that I could hear the low-profile Michelins blustering and booming as they coped with strange, arrhythmic changes in the road surface. The competition ride-pack made every mile seem corrugated. My shoulders ached. I wondered if it would rain. Part of me hoped it would.

'Mickey, we're up at a hundred and thirty-eight miles an hour here. What can I say? No police and right on schedule.'

I put on 'You Won't Fall'.

'Mickey, it's been real. Have a nice life.'

One Saturday morning I made a pick-up not far from home, at a discreet office near the Scandic Crown Hotel, part of a mass of new building which cuddles into the southern curve of the river at Rotherhithe. It was more like spring than winter, a cool, wide day, with a breeze off the water fluttering in the masts and rigging of the dry-docked clipper *La Dame de Serk*. I arrived too early, sat for fifteen minutes in the car, then locked it and went to see if I could find the river behind its retaining wall of film studios, local history resources and entry-level postmodern housing. A Russian blue cat sat in the middle of the sunny deserted street. 'Puss,' I called softly and, when it ran off, I followed it. Suddenly there was the smell of water and space, a sense of windy April softness in the air. Pageant Stairs. The tide was out. Rotting wooden piles led across an acre of mud towards the brown and shrunken Limehouse Reach. A gull planed overhead, banked towards Tower Bridge, a mile west and hidden by a bend in the river. Behind me, Rotherhithe Street was waking up; by then HDC Biotech had the girl ready for me.

Twenty years old and five feet six inches tall, she wore a sweatshirt and grey Levis, holed at the knee, under a dirt-glazed olive-drab parka, the sleeves of which were so long she had to clutch the cuffs continually to keep them from falling over her hands. Her hair, a dirty yellow colour, tired of being treated, fell into loose dreadlocks streaked here and there with faded purple. Her face still retained some of its adolescent fullness; her skin was still good. Her nose and eyebrows had been pierced for Camden silver rings as thin as hairs.

'What's this?' I asked the HDC people.

'Is there a problem?'

'Only that she was begging outside Turnpike Lane tube station the day before yesterday.'

'And that's a problem for you?'

'Look at her.'

Someone flipped open a mobile phone.

'Would you like an espresso,' they offered, 'while we discuss it with Mr Ashton?'

I shrugged.

'There's no need for that.'

'Fuck you,' said the girl, as if she had just noticed me. Her eyes were round and grey, very young and direct. A light cold had reddened the fleshy part of her nostril around the nose-ring and given her voice a husky edge. I told her:

'I'm not having your dog in the car.'

The HDC people looked puzzled.

'Dog?'

'The Alsatian-cross puppy on the piece of string,' I reminded them.

She laughed.

'Fuck you,' she said.

'There's no dog,' they reassured me.

'Luggage?'

'There's no luggage.'

'Fuck you.'

A good weather forecast had clogged the outside lane of the M1 with bulbous M-registered hatchbacks making a steady seventy-five miles an hour. I looked at my watch – eight-thirty – and began to pass on the left. The edge had gone off the day. Luton preceded Newport Pagnell, which gave way in its turn to Watford Gap. My passenger spent this part of the journey curled up on the back seat. She sneezed or coughed, or sang softly and tunelessly to herself and, when I tried to talk, ignored me. I watched her in the driving mirror. After an hour she sat up, stretched and said contemptuously:

'You can't catch it, you know. I'm not a pariah.'

'What's a pariah?' I said. 'Is it some kind of fish?'

'Fuck off,' she told me, and that was it for another half-hour. What she seemed to like most was watching the scenery fly past. Staring at low-lying fields, thunder clouds, rain, she showed all the unguarded delight of a child. Eventually I asked:

'Catch what?'

'How do I know? Some fucking thing. I need a Kleenex.'

I pretended to root about under the dash.

'I had some here somewhere. Do you want to steer while I look?'

'Very funny,' she said. 'I'm hungry.'

'I'll find you a McDonald's.'

'Fuck off.'

Sometimes you leave a motorway and return to ordinary human perspectives and are struck by how mad the whole thing is – the dirt, the disturbed air, the noise, the speeds people travel at. It seems inhuman and incredible, and you wonder if you'll ever manage to make yourself do it again. As we sat in a Little Chef above the motorway watching the traffic streak past beneath us, the girl said in a voice angry but puzzled, 'Most of them don't look bright enough to drive in the first place.' And then, as if the two ideas were connected: 'What would you do if you had a lot of money?'

I wasn't sure how to respond.

'How much money?'

'Enough to get everything you wanted,' she said with the exaggerated patience of a five-year-old, and looked down at the motorway again. There was a silence. Then she asked me:

'Where is this?'

'Leicester Forest East.'

'It's nice.'

We ate. She looked happier for a moment, then suddenly white and sick. 'Where's the toilet?' While she was away I raised Shogun Cars on the Vodafone.

'This job stinks, Choe. I'd rather drive veal calves to Dover.'

'Sorry Mick, I can't hear you.'

'Oh yes you can, Choe.'

'Could you say that again?'

I was still trying to talk to him when the girl came back. She seemed shaken. She sat wiping her mouth repeatedly on a paper napkin, glancing across at me every so often with an expression half aggressive, half miserable. Her face had a damp sheen. What comfort could I offer? I didn't feel I owed her anything, and Choe's bland evasions were making me angry and distracted. In the end, sick of the pair of them, I suggested, 'Have a word with this mouse, Choe,' and passed the phone over.

'Hello?' she said.

He rang off.

She wiped at her eyes suddenly.

'Why are you fucking me about like this?'

I said, 'I'm not.' I got her a packet of tissues and a bottle of Evian water and walked her out to the car-park.

'I had a lot of money once,' I told her.

She smiled for the first time.

'Oh, great,' she said. 'What did you get?'

Without thinking, I said: 'I bought a Romeo Gigli frock.'
'What?'
'Not for myself, of course.'
She stared at me in disgust.
'Being rich isn't like Christmas,' I told her. 'You just buy houses and things.' Even to me it sounded like a counsel of despair.

Out on the windy tarmac there was a real public holiday in progress: the RAC booth doing brisk business against a photographic background of wrecked and tangled Fords; two men with accordions and a plastic bucket collecting for the blind; people wandering dreamily about in front of each other's cars, treading in an ice cream or treading on the brakes, blinking in the sunshine as they tried to find 'Fuel' and get back on the road again. Their children had gone to the wrong Mondeo (metallic plum) and waited by it for twenty minutes and were still crying. They were up to here with it, they told one another: right up to here. Out on the motorway they would drive slowly and woodenly, and refuse to give up their lane. Meanwhile, a very fat woman with straggling grey hair had lost her way in the middle of the zebra crossing, a notional causeway connecting restaurant to car-park, and now stood grasping the front of her floral-print dress repeatedly, and pulling it down over her belly to reseat it. She smiled happily around until somebody came to fetch her.

The girl watched, puzzled as a Martian, then said: 'They're thick and they love it. It's such a revenge for being alive, isn't it? To be thick and in the way.' Waiting for me to unlock the BMW she added:

'What sort of shit car is this anyway? They said I'd get a limo.'

It was my turn not to talk.

Leicester preceded Nottingham, which gave way in its turn to Mansfield, where the clouds, as they say, opened. The traffic slowed, curdled across all three lanes, then, finned with spray and blinking its hazard lamps, went nose to tail at twenty miles an hour into the rain. The sky was dark, the motorway silver:

cold air filled the car. The girl looked out. She tucked her hands into her armpits and curled up so tight she barely occupied half the rear seat. Every so often she shivered briefly, like a wet dog. At Rotherham I took the M18 east and then the A1(M) which I intended to follow to Edinburgh. Doncaster, Pontefract, York, said the roadsigns: A630, M62, A64. Despite that, I soon found we were heading into unmarked territory. The girl sat up abruptly. She pushed back the cuff of her parka to reveal a gold Breitling Chronomat.

'Where are we?'

'Darlington,' I said. 'We've just passed Scotch Corner. You can go back to sleep: we won't be there for another two or three hours.'

'Yes we will,' she said.

'What?'

'Take the A68.'

'Too much local traffic to be any quicker.'

'Are you stupid?'

'Let me explain. I was hired to drive. You were hired to sit in the back.'

'You are stupid,' she said.

She shook her head. 'Look, *we aren't going to Edinburgh.* OK?'

The Vodafone rang.

I answered it. Choe's voice said: 'Where are you, Mick?'

I told him.

'Good,' he said. 'I thought you'd be there about now.'

'Choe, there's a problem.'

'It's not ours, Mick. Do what she wants.'

'Choe, what's going on?'

'There's no problem, Mick,' he said.

He rang off.

Perhaps half an hour later we were pushing into the raw North Pennine hillsides above Consett. Tired and withdrawn, the girl rested her cheek against the nearside rear window and watched the summit of Bolt's Law, axle of our shallow north-western sweep, shredding the rainclouds. 'Turn left here. And now right.' She kept us in the valley of the South Tyne, which on a wet day is the bleakest, most useless place you've ever been: groups of sodden pedestrians plodding along in the grass beside the road, empty petrol stations and tea-rooms, the watery glint on the long pathways between vanished Roman settlements; then suddenly a glimpse of Hadrian's Wall like excavations for a new Sainsbury's. 'Now right again. Now stop. Stop here.' She had me pull into a gateway somewhere on the edge of the Spadeadam Forest. Behind us, the valley spread out to where Crag Lough lay like a mirror in the grey light; beside us, a steep tussocky drop into the Irthing. It was raining steadily. Mist breathed out of the trees to meet the low cloud. The road curved away gently uphill between drystone walls and dense stands of conifer. I could see a lay-by six hundred yards ahead, and in it a black car much bigger than mine.

The girl said: 'I change rides here.'

She got out and slammed the door. The BMW was filled briefly with a smell of woodland and damp bracken.

I wound my window down.

'I hope you live long enough to get what you want,' I called after her.

She sneezed. Without turning round she said:

'I wouldn't wear a Romeo Gigli dress if I was paid to.'

'Frock,' I said. 'I think you say frock.'

'Fuck you.'

She walked slowly and tiredly away up the hill, stopping once to massage the small of her back, the way a pregnant woman often will. Five minutes later the car ahead left its position in the lay-by and coasted silently down past me. It was long and black, and awkward to drive in a Northumberland lane: a Moscow car covered in chrome, as American as a Dead Kennedy playing card. *Zil 117*. I saw the girl's tired smile, I saw her hand lifted to me. I saw Ed Cesniak sitting beside her in one of his plum-coloured suits, and I saw him grin across at me. I saw how much room they had between them on the cheap leather seat.

Well, I thought: At least you got your limo.

*

In my dreams I soon catch them. White faces stare back at me down all the narrow lanes. 'Your driver's no good,' I tell them. Trying to get away from me, he has put the power on too hard and come out of the turn in radical oversteer. 'Your car's no good either,' I say, watching it wallow on its diplomatic-grade shocks: but I don't think they can hear me. I stick to them like shit all the way across country to Preston, where they turn south on the M6. It is beginning to get dark, squalls of rain are blowing almost horizontally across the road. Suddenly the Vodafone chirps. It's Choe.

'What are you doing, Mick?'

'Oh, hi Choe,' I say. 'I thought you couldn't hear me?'

'Mick, Ed says you're tailgating him at a hundred and ten miles an hour. He says he's not worried but he thinks you might get hurt.'

'Does he now?' I say. 'Would he like his wing mirror ripped off?'

I slip the M3 a bit closer and switch the halogens on to main beam. I switch on the fog lights. I switch on anything else I can find, including Lenny Kravitz, making his way with a kind of psychotic self-control through 'Mama Says'. The driver of the Zil raises his hand to cover his interior mirror, brakes heavily and swerves back into the middle lane. I go up on his nearside, wind my window down, stick my head and one arm out into the airstream and grin at him.

'I tell you what, Choe,' I shout into the Vodafone. 'Do you bet I can? Rip it right off?' It's getting hard to speak to him if I want to steer as well.

'Mick, stop that!'

'Do you bet me?'

Choe says quietly: 'The girl wants you to leave them alone, Mick.'

'The girl doesn't know what she fucking wants. And what are they going to do with her when they've finished with her, Choe? Dump her on the Lancashire waste tip with all the other used rubber gloves? Remember that tip, Choe?' By then we are down at eighty miles an hour and the Zil has hustled me on to the hard shoulder. I say: 'I'm sick of these fuckers, Choe.' I brake irritably, drop a gear and get eight and a half thousand revs, all in the same gesture; and in that gesture depart. At a hundred and forty I am still trying to accelerate.

Nothing like that happened, of course: or ever will. The Zil and its occupants are long gone in the dirty rain, en route to Budapest or Zurich. Who was screwing who? Did the girl have herself kidnapped? Or had HDC Biotech intended to sell her to Cesniak all along? How far was Choe involved? When I got back to Shogun Cars it was late; everything stank of kebabs. I leant over the dispatcher's desk and told him, 'I'll drive a cab from now on.'

'Whatever you want, Mick.'

'She was a live host. She was a live host.'

'Fucked if I know what that *is*, Mick,' he said puzzledly. 'Do you?' He pretended to look through the paperwork. 'They told me it would be an "industry executive".'

'I'll drive a cab from now on.'

'Whatever you want.'

Because minicab work requires a very specialised vehicle I bought a Mercedes 230TD with 110,000 miles on the clock, equipping it with 'No smoking' signs and a Magic Tree airfreshener ('You'll find one in every car'), despite which its blue-grey nylon upholstery soon soaked up the smell of ocakbasi, sweat and patchouli oil. A powerful heater kept the inside too warm. I practised asking, 'Where do you want to go?' in a voice of neutral exasperation; driving with my eyes fixed on something in the top left-hand corner of the windscreen, especially at complex junctions; and repeating the words 'King's Cross' as if I had never heard them before. I liked night work because there was no pressure from other motorists. I could encourage the Merc amiably out on to some vast empty interchange in

Tottenham Hale or Harlesden – where the wet tarmac and tall buildings looked like another country inhabited by another race of people – and take time to misread 'Neural History Museum' on a torn and flapping poster under a bridge. Wherever you are in London at two in the morning, there is always someone coming out of a late shop reaching into a brown bag of groceries. 'AH. FORKEY,' the dispatcher will say suddenly and very loudly: 'Is anyone near Colyton Road? FORKEY; Colyton Road, anyone do me Colyton Road? GRON,' and be lost in a burst of static. Then all is quiet again.

I got home from these night rides feeling at the same time rested and lively, to make espresso on the stove; load the dishwasher with Cuisinox cookware and the washing machine with Hanro knickers; wipe the kitchen top, upon which Isobel had been spilling milky tea all day; and at last go quietly upstairs to tidy her clothes and watch her while she slept: or talk if she was awake. 'China,' she would whisper in delight; 'Hello, China,' as if I had been absent for months – expected back, like a child from boarding school or a husband from a business trip: but not so soon. She might be reading: Camille Paglia one night, Françoise Sagan the next. (Her tastes yawed. She could always mix a paragraph of a self-help text called *The Road Less Travelled* with two or three of Baudrillard, *The Evil Demon of Images*. It was disconcerting.) Sometimes she took my hand tightly in hers; and sometimes she seemed so pleased to see me I couldn't look into her eyes. One morning I came in and found her convulsing.

She had fallen off the bed, pulling the quilt with her and knocking down the African table again. Barleywater and drugs had gone everywhere. Isobel was lying on her back looking startled and panicky. Sweat ran off her. She couldn't speak, but she could grunt, and anyway everything was there in her round white staring eyes – fear, confusion, loneliness. I wondered if she could see me: I knew she could. Her spine arched and relaxed, arched and relaxed, quite slowly, in a way that had nothing to do with her. She seemed most of all to be trying to convey that:

This is nothing to do with me. At the crux of each spasm I could hear her teeth grind with the effort of denying it. She had wet herself. The smell of her, breathing from every pore and aperture on a long, languorous swell, changed from moment to moment: ammonia to sloe gin, expensive shoe cream to cheap banana milk. I bent over her there in the dark room, not quite knowing what to do, while Isobel unpacked herself, like a Victorian medium, of these ghosts and ghost-locations: the smell of a zoo; the smell of a tidal pool; moist earth, torn leaves and uprooted sticks; stale bread; bruised grass in a wedding marquee; plastic and frankincense; fennel, fenugreek and burnt cork. Beneath that, deeper, more bodily odours, oils, waxy secretions, bloods and fluxes, things glandular and hidden. I didn't know what was happening. Was Isobel *remembering* puberty? A wet dog on the White Downs? The miasma of old tobacco in some deserted hotel lounge? It was as if the Alexander treatments had unsettled old emotional sites within her, so that they flickered and flared up. Suddenly the convulsion let her go, dropped her at my feet without a gesture and walked away. Her eyes widened, brightened, as if they had seen something preternatural, closed again: and she was able to speak. 'No. They wait here for people,' she insisted, trying to warn both of us about something. 'China! The screen! We can fly!' I bent over her to listen. She choked on a plug of mucus and writhed away from me. 'No! Oh no!' She changed her mind and held out her arms like a toddler for comfort, and when I recoiled, because she reeked like a mare on heat, could only wail: 'Oh China.' I picked her up and put her back in bed. Her body was rigid, slippery to touch, fantastically hot, hotter than a human being should ever be. She smelt of lemon, and something glutinous beneath – albumen, or perhaps semen, caught at the point of drying; then, briefly, milk from a dandelion stalk broken on a late spring day. With that, all the tension went out of her. 'Have me, Brian,' she said, in a clear, sane voice, a voice almost conversational: and slept. I was left trembling in the growing light, tears of rage and misery running down my face. Whatever Brian Alexander had promised her, it wasn't this. I saw with a sudden hopeless clarity that whatever either of us had promised her, it wasn't this.

15
Hi-pad London

Jealousy is malarial because:
   It recurs.
   It is unpredictable in both frequency and ferocity.
   It causes you to hallucinate.
   Nothing you think or predict or imagine, no conclusion you reach in a condition of jealousy, can be trusted. Jealousy builds a housing project of logic from a single brick. What can you do? Wander the ramps and serviceways of your private Broadwater Farm like any other puzzled debt collector. Every floor looks the same. Knock on the right door and there is a sudden tense silence inside. You want something from the occupant, but you no longer understand what it is, let alone how to get it.

Isobel had passed the crisis, and now improved daily. Her skin began to heal. All her different fevers broke. She collected her medication together, took it to the bathroom and arranged it on the shelves, where it could gather dust. Her appetite increased, and she put on a little weight.
   'Work days now,' she ordered me. 'Work days now, China. I want to do cooking again.'
   'Shall I hire a video tonight?'
   'Yes. Get *Moonstruck*. No, get *Three Colours White*.'
   'I'll get them both.'
   'Bring popcorn. Bring lots of popcorn.'
   'I thought you wanted to cook.'
   'Bring Maltesers.'

When I got back, she was frying chicken livers for pâté, stirring them with a wooden spoon held at arm's length.

'Isabel, what are you doing?'

'Standing well back, in case I see them.'

'What did you think about at work today?'

'Nothing much.'

'China, you must think about something.'

'Not really.'

'China, tell me.'

'I drove around imagining you in a hospital smock.'

'Oh yes? That's what you do all day, is it?'

'Yes. It was open at the back. "HOSPITAL PROPERTY" was stencilled on the front of it in red, in case someone stole it.'

'Why would someone want to steal that, China?'

'They might want to steal you.'

'And why would they want to do that?'

'They might. Anyway, in the end, you and I met—'

'Oh, we met, did we?'

'—in some dusty little consulting room with a filing cabinet and a desk, which you bent over almost immediately.

'*Bent over?*'

'I was a doctor—'

'Of course you were. *Bent over?*'

'Well, that's cheered you up a bit,' I said.

Half-past three in the afternoon. Pink clouds over the trees round the communal garden. The crows complain from their perches on top of the flats across the road. The sky is greying away from blue. In ten minutes it will be grey with a greenish tinge, a much flatter, less illuminated, colour, like the difference between the scales of dead and living fish. A breeze gets up and moves the branches of the London plane outside our house. A dog yelps, running in circles on the darkening grass. It is a neatly clipped Old English sheepdog, barely more than a puppy, whose favourite game is to run three or four times round a thick group of shrubs, then turn round and run three or four times in the opposite direction. It is happiest if another dog will join in, but content to run in any case. Eleven lights come on, one above the other, on the eleven landings of the apartment block. One drowsy fly, woken perhaps by the brief sunshine earlier in the day, buzzes and taps at the sash window. The block of flats, the trees, the Victorian houses on the other side of the square, are now silhouetted against the sky, completely black.

I stare out. I hear her in the room behind me. I wait for the right moment. I say:

'Are we back together again Isobel?'

'I do love being with you, China.'

It wasn't enough.

'She never makes an effort, Choe. I make all the effort.'

'I told you, Mick.'

'She won't come an inch towards me.'

'She's got you by the cock.'

'It's not that, Choe.'

How can I admit this?

I was terrified that, recovered, she wouldn't need me.

A mild winter made London intimate and cosy. The residential streets seemed to become narrower, the brickwork warmer. I knew it was nearly Christmas when I dropped a fare in Camden and the whole of Inverness Street market smelt of Christmas trees. Vanloads of them were coming in, with shouts and palaver as the drivers tried to manoeuvre in the confined space between the stalls in the afternoon gloom. By then, Isobel and I were shouting at one another late into the night, every night. I slept on the futon in the spare room. There I dreamed of Isobel and woke sweating.

You have to imagine this:

The Pavilion, quite a good Thai restaurant at the corner of Rupert Street and Shaftesbury Avenue. Isobel orders beef panang. 'Can I have a red curry as well? Would that be really greedy?' she asks me. And, before I can answer: 'I'm going to.' She gives me a jacket wrapped in birthday paper. She leans across the table. 'Ally Capellino, China. Very smart.' The waitresses, who believe we are lovers, laugh delightedly as I try it on. But later, when I want to buy Isobel a red rose, she says, 'What use would I have for that?' in a voice of such contempt I begin to cry. In the dream, I am fifty years old that day. I wake thinking everything is finished, even my life.

Or this:

Budapest. Summer. Rakoczi Street. Each night Isobel waits for me to fall asleep before she leaves the hotel. Once outside, she walks restlessly up and down Rakoczi with all the other women, waiting for Ed Cesniak to pick her up and take her back to the decaying courtyard off Damjanich and there discover that beneath her beige linen suit she has on grey silk underwear. She is always hot. She cannot explain what has failed in her life. I wake and follow her. All night it feels like dawn. Next morning, in the half-abandoned *Jugendstil* dining room, a paper doily drifts to the floor like a leaf, while Isobel whispers urgently in someone else's voice:

'*It was never what you thought it was.*'

Or this:

Isobel and I were in a room with bare floorboards, and Brian Alexander was in there with us.

Appalled all over again by their directness, astonished to find myself so passive, I would struggle clear of dreams like this thinking: What am I going to do? What am I going to do? It was always early. It was always cold. Grey light outlined a vase of dried flowers on the dresser in front of the uncurtained window, but the room itself was still dark. I would look at my watch, turn over and go back to sleep. One morning just before Christmas I got up and packed a bag instead. I made myself some coffee and drank it by the kitchen window, listening to the inbound City traffic build up half a mile away. When I switched the radio on it was playing Billy Joel's 'She's Always A Woman'. I turned it off quickly, and at eight o'clock woke Isobel. She smiled up at me.

'Hello,' she said. 'I'm sorry about last night.'

I said: 'I'm sick of living with the two of you. I can't do it. I thought I could, but I can't.'

'China, what is this?'

I said: 'You were so fucking sure he'd have you. Four months later it was you crying, not me.'

'China—'

'It's time you helped,' I said.

I said: 'I helped *you*. And when you bought me things out of gratitude I never once said, "What use would I have for that?"'

She rubbed her hands over her eyes.

'China, what are you talking about?'

I shouted: 'What a fool you made of yourself.' Then I said: 'I only want to be something to you again.'

'I won't stand for this,' Isobel whispered. 'I can't stand this.'

I said: 'Neither can I. That's why I'm going.'

'I still love him, China.'

I was on my way to the door. I said:

'You can have him then.'

'China, I don't *want* you to go.'

'Make up your mind.'

'I won't say what you want me to.'

'Fuck off, then.'

'It's you who's fucking off, China.'

This time I had some cardboard boxes delivered by a firm in Camberwell, packed all my stuff up in them and drove them across the river in a Luton van. I threw away the things she had bought me. When she asked, 'But don't you want any of the photographs?' I shrugged. 'What would be the point?' I asked her. She looked down at her feet. She was crying silently. 'I just thought you might want to keep some of it.' She left the room and came back with two prints we had bought in New Orleans; a ceramic bowl from Tenerife in which she had piled Clementines to remind us of the sun. 'I thought you might want these. You did like them.' She brought me the brand new steam iron and stood there holding it awkwardly in front of her, her thin wrists trembling with the weight of it.

'This is yours, anyway.'

I returned to Haringey and unpacked in Choe's spare bedroom. 'Unpacked' is a misleading word. There were things there I had never got round to taking with me when I moved back in with Isobel – a small shelf of unread books; an ironing board and a lot of wire coat-hangers, one with a pair of easyfit Levis folded over it; a carrier bag from the Conran Shop. There was also a stove-top espresso maker still in its packaging. I stacked the boxes on top of one another until they made a kind of Alamo round the cheap futon. They were big, stout boxes, thirty inches on a side, stamped QTY 20PCS GW 15.5 KGS. Suddenly I couldn't see the point of opening them. Neither did I look back much on the life they contained, the one I had planned with Isobel. 'Nostalgia's first meaning is the yearning for a lost home,' claims Jonathan Meades. I was beginning to get used to living out of my own head, like a sales rep out of a suitcase. There were no curtains at the window, so I hung my jackets up there instead. They faded steadily in the light. The boxes loomed over me. GW 15.5 KGS, I read: HI-PAD LONDON.

Choe hardly acknowledged my arrival. Preoccupied and irritable, he talked long-distance on the telephone far into the night. Bulky packages were delivered for him by bike messenger in the afternoon when he was out. He borrowed the BMW and when he brought it back, sometimes two or three days later, the footwells were littered with plastic cups and half-eaten food and it smelt somehow of Eastern Europe. Plumes of grey mud, hardened to concrete and full of pinkish salt crystals, had sprayed up from the front wheel arches to customise its side panels. He lost interest in the minicab business, and promoted the wife of one of his drivers to dispatcher – a fat woman with thick red creases in her elbows, who wore her hair in a kind of black crocheted bag, ticked the pages of *Puzzler* magazine with a leaky biro and drank sachets of flavoured hot chocolate all day. A handwritten notice appeared in the window, next to 'DRIVERS WANTED'. '*Customers not known to this company,*' it said, '*will pay their fare before they get in the cab.*' On his rare visits to the office Choe spent the afternoon staring disgustedly at the TV.

'Just fucking look at that.'

This time, it was Isobel who wrote the letters. Shortly after I moved back I received a notecard with a Picasso dove on it. 'This is my favourite card,' she wrote. 'I hope you like it too.' Soon, she was writing every other day. 'I miss the way we used to wake up together,' she finished one letter; and began the next: 'Do you remember when we went to Windsor and got a boat, and you laughed because even though it rained I kept saying, "Aren't we lucky. Aren't we *lucky*."' (I did. If I closed my eyes I could remember clearly the way she had trailed her bare feet in the water, laughing delightedly as the little yellow boat, its outboard droning like a toy, bobbed in the wake of a larger one. I remembered the humid late-summer air; willows 'like a jungle,' as Isobel described them, on the south bank; a man swimming with his two dogs from a tiny sandy beach; lightning far down the Thames towards Staines. I remembered being astounded by the simplicity of her joy in these things.) 'Well we were, China. We were lucky. And I miss the fun we had.'

She seemed confused. 'I love Brian,' she wrote, and only a paragraph away in the same letter: 'It's you I love now. Please come back.'

'No thanks,' I replied.

What did I care if Isobel was sad? I was bankrupt, fifty years old and living near Tottenham with a sociopath. I couldn't quite understand why she was hurting me like this. Perhaps she didn't know that she was hurting me. It wasn't really something I could tell her. It wasn't really something I could tell Choe either. 'You can get a tart anywhere,' he said. His patience was gone. 'Just shut up about her.'

'I've got to talk to *someone*, Choe.'

Two or three days later Isobel began telephoning.

'China? I'm not very well.'

'Phone the doctor,' I said. I left a careful pause, then advised: 'That's what I'd do.'

She took this in.

'But would you come and stay? Just until I feel better?'

'I don't think I want to do that,' I said.

'China, I think it's started to work at last.'

'What has?'

'The Miami treatment. China, I don't know what to do if it's started to work.'

'Phone the doctor. He'll be pleased.'

There was a silence. I was going to hang up when she said:

'China, can't we be friends?'

'Friends is one thing. This is another. Either you want him or me.'

'Nothing's ever that simple,' Isobel said. She sounded empty and depressed.

'Yes it is.'

There was a pause.

Suddenly she said: 'I haven't been in touch with him anyway.'

My heart seemed to shift painfully in my chest.

'Why don't you leave me alone?' I said, and put the phone down.

'If it rings again,' I told Choe, 'I'm not in.'

He stared at me incuriously. Then he shrugged and said, 'I'm surprised the fucker's still connected. I haven't paid the bill.'

Christmas. Central London. Traffic locked solid every late afternoon. Light in the shop windows in the rain. Light in the puddles. Light splashing up round your feet. I couldn't keep still. Once I'd walked away from Isobel, I couldn't stop walking. Everywhere I went, 'She's Always a Woman' was on the radio. Harrods, Heal's, Habitat, Hamleys: at each stop Billy Joel drove me out on to the wet pavement with another armful of children's toys. I even wrapped some of them – a wooden penguin with rubber feet, two packs of cards, a miniature jigsaw puzzle in the shape of her name. Every time I saw something I liked, it went home with me.

'I bought you a present,' I imagined myself saying. 'This fucking little spider that really jumps:

'Look.'

Then quite suddenly I was exhausted. Even if I had wanted to go somewhere for the holiday I wouldn't have been able to: Choe had the BMW, and was pushing it through the night to Switzerland on a simple, face-bursting fuel of crystal meth and adrenalin. Christmas day I spent with the things I'd bought. Boxing day, and the day after that, I lay in a chair staring at the television. Between shows I picked up the phone and put it down again, picked it up and put it down. I was going to call Isobel, then I wasn't. I was going to call her, but I closed the connection carefully every time the phone began to ring at her end.

I wondered if I should go and visit Christiana Spede.

Once I had the idea, I felt as if I would lose my nerve unless I carried it out there and then. I left the house quickly. Halfway to the tube station I ran back, wrapped the wooden penguin with rubber feet and put in a card saying, 'Merry Xmas. I hope it all turned out well.' I went out the second time via the corner off-licence, where I bought two bottles of a nice California chardonnay, 1991.

Turnpike Lane, King's Cross, Chalk Farm. The stations were deserted and cold: tiled and dirty, forsaken, far underground. Sudden winds; those ads for bestselling books and designer underwear; an aluminium beer can rolling and dancing at the bottom of a completely deserted escalator. Braided cables a wrist thick lined the tunnels, yellow, violet, green. Tired middle-aged schizophrenics, retreating from quality lives in the Home Counties, haunted the lower platforms with their dogs and bags of clothes. As I passed, an educated look sprang from nowhere into their eyes, and suddenly they were talking loudly to themselves on various disconnected topics – the KGB; Oxford; change. At

Chalk Farm the lifts were out of order. In the street it was raining heavily. I turned up my coat collar and stepped out with reluctance.

Chalk Farm was deserted. Rain dripped from the shiny black branches of the flowering cherry outside Christiana's house. I rang her doorbell. After a minute, I knocked. I felt certain she was in. I knocked again, then knelt and shouted through the letterbox:

'Christiana! It's Mick Rose.'

Nothing.

'Merry Christmas.'

After a moment, I thought I heard a second-floor sash window sliding up, and then a quiet voice saying: 'Fuck off, China.' But there was no one there; and when I stood back on the wet pavement, I could see clearly that all the windows were dark and none of them were open. Street light flared back at me when I raised my head, like the light reflected off someone's spectacles. I felt slightly dizzy. I stepped backwards off the kerb and into cold water. It seemed a long way down. I said, 'Christiana?' A train made its stealthy, thoughtful grinding noise as it rolled in a slippery haze of halogen light along the rails behind the house.

'Christiana?'

No answer.

After a while, I pushed her present through the letterbox, tearing the wrapper only a little; arranged the bottles of wine on the doorstep like an eccentric milk delivery; and walked back to Chalk Farm tube.

There were less than two days of December left to run when Choe returned from Europe. He was dressed in Thierry Mugler slacks and a white dress shirt. He hadn't shaved since he left the house on Christmas Eve. The speed had worn off but he still couldn't seem to settle. He walked nervously about the flat as if it belonged to someone else, picking his own things up and putting them down again like someone who didn't approve of them very much and was wondering who might buy stuff like that. 'Fucking shit people, the Swiss,' he repeated several times. He wanted to talk, but was clearly reluctant to allow himself; in the end all he would say was, 'I get so fucking tired of this. You know? If people deal, they deal, that's all there is to it.' We had pizza delivered. He sat at the kitchen table, eating American Hot with his fingers and finishing a case of Budvar he had opened in the car on the way back. Over the last three months he had let his hair grow, and now wore it pulled back from his forehead into a short, oily pigtail, which gave him a brutal look. The fluorescent light, though, revealed him as haggard and tired. I was shocked to see grey hairs in his stubble.

Much later that night I decided for some reason I would phone Isobel again. I would have it out with her this time. I would tell her just what a shit I thought she had been. Her Miami postcard – with its naive injunction, 'Wish me luck!' – was propped up on the dusty side table in front of me as I dialled. I let the phone ring fifteen times; pressed the redial key and let it ring twenty: but no one answered. I replaced the receiver, waited five minutes and dialled again. Nothing. Whenever that happens, I think of a long hallway, old-fashioned wallpaper, a smell of lavender floor polish, an old black Bakelite telephone with a dial. I don't know why. Outside, three steps down into the deserted street, it is raining steadily. Upstairs the rooms are neat but untenanted, full of very large furniture. All unanswered telephones ring in this space. I put the handset down and stared for some minutes at Choe's collection of used theatre tickets, BFI tickets, receipts from Waterstone's and Murder One for novels by Harry Crews, James Crumley and Tim Willocks. Some dusty paperclips and pencils in a jar. An unopened packet of incense sticks. Then I went into the kitchen, made a pot of espresso and drank it while I watched an *X-Files* rerun on TV.

'Fuck,' I said.

Suddenly I wanted to hear her voice. I was filled with an unreasonable fear for her: but more than anything I just wanted to hear her voice.

I said, 'This fucking phone.'

Choe, who had been aimlessly cutting lines on a mirror while he soaked Europe off in the bathtub, came part of the way into the room and leant on the door frame looking at me. I was already dialling again, letting her phone ring four or five times, then dialling again.

'I'm worried, Choe.'

He shook his head.

'One thing or the other, Mick,' he said tiredly. 'Sort her out or leave her alone.'

I looked at my watch.

'I'm worried about her,' I said.

'I'll drive you over there,' he offered.

I stared at him in surprise.

He shrugged.

'What the fuck,' he said: 'I get to drive the heap again.'

He said: 'Hang on a minute.'

When he came back he was sniffing and wiping his nose. He had got dressed in his black Levi 620s, now glazed with dirt along the front of the thigh; sixteen-hole DMs with red laces; and the old cap-sleeve T-shirt which best showed off his hard little shoulders and rose tattoo. On the way out he picked up a nice Comme des Garçons jacket.

He said: 'Good deed for the day.'

So that was how we came to be in Stepney in the early hours of a wet New Year's Eve, full of fancy foreign lager and some quite decent blow Choe had picked up outside a *routier* on his way through France to Zurich. We talked about Isobel. I said everything I always said. Choe said everything he always said. Then he surprised me by adding, 'I've always fancied her. But I suppose you knew that'; and ended up weirdly:

'You want to dump her, Mick, and get someone nearer your own age.'

At the time he was chopping down through the gears to leave the A102 for Victoria Park. Engine noise batted back off the dark buildings, *oom, oom, oom*, then fell away behind us down the empty streets, as if it was after all possible to leave yourself behind in this life. I stared at his face, underlit by the dashboard instruments, further from understanding him than I had ever been.

'You what?' I said.

Imagine this:

Two a.m. The house was quiet.

Or this:

I stood on the pavement. When I looked in through the uncurtained ground-floor window I could see the little display of lights on the front of Isobel's CD player.

Or this:

For a moment my key didn't seem to fit the door.

Imagine this:

Late at night you enter a house in which you've been as happy as anywhere in your life: probably happier. You go into the front room, where street light falls unevenly across the rugs, the furniture, the mantelpiece and mirrors. On the sofa are strewn a dozen colourful, expensive shirts, blue and red and gold like macaws and money. Two or three of them have been slipped out of their cellophane, carefully refolded and partly wrapped in Christmas paper. 'Dear China,' say the tags. 'Dearest China.' There are signs of a struggle but not necessarily with someone else. A curious stale smell fills the room, and a chair has been knocked over. It's really too dark to see.

Switch on the lights. Glasses and bottles. Food trodden into the best kilim. Half-empty plates, two days old.

'Isobel? Isobel!'

As if in answer, I remembered her voice on the telephone, whispering:

'I think it's started to work.'

The bathroom was damp with condensation, the bath itself full of cold water smelling strongly of rose oil. Wet towels were underfoot, there and in the draughty bedroom, where the light was already on and Isobel's pink velvet curtains, half-drawn, let a faint yellow triangle of light into the garden below. The lower sash was open. When I pulled it down, a cat looked up from the empty flowerbed: ran off. I shivered. Isobel had pulled all her favourite underclothes out on to the floor and trodden mascara into them. She had written in lipstick on the dressing-table mirror, in perfect mirror writing:

'Leave me alone.'

16
The Signs of Life

I found her in one of the bigger blanket boxes. When I opened the lid, a strange smell – compounded of blood and beeswax, pot-pourri, vomit and whisky – filled the room. To fit herself in, Isobel had curled up, scrawny and foetal, with her head pillowed on one hand, in the pained attitude of a thirteenth-century peat-burial. Beneath her was a litter of brochures ('The Alexander Clinics Welcome You'; 'How We Can Help; Grow Your Way to Freedom!'), Polaroid snapshots and sodden tissues. She was clutching an empty Jameson's bottle. She had torn the waxy machine-varnished covers off the brochures and then thrown up on them. The photographs were all of Isobel (seen arranging flowers at the Peckham flat; perched smilingly on a slab of rock at St Govan's Bay, while the great waves broke not twenty feet from her; caught drinking milky coffee in a pink towelling robe with a row of hand-washed Marks and Sparks cotton knickers drying on the radiator beneath the window behind her – that was a very early one). She had discarded two cans of Gillette shaving foam, an old-fashioned safety razor of mine and some spare blades. She had slit her wrists. But first she had tried to shave the nascent feathers from her scalp, upper arms and breasts, hacking at the keratin until her skin was a mess of bruises and abrasions, indescribable soft ruby scabs, ragged and broken feather sheaths like cracked and bloody fingernails. Miami. In a confused attempt to placate me, Isobel had tried to get out of the dream the way you get out of a coat.

She was still alive.

'China,' she said.

Sleepily, she held up her arms. As she moved, the down of twenty different birds puffed up out of the blanket box into the air around us like grey smoke. It fell back into her wounds and clung there, turning red. For a second I was breathing it. It was as if a quilt had burst in my face, and I was breathing feathers. They had a strange odour, musty yet exotic, dry but full of musk. For a fraction of a second I felt as guilty as if I had smelt the private smell of someone I hardly knew.

Suddenly I heard wings. They were soft and distant. They were close and panicky. They seemed to circle the room, then fade.

'China.'

Here at the Alexander Clinics, we use the modern 'magic wand' of molecular biology to insert avian chromosomes into human skin-cells. Nurtured in the clinic's vats, the follicles of this new skin produce feather-sheaths instead of hair. It grafts beautifully. Brand-new proteins speed acceptance. But in case of difficulties, we remake the immune system: aim it at infections of opportunity: fire it like a laser.

Our client chooses any kind of feather, from pinion to down, in any combination. She is as free to look at the sparrow as the bower bird or macaw. Feathers of any size and colour!

THE ALEXANDER CLINICS WELCOME YOU

Isobel, poring over these brochures in nicely appointed waiting rooms in Miami and west London, had chosen for her breasts muted weights and shadings of grey into pale turquoise, grey into pink, worked in the body feathers of lovebirds and parakeets. On her upper thighs, she had decided, the base grey would darken to a browny charcoal she had picked from a tufted duck; and then into the dense black pubic stripe. Across her shoulders and along the backs of her arms she had opted for a sheaf of primary flight feathers from the biggest birds in the world, set in such a way as to mimic the wings of a peregrine falcon half-folded for the stoop. Finally, to cup her head like the hands of some exotic lover, the curved main coverts of Contamini's desert owl.

The design team were disappointed.

Running new graphics software on an office Mac upgraded to three gigabytes of RAM, they had used an ordinary Wacom tablet and 20-inch display to match the cobalt blues and iridescent greens of mallard speculum to a dense metallic black lifted from the African starling. A tall and bizarrely proportioned figure, all bars and chevrons, stared at Isobel out of the monitor – Twenty-First-Century Transgenic Woman. Isobel stared back with contempt.

'It looks like a car.'

They tried again. A riffle through the current issue of *Harper's* unsettled them, though they did like what they saw. In response they split the difference between Gaultier and *animé* art, assembling a short skirt and two-stripe crop from the greasy-looking primaries of a South American vulture.

'No,' said Isobel.

'There are some amazing things here by someone called Wendi Hoey—'

'No.'

'It's "deconstructivist fashion".'

'No.'

'We could try this—'

'Not on me.'

'Or this—'

'No.'

When they weren't doing couture they liked facts. 'Twenty-five thousand feathers on a swan,' they informed her. They explained filoplumes. They explained structure: 'Under high magnification the barbs themselves look almost like tiny feathers.' At lunch she overheard them telling one another how, where the eyes of the predator tend to look only forward, those of the prey can see all around and above. They were impressed by extremes. 'Really big lifters,' they would boast, 'like Canada geese . . .' as if they had once shaken hands with some. They offered her a kind of stole made from ostrich feathers. They offered the long unbarbuled plumes, soft and trailing, of Count Raggi's bird of paradise.

Later she would complain:

'They were idiots. This wasn't a *frock*. It was my life, and they wanted me to look like Sarah Bernhardt.'

In fact they were only postgraduate biologists in the storefront of a new technology, a bit dishevelled by success. They liked Isobel, though her diamond gaze and outright sexuality had frightened them at first. They admired her. But they were always having to be off to weekend conferences in short-sleeved shirts, chinos and blazers: so in the end they taught her how to use the Mac. She loved it. It was as if all along her dream of flight had been a dream of sitting in front of this machine. She had an immediate sense of *déjà vu* (she said): brushed a key. A million red and blue parrots burst out of the digital forest into the morning air. She touched the Wacom tablet with the pen and looked up just in time to watch a million colours wash across the screen. She toyed with lory and macaw, oriole and crimson rosella: discarded them. She scanned in her favourite photograph of herself – Isobel shown meditative in a Monsoon dress as exotic as the Guiana jungle in 1595 – stretched and tugged it into the strangest shapes, reinventing herself as wren; as swan ('Come and live with me and be a swan!'); as Lady Amhurst's pheasant. It was, in a way, the happiest time of all: that hinge or pivot in your life at which it seems you can have everything, that precarious moment of delight before the fall into choice. She was in the studio thirteen hours at a time. If she looked up from the screen she could see Miami stretching away, night and lights and water. Suddenly she yawned. It was midnight and she had had nothing to eat since lunch.

She always wound up with her original idea.

'I want this,' she told the design team. 'I really do.'

The team had hoped for a platform. They had hoped for a

showcase, something that would demonstrate the breadth of the technique.

'I want this.'

Half of them were in love with her anyway; and the other half were in love with fashion.

'It's nice,' they said.

Feathers of any size or colour! But the real triumph is elsewhere . . .

Designer hormones trigger the 'brown fat' mechanism. Our client becomes as light and as hot to the touch as a female hawk. Then metabolically induced calcium shortages hollow the bones. She can be handled only with great care. And the dreams of flight!

HOW WE CAN HELP.

Telling me about herself as a child, watching guillemots and black-backs hover and dip against the grey sea light, Isobel had once said:

'How I hated it all.

'I willed myself away. I didn't know where, just anywhere.'

And then:

'At least the gulls could get away.'

What had she wished, a seven-year-old thinned by growth and ambition, blown about after school by the blustery winds of Aire Point? To be as free as the father who had brought her into the world at Sennen Cove only to maroon her in the same gesture, in that small ice-cream business – in that world of small business – and who now, easily released by his adulthood, flew like a bird every Wednesday in a toy Cessna from a toy aerodrome near St Just? What fantastic resentments a seven-year-old must bear. What did she promise herself, watching the gulls brace themselves against the sky then turn impassively out to sea and let the cold air slip by them? What did she dream, running down the hill with her arms outstretched in a classic bank-and-turn? Whatever it was, she never banked on this . . .

A gull needs a keel. A gull is a machine for levering the air.

Something must anchor the huge packs of muscle that operate its wings. Gulls need an armature, complex and Victorian, and inside they must look much as the turkey does, a curious cage of bone, stripped and bared after Christmas dinner.

This is not to mention a beak.

Isobel had none of these things. Oh, her heart beat three hundred times a minute. In those days she ran hotter than any other human being. And she looked so beautiful and eerie in her plumage. But despite all that she was a thinnish woman of the Thatcher middle classes who liked to have an income of between fifty and a hundred thousand pounds a year. Alexander had made her resemble a bird. But underneath the cosmetic flourish, the DNA treatments, the Miami cut-and-splice, she was still Isobel Avern. Whatever he had promised her, she was only Isobel. Eventually she would shop again at Harvey Nichols.

> Engineered endorphins released during sexual arousal simulate the sidesweep, swoop and mad fall of mating flight, the frantically beating heart, long sight. Sometimes the touch of her own feathers will be enough.
> GROW YOUR WAY TO FREEDOM!

Whatever he had promised her, she could never have flown.

Some events take language away from you. The pieces of the world settle into a shape that won't be said. It is a kind of vertigo. The endless panic bubbles up but it doesn't seem to show. I stared down into the blanket box. After a long time I managed to pick Isobel up and carry her carefully down the stairs. Then I was running across the pavement towards the M3, and Choe was blinking muddledly at the sight of her, throwing the nearside rear door open and beginning to say, 'Christ, China.'

I couldn't get her into the seat. Her arms and legs were everywhere, pivoting loose and awkward from the hips and elbows. I didn't panic until then.

'Isobel, you'll have to help . . .'

'China.'

'What, love? What?'

'China.'

She could talk but she couldn't hear. Blood ran into my shirt where she had put her arms round my neck. I slammed the door behind us. Choe started the engine.

'Drive,' I urged him.

He looked surprised. Then he said mildly, 'OK Mick.'

At that the BMW seemed to slither away from the kerb of its own accord, fishtailing out into the empty arcade-game of Whitechapel, where we began to pass the scattered traffic on either side at eighty or ninety miles an hour. Some radio station I didn't know was playing the protracted, formal opening of the old Who song 'Baba O'Riley'. Choe turned up the volume. Suddenly London was falling away from us at odd angles, as if it had achieved the topological values of a Vorticist painting. Lumbering taxis, wry hoardings, white faces of pedestrians fearful on traffic islands splashed with halogen pink, rushed upon us and were snatched away in the nick of time.

'*Yes*,' said Choe to himself.

He had the carbon-fibre front seat set right forward and his face up near the windscreen. Driving was a physical thing for Choe. Cars loathed him, I now saw. He never let up. They always had to be forced. They had to be contained somehow between his hands and feet, held in a vice constructed out of revs and brakes, revs and brakes. They always had to be driven on and held back both in the same moment, the same gesture. Choe ground his teeth and, purple in the face from coke and aggression, aimed his cars like guns, from hazard to hazard.

After a bit he asked in a conversational voice, 'Where we going?'

'Oh, *come on*, Choe.'

'Honest question, Mick. Be fair.'

Something took his attention and silenced him for a while after that. I sat in the back with my arms round Isobel. I talked to her but she didn't answer. 'Do you remember the time we stayed in St Ives for Christmas, and to cheer me up you bought me a pushalong duck, with rubber feet that flapped?' I kept catching glimpses of her in weird neon shop lights from Wallis or Next or What She Wants, lolling against my chest with her mouth half open. She knew how bad she was. She kept trying to smile up at me. Then she would drift off, or cornering forces would roll her head to one side as if she had no control over the muscles in her neck and she would end up staring and smiling at the back-seat upholstery whispering:

'China. China China China.'

'Isobel.'

She passed out again and didn't wake up.

It was twelve minutes since I had found her. We were nearly there.

I said: 'Can't you get a move on, Choe?'

'Fuck off Mick,' he said.

After a moment he added matter of factly: 'I've lost it, I'm afraid.'

A late taxi had forced him to brake in a turn. Instantly the rear-wheel drive was all over him, flicking the back end around so fast we could almost see it catching up. Three in the morning, New Year's Eve: Hammersmith Gyratory. The piers of the flyover loomed above us in wicked orange light, stained grey concrete plastered with anarchist graffiti and torn posters. The M3 waltzed sideways towards them, ballistic at last, a car glad to be out of Choe Ashton's hands. I curled my body over Isobel's, trying to cradle her head. G snatched her away from me. G for gravity. G for the gravity of things. I could hear Choe repeating 'fuck' in a monotone: 'Fuck, fuck, fuck, fuck.' We tipped the kerb, tripped over our own feet, and began a long, slow roll like an airliner banking to starboard. We hit a post box with an extraordinary noise, like someone stamping on a cardboard box. The BMW jumped in a startled way and righted itself. Its offside rear suspension had collapsed. Uncomfortable with the new layout, still trying to get away from Choe, it spun twice and banged itself repeatedly against the opposite kerb with a sound exactly like some housewife's Metro running over the cat's-eyes on a cold Friday morning. Something snapped the window-post on that side and broken glass blew in all over Isobel Avens' peaceful face. She opened her mouth. Thin vomit came out, the colour of tea: but I didn't think she was conscious. Then she said, quite clearly: 'I went too far, China. I went too far.' Until that moment everything had seemed to happen in slow motion, some Hollywood choreography featuring an obsolete BTCC racer which dismantles itself to the long, romantic, yet interrogative guitar lines of Joe Satriani's 'Always With You, Always With Me'. Now, things came back up to speed again. Hammersmith Gyratory, ninety-five miles an hour. Choe dropped a gear, picked the car up between steering and accelerator, and shot out into Queensborough Road on the wrong side. The boot lid popped open and fell off. It dragged along the road for a minute, then went backwards quickly and disappeared.

'Christ, Choe.'

'Not many cars would do that.'

'China.'

Draped across my arms, Isobel was nothing but a lot of bones and heat. I carried her up the steps to Alexander's building and pressed for entry. The entryphone crackled but no one spoke. 'Hello?' I said. After a moment the locks went back.

Look into the atrium of a west London building at night and everything is the same as it is in the day. Only the reception staff are missing, and that makes less difference than you would think. The contract furniture keeps working. The PX keeps working. The fax comes alive suddenly as you watch, with a query from Zurich, Singapore, LA. The air-conditioning keeps on working. Someone has watered the plants, and they keep working too, making chlorophyll from the overhead lights. Paper curls out of the fax and stops. You can watch for as long as you like: nothing else will happen and no one will come. The air will be cool and warm at the same time, and you will be able to see your own reflection, very faintly, in the treated glass.

'China.'

Signs of Life

Upstairs it was a suite of open-plan offices – health finance – and then a suite of consulting rooms. Up here the lights were off, and you could no longer hear the light traffic on Queensborough Road. It was two-fifty in the morning. Choe got into the consulting rooms and then Alexander's office, and ranged about breaking things, while I walked up and down with Isobel in my arms, calling:

'Alexander?'

No one came.

'Alexander?'

Someone had let us in.

'Alexander!'

Alexander's desk, an oiled sweep of top-end hardwood, was stacked with computer printout and brochures. 'For fuck's sake Choe,' I called. 'Stop that and come and help me here.' We swept everything off on to the floor and tried to make Isobel comfortable by folding my coat under her head. 'I'm sorry,' she said quietly, but not to me. It was part of some conversation I couldn't hear. She kept rolling on to her side and retching over the edge of the desk, then laughing. I had picked up the phone and was working on an outside line when Brian Alexander came in from the corridor. He had lost weight. He looked vague and empty, as if we had woken him out of a deep sleep. You can tear people like him apart like a piece of paper, but it doesn't change anything.

'Press nine,' he advised me. 'Then call an ambulance.'

He glanced down at Isobel. He said:

'It would have been better to take her straight to a hospital.'

'Shall I twat him one, Mick?' Choe said.

I put the phone down.

Isobel woke up, saw Alexander, and put her arms up imploringly to him. '*Brian*,' she said. She threw up again. 'Sorry.'

I rubbed my eyes.

'Just talk to him, Choe,' I said.

Choe took Alexander's arm and, murmuring, 'This is a really nice suit you've got on,' guided him over to the window. There he continued, 'See that? The traffic is really bad tonight.' Alexander looked at Choe, then down at the sleeve of his own suit, and then out of the window at the BMW, half up on the pavement with smoke coming out of it. Choe said: 'You've got to agree that's a perfectly good car, haven't you? Well, look, I just *stuffed* the fucker into a post box.' He smiled reminiscently. 'Drugs and classic oversteer. The two best things in the world.' He added, as if he was discovering it for the first time: 'Mick's a wanker but he knows a good car.' Without taking his eyes off the doctor, he reached round behind him with one hand and picked up a copy of 'The Alexander Clinics Welcome You'. 'And another thing,' he said. 'What's all this crap?'

'Leave it, Choe,' I told him. 'That's not the point.'

'No, be fair, Mick. Let him explain himself.'

He waved the brochure in front of Alexander's face, in such a way that it fell open at random. Alexander, under the impression he was being invited to read the paragraph which began, 'Here at the Alexander Clinics,' misunderstood him comprehensively.

'Oh, that,' he said. 'Grafting turned out to be unnecessary. It was a very early idea. Do you know anything about this? Genome mapping was the difficult thing. By the time we'd done sufficient mapping to give us a vocabulary of fifty or a hundred birds, someone had found a way we could simply punch the new genetic material directly into the patient's cells, tethered to regulatory sequences which switched the correct ribosomes on only in hair-follicles. We had no trouble, even with the hormones.'

He shrugged.

'Grafting was just expensive and unnecessary. We left it in the brochure because the patients are already familiar with cosmetic surgery.'

He produced a faint smile.

'Molecular biology excites them, but it makes them feel less comfortable.'

He stared at Choe. Choe stared back.

'For fuck's sake,' Choe said. 'I said, you know, *explain.*'

He pulled Alexander's face quickly down towards him and butted it. A long dollop of blood shaped like a very streamlined dumb-bell shot out of Alexander's nose, turned over once or twice in the air, stretching elegantly, and landed on the arm of Choe's beige Comme des Garçons jacket.

'Fuck,' said Choe.

'Choe!'

'How am I going to get this off, Mick?' Choe appealed.

I stood between them and gave Alexander a wad of Kleenex for his nose. Wiping blood across his face so that it left an oblique brownish smear, fading where it reached the dark granulated skin above his cheekbone, Alexander focused shakily on me. I had been moving things about for him since the old Astravan days; since before Stratford. And if I was just a contract to him, he was just some writing on a job sheet to me. He was the price of a 1985 competition M3 on to which I had had someone bolt a Garrett turbocharger. He blinked.

'I know you,' he said. 'You've done work for me.'

'But you did this,' I reminded him.

I got him by the back of the neck and made him look closely at Isobel. Then I pushed him against the wall and stood away from him. I told him evenly: 'Now I'm glad I didn't kill you when I wanted to.' I said: 'Put her back together.'

He lifted his hands.

'I can't,' he said.

'Put her back together.'

'This is only an office,' he said. 'She would have to go to Miami.'

I pointed to the telephone.

I said: 'Arrange it. Get her there.'

He examined her briefly.

'She was dying from day one anyway,' he said. 'The immune system work alone would have killed her. We did far more than we would normally do on a client. Most of it was illegal. *It would be illegal to do most of it to a laboratory rat.* Didn't she tell you that?'

I said: 'Get her there and put her back together again.'
'I can make her human again,' he offered. 'I can cure her.'
I said: 'She didn't fucking want to be human.'
'I know,' he said.
He looked down at his desk; his hands.
He whispered: ' "Help me to fly. Help me to fly!" '
'Fuck off,' I said.
'I loved her too, you know. But I couldn't make her understand that she could *never* have what she wanted. In the end she was just too demanding: effectively, she asked us to kill her.'
I didn't want to know why he had let me have her back. I didn't want to compare inadequacies with him.
I said: 'I don't want to hear this.'
He shrugged.
'She'll die if we try it again,' he said emptily. 'You've got no idea how these things work.'
'Put her back together.'
You tell me what else I could have said.

I lived in a hotel on the beach while it was done. Miami. TV prophecy, humidity like a wet sheet, an airport where they won't rent you a baggage trolley. You wouldn't think this listening to Bob Seeger. Unless you are constantly approaching it from the sea, Miami is less a dream – less even a nightmare – than a place. All I remember is what British people always remember about Florida: the light in the afternoon storm, the extraordinary size and perfection of the food in the supermarkets. I never went near the clinic, though I telephoned Alexander's team every morning and evening. I was too scared.
Infections were racing through her again as her immune system went down block by block. Contamination from bacterial soups employed in the original treatments had filled her with fragments of a strange or damaged DNA. Her blood was a junkyard of proteins. In addition there were problems with the engineered hormonal chemistry. Most of the bird hormones had one or two more amino acids than their naturally occurring

counterparts: some had as many as ten. Worse: because they had been manufactured on human robosomes, they all had radical differences in topology. It was a language problem. Unable to make sufficiently fine grammatical distinctions, or indeed fully separate signal from noise, Isobel's biology, unsure what kind of animal it might now support, was spiralling into total metabolic collapse even as it tried to understand the new messages raging through it. Intubated and strapped down, she fluttered and thrashed like a sparrow trapped in a room; or lay still, breathing at some impossible rate.

One day the team were optimistic, the next they weren't. They seemed like children to me; smooth yet aggressive: full of themselves. 'You want to call in a veterinary?' they asked one another every morning. 'Ha ha, ah ha ha ha.' But in the end I knew they had got involved again. They were intrigued by the chemistry, excited by its implications. They were going to stabilise her. She was going to have what she wanted. They were going to do the best they could for her, if only because of the technical challenge. All I needed to do was wait.

In your early forties the summers rush past. Before you know it, November has ended everything. By contrast the winters seem long and dreary. Then in your early fifties, winter begins to rush past, too. You are just settling down to endure February when you notice buds on the trees: it's March, and if the air is still cold and northerly, well, the sunshine is warm. Two kinds of subjective time have suddenly meshed like gears. The first kind is an illusion of acceleration – the older you get, the smaller a proportion of your life a single summer becomes. The second kind is an illusion of duration – the sense we have that something unpleasant takes longer to pass than something pleasant. Once these two kinds of time have equalised or changed gear, waiting for anything becomes much easier.

Isobel slipped in and out of the world until the spring. But she didn't die, and in the end I was able to bring her home to the blackened, gentle East End in May, driving all the way from Heathrow down the inside lane of the motorway, as slowly and

Anima

carefully as I knew how, in my new off-the-peg 7 Series. I had adjusted the driving mirror so I could look into the back of the car. Isobel lay awkwardly across one corner of the rear seat. Her hands and face seemed tiny. In the soft wet English light, their modified bone structures looked more rather than less human. Lapped in her singular successes and failures, the sum of her life to that point, she was as calm as I had ever seen her.

About a mile away from the house, outside Whitechapel tube station, I let the car drift up to the kerb and stop. I switched the engine off and got out of the driving seat.

'It isn't far from here,' I said.

I put the keys in her hand.

'I know you're tired,' I said, 'but I want you to drive yourself the rest of the way.'

She said: 'China, don't go. Get back in the car.'

'It's not far from here,' I said.

'China, please don't go.'

'Drive yourself from now on.'

If you're so clever, you tell me what else I could have done. All that time in Miami she had never let go, never once vacated the dream. The moment she closed her eyes, feathers were floating down past them. She knew what she wanted. Don't mistake me: I wanted her to have it. But imagining myself stretched out next to her on the bed night after night, I could hear the sound those feathers made, and I knew I would never sleep again for the touch of them on my face.

EPILOGUE
In Jumble Wood

A kind of paralysis gripped me whenever I thought about Christiana Spede. In the end it was she who got back in touch. She returned two books I had lent her with a little note written carefully on the brown-paper wrapping. It was an act of language, an invitation to treat. Her operation, she said, had been successful; and she was recovering well. Would I send back the denim jacket I had borrowed in October? I would. I was curious. 'Did you feel it would be *inappropriate* to put your note inside the package?' I enquired carefully. 'Or did you just forget?' She replied on a postcard of Chagall's *Garden of Eden*, in which it is Adam who tempts Eve with the apple:

'I wasn't sure you'd want to hear from me.'

It could easily have rested there, but one thing led to another, and we met at Camden Lock on an unseasonable Sunday afternoon in May. It had been raining for a week. Under a sky marbled lead and silver the markets had reverted to type – stalls flimsy and bricolaged, sheets of heavy-gauge plastic flapping madly in the wind, the tourists wincing and ducking away. A pair of lace gloves blew down a crowded aisle and adhered, disfigured, to the muddy cobbles underfoot. No one noticed. 'Sorry,' a jeweller told us shortly, when Christiana asked to look at some little turquoise and silver ear-rings, 'I'm closed.' So we walked up to Inverness Street and ate at the Mimico Bistro, now defunct. Among the middle-class adolescents and Spanish tourists, an old lady in a thick maroon woollen coat was eating fried eggs, carefully dipping chips into them one by one.

Anima

'Look at that,' said Christiana. 'There's something about the way old people eat, even when they're greedy. Do you know what I mean, China? Dignified, and with a steady concentration.'

'I'm an old person,' I said.

All this time we hadn't touched.

'Christiana—'

'Camden is still worth it because of that,' she said.

Suddenly she looked away and blinked. Her hand came out and held mine across the table.

'China?'

'Christiana, I—'

'I couldn't understand what had happened,' she said. 'I felt totally alone.'

Suddenly I got up and went round to her side of the table. She scraped her chair back and started to get up. We embraced awkwardly, and then she pushed me away. She laughed. I must have looked terrified.

We live together now, although perhaps 'together' is the wrong word. We turned the Chalk Farm house back into separate dwellings. Christiana kept the garden and her little bare blue and white bedroom looking out on to the railway. I thought about it for a while, then hired a design partnership to do my half. They put in a Japanese cedar bathtub, Seimatic worktops, ARCO taps by Hansgröhe; floors of Douglas fir. By the time they'd finished, it was austere yet sensual, Pawson-like (though I couldn't afford Pawson himself). Less a home than a clean slate. Christiana hates it. While her snobberies are no longer those of the woman I knew in the early eighties, they present as political even when their content is domestic. Sometimes she will admit grudgingly, 'At least it's an easy place for you to keep clean.'

We have separate entrances and telephone accounts and grocery bills. We are careful with one another's privacy (which she calls 'space'). Even so, things are sometimes bad between us, and when they are she remembers how I abandoned her to King's College Hospital, and she says:

'You turned out to be a bigger bastard than Choe in the end.'

I never respond to that. What can I tell her? That in forgetting her I remembered Isobel, as if they were two halves of the same woman? That to me, then, it was as if one woman had gone into hospital and immediately, in a single fluid, seamless movement, returned to convalesce? As if she had entered by the front door at King's and come out by the back door of the Alexander Clinic, Miami?

'A much bigger bastard, China.'

What can I say about Choe Ashton?

During Isobel's second term in the Miami clinic I had taken a week off here and there to set up a new business, flying back steerage from Miami. By then, I suspect, I already knew that I wasn't going to be there for her when she came out; that whatever I did now I would do for myself. They still remembered me in Soho. Fifty years old and full of a visible – if at times undependable – energy, I was able to borrow enough to get back into the production side: ads, corporate videos, pop promos. After I walked away from Isobel in the spring, it was easy to immerse myself in that. It was hard work, and I felt too empty and distanced from everything to want to get involved with Choe again. But I did go looking for him on one of those trips back, and I did find him.

Haringey, late April: 10 a.m., and I was walking down towards the Salisbury Hotel. The rush-hour traffic had diminished to a trickle and the morning queues were in the Cypriot banks. There had been an early frost, but now bright sunshine was spilling into the slot of Green Lanes, pouring off the grimy buildings and splashing on to the exotic vegetables stacked outside the Turkish shops, some of which had been closed for barely eight hours. (This brought me a quick, aching memory of Budapest: paprika and flowers in the open markets, then Dohany Street east of the synagogue, ablaze with morning light. You stand dazzled, almost afraid to cross the road; then, looking north up Klausal, catch a glimpse of scaffolding, trees,

Klausal Square in a resplendent haze. Happiness and beauty are the worst things you can have in a life, because you never forget them. They go on and on ambushing you, presumably until you die.) Ten minutes later I was outside the minicab office. The locks had been changed at Choe's flat. Choe hadn't returned my calls. Shogun Cars had responded with a disconnected tone. Now I saw why. A fire in the night and Choe's enterprise had burnt to a shell.

There were scorch marks on the pink walls above the empty casements. Parts of the roof were open to the air. The first floor had fallen through into the minicab office. Blackened, eroded beams barred the doorway. But I ducked and shoved my way in and stood in a puddle of water in the middle of the room and tried to locate the dispatcher's desk, the filing cabinet, the pool table. Not much left to see. It was cold and dark in there, yet somehow comforting, and I stood for quite a time feeling grateful that nothing was required of me. Then beneath the acidic smells of charred wood and melted plastic, the residue of burnt petrol, I caught a faint, stale reek of something else. I heard a stealthy noise; looked up in anxiety. Pigeons. Pigeons had already moved in from the abandoned cinema across the road to breed. They shifted their pink, mangled feet awkwardly among the rafters high up.

'Don't do that,' I begged them.

Then Ed Cesniak, who'd been standing at the edge of the room all along, coughed and said:

'Hi, Mick.'

'Jesus Christ.'

I remembered his face as pale. Now, as he stepped out of the shadows, it was a white on the edge of green – an albescent, almost radiant green. I felt an extraordinary fear and stepped back.

'Mick, Mick,' he said softly, as if to calm me.

'My name's China.'

'Hey, China,' he said. 'Look, whatever you do, don't feel scared. You were only the driver. You weren't involved. We know you weren't involved.' He laughed. 'Even Choe wasn't really involved,' he said. He looked round at the devastated office. 'Pity about this. It was a nice little place.' He shrugged. 'Look,' he said, 'tell Choe, "No hard feelings." He won't be hurt. But he should stay away for a while.'

He pushed up his cuff to look at his Breitling Chronomat.

'Hey,' he said. 'I'm late. Look, it was good to see you, China. Sometime soon, yeah?'

He held out his hand.

'Where's your Walkman, Ed?'

He smiled.

'Choe liked that more than anything, didn't he? Robert Johnson.'

A long black car drew up quietly in the street outside. Ed picked his way with care over the puddled TV, the bubbles of silver metal that had been cable and chassis of the microwave oven, all the gluey, melted rubbish of Choe's ambition, over the threshold and into the bright April light. 'Do you all need a *lift*?' he called back. 'I'm going west. Or is it east?' he asked himself. When I told him no, he raised his hand goodbye; then, changing his mind suddenly, turned to speak again. The light caught his eyes and made them so blank, so empty, so very transparent that I could see right through to the imp bottled in there. That imp; it's never so much the other person's ego as something escaped from our own. Some residue of personality we never wanted to acknowledge which slips over to people like Ed and, suddenly able to be honest about itself, becomes a real goblin.

'The Walkman was for Choe,' I heard him say. 'All for Choe.'

Someone told me Choe had moved to Chiswick; someone else that he had left Britain altogether. One day in July I got a call from him.

'Hello?'

'Don't be a prat, Mick.'

'Choe. Nice to hear from you.'

'You could get your head stuffed in a litter bin just for talking to me.'

'It was you who phoned,' I pointed out.
'I'm not kidding, Mick.'
'I know, Choe.'
I said I would like to talk anyway.
'Can you get up here?'
I said I could, and we arranged a meeting. He was living in his home town again. *I fucking hated that place*, I remembered him saying; and wondered how he could be getting on there. 'Does that seem like a good idea?' I asked. 'Given how you felt?'

No answer.

He rang to cancel the arrangement three or four times. Each time it was back on within an hour or two. First I was to meet him at a pub called the Bear's Paw. Then, if I was bringing a car, the place where he lived – though he seemed reluctant to give me its address. Finally he agreed to be in the town-centre car park at one o'clock the next day. He was distracted, I thought by fear, although I see now it wasn't that. He seemed to have forgotten about Isobel, because once or twice he asked me:

'How's your tart, Mick?'

I drove up in Christiana's battered Citroën Safari, leaving the M1 at Sheffield and following the Snake Pass west. At that time of the year the moors seem burnt and derelict in the sun. Then you look into the deep little cloughs that run away up into the peat and you see how full of trees they are – green oaks, green turf, yellow tormentil, silver water running over stones. From its summit the Snake slipped back down through a series of tight hypnotic curves to farmland. I turned south and took the A6 for a few miles, and the next thing I saw was a tall steel chimney, elegant as a rocket, towering above the rows of do-it-yourself warehouses and light chemical plants which had moved in on the quarry companies in the late eighties and now lay calm and exhausted under the sun, caught between boom and bust.

Otherwise it was Choe's nightmare: Woolworth's, Sainsbury's, the record shop, the bus station. *Only the recently dead use a bus station.* I found him sitting on the broken-down brick wall of the car-park, kicking his feet in the sunshine. His jeans were rolled up to show off a pair of paint-splattered workboots. He had shaved his head, then let the hair grow two or three millimetres so that the bony plates of his skull showed through, aggressive and vulnerable. I thought he was nervous, but bored and lonely too, as if he had been sitting on his own all morning. He seemed reduced, as if the town had already done its work on him, peeling him back along his own lifeline to first display and then dismiss every self-reinvention since adolescence.

He jumped off the wall when he saw me.

'Where's the car?' Then, realising that the BX was mine: 'Jesus Mick, what's this? It looks like a fucking minicab.'

'Where to, mate?'

'Look Mick, I really meant that about the litter bin.'

'Ed sends you his love.'

'Oh yes?'

'Let me see if I can get this right. He says he could swallow you with a glass of water, but he won't. He says to tell you, "Don't be a wanker all your life, Choe."'

Choe grinned wanly.

I said: 'I think that was it.' I said: 'Does that sound about right?' I said: 'So where do you want to go?'

'When I was young,' he said, 'my parents kept chickens in a hutch in the back garden.' He watched a woman carry two supermarket bags across the car-park and stand by the door of her little red Corsa as if she expected someone else to come and unlock it for her. 'They named a chicken after each of us. Then they served them up for dinner, once or twice a year.' He blinked up into the sun. 'Alan, Andy, Edie, Choe,' he recited. 'I got mine at Christmas. Do you believe that?'

Well, do you believe that? I thought. He had asked as if my answer was important to him – as if it might help him understand the way he had seen the world since.

'No, Choe. I don't.'

'I really like housewives,' he said. 'Don't you?'

'Where do you want to go, Choe?'

'Jumble Wood.'

I stared at him.

'Are you sure?'

'I live there now mate. It's where I live.'

'You'll have to direct me.'

At its southern edge the town petered out into a labyrinth of narrow lanes between tall, honey-coloured gritstone walls. The road would dip suddenly into a valley, turn two hundred degrees, then lift up to some empty, open little bit of land with a wind-farm on it. Blind junction followed blind junction, each marked by a white, abandoned-looking pub. Soon I had no idea where I was. But summer had brought the flowers out; horses were up to their knees in moon-daisies in every field. The verges were fat with clover and cow parsley. The foxgloves were like girls. Thick clusters of creamy flowers weighed down the elders, and wherever I looked there were wild roses, the most tremulous pink and white. Every field's edge was banked with red poppies. That would have been enough – fields of red poppies – but among them, perhaps one to five hundred, one to a thousand, there were sports or hybrids of a completely different colour, a dull, waxy purple, rather sombre but fine.

'Stop here,' ordered Choe.

A quiet road of stone three-bedroomed houses, mature horse chestnut trees and neat, rather unimaginative gardens bright with stonecrop, pelargoniums and lobelia, curved up and round to oak woods suspended on the lip of a steep little gritstone scarp. It was much as I remembered it. If the roadway looked in need of repair, that rather added to its comfortable quality; if the woods looked a little dustier, they were just as tangled, just as secretive. Birds were flocking in the hot blue air above the trees, dipping, sweeping, hovering; a coherent, noisy wheel of gleaming white specks.

I turned the ignition off. The Citröen dieselled briefly into silence.

'Gulls,' I said. 'They're seagulls.'

'This car sounds like shit, Mick.'

'It's French, Choe. That's how they sound.'

He got out.

'It's crap,' he said. 'That's how crap sounds.' And then: 'Jumble Wood.'

When you got closer, you saw he had fenced it in with chain link. There were tall, heavily padlocked gates of galvanised metal, big enough to admit a truck, and from there a raw-looking lane, surfaced with limestone chippings and lit at night by halogen lamps on concrete standards, had been cut through the wood. The sign on the gate, green letters on a white wooden board, had originally read: 'SHOGUN SERVICES'. Some local child had added a T to the first word.

'Shotgun, eh?' boasted Choe. 'Shotgun Services, that's me.'

'Choe—'

'Come and have a look.'

Jumble Wood was still meditative. But now it was full of small black flies too. Dust thrown up by days and nights of contractors' traffic had greyed the bark of the oaks, which seemed suddenly dwarfed and contorted in the face of it all. An oppressive breeze rustled through branches strung with heavy-duty electrical conduit. We walked up the hill in silence, Choe smiling and grinning at me, while the seagulls circled above something perhaps two hundred yards in front of us, crying rawly into the heated afternoon air. At the geological divide, where millstone grit gave way suddenly to limestone, the trees had been bulldozed out of the way. We stood and looked across to the spot where Choe's fat girl, his green woman, had come up from out of the earth.

'What do you think, Mick?'

The dump had almost filled the little valley. It was the usual stuff. Grey earth and burst cardboard boxes. Cascades of used pippettes, gel-loading tips and sample combs. Empty nucleotide phials with poster-coloured lids as bright as toys for very young children. A Lego of transparent plastic trays and cheerful red flipper racks. Puddles of run-off solvent, detection-reagents and electrophoresis gels. It was stuff that would glow in the dark. It was carbon tetrachloride, a rainbow in your head at night, hallucinations like the dimples in oil. It was the diamondy glitter of smashed borosilicate glass, the remains of a consignment of flasks with characteristic blue polypropylene caps. Where the wood avens had grown, someone had got rid of a dozen plastic dustbins stuffed with computer output, now sodden, caky and unreadable – though I picked out the words 'microfiltration zones'. Where Choe had rucked the green girl and, panting, sealed her with his adolescent kiss, a small rusty-yellow bulldozer rested hull-down among heavy-duty waste tubs sealed 'Burn Without Opening'. The trees that remained were leafless, decorated with nests and tangles of biohazard tape, or strips of polythene floating like good-luck charms in the hot breeze. As I watched, a flimsy white plastic bag drifted past at eye level, turning over and over on itself, expanding and contracting like some formless, slow-moving creature of the sea, until it became tangled in the upper branches of a sycamore. Even then it seemed to have achieved, rather than death, development: as if it might settle down now for some years to sift the wind for food, produce spores, change shape, and only then die.

'I come here a lot,' Choe said vaguely.

He waved his arm.

'Look at those fucking gannets.'

Thinking perhaps that he had thrown them something, the circling gulls dipped and veered abruptly in their flight.

'They could wait forever.'

'They're big strong birds,' I agreed.

He stared at me.

'I'm fucking scared of them,' he said.

'I thought you were scared of nowt.'

He laughed.

'Come and have a beer.'

About four hundred yards down the track he had bulldozed a little clearing in the oak wood and that was where he lived, in an old green caravan about thirty feet long, sitting askew on a broken axle and deflated tyres. Moss grew from its aluminium window frames, but there was a good Honda generator at the back, and a brand-new satellite dish beside the door. Inside – though a disturbing light filtered in through the oak trees, as of a storm always approaching but never arriving – I found it quite comfortable. Refrigerator, microwave and telephones were installed at one end; at the other a gigabyte Mac on a cheap white stand, more phones and five Sony TVs bolted into the kind of display rack popular in bars in the mid eighties. He had brought his Harry Crews collection with him from Haringey. He had books by Robert Stone, Jayne Anne Phillips and Harold Bloom. He had a shelf of *Internet* magazines and novels with titles like *Snow Crash*. Where he slept, I couldn't see. Perhaps he didn't sleep.

'What's on TV?' I said.

He picked up a remote control. All five screens sprang silently into life. They showed: poor-quality video images of the *Titanic* – anchor chains, winches and capstans which resembled nothing so much as shots of some heavily moulded ceiling discovered in a country house; a live mouse with a full size human ear growing out of it; Isobel Avens' face in close-up, her lips making the word 'China' over and over again; the credits of a film called *Leningrad Cowboys Go America*; and a single magpie, which seemed to wear its wings like an iridescent cloak, flapping up in slow motion from a grass verge into a hedge.

One of the pictures changed and the rest stayed the same. Then the rest changed, and nothing was the same.

'Is that a prophecy?' I asked.

Choe shrugged.

The refrigerator was full of bottles. I took one out and opened it. Choe already had one.

'I bought a case of this,' he said.

'Giraffe beer. Ah.'

'Why drink anything else?'

'Why indeed.'

We sat down and watched the TVs for a while. Eventually, when he realised I wasn't going to say anything, Choe got up and switched them off. He was desperate to get my attention. 'The thing is,' he said, making a gesture intended to include the caravan, Jumble Wood and the waste tip he had made of it, 'that the whole world's going to be like this soon.'

'Choe. How clever of you to guess that.'

'At least I can live with it, Mick. You were just a fucking hypocrite all along.'

I began to turn away, but he got hold of my sleeve. 'A fucking hypocrite all along.' He wanted me to be angry with him because he had spoilt the valley; he wanted me to be angry with him because he couldn't grow up. Neither of those things seemed to be the issue any more. 'Mick, I only told you all that stuff about the girl to get you going,' he said. 'Really. None of it was true. I never believed it.' He nodded back in the direction of the town. 'I lived down there, and I used to come here just to get away. Just to sit on a Saturday afternoon. Have a wank. You know.'

'Do you think I care?' I said.

He looked upset and ran out of the caravan. I drank the rest of my Giraffe beer and smashed one of the TV screens with the empty bottle. It was getting late by then. I went out. Horizontal sunlight gilded the tops of the oaks, and Choe was back at the tip. Twenty or thirty herring gulls had gathered shrieking above him, and he was throwing stones at them with single-minded ferocity. It was some time before he noticed me.

'These fuckers,' he said. They can wait forever.' He rubbed the inside of his elbow. 'I've hurt my arm.'

'They only live a year or two, Choe.'

He picked up another stone.

Whatever he says now – and whatever you and I might think – something happened to Choe in Jumble Wood when he was young: something that centralised itself in his life so thoroughly that for over twenty years, puzzled, charmed and frustrated, he was compelled to return there yearly on the anniversary of the event. In doing so he reassured himself less perhaps of the green woman's existence than of his own.

Signs of Life

I imagine him standing there all afternoon as the sunlight angled across the valley. Seen in the promise of that light, the shadows of the sycamore saplings are full of significance; the little crag still resembles a white church. Behind him, on the gritstone side of the divide, the wood is hot and tranquil and full of insects. He rests his hand on the rough bark of an oak. He appeals to whatever lives in that place, or at least in that part of his heart, 'Bring her back. Bring her back to me,' only to be hurt time and again by its lack of response. Then one day, tiring of the long wait, and finding himself in a position to do something about it, he buys the valley and buries it forever. To understand how completely Choe jumped ship on his own dream is to understand the confidence which Isobel Avens maintained in hers.

For a time I didn't dream at all. This wasn't entirely Isobel's doing, though I suppose she made my life a dream in itself, one so surprising and gracile that until I lost her I was always moving from moment to moment, incident to incident, in a kind of warm seamless daze. I never wanted anything until Isobel. I've not really wanted much since.